DAY OF RECKONING

A POST-APOCALYPTIC NOVEL

G. MICHAEL HOPF

DOOMSDAY
PRESS

Doomsday Press, a division of Beyond The Fray, LLC, San Diego, CA

www.doomsdaybooks.com

DOOMSDAY
PRESS

To the men and women of law enforcement.

Hard times create strong men.
Strong men create good times.
Good times create weak men.
And weak men create hard times.

G. MICHAEL HOPF

PROLOGUE

South Atlantic
January 14, 2000

BARRETT SCHUMARR STARED through the thick glass that separated him from test subject three eighteen.

Three eighteen squirmed, but the restraints held him tightly to the chair.

Schumarr glanced at his pocket watch with anticipation that soon the minor squirms would evolve into violent spasms. If three eighteen was like the previous test subjects, the spasms would be closely followed by death.

The room rolled to the left.

"The storm is getting closer," Charles said, referring to the ship's dramatic rolling and pitching caused from the building waves.

Charles was Schumarr's assistant and often a harsh critic and skeptic of his.

Schumarr paid no attention. His gaze darted between his watch and the man.

Three eighteen quit squirming.

1

"He's stop moving. Make a note on the time," Schumarr ordered.

Charles did as he was commanded and jotted down notes on a clipboard.

Schumarr exited the observation room and started towards three eighteen but stopped when the man's head quickly lifted.

"Can you hear me?" Schumarr asked.

Three eighteen opened his eyes and looked in Schumarr's direction.

Schumarr could see he wasn't looking at him, he was looking *through* him. "Can you hear me?" Schumarr asked again as he snapped his fingers loudly near three eighteen's ears.

Three eighteen jerked his head. Thick drool dripped from his lips and sweat streamed down his stubbled face.

"Make a note that three eighteen is nonresponsive to my commands. He appears to be lucid, but he's displaying some sort of catatonic state. This is a different response than before. This is interesting, very interesting," Schumarr said looking at his watch. "We've past the time of when the other subjects began violently thrashing."

Charles feverishly wrote.

Schumarr bent over and looked closer in his eyes. "His pupils are dilated, fully."

Three eighteen continued to stare ahead.

"Hello, are you there?" Schumarr said and clapped his hands inches from three eighteen's face.

This time he locked eyes with Schumarr.

"There you are," Schumarr said with a broad smile.

Three eighteen furrowed his brow as a look of anger grew on his face.

Schumarr cocked his head and asked, "Tell me what you're feeling?"

Three eighteen matched Schumarr's gesture by also cocking

his head.

"Tell me, how do you feel?"

No response.

Three eighteen's eyes rolled back into his head and his body tensed.

Schumarr wondered if this was the beginning of the end. *Is he about to spasm then stroke out like all the others before him?* Schumarr looked over his shoulder to see Charles staring. "Don't gawk, write! Write everything you're seeing here!"

"But we're filming too!" Charles fired back.

"Write, damn it. Put down everything you're seeing in the moment. It's important! And don't argue with me."

Charles went back to scribbling quickly.

A loud snap caught Schumarr's attention. He turned to find three eighteen had broken the leather strap holding his right arm. With his right arm free, he reached across and undid his left.

Schumarr stepped forward to stop him but was pushed back hard. He stumbled backwards and fell, hitting his head against the bulkhead.

Charles looked on in horror as the leg restraints were the next thing he undid.

"Stop him!" Schumarr barked.

Charles came into the room but froze when he saw three eighteen stand and turn to face him.

A look of pure anger was etched on three eighteen's face. He stepped away from the chair and stared at Charles. Thick drool spilled from his gaping mouth and ran down his shirt.

Charles tried to flee but wasn't fast enough.

Three eighteen caught him at the door and dragged him to the floor.

Schumarr watched in fascination as Charles was beaten mercilessly.

Charles tried to fight back but the onslaught was too much.

Three eighteen pinned a wailing Charles down by holding his shattered arms to the floor. He opened his mouth and spit a large amount of saliva into Charles' face much of which went into his mouth.

Charles gagged and threw up.

Displaying incredible strength, three eighteen reached down with his right hand and ripped Charles' jaw off and tossed it aside.

Blood poured from Charles' now gaping face. He gasped a few times then died.

With Charles dead, three eighteen turned his attention to Schumarr who had crawled to the far corner of the room.

Schumarr's eyes widened with an odd joy. Deep down he was happy; it appeared he had finally succeeded at creating something unique and equally terrible.

The door burst open. Two armed men raced in.

Three eighteen turned towards them.

They raised their rifles, but just before they could open fire, Schumarr yelled, "Don't kill him. I need him alive!"

With vicious intent, three eighteen charged the guards but only made it to within arm's reach before being hit in the head with the butt of a rifle. He fell to his knees, grunted and lunged again. A second hit to his left temple knocked him out. He fell to the floor unconscious.

Schumarr stood, wiped his hands on his white lab coat and said, "Outstanding!"

The guards gave Schumarr a perplexed look.

Unsure of how long he'd be out, Schumarr ordered, "Take him back to his cell."

They slung their rifles and scooped up three eighteen's limp body.

"And triple restrain him," Schumarr barked.

"Yes, sir," one replied.

"And make sure you wash. Toss, better yet, burn those clothes," Schumarr warned.

The men looked at their clothing, each other and back to Schumarr. They nodded and exited, three eighteen's bare feet dragging across the blood-covered floor, leaving a trail out the door.

Franz, Schumarr's senior assistant, stepped into the room carefully avoiding the gathering pools of dark red blood and not giving a care for his fellow assistant's death and said, "Dr. Schumarr, Mr. Clayton has requested to see you immediately."

"See?"

"Yes, he's here. He just landed."

The ship shook and heaved again.

Franz cringed and gave Schumarr a distressed look.

Schumarr stepped over Charles' dead body and patted Franz on the shoulder. "Don't be concerned. This ship was made for such storms."

Franz replied with a sheepish smile.

"I'm glad he wants to see me because I want to see him."

"What do I do with Charles' body?" Franz asked.

"Take it to examination room four," Schumarr said as he exited. He paused, turned around and looked at Charles' body. "And make sure you confirm he's dead. If he's not, restrain him too. I'll be back down later to conduct an autopsy."

"Shut down?" Schumarr howled.

"Dr. Schumarr, our benefactors have pulled their funding. We're out of money."

"But I've finally made significant progress with Project Sleeper," Schumarr exclaimed.

Clayton shook his head. He didn't come to debate, he came to ensure the project was shut down.

"Don't you see? We've been searching for the perfect formula, the perfect combination to make the perfect bioweapon and I'm very close."

"That's a lot of *perfects*," Clayton mocked.

"I just need more time."

"You've had plenty of time," Clayton said.

"We're close. I just need more time. These sorts of things don't happen overnight!" Schumarr snapped.

"Dr. Schumarr, enough, you've had five years. They're cutting us off. It's over!" Clayton yelled, his nostrils flared with anger.

"It's not over! Find money somewhere else."

"I know your brown-skinned friend, Yasser, loved this project. He blinded his father with the vision of creating the one, and I'll use your word, perfect solution. But it's cost us five years and half a billion dollars. While you fiddled away years experimenting, precious financial resources that could have gone to financing real attacks were squandered. Enough of the games, I'm tired of it. We're fighting a war against the imperialism of the United States. It's a real war, a war fought with real weapons, not weapons only found in science fiction."

Schumarr's spine tensed. He stood tall, clenched his square jaw and slowly ground his teeth. Anger began to well up inside him.

Seeing a change in his composure, Clayton shifted his tone and said, "Doctor, we all appreciate your efforts, it's just too late now, I'm sorry. Our alliance with your friends, the sheep-herders, hasn't been this fragile, we need to preserve what we can. We must go back to more conventional means if we're to see our vision of a one world socialist order established. Our efforts need to be refocused on taking control of one of their political parties and from there we can destroy America from the inside out."

Schumarr didn't reply. He narrowed his eyes and stared past Clayton out the window to the high waves cresting on the rolling ocean.

"Go pack your personal belongings," Clayton ordered.

"Give me at least another week," Schumarr pleaded.

"We don't have another week. I have helicopters picking us up tomorrow once we clear the storm."

"You go, leave me, I need to finish this, please," Schumarr begged, his hands clasped as if he were praying.

"I can't leave you. We're scuttling the ship tomorrow. Charges are being set now. We can't leave any evidence," Clayton said. He hung his head and began to feel sympathy for Schumarr. He too had been convinced about the project in the early days, but lost faith when the years dragged on with no results. "I'm sorry, Barrett."

"This was your idea, wasn't it?" Schumarr asked.

"Honestly, yes. I'm done," he answered and paused. He took a step towards Schumarr and said, "I should tell you before you hear it once we make landfall tomorrow."

"What?"

"Project Titan," Clayton said.

Schumarr shook his head and grumbled something unintelligible under his breath.

"What did you say?" Clayton asked.

"How do you know about that?"

"Someone on your team has a big mouth."

"Who?"

"So it's true?" Clayton asked.

Schumarr lowered his head and shoulders. He sat down on the chair next to him and sighed.

"What were you thinking?" Clayton asked.

"I'm a scientist. We never throw out findings. You never know where they might lead you. New discoveries, rewriting history," Schumarr mumbled.

"Christ, if that thing gets out, it will kill us all. Are you crazy?"

"I was merely exploring a different angle. I meant to discuss this with everyone later."

"Well, your assistant Charles thought it best we all know *now*. I'm sorry, Barrett, I really am, but you've turned this into nothing more than a shit show. You were tasked with creating a lethal virus that would cripple America; instead you turned your attention to making monsters."

"I'm sorry, I was just going where the science led me."

"Where is it?" Clayton asked.

"Down below. He's secure, I swear," Schumarr said, looking up with weary eyes.

"He's secure? What does that mean?" Clayton asked, his tone showing concern.

"Today we had a breakthrough. It was marvelous. Project Titan took a big step today."

"Destroy Project Titan, Project Sleeper, all of it!"

"No, please, I have years' worth of data, findings. They might reconsider."

"It's not your work, they own it, they paid for it. No, it must all be destroyed."

"Why? Please!"

Tired of the debate, Clayton walked to the door of his stateroom, opened it and simply said, "Be ready to leave tomorrow."

January 15, 2000

"YASSER, listen to me. We cannot let this end now. Go tell your father, please," Schumarr begged. His hand gripped the phone receiver tightly.

"Dr. Schumarr... Barrett, I'm sorry, my father made up his mind. We are moving in a different direction now."

"At least let me save all my findings, my logs."

"My father gave specific instructions to have it all destroyed."

"Why? It doesn't make any sense. Why have me even work on this only to destroy it all when we're so close?"

Yasser paused.

"Are you there?" Schumarr asked.

"Yes."

"At least tell me why."

"Barrett, we know about the other thing you were working on. We didn't fund you so you could create something none of us have control over. You see, my father likes control and this, this he can't be. We have no assurances that once this gets out it won't destroy us too."

"I'll get rid of it, I promise, but keep Sleeper alive, please."

"I'm sorry but no. We're focused on more conventional means to strike at the United States and its allies. Ones that use commercial airliners."

"Jets, commercial jets? No one hijacks anymore."

"It's more than that, you'll see. We hope to execute that plan sometime in late 2001."

Schumarr shook his head wildly and said, "Yasser, I've known you for how long? Six years, seven. You know I can do this."

"Barrett, I consider you a friend, but I'm sorry, my father is no longer interested in your project. You're a world-class virologist; any university or big pharma lab would take you. Your life isn't over."

"This is my life's work. I don't care about universities or big pharma."

"*I have to go. Let's get together soon. I'll be in Berlin to open a new Muslim cultural center this June. I'll send you an invitation. I'd like you to come.*"

Schumarr hung his head in despair. "Fine."

"*Thank you for your hard work.*"

"Sure."

"*Goodbye, Barrett.*"

SCHUMARR SOMBERLY WALKED the narrow and darkened passageways until he reached the lower decks where his research facility was located. He searched his thoughts for how he could save his work but nothing came.

He looked at his watch. There was thirty-seven minutes to go before the choppers arrived and ferried them all away. He hated the thought of abandoning years of work, but with Clayton overseeing the shutdown, he'd never be able to get one scrap of paper off the ship without him knowing about it.

"Dr. Schumarr, Dr.Schumarr!" Franz yelled from the other end of the passageway.

Schumarr looked up. He could see the distress on Franz's face.

"What's wrong?" Schumarr asked.

"It's Clayton. He's in your office...and he's destroying everything," Franz replied, out of breath.

Schumarr's eyes widened in shock. He sprinted past Franz and into the laboratory. His office lay in the far corner and there he saw Clayton and two other men ripping apart his logs and shredding the contents.

"No!" Schumarr barked, racing towards them.

"Stop him," Clayton ordered.

The two men who were helping Clayton grabbed Schumarr.

"Stop it!" Schumarr blared.

"I gave you the opportunity and I see you haven't done one thing," Clayton said, stuffing a stack of papers into a shredder.

"What does it matter? You're blowing up the ship!" he yelled.

Clayton grabbed another tall stack and began feeding the shredder. "I'm not taking any chances."

Schumarr tried to resist the grips of the men. "You're hurting me."

Clayton leaned close to Schumarr and barked, "Bring me everything of value. I need to destroy it myself."

A howl came from down the hall.

Clayton looked past Schumarr. "What was that?"

"That's Project Titan," Schumarr replied.

A devilish grin spread across Clayton's face. "I'd like to meet him." He stepped over stacks of binders and exited the room. "Where is he?"

"Let go of me. I'll show you," Schumarr said still struggling.

Clayton looked at his men and nodded. "Let him go."

Schumarr brushed himself off and straightened his wrinkled clothes. He reached into his pocket and removed a ring of keys. "Follow me."

Clayton and the others did just that.

Schumarr took them through a short maze, which ended in front of a large door. He peered through the small window in the door and saw three eighteen pacing; the triple restraints dangled from his wrists. In the far corner of the room, Schumarr took note of the observation window. Suddenly, an idea popped in his head. "He's in there, but we need to go to the observation room, this way." Schumarr took them around the corner and led them into a small darkened room. A single table with two chairs faced a large window.

"Here you'll get a better view of him," Schumarr said, pointing into the room.

Clayton and the two men walked in.

Three eighteen stopped pacing and looked around.

Schumarr turned on the light in the observation room.

Three eighteen snapped his head in the direction of the window. He sprinted towards it and launched himself forcefully but bounced off and fell to the floor.

Clayton and the others flinched but Schumarr didn't. "Bullet-resistant reinforced glass, level five like in armored vehicles."

Clayton replied with a simple grin. "You're prepared, I see."

"Yes," Schumarr said, taking a few steps back towards the entry door.

Three eighteen picked himself up, walked to the window and stared at everyone. Blood streamed down his face from a gash where his head had impacted the glass. His fully dilated eyes examined each of them on the other side.

"What's he doing?" Clayton asked.

"I'm not sure, as I haven't had ample time to study him, but if I were to guess, he's *studying* us."

"Fascinating," Clayton said.

"Fascinating, indeed," Schumarr said.

Three eighteen looked to his right and saw a door next to the window, which opened into the observation room. He stepped over and tried the handle but found it locked. He returned to staring at them.

"Does he always drool like that?" Clayton asked.

"I think so. Again, I haven't had time to examine him. He's unique," Schumarr said proudly.

"And what was it that made him this way?" Clayton asked, his eyes glued to the staring test subject.

"A parasite, a simple single-cell parasite."

Clayton craned his head towards Schumarr and said, "Parasite?"

"Yes, a common one too."

"What do you mean? Explain?"

Schumarr looked at his watch and saw the time. The helicopters would be arriving in twenty-three minutes. He needed to act and fast.

"Two years ago, I read a research white paper on a common parasite called *Toxoplasma gondii*. It's been known for a while that it has the ability to control rats. What I found intriguing from this research was they believe it can affect humans too."

"How so?"

"By creating rage. They discovered that half of the people who display unprovoked anger issues are infected with this parasite. I found this fascinating. I began to think that if it could be sequenced properly, we could use this parasite to our advantage by creating a type of super soldier. With that in mind, I endeavored on doing just that. I took the parasite and enhanced its effects on the human hosts. Three eighteen is the first one to survive to this phase of testing."

"You're telling me this guy has a parasite in his brain?"

"Yes, one I've enhanced synthetically, a *Toxoplasma* on steroids, you could say."

"But...exactly how were you planning on weaponizing this?" Clayton asked. His face showed the confusion that was going through his mind. "You told us you were working on a virus, some sort of bioweapon but you were just making Frankenstein-type shit here."

"I'm working on Sleeper, but this can be weaponized. I'm just not there yet in my research. I need more time, but we could create a super soldier who is stronger, faster and wants nothing but to kill, imagine that."

"What's wrong with him? He just stands there staring," Clayton asked, facing the window again.

"I can only guess but the parasite seems to want to spread by attacking uninfected. It attacked and killed my assistant Charles but before Charles died, it appeared he was trying to infect him."

"Infect? What have you made here?" Clayton asked.

"Like I said, I need more time," Schumarr said.

"How dare you create this...whatever this is. When were you planning on telling me?" Clayton asked.

Schumarr didn't answer. He stepped out the door, slammed it shut and locked it.

"Dr. Schumarr, what are you doing?" Franz asked standing in the hallway.

"Ensuring our work continues," he replied to Franz.

Clayton ran to the closed door and began slamming his fists against it. "Open the door!"

"Sorry, but my work is too important," Schumarr said and slapped a large red button on the wall.

Inside the room, Clayton heard an audible click coming from the door that connected their room and the holding cell. He looked at the door then the window.

Three eighteen cocked his head at an angle and gazed upon the door. He reached for the handle, turned it and this time it opened.

"Schumarr, let us out of here!" Clayton yelled.

Three eighteen threw the door open, stepped into the open doorway and stared at Clayton and the two men.

"Kill him, kill him now!" Clayton ordered the two men.

The men stood frozen in fear.

"Kill him, damn you!" Clayton screamed.

Schumarr didn't wait to watch. He had little time to get what he needed and rushed off.

Three eighteen sprang on the first man and ripped his throat out then leapt onto the next.

Clayton frantically kept trying the handle of the locked door in a fruitless effort to open it. "Schumarr, open the door, please. I'll let you take your work, but please open the door!"

Schumarr raced to his office and grabbed a stack of his personal diaries and all the logs which represented years of work. He turned to Franz and ordered, "In the lab, get all the discs, hurry."

Screams came from the observation room.

Schumarr paused. It gave him pleasure when he imagined three eighteen ripping Clayton apart.

A loud crash came from down the hall.

Schumarr grabbed what he needed and ran out of his office. Movement down the long passageway caught his eye. He turned to see three eighteen's arm dangling out the small window in the door. *What have I created?* he asked himself a bit freaked out.

Franz came around the corner. "I have the discs."

"Let's hurry, come on," Schumarr said.

The two men sprinted until they reached a hatch that led to the flight deck.

Franz cranked the lever and pushed the heavy hatch open.

Daylight washed over them.

The first of two helicopters had landed and the crew were boarding.

"Our timing couldn't be better," Schumarr said with a smile.

The two made their way but were stopped by Steffen, the captain of the ship. "Where's Clayton?"

"Oh, he's down below. He'll catch the second helicopter," Schumarr replied. Beads of sweat poured down his face.

Steffen raised a single brow. "Really?"

Schumarr could see the doubt in Steffen's face. "Can we get on board now?"

"No, I was given specific instructions not to allow you on one of those birds unless Clayton was present. He's your escort off this thing."

"That's ridiculous," Schumarr rebuffed.

"No, what's ridiculous is you were working on a fucking uncontrollable monster that could have killed us all and you didn't seem to think you should tell me, the captain," Steffen reprimanded.

"I don't care what they told you, it's all a lie," Schumarr railed.

"Doesn't matter what you say, I listen to whoever pays me and that's not you. Now go over there and wait until Clayton comes up," Steffen ordered as he pointed to a crate fifteen feet away.

Schumarr clenched his teeth in frustration. He was so close to getting away but Clayton had covered all his bases.

"What now?" Franz asked.

THE FIRST HELICOPTER LIFTED OFF; within minutes the second landed. The remaining crew boarded and were now waiting for Clayton and his two men to appear but, of course, they weren't coming.

Steffen walked over to Schumarr and asked, "Where is he?"

"I don't know what you're talking about. Last I saw him was in my lab. He was destroying stuff."

"Stuff like that?" Steffen asked, pointing at the logs Schumarr was cradling like a small infant.

"No, these are my person diaries," Schumarr replied.

"Let me see," Steffen ordered, his hand stretched out.

"These are personal diaries," Schumarr barked.

"We don't have time for your bullshit. The first charge is set to go off in ten minutes and we were supposed to be airborne five minutes ago. Now tell me where Clayton is."

A figure stepped out a hatch and onto the deck.

Steffen turned but the sun was in his eyes. "Clayton is that you? Where the hell have you been?"

Schumarr nudged Franz, leaned in close and said, "Run."

And run he did. Franz sprinted for the helicopter with Schumarr just behind him.

"Hold on, where are you two going?" Steffen asked.

Schumarr didn't look back. He knew what was coming. When he heard Steffen wail in pain he ran harder.

The two reached the helicopter. Schumarr climbed on, but as Franz was, he dropped the dozens of floppy discs. "Shit!"

Frantically he began picking them up.

Schumarr looked and saw three eighteen sprinting towards the chopper. He yelled, "Lift off, lift off now!"

"Your friend?" the pilot hollered over the noise of the rotating blades.

"Go!" Schumarr snapped.

The chopper lifted, but Franz didn't notice, as he was focused on gathering the dozens of discs. When the chopper was a foot up and climbing, Franz looked up. "No, wait!"

"Leave him, go!" Schumarr wailed.

Franz reached, but Schumarr offered the sole of his shoe and kicked him. Franz fell back onto the deck. He turned to get up, but three eighteen was on him before he could react.

"Hurry, go, go!" Schumarr yelled.

The pilot did exactly that. He accelerated the chopper's ascent and in seconds was several hundred feet above the aft of the ship and climbing.

Schumarr looked down as three eighteen ripped Franz's body apart.

The man in the copilot chair tapped Schumarr on the

shoulder and handed him a headset.

Schumarr put on the headset and was greeted by the pilot. "What was that thing on the deck?"

"It was beautiful," Schumarr replied.

A voice with a thick Middle Eastern accent then asked, "Are you Dr. Schumarr?"

Schumarr looked at the several faces on the chopper. They were all familiar; he had known them for years and none had accents like this. Confused he asked, "Who's this?"

"My name is Aashiq. I'm a friend of Yasser," the voice said.

Schumarr kept looking at the faces in the back with him but no one was talking. He turned to the cockpit and stared.

The man in the copilot's seat turned and removed his sunglasses. "Hi, Dr. Schumarr, I'm Aashiq."

"Yasser didn't say anyone was coming."

In a slow but steady voice, Aashiq asked, "What did we just witness on the deck of the ship?"

"That was Project Titan," Schumarr replied.

"And what are you carrying with you?" Aashiq asked.

"Oh, um, these are my private diaries," Schumarr lied.

"Good Doctor, you were given specific instructions not to take anything off that ship."

"But these are my private and personal journals, nothing more," Schumarr pressed.

"And what happened to Mr. Clayton?"

"I think we can assume that subject three eighteen killed him," Schumarr said.

Distant explosions distracted Schumarr. He craned his head back to see the ship now engulfed in several large orange fireballs. When he faced Aashiq he was greeted with the muzzle of a semi-automatic pistol.

"Give me the journals," Aashiq ordered calmly.

"But they're—"

Aashiq leveled the muzzle at Schumarr's face and repeated, "Give me the journals."

Schumarr gulped. He thought quickly about what he could do, but now he had zero options save throwing himself and his journals out the open doorway of the helicopter with hopes he'd survive the fifteen-hundred-foot fall.

"Now," Aashiq pressed.

Schumarr couldn't hesitate anymore. He loosened his arms and handed over the logbooks.

Aashiq took them. He holstered the pistol and opened the first book on the stack. He read for a minute then began to flip through quickly.

"Project Sleeper is in book three," Schumarr said.

"I don't care about that. Where can I find everything on Titan?" Aashiq asked his attention still on the books.

"Titan?"

Aashiq looked back at Schumarr and asked, "Where's all the information on Titan?"

"If you wanted it, I could have just given the real thing to you," Schumarr said.

"You have it on you?"

"Um, no, I didn't get a chance to get a live sample but everything you need to know to replicate it is in book seven," Schumarr answered.

Aashiq put book seven on top and opened it, he flipped until he found a tab that read *TITAN*. "Of course. This is good, really good." Aashiq excitedly read, his finger tracing the words.

Schumarr relaxed into his seat. The fear he had that his life was on the line melted away.

Aashiq read for ten minutes, closed the book, faced Schumarr and asked, "This is everything?"

"Everything...So Yasser *is* interested in Project Titan and not Sleeper?"

Aashiq held up book seven and asked again, "This is everything one needs to replicate the Titan parasite? How does it work? What's the R naught? Incubation?" Aashiq asked, rattling off questions.

"You seem to know a lot about this sort of stuff," Schumarr said.

"PhD in microbiology from Oxford."

"Impressive," Schumarr said with a half grin.

"Yasser speaks highly of you. I can see why, you're brilliant," Aashiq said.

"So you and I will be working on this?" Schumarr asked.

The helicopter turned left.

Schumarr looked through the cockpit window and could see the shoreline coming into view.

Aashiq tapped the pilot's arm and said, "Put us down on the far west side of the bay. There's a landing zone over there."

The pilot nodded.

"Where are we going?" Schumarr asked.

Aashiq turned back around and asked, "What I asked before, it's all in here? Incubation time, everything?"

"Yes, you'll see I'm thorough and detailed."

"And it does exactly as you say it does in here?"

"If you mean does it work to change a host, yes; however, I don't know if it can spread from host to host and the incubation time is long. If I were to continue working on it, I'd dedicate time and resources to enhancing or accelerating the parasite's maturation."

"How did you create such a beautiful thing?" Aashiq gushed.

"Like I told Clayton, I follow where the science takes me." Schumarr glowed.

Aashiq couldn't believe his good luck.

"I still think some additional testing is needed to see how it mutates. And I need to see about creating a vaccine," Schumarr replied.

"But it's all here, it just needs to be perfected?" Aashiq asked still in shock at this discovery.

"It's all there. And you saw it with your own eyes. That was a man infected with the Titan parasite. It's real, it works."

Asahiq tenderly touched the cover of the logbook.

"Why didn't Yasser tell me earlier he was interested in Titan?" Schumarr asked.

"He's not, but when he told me about it, I was beyond thrilled. What's in here will ensure our caliphate rules the world and stamps out the infidel. This is it, this will bring about the end of days."

"I'm confused," Schumarr said.

"You're a brilliant scientist, Dr. Schumarr. Do you wish to continue your work?"

Not believing his luck, Schumarr smiled and said, "Nothing would give me more pleasure."

"Good."

"But on one condition," Schumarr pressed.

"And that is?" Aashiq asked.

"That I be allowed to take Titan to its fullest potential."

"Good Doctor, you'll be given every resource. We want nothing more than Titan to be as powerful as it can be," Aashiq replied.

"Excellent. When do we begin?"

"As soon as we land," Aashiq said and held his hand out to Schumarr. "It will be an honor to work alongside you on this most holy of endeavors."

Schumarr firmly grasped Aashiq's hand and shook it. "The honor is mine."

Aashiq turned towards the front. He cradled book seven against his chest, closed his eyes and said, "Praise be Allah."

CHAPTER ONE

Friday, April 21
San Diego, California

BRETT PULLED the tank top over his head and stretched it with hopes his slight belly bulge wouldn't show. He and his wife, Madison, had committed to working out regularly once they had finally admitted they were not looking like the spring chickens they once were.

He headed towards the kitchen and caught a reflection of himself in the hall mirror. He paused and admired the changes in his body. Yes, he still had some pounds to lose but overall his faithful commitment had been paying off. His arms were muscular and his chest proudly extended past his belly. He was getting close to his goal, but one thing he didn't factor in when they had decided to begin working out was how good he would feel emotionally. His spirit was higher and there was a notable pep in his step.

His youngest son, Will, had even noticed and exclaimed two mornings ago that 'Daddy is looking tough.'

Hearing this added to his motivation to continue; however,

there was one thing he couldn't change—his ever-thinning hair. He leaned closer to the mirror and ran his fingers through his dark brown hair to cover the spots where he could see his scalp. He stepped back and saw his efforts were futile, either he lived with growing old gracefully or go get plugs. Not allowing this reminder to bring him down, he grinned and stepped away; instead he'd focus on the successes he had now. "One thing at a time."

Madison raced down the stairs and whirled past Brett. "Come on, we're running late." She grabbed a large bottle of water and took a drink. Her thick blond hair was pulled back into a long ponytail that dangled down and touched the back of her slender neck. She too had been seeing results from the workouts and just like Brett was full of energy and vigor.

"I'm coming, just admiring these things!" Brett exclaimed as he raised his arms and flexed.

"Oooh," she purred as she touched his biceps.

"Maybe we should run upstairs and get a workout there instead today," he teased grabbing her around the waist and pulling her close.

Madison kissed him on the lips, looked into his green eyes and replied, "Sounds tempting but the elliptical sounds better right now."

"What?" Brett howled.

She pulled away and said, "Come on, let's go. I have to be back soon to pick up the boys."

"Are you serious?" he asked, still standing where she had left him, his mouth hanging open.

She stopped and asked, "Were *you* serious?"

"Um, no, but how did you know I wasn't?"

She approached him, took his hand and softly said, "I know you better than you probably know yourself, now come on."

Brett chuckled because she was right; there wasn't anyone

in the world who knew him better. After twelve years together, not one person could claim they knew him more. They had their ups and downs like any relationship but at its core they were rock solid. Their relationship had started out as a deep friendship and grew from there. They had varying different likes and dislikes but their values were exact, from how they viewed the world to how they mutually raised the boys, Eddie and Will.

Knowing she was right and they needed to leave, he grabbed his backpack along with a large water bottle and his smart phone.

Already in the car, Madison grew impatient. She leaned over and honked the horn.

"I'm coming!" he hollered. In his right hand, he felt his phone vibrate. He looked down and saw a news flash on the screen. 'Several people shot in a café in Copenhagen.'

THE GYM WAS a short ten-minute drive away. They chatted and discussed a party they were having at their house the next day. It had been a while since they'd held a house party and preparations for it were the overriding issues they had been dealing with the past few days.

Holding her phone, Madison scrolled through a list she had created. "Now you're picking up the rest of the food tonight, right?"

"Maddy, my answer hasn't changed since I said yes earlier today and the day before." Brett laughed. He glanced at her and could see the strain on her face.

"I'm just making sure."

"You know this party will be fine. They always are, stop stressing. You're too worried about these little things."

She shot him a hard look, scrunching her face. "They're not

little things. I want it to be perfect. I don't want my friends to think we're..."

"We're what?"

"Nothing."

Brett leaned over and patted her leg. "Honey, our friends love us. They won't judge us for anything. Good God, we're not serving dog food and piss to drink."

"Don't mock me," she snapped.

"I'm not, I'm just saying everything always works out."

"There's no reason we can't make it a great party."

"I agree, but there's no need to stress."

Madison sighed and looked out the window.

Brett stopped at a red light and heard his phone vibrate again; he looked down and saw another news flash on the screen. *Dead in Copenhagen attack rises to twelve.* "Wow," Brett said out loud.

"What?"

"Oh, there was some sort of mass shooting in Copenhagen."

"Hmm. You don't really hear about such things," Madison said.

"They happen; just last year they had that terrorist attack at a mall. A lot of people were killed," Brett said reminding her of a very prominent attack.

"I thought they killed only a couple of people," Madison replied.

The light turned green and Brett hit the accelerator hard, propelling their BMW 5 Series down the road at a high rate of speed.

"Class starts in less than ten minutes, hurry up," Madison urged, referencing the spin class she had scheduled.

"Just so you know, they killed more people than a couple."

"Whatever, I can't remember," Madison said her head down again in her phone. "Um, should we make a special cocktail?"

26

Brett cocked his head, choosing to remain silent, as the nonstop party planning was wearing thin for him. His phone vibrated and lit up one more time, catching his eye. He quickly glanced down and saw it was another news alert. *'Death toll rises to more than 25 as attacks spread across Copenhagen.'* "What the hell is going on?" Brett blurted out.

"Huh?" Madison asked, her head down.

Brett pulled into the parking lot of the gym and parked. "This," he replied, handing her his phone.

She took it and said, "Oh no."

"Yeah, this is crazy, this is some sort of terrorist attack, not a random mass shooter," Brett declared as they walked inside.

Madison's attention quickly turned to her spin class. "Okay, sweetie, have a good workout." She kissed him on the cheek and rushed off.

"Sure," Brett said, not paying attention to her. He opened his web browser and went to the news. There the headlines shouted out in big bold black letters: **TERROR STRIKES COPENHAGEN**. He walked to the bench and sat down and scrolled through the preliminary reports coming in. His heart rate elevated. He felt so badly for all those who were suffering. His thoughts then shifted to his youngest brother, David, a photographer and documentarian who contracted out his services to various news outlets. The last he heard from him, he was somewhere overseas. He didn't know why exactly but a sudden concern came over him. He flipped to the phone, scrolled to his brother's contact information and hit the call button. Putting the phone to his ear, he listened. The typical pause between connections was replaced with two clicks then a long hum. This told him David was overseas. After several long tones the line clicked and David's voice came on.

"This is David. You know what to do."

"David, hey, it's Brett. I, um, just seeing if you're okay. I'm sure you're probably smack dab in the middle of this horrible stuff. Um, anyway, give me a shout when you have time. It will be nice to hear my baby brother's voice," Brett said and disconnected. He looked at the screen when suddenly another news alert popped up.

'Explosions and gunfire rock Copenhagen.'

He couldn't help but feel emotion when looking at the headlines. He and Madison had just spent time in Copenhagen not eight weeks before and had fallen in love with the city and the people. He thought about all the places they had gone and wondered if those sites and, more importantly, anyone they might have met might be a victim.

"Hey, are you using the bench?" a man boomed above him.

Sheepishly, Brett looked up and replied, "Ah, no, go ahead." He stood and walked away. He needed to get his mind off the horrific news and a hard workout would do that.

Copenhagen, Denmark

DAVID RACED down the cobblestoned alleyway towards the rattle of automatic gunfire. His heart was pumping hard and sweat was streaming down his stubble-covered face. He hoped he had charged his camera but his mind wasn't thinking clearly when he'd first heard what was too recognizable to him. Years of working in combat zones gave him a sixth sense, so the second he heard the first volley, he took off towards the sound. He had been a foreign correspondent for Reuters for ten years, and when asked if he liked what he did, he'd always grin and say, "Best job in the world."

When he exited the alley, the unfiltered sounds of terror hit his ears. Bursts of gunfire mixed with screams filled the air. The wailing sirens of police were drawing closer and a rush of people pushed past him. He paused to orientate and looked towards the corner of two streets over three hundred feet away. There he saw two men holding AK-47s. They were calmly walking back and forth on the sidewalk firing into a corner café. Unafraid, he did the opposite of everyone else; he ran towards the horrific scene unfolding. He covered two hundred feet and took cover behind a parked car; he pulled off his backpack and reached inside to grab his camera. Instinctually he turned it on without looking and popped his head above the hood and looked towards the café that was under attack. Harrowing screams bounced off the buildings with the roar of another volley of gunfire being amplified by the acoustics of the mid-rise buildings that lined the street corner.

The men were still there, their behavior so calm and patient as if they were just going through a mundane act.

David raised his camera and zoomed in the lens on the man closest to him. He placed his trembling finger on the button to snap a photo but paused. Through the lens, he saw a woman, bloodied, sobbing and desperately crawling away.

The terrorist spotted her and casually approached her.

Shocked by what he was seeing, David lowered the camera and did something he had never done in his many years as a correspondent. "Hey!" he hollered towards the terrorist to draw his attention.

The terrorist didn't hear him and continued towards the woman.

Seeing that he wasn't successful, he stood up. "Hey, shithead, over here!" David yelled and started waving his arms.

The second gunman appeared from around the corner, further away, and sprayed a volley of bullets into the café.

Again, seeing his attempt failed, David looked for something to throw.

The woman placed one blood-covered hand in front of the other and dragged herself along the uneven sidewalk.

The terrorist stepped in front of her.

She looked up, her eyes telling the horror of what stood in front of her. With a sorrowful moan, she said, "No, no!" Tears streamed down her blood-covered face. Unable to run because of wounds to her legs, she did the only thing she thought would help, beg for her life.

Emotionless, the terrorist raised the muzzle of his rifle and leveled it at her head.

Not giving up, the woman raised her hand in a gesture for mercy.

Scrambling to find something to throw, David saw the bottled water tucked on the side pocket of his backpack and pulled it out. He stepped forward and threw it as hard as he could.

As the bottle spun through the air, the terrorist pulled the trigger.

A short burst exited the barrel and struck the woman in the face.

Her head snapped back and her body fell to the ground, lifeless.

The bottle finished its spin and hit the terrorist squarely in the back. He spun around to see David standing fifty feet behind him.

Not often was his timing off, but when it really mattered, it had been this time. David gulped and stood staring at the mass murderer. All the sounds around him suddenly vanished. The sirens, screams and cries just went mute and his vision narrowed to a tunnel as he focused on the barrel of the AK-47 that was now pointed at him. He knew he should run, but for whatever reason he was frozen to the spot, unable to make a move.

The terrorist pulled the trigger, but nothing happened. He looked down and saw the slide was back, indicating he was out of ammunition. Calmly he removed the empty magazine, allowing it to fall hard to the ground, and pulled a fully loaded one from his pocket and inserted it.

Suddenly and unexpectedly a car raced past David and stopped next to the terrorist. An unintelligible voice blared from the car. The second terrorist ran up and got in. The first kept his eye on David.

A deep feeling of regret came over David as he second-guessed his decision to involve himself. He had broken a journalistic rule of becoming part of the story, but how could he just sit and watch a murder without doing something? It was the honorable thing to do, but with his life in the balance he couldn't help but wish he hadn't.

More yelling came from the car.

The terrorist yelled back, lowered his rifle and stepped towards the car. Just before he climbed in, he gave David one last look and grinned.

The car accelerated away and made a hard left disappearing into a narrow alleyway.

David slowly walked towards the woman's lifeless body, but stopped when he came upon the bottle of water he had thrown.

If asked how long it was in between the terrorists' departure and the police arriving, David wouldn't be able to honestly answer. What must have been seconds seemed like minutes, but soon the entire street corner was swarming with police, the blue lights of the cars dancing off the cobblestone streets and stone facades of the buildings.

David reached down and picked up the bottle of water. It was cool to his touch. He couldn't believe what had just happened to him because of this little bottle of Evian. He opened it, took a drink and a moment to calm his nerves before doing what he came to do, document the news.

London, United Kingdom

JORGE SOROSSI WAS NOT a man with the patience to wait for anyone because a man of his extreme wealth, status and reputation kept everyone else waiting. Today was different and he wasn't enjoying the role reversal.

He tapped the fingers of his left hand firmly on the leather chair while his right hand swirled the forty-year-old scotch his assistant had just poured.

"Where the hell are they? They're now an hour late," he barked at his Harris, his longtime personal assistant.

"Would you like me to call them again?" Harris asked.

"No, I'm just tired of waiting like a common servant," he snapped. He took a long drink and set the glass down. "Turn on the television," he ordered.

Harris did as he asked.

"...the horrific attacks earlier are now being attributed to a radical offshoot of Islamic State, a group that reportedly goes by the name The Bloody Hand. Not much is known about them as of right now. According to the Danish Intelligence Service, they've received credible information on the terrorists who committed these attacks and have linked them with this new group, but nothing else as of now. As of minutes ago, the death toll has reached two hundred and thirteen dead and many more wounded, many of which are critical. We know the death toll will rise as they haven't been able to get a full accounting of dead at the stadium. We're now hearing the death toll could rise to well over five hundred," the BBC newscaster said.

"Sir, call for you," Harris said holding a mobile phone.

"Is that the encrypted line?" Jorge asked.

"Yes, sir."

Jorge took the phone and asked, "Who is this?"

"Some of our people were a bit too eager to begin phase one," a mysterious voice said.

"Who is this?" *Jorge asked.*

"We're moving up the operation. Phase one will begin soon."

"Who the hell am I speaking with?" Jorge snarled.

"We need more money so we can finalize phase two."

"Who is this?" Jorge again asked, frustrated that the person wouldn't identify himself.

"Your friends, of course."

"We had a meeting. I was to meet Israfil."

"We said we'd talk, and we're talking," the man said.

"Is this you, these attacks? This stuff won't work. You told me you had something else, something big planned. Not shit like this. I said this sort of strategy will only embolden them. I insist on speaking with Israfil and who the hell is this *Bloody Hand.*"

"We're all part of The Bloody Hand. You, me, those fighters tonight in Copenhagen."

"This strategy won't work. You promised something dynamic," Jorge growled.

"It's coming, I promise."

"I want to speak to Israfil," Jorge barked.

"You'll hear from Israfil soon enough. We need additional funds so we may complete phase two."

"Not until I speak with Israfil."

"Today's attack was premature, but you'll see more coming soon and the reason is valid. I don't expect you to understand, but it will do what we need them to do."

"You're playing into Shade's hands with this sort of stuff. Now, I demand to speak with Israfil," Jorge snapped.

"You're not in any position to make requests. You came to us, but to complete the plan we need the additional funds to do so. We are very close."

Jorge clenched his fist and gritted his teeth. "How much?"

"*Another ten million.*"

"I've given you over one hundred thirty. What are you doing with all my money?"

"*You'll know soon enough what comes of it.*"

Jorge went to respond but stopped when the newscaster cut to news from the United States.

"*President Shade has called the Danish prime minister and offered condolences and pledges support. He also said he will finally push through on a campaign promise and issue an executive order that will totally ban travel from all Muslim nations with ties to recent terror incidents in Europe. He will also increase vetting procedures for all incoming non-US passport holders coming from anywhere. This is a huge step for the already controversial president and will surely cause outcries from civil liberty and immigrant advocates,*" the BBC reporter said.

"*Mr. Sorossi, we need something else from you,*" the man said.

"What?"

"*We need you to contact the groups you're financing in the United States. We need them to increase their displays of civil disobedience. We need them to take to the streets; we need them to create mayhem, discontent.*"

"I don't think I'll need to tell them to do anything, Shade's response to this attack will have them riled up, but I'll make the call."

"*Just make sure they take to the streets. We need law enforcement focused on them. And one final thing.*"

After a long pause, Jorge asked, "Yes?"

"As soon as President Shade implements his executive order, we need one of the federal judges on your payroll to block it. We can't have anything in our way."

"What are you planning?"

"Mr. Sorossi, you'll see soon enough. Just do as we ask and we'll give you what we both want, the toppling of the United States."

"Just tell me."

"When it happens, you'll know. Goodbye."

Ramona, California

"CHEERS!" the group joyfully said in unison as their glasses clanged together.

Cassidy looked at each person sitting at the table, stopping on Sophie. He mouthed, *I love you.*

Sophie winked at Cassidy.

Laughter broke out.

Cassidy relaxed in his chair, taking in the moment. Surrounding him were the most important people in his life. Sophie, his beloved girlfriend; her brother, Scott; and Jim Ramsey, an old friend from his days in the Marine Corps.

"Dinner was amazing, thanks so much," Ramsey said, rubbing his belly.

"I'm happy you enjoyed it," Sophie said, her chin resting on her hands. A pleasant smile graced her face.

Cassidy looked at Sophie and said, "She's an amazing cook. That's why I've tacked on a few extra pounds."

"You know what they say, belly full, balls empty, that's how you keep a man," Sophie joked.

"I love her even more." Ramsey smiled.

She reached and took Cassidy's hand, squeezed it and replied, "I'm blessed. He's a good guy."

Scott looked at his watch and said, "Dinner was so good and the company better, but I need to call it a night."

"No, not yet," Cassidy urged, shocked to hear Scott was leaving.

"Yeah, I got a text just before dinner. I've got to report to Otay tomorrow," Scott replied. He worked for the San Diego Port Authority.

"Wait, does that mean you're not going hunting with us tomorrow?" Cassidy asked.

"Sorry, but I got to go in," Scott said, standing.

"We've had this planned for months," Cassidy complained.

"Duty calls. You know this better than me," Scott said.

"There has to be someone who can take this," Cassidy said.

"When you're the manager of operations and one of your employees calls in sick, someone has to step up and that person is me."

"Total bullshit," Cassidy said.

"But there's good news, I can join you later tomorrow night at your campsite," Scott said.

"Good, so it's not a total loss," Cassidy said.

"I have to ask, is it really a sick call or something to do with this terrorist stuff?" Sophie asked.

"Now, Sophie, you know I can neither confirm nor deny," Scott quipped.

"I'd like to say I'm shocked but I'm not," Cassidy injected.

"I'm just waiting for big attacks like that to come here," Ramsey chimed in.

"It's scary. I can see it happening here though too," Sophie added.

Scott glanced at his watch but didn't leave. "Schools, that's what I think. Why not hit schools?"

All eyes turned to Cassidy.

"It's our soft underbelly. I'll be honest, I not only sweep the floors but play security guard, and let me tell you, that's a tall task to accomplish with a school administration that's clueless. I was only just able to convince them to lock the gates when the bell rings. I wanted to restrict access but they wouldn't have it. I was told to mind my own business and go back to the job I was hired for."

"Idiots, we have more security at a jewelry store than at our schools." Ramsey sighed.

"No one cares until they have to care then everyone wants to cast blame somewhere else," Cassidy groaned as he took a drink of his beer.

"That's gotta be so frustrating for you," Ramsey said.

"It is, from being a squad leader with combat experience to sweeping floors, cleaning toilets and having middle-aged women with master's degrees in elementary education telling me how to best secure the school is quite frustrating. Get this, I've seen this one vehicle, the same car almost every day for the past two weeks, cruising the school, a single guy driving. Sometimes he's parked and just staring at the school."

"A ped?" Ramsey asked.

"Could be, but dude, he looks like a Hajji. Like I could see this guy driving by us in Sangin, but his car would have a bomb in it," Cassidy said.

"Let me get this straight, you've spotted a single Muslim-looking guy cruising by your school or parked close by the past couple of weeks and you thought not to tell me?" Sophie asked.

"I didn't want to alarm you. I told the administration. At first they were interested until I said the magic get-out-of-jail words in liberal California."

"Let me guess, illegal, no undocumented," Ramsey joked.

"Close...Muslim. The second I think this guy could be a fucking terrorist casing our school, they get butt hurt and ask me to stop. The principal even suggested I go see counseling and that they don't profile, period." Cassidy laughed and continued. "I took down the pertinent details and contacted the SDPD. Hopefully they'll check on him."

"Good, but what's up with the admin? It's like the world is

upside down. What's good is now bad, and what's bad is now good. It's like we're living in the *Twilight Zone*," Sophie said.

"Ha, good cultural reference but how would a twenty-five-year-old know the *Twilight Zone*?" Ramsey asked, chuckling.

"Netflix," she answered.

Cassidy sighed heavily and said, "Every day I kick myself for getting in that damn car. I knew I should have called Uber or a cab, but I just thought I was only driving a couple of miles away. My damn fool hubris got the better of me and now look at me. I'm a total failure."

"Don't say that," Ramsey said.

"You're solid, bro, don't let the past get you down. You're gainfully employed, you have benefits and that job is not the last one you'll get. Please don't beat yourself up over it," Scott said.

Sophie rubbed his arm.

"Enough of the pity party, let's all toast to loved ones and friends," Cassidy said. He jumped up, went to the freezer and removed a chilled bottle of Fireball.

"Oh God, not Fireball," Scott said. "Sorry, I'm out."

"Fine, you're out, but you two, you're having one with me," Cassidy said to Sophie and Ramsey.

"I hate you," Sophie joked. She detested the taste of Fireball.

He blew her a kiss and poured three full shot glasses.

Ramsey took his and raised it.

Cassidy did the same with Sophie joining.

Scott grabbed a glass of water so he wouldn't be left out.

"To friends and loved ones!" Cassidy cheered.

The others tapped their glasses and repeated what he said.

CASSIDY STEPPED into the bedroom and closed the door. "He's all tucked in," he said referring to Ramsey.

"What a good friend. Did you read him a story too?" she joked from behind the glow of her iPad.

"No, but I did sing him a lullaby," Cassidy replied, jumping into bed and crawling next to her.

"He's a nice guy, I like him," she said.

"Me too, but I'd rather talk about you now," he said with a softer tone.

"Oh really?"

"Whatcha doing?" Cassidy asked after taking notice she was fully intrigued by whatever was on her screen.

"Did you know that babies in the womb can recognize the voices of their parents?" Sophie asked.

"Yeah, I'd heard that before, but why are you reading about babies? Do you have something to tell me?" Cassidy said as he slowly lifted her pajama top.

"Um, what are you doing?" Sophie asked glaring at him.

"Role-playing what I'd do if you were pregnant by talking to your belly," Cassidy said lowering his head to her belly. "Hi, this is Daddy. Are you nice and warm in there?"

Sophie put the iPad down. She longingly looked at Cassidy.

"Daddy, can't wait to meet you," he said softly.

"You're so silly." Sophie laughed as she ran her fingers through his thick dark hair.

"Why are you reading about babies? Shouldn't you be responding to your regional manager's e-mail concerning the position in Boise?" Cassidy asked.

"I should. I've been doing a ton of research on Boise. It looks nice and the cost of living is so much lower than here. We could get a big home, with a yard."

"I'll support anything you do. It's not as if I have a real job," Cassidy said.

"Don't say that."

"It's true."

"Whatever."

"Let's get back to why you're reading about babies," Cassidy said.

"No reason, just saw it on Facebook. But if we were to have a baby, Boise has decent schools, but more importantly, the quality of life looks so much better. I'm just torn, as my family is all here."

"They could always come visit," Cassidy said.

She took his face in her hand and turned it left and right. "I hope they get your looks."

"Your family?"

"No, our baby...if we ever have one."

"My looks, are you crazy? Could you imagine me with long hair and lipstick? Poor little girl would be tortured."

"What are you talking about? You're the most handsome man I've met," she said softly.

He shot her a look, smiled and joked, "Are you being nice so you'll get lucky tonight?"

"And you're smart," she said with a devilish grin.

He sat up, tore off his shirt and said, "Fine, twist my arm."

She pulled him close and gave him a kiss.

San Diego, California

"Turn the TV off and come to bed," Madison groaned.

"Just another minute," Brett mumbled, his eyes glued to the scenes of death and mayhem on the television screen.

"Nothing new is going to be reported and I have to say, it's depressing me. Please turn it off," Madison complained.

Brett cocked his head and said, "Depressing you? So sorry a tragedy like this is annoying and inconvenient."

"I didn't say that. Stop putting words in my mouth," Madison shot back.

"You haven't had any interest in what's happening, not one bit."

"Because I don't need to drown myself in the news. I heard what happened, there's nothing I can do about it, but I'm informed. That's all I need to do."

Brett put his attention on the screen again and thought about what she had said, specifically, the point about not being able to do anything about it. *Is that true?* It was in the sense that there wasn't anything they could do for these people in Copenhagen, but what about ensuring he and his family were safer? *Can I be more proactive at home?* He turned the television off and came to the bedroom.

Madison was sitting up in bed with her iPad, flipping through Pinterest, looking for a drink recipe.

Brett got into bed and scooted next to her. "What are you doing?"

"I want to have a special drink for the party, something fun and bubbly."

"Hmm."

She sighed, looked at him and rolled her eyes. "This is why I hate you watching too much news, you get grumpy."

"I'm not grumpy."

"Then what was that little noise you just made?"

"It was nothing."

"Yes, it was."

"You want to know?" he asked.

"I'm sure you'll tell me regardless," Madison groaned.

"What's up with you?"

"Nothing, I'm just a bit done with the Copenhagen thing. It's all you've been talking about since we left the gym. I get it, it's a bad deal, it sucks but I still have my life to live. I feel horrible for those people, but like I said, there isn't anything I can do about it."

Brett thought about countering her but held his tongue. He knew Madison well enough to know she would only fight about it.

She reached out, touched his arm and with a softer tone said, "Don't stress so much. Everything will be fine, we'll be fine, the kids will be fine."

He trusted her words before, but this time they didn't provide the comfort they normally did. He scrunched his face and replied, "What happened just makes me sick. I worry that something will happen here and I'm just not prepared."

Seeing the stress and concern, she moved closer and planted a kiss on his lips. "Oh, honey, we're as prepared as we need to be. We have everything we need, you're a great provider, our family has everything it needs."

"Do we?" he asked, referencing the attacks and questioning if he was truly ready to handle a situation if it came to his world.

She leaned back slightly and asked, "What do you think we need?"

"I don't know. I'm just worried. Those poor people were just sitting ducks; there was nothing they could do."

"What do you expect them to do when some madmen with guns start shooting?"

"Fight back," he blurted out.

"Fight back, like pull their own guns out or give them a karate chop? That's lunacy," she snapped, her soft tone melting away instantly.

"What's wrong with fighting back?"

"That's not our job, that's the police's job. Civilians don't fight," she boldly declared.

"What if someone had fought back, maybe they could have

prevented more people from getting killed. Look at September 11."

"What are you talking about?"

"The plane that crashed in Pennsylvania, that plane was headed to Washington and was supposed to hit a building. If those passengers hadn't fought back, others would have died."

"Yeah, but those people died."

"They did, but they sacrificed themselves to save others, that's honorable. And they were going to die anyway. That plane was going to smash into a building."

Madison pulled further back and asked, "What's gotten into you? Never in my life have I ever heard you use such language. Honorable?"

He could feel his blood pressure rising as her typical condescending tone began to irritate him. Knowing if he kept countering her, she wouldn't stop and the discussion they were having would turn into a fight.

Madison sighed heavily and picked up her iPad.

He looked at her and wished she could feel the way he did. She was smart but equally stubborn. Doubt then entered his mind. Maybe he was being foolish; maybe his emotional response to the grisly attacks in Copenhagen were nothing more than an emotional overreach on his part. Like he did with other things, he would need to sleep on it and let some time come in between the events and him. He slipped further under the covers and clicked his light off. As he laid his head on the pillow and closed his eyes, the images he had watched earlier flashed. He worked out different scenarios if he had been there until he drifted to sleep.

Rancho Bernardo, California

Mo RELAXED into the heavily cushioned chair. The movie he and his parents were watching was either boring or he just couldn't focus. Who knew, but for seventeen-year-old kids, focusing was an issue unless they were playing the latest game, and for him that was HALO.

"Put your phone down and watch the movie. I rented this just for you," Mo's father snapped.

Mo put his phone down and put his attention back on the movie.

A ping sounded on Mo's phone.

He looked down and saw his friend Malik had sent him a text. He swiped and pulled it up.

"Check this out. AWESOME!!!" Malik wrote.

Below was a link to a video.

Mo clicked the link. His browser pulled up and shortly after a video feed began. He leaned closer to see what it was. The video was dark and it was hard to hear clearly over what to him sounded like screams, shouting and gunfire.

His phone pinged again.

"Go to 1:56. Watch the bitch INFIDEL cry. HILARIOUS!"

Mo went to the time on the video. On the screen, a woman was on her knees, her arms up, and on her face tears streamed, but more importantly her face told the story of a woman terrified.

"Please, no, don't do this," she begged.

Several men offscreen were laughing and speaking in what was clearly Arabic.

"Please don't."

A man entered the screen and grabbed the woman by her thick blond hair and pulled her head back hard.

She wailed in pain and terror.

The man brandished a six-inch knife. He held it closer to the camera lens and shouted, *"Allahu Akbar!"*

44

The men off camera began to holler the same.

The man without hesitation took the blade and slid it across the woman's bare throat. Blood spurted out.

The woman gurgled and choked.

He pulled her head back farther and put the knife again on her throat but this time he sawed at it until he ripped her head off her shoulders.

The men offscreen cheered.

The man with the knife held up her dismembered head and hollered, "*Allahu Akbar, Allahu Akbar!*"

An unknown number of men entered the screen. They placed their open palms in the blood and showed it to the camera. In unison they began to chant, *wamin nahiat alddamawia*.

The video ended.

Mo was wide-eyed. He was in between a state of shock and delight.

"What was that!" his father yelled and smacked the phone out of his hand.

Startled by his father's sudden appearance over his shoulder, Mo jumped and said, "What? Nothing."

"Nothing! I saw it, don't lie! What are you doing? What are you watching? Huh? Is it your friend Malik? Huh?"

"Dad, no," Mo denied.

"Don't lie to me," his father said and picked up the phone. He rewound the video a few seconds and watched. He cringed and looked away when the man sliced the woman's throat. Angered, he tossed the phone against the wall. It shattered. "What are you doing watching that sort of stuff in this house on your phone? Huh?"

"It's news," Mo said in a weak attempt to defend his actions.

"News? That's terrorist propaganda. And your friend Malik

G. MICHAEL HOPF

writes *awesome*. Son, what's wrong with you? Those people are killers, murderers. We are not them."

"Maybe we should be!" Mo shot back defiantly.

"What did you say?" his father asked angrily, taking a step towards him.

"Americans are over there killing *our* people every day. They bomb them all the time. Killing innocents! We can't just sit by and do nothing."

"Our people? Are you an idiot? We're Iranian. I fled after people like that began to kill your relatives. Your great-uncle was executed by those types of people. Fortunately, I was given asylum and only because I could help the effort to rid my people of the scourge in Iran. Don't you dare say those are our people. We're Persian, they're Arabs, and on top of that, we're Americans. You were born here, you're an American, you're not an Arab, you're not even Iranian. You've never even been to the Middle East."

"I hate America and you...you're a traitor to the prophet!" Mo screamed.

His father slapped him across the face hard.

Mo's mother screamed, "Stop it!" She ran to Mo.

"Mohammed, you take that back. You take back what you just said!" his father blared.

"No, I won't!" Mo yelled. He picked himself up and marched out of the room.

His father wasn't done with him. He grabbed Mo's arm and gripped it tightly. "Don't you dare walk away from me. You live in my house and under my rules." He began to slap him repeatedly on the back of the head with an open hand.

Mo cowered and tried to shield himself from the hits but his father was relentless.

After a flurry of smacks, his father released him and yelled, "Go to your room. You're on restriction. You're to only go to and

46

from school. No more hanging out with that kid Malik. You hear me?"

Mo stood up, glared and raced off.

USS *Anchorage*, Arabian Sea

Sergeant Rich Brennan lay in his rack, resting. To say he was tired was an understatement. He was worn out, but he found a minute's worth of energy to gaze upon Jenna's face. He swiped from one photo to the next on his phone until he came to the photo of the ultrasound.

Jenna and he had once had a turbulent relationship. It had all started in high school. They'd started dating the beginning of their junior year and continued their romance long distance when he joined the Marines. However, she had found being a deployment widow difficult so they broke up soon after he made it to the Fleet. They rekindled the flame when he returned home from leave after his last deployment to Afghanistan and, from then on, kept it lit. Of course, it required he come home more and bring her to Camp Pendleton as often as he could.

At first the news of her pregnancy scared him; then over time he settled into the idea of being a father, but with weeks to go in the pregnancy, the fear began to return. He loved the Marine Corps and knew being married with a kid would change his experience of it. In fact, he hadn't contemplated getting out until he found out he was going to be a father. He had seen over his many deployments how a family at home affected those Marines. While they provided comfort, they also seemed to bring pain. He never could get any of those Marines to admit it but he could see it in their weary eyes as they boarded transport to deploy knowing they may never see their loved ones again. The questions he knew that plagued them popped into his own head. *How will I provide for them? What will happen to them if*

I die? How will Jenna and the baby manage on the next deployment I'm sure to go on? Never did he dread a deployment until now, and being infantry, he was assured to deploy every eighteen to twenty-four months.

When he tried to discuss his troubled thoughts with his two best friends, Corporals Viktor Vickers and Kevin Klyde, they'd only return his beleaguered questions with taunting answers like, *'Maybe next time you'll be mindful of where you stick your dick.'* Or, *'If you kept it wrapped, you wouldn't be in this predicament.'* Often, they were good counsel until now and he hated it. But alas, it was his situation to deal with and he would deal with it with an open mind and a commitment to be the best he could be.

"Sergeant Brennan, did you hear?" Lance Corporal Dietz asked, stepping next to his rack.

"Hear what?" Brennan replied, lowering his phone.

"Some douchebag terrorists attacked and killed hundreds in Europe somewhere."

"That sucks," Brennan said as he lifted his phone.

"Do you think it will change our going home?" Dietz asked.

"No."

"You sure? Several people are saying it will."

"Dietz, I highly doubt it. Now leave me alone. I want some private time," Brennan said drawing the blinds on his rack.

"Goodnight, Sergeant Brennan. I hope you're right."

CHAPTER TWO

Saturday, April 22
Copenhagen, Denmark

DAVID SHRUGGED HIS SHOULDERS. A deep ache emanated from the center of his back and into his shoulders and neck.

The sun hit his face and warmed it. A grateful feeling rose in him. Seeing the sun made it even more special. He had survived, but why?

The adrenaline that had coursed through his veins during the long evening and early morning hours was waning. A great fatigue was bearing down on him, but leaving the scene to go find his bed felt like a dereliction of duty. However, he was finding it hard to focus and if he was going to be at his best, he needed a few hours of rest.

He walked down the nearly empty sidewalks of Copenhagen, heading towards his hotel. What would have normally been a bustling Saturday late morning was eerily quiet. A heavy sense of dread hung like a thick cloud over the city and there was no escaping it. Each turn down a street and each person he saw displayed the dreariness.

A buzz in his upper jacket pocket tore him away from the fog of the hours before. He reached and pulled out his phone. He expected to see the screen of his iPhone full of notifications and his assumption proved correct. As he thumbed through the typical numbers and texts, he stopped when he saw his brother Brett's phone number with a notification there was a message. He clicked the message and put it to his ear. When his brother's concerned voice came over, it tugged at him. He and Brett were close but didn't stay in constant contact. They had a relationship that could go for months without conversation, but the instant they talked, they could pick right up from where they had left off before. When the message ended, he went to hit the call back then remembered the time difference. The last thing he wanted to do was wake him but he questioned the hesitation. The minimum he could do was text, so he did and stated he'd call later when the time was more appropriate.

The phone vibrated the second he pushed the send button.

He saw it was one of the numbers that had called him countless times. He knew the number well. It was his agent calling.

David accepted the call and said, "Hi, Max."

"David! Thank God you're okay!" Max bellowed with his thick New York accent.

"I'm good. Max, it was horrible, it was fucking horrible."

"So the reports are correct," Max said.

"What do you mean?"

"The reports that you were at one of the cafés when one of the attacks was going down."

"Who told you that?" David asked.

"David, how long have you known me? I have my sources. You gave a statement to the police and, well, we found out. How come you didn't do an interview? This is pure gold."

"It didn't feel right. I'm not the story."

"The hell you aren't. Now I've got you set up for airtime with all the top shows. I need you available later, okay?"

David grunted but knew the importance of him telling his story. It not only helped others understand the brutality of the terrorists with a firsthand account, it also selfishly benefitted him. He had been working on a film documentary about ISIS but his financial resources had dried up after many in the mainstream media outlets turned a cold shoulder to anything they perceived might tarnish Islam. It infuriated David, but it was the reality of what he was dealing with. With his financial backers gone, his film died.

Max was a godsend and was always looking out for him. He knew that any exposure David could get might help bring in some much-needed money for his project.

"When and where?" David asked.

"I'll e-mail the details. You should try to get some rest."

"That's what I'm about to do."

"And get me all your shots. I've got some hungry news outlets. And please get some of those bloody handprints. I hear they're everywhere."

"I will as soon as I get to the hotel. I'll send them to the FTP server."

"Sounds good. Thanks and, Dave, good job, bravo."

"Yeah, yeah."

"Be safe. I can't risk having you end up horizontal," Max joked.

Ignoring Max's attempt at humor, David replied, "Talk with you later." He ended the call and put the phone back in his pocket. He paused on the corner and caught a glimpse of a canal. The waterways and colorful buildings that lined them were iconic to the city. He loved this city and its people. What happened to him was something he would never forget but what would be seared into his memory forever was the woman he'd witnessed being executed. Her pleas for mercy going unheeded made his heart ache. It also was a clear message to him that he needed to do more. He wasn't sure what he could do but he couldn't be a bystander in history anymore, he needed to bring awareness, real awareness, to the threat that was spreading around the world.

Lake Arrowhead, California

THE SUN's early light crested the horizon and with it brought the promise of a new day but more importantly for Trevor Cassidy, the sun brought warmth. It was a welcome sight to see the orange glow as his numb fingers and toes ached from the cold air.

Spring, or mud season as the locals called it, was merely a light winter because on some days it could be in the low fifties and on others you could wake to six inches of fresh snow.

Cassidy, a native of Lake Arrowhead, disliked spring just for that reason, but one event each year kept bringing him back, spring gobbler season. He had grown up hunting and the first chance to get out with his bow to snag a turkey, he was there.

Cassidy was proud of his native home so having his best friend, Jim Ramsey, to show it off to made it more special than before. He hadn't seen Ramsey since he left the Marine Corps four years before, so the two would be able to spend much-needed time together.

Ramsey had just ended his active service with the Marines and was on his way home, but not before spending the weekend with Cassidy. Like Cassidy, the two had served with the First Battalion, First Marine Regiment in Weapons Company as heavy machine gunners.

After exiting the Corps, Cassidy had big plans, he was going to join the State Department, but those plans all came crashing down after one bad night and a DUI. With his dreams of being an agent dashed, Cassidy came home and found the one job he could get, a custodial job at the local elementary school. His fall from grace was profound.

Ramsey hadn't admitted it to Cassidy, but one reason for his stopping by was to ensure his friend was coping.

Cassidy often commented that hunting and combat were similar in some ways; both included hours and hours of sitting around, accompanied by boredom, all offset by brief but intense moments of action. When Cassidy invited Ramsey to go turkey hunting, he gave him that exact comparison but added the one advantage of turkey hunting was that they didn't shoot back.

The sun's first rays touched his chilled face. It felt good, so good, in fact, that he began to doze off.

His head bobbed up and down as he tried to fight the sleepiness.

The crack of a branch behind him brought him out of his slumber.

He quickly glanced right and peered towards a grove of aspen trees. There he saw a young spike buck mule deer grazing.

A smile creased his rugged face. Seeing the majestic animal made him so happy to be home. He loved the wilderness and all that inhabited it. Hunting for him wasn't just the kill; it was more about the appreciation of the outdoors and the animals that lived there. He never took a shot he couldn't make and he never killed for the pleasure, he left that for the battlefield. Cassidy, like many warriors who served with him and those who had come before, didn't join the military for the benefits, the GI Bill or even for love of country. Yes, he loved his country, just like many Americans, but truth be told, he joined the Marines and specifically signed up for infantry so he could be among the few who knew what combat truly was. It was hard for him and others like him to explain that to the civilian population. It wasn't politically correct to say you wanted to see combat, somehow that defined you as being deranged or delusional. It seemed all the civilian population understood about combat was four letters, PTSD. He and many others hated that their sacrifice had been summed up to mean only that. What also irritated him was that those very broad definitions came from people with no experience in the matter. How easy it was for society to lump him and his brothers into a neat little box wrapped in phony sympathy and tied up nicely with a bow of skepticism. It was true that some of his comrades had a difficult time transitioning from the battlefield and needed help, but to say all veterans were disturbed was one of the biggest lies perpetrated by a society against a group of people who had given so much and asked for nothing in return. It was the very definition of groupthink and represented the wide disconnect that separated society and the warrior class who protected them.

Cassidy enjoyed the tranquility of the wilderness. There he could reconnect with nature and clear his head while enjoying the fraternity of brotherhood.

A cool crisp breeze swept in from the north and enveloped him with bone-chilling air. He shivered and resisted the urge to adjust in the tree stand for fear his movement would spook the deer.

He admired the lone spike buck and wondered if he was the fawn he'd seen last year wandering these parts.

With his mind drifting, he didn't see the two turkeys appear over the rise to his left until the deer took notice of them. Curious as to what the deer found so interesting, he slowly moved his head until he spotted the two gobblers.

His heart fluttered with excitement.

The birds were moving towards him and soon would be in range.

Ever so carefully, he raised his bow until it was out in front of him. His arrow was nocked and ready, so he pulled back on the string. The cams creaked and his muscles tensed until he reached the breaking point where the pull weight reduced. He placed his index finger knuckle behind his ear and peered through the peep sight.

Turkeys were some of the dumbest birds he'd ever hunted, but they had a keen eyesight and could pick up on any subtle movement.

Fortunately, Cassidy was smooth with his draw and now only needed them to walk into a safe range.

The turkeys kept meandering down the slope towards him and soon would be thirty yards from his position, a proven and accurate striking distance for him. He could go further but again didn't want to take the chance of only wounding the animal. He prided himself on his hunting ethic.

The slow-moving birds were taking their time and putting strain on Cassidy's muscles.

Come on, stupid birds, he thought to himself.

Just a few more yards and the turkeys would be past a felled tree and in clear sight and range.

Cassidy couldn't wait nor could his arms, shoulder or back.

One bird jumped on the rotting tree and looked in Cassidy's direction. It was just about where he needed it, but the scrawny branches of a fir were blocking a clear shot.

"Argh," Cassidy grunted.

Just to be a pain in Cassidy's ass the turkey didn't move from his perch on the tree.

"Jump, move," Cassidy said under his breath.

A vibrating sound emanated from Cassidy's backpack. It was his mobile phone.

Cassidy ignored it and kept his bow drawn.

The phone stopped but quickly began vibrating again.

Oh, come on, He thought.

The phone stopped again and in seconds began vibrating once more. It was clear someone needed to talk to him, but he wasn't going to answer. He was just a few branches and feet from bagging a turkey. He could taste the basted meat already; he just needed the turkey to come into range.

Over and over the phone vibrated.

The turkey finally jumped down and came into clear view.

Cassidy aimed.

A loud crashing sound to his right startled him and the turkeys.

The birds looked and took off at a sprint away from Cassidy and the noise.

Cassidy retracted the arrow and looked to see what or who was coming towards him. From behind a tree a couple came holding hands and giggling.

"You gotta fucking be joking," he snarled.

The young couple walked underneath his tree stand and towards the creek beyond, oblivious to Cassidy being up in the tree.

He was half tempted to get down and give them a piece of his mind, but why bother. Frustrated and tired, he eased back against the tree and tried to enjoy the warmth of the sun with hopes the turkeys might just return.

San Diego, California

UPON WAKING, the first thing Brett did was look at his mobile phone to see if he had any messages from David. When he saw the pithy response from his brother, which was typical of him, he felt a weight ease off him.

However, his anxiety concerning the attacks in general multiplied by seemingly endless news flash notifications. He thumbed through the list and clicked on the most recent one. As he read his heart sank.

"Daddy, you awake?" his son Will asked from the bedroom doorway.

Brett looked over and saw his youngest son and smiled. "Hi, buddy."

"Eddie and I want to know if you're making pancakes this morning?" he asked then wiped his nose on his sleeve.

"Sweetheart, you don't wipe your nose on your clothes. Go get a tissue," Madison scolded.

"You're awake?" Brett asked, surprised to see her awake. She normally slept in late on weekends.

"How can I sleep with you two talking?" she snarled.

"Talking? He just asked a simple question, and it was just above a whisper," Brett countered.

"Sounded loud to me. Can you two please go away?" Madison said as she fluffed up the pillow.

"Sure," he said swiftly getting out of bed. He wasn't leaving because she asked, but because he couldn't stand being around her when she was like this. He walked over to Will and said, "Come on, son."

The two left the room with Brett closing the door behind him.

Brett enjoyed his weekend mornings. It was quality time he could spend with his sons.

"WHAT KINDA PANCAKES are you guys wanting this morning?" Brett asked, a broad smile stretched across his face.

"Chocolate chip!" the boys cheered in unison.

"How about doggie-shaped chocolate-chip pancakes, who wants those?" Brett asked cheerfully.

Both boys raised their arms and squealed, "Me!"

"Perfect, let me get to it," Brett said and immediately went to making the pancakes.

———

WHEN WILL TOOK the last bite, he leaned back in the stool and smiled. "Yummy, that was good." Melted chocolate was smeared across his pouty lips and chin.

"You're awful quiet, Eddie?" Brett said.

"They were good," he replied.

"What's wrong?" Brett asked.

"Nothing," Eddie answered.

Nothing always meant something, Brett thought.

"Can I go play?" Will asked, lifting his arm to wipe his face on his sleeve.

"Stop right there," Brett said and pointed at his arm.

Will's eyes widened. Slowly he lowered his arm and asked, "Napkin?"

Brett tore a paper towel and handed it to him. "That was a close call. Your mother is getting tired of you staining all your clothes. Please use a napkin."

Will wiped his face and said, "Okay." He jumped off the stool and raced down the hall, the pitter-patter of his small feet on the wood floor the only sound in the quiet house.

Eddie jumped off the stool and turned to head off.

"Hold it right there," Brett said.

"What, Dad?" Eddie scoffed.

"Don't give me a tone. You seem out of sorts and I want to know why."

"I said it was nothing."

"Not true. Now the quicker you tell me, the quicker you can go to the playroom."

Eddie stood quiet, his head down.

Brett walked over and squatted down. "What's wrong, buddy?"

"Are terrorists going to kill us?"

The question shocked Brett. "Why are you asking that?"

"Tony said terrorists killed a bunch of people in another country and they will try to kill us too."

"Whoa, whoa, why would Tony say that?"

"Did a bunch of people die yesterday?" Eddie asked.

Brett cocked his head and searched for the appropriate answer to give his ten-year-old.

"They did. I heard the news," Eddie said.

"Yes, some very bad people killed and hurt many others yesterday."

"Are they going to kill us next?"

"No, we're safe."

"You promise?" Eddie asked.

Brett recoiled. *Can I promise honestly?* His thoughts had been plagued by such questions. However, he didn't want to frighten Eddie, so he did what parents often did, told a white lie, "I promise."

BRETT CLEANED up and turned on the television. He flipped past the children's shows and put on the news. Like a drug addict, he couldn't wait to get his next fix. Like the night before it was an endless loop of harrowing stories concerning the attacks and updates on new threats.

"*...information is trickling in concerning this new terror group The Boody Hand. We're getting reports their leader is a man named Israfil. He and his followers consider him the twelfth imam. I know many viewers may not know what that means, but* *in Islamic prophecy, the twelfth imam is the final prophet who will appear just before the end of days..."* the newscaster said.

His phone vibrated on the counter behind him. By the sound, he could tell it was a text. Thinking it might be David, he pulled himself away from the television and picked it up. A chuckle came when he read it.

'Turn off the TV and come upstairs and turn me on!!!'

He replied, 'Who is this?'

'Someone who is sorry for being a butthead last night and this morning.'

'Oh, the grumpy person who's masquerading as my wife,' he texted back.

'Now come upstairs and let me show you how sorry I am.'

Brett didn't hesitate; he turned off the television and raced upstairs.

Copenhagen, Denmark

"THANK you for sharing your story. I'm happy you're okay," the primetime reporter said.

"Thank you for having me on," David replied.

The glaring lights from the camera went dark, leaving David in the shadows two blocks away from the very spot he'd almost lost his life the night before. He unclasped his hands, which he had tightly locked together to prevent them from shaking. He looked down and willfully tried to make his hand stop trembling, but it didn't work. Frustrated, he stood up, jammed his hands into his pants pockets and looked around.

The CNN crew quickly packed up and exited as fast as they had set up. To either side of David were others being interviewed by other networks. The flurry of activity had grown substantially since the night before, with news crews and reporters flooding the still, quiet streets.

With his high-profile interviews out of the way, David had a deep sense of weariness. In the past, he would have had his next steps planned but tonight he didn't. He had his cameras with him but the desire to document the aftermath of the attacks had vanished. He kept telling himself to do something but he just couldn't conjure up the motivation. The old saying *'fake it till you make it'* popped in his head and he tried but failed miserably.

Feeling very uneasy, he thought about ways to combat or at least subdue those debilitating feelings. Two things came to mind but they were vices he had long since quit. Determined to calm his mind and his nerves he hiked to the closest store. Inside he stepped to the counter and said, "Cigarettes."

The cashier looked at him and then to the vast display of two dozen varieties.

"Marlboro reds," David grumbled.

The cashier got him the pack and rang it up on the cash register.

David didn't pay attention to the cost; he gave the man twenty euros and exited the store, grabbing a pack of matches on the way out. His hands shook as he opened the pack. It had been three years since he smoked and he knew if he had one, he could fall easily back into the pack-a-day habit he used to have. With a trembling hand, he put the cigarette to his lips. The sweet taste of the filter brought back memories, good ones; he pulled a match and lit it on the first strike. He lifted it towards the tip of the cigarette and paused. His mind was screaming at him not to do it. His pause was longer than he thought, allowing the match to burn his finger. "Ouch, damn!" he barked, dropping the match. He tore the cigarette from his lips and threw it on the ground. "No," he said, marching away, determined not to fall victim to his own weakness.

A police siren blared in the distance followed by three more.

He stopped; a queasy feeling came upon him. He opened the pack, pulled out another cigarette and without further delay lit it. The first inhale was perfect. The smoke filled his lungs, with the nicotine almost immediately giving him a slight buzz. "Ahh," he sighed. The smoke wafted over him and again fond memories of his days smoking *and* drinking came to him. With one part taken care of, he needed another. Time to find a bar.

USS *Anchorage*, Off the Coast of Somalia

BRENNAN SAT BACK and readied himself for the surprise briefing.

After just returning to the ships from a two-month operation in Afghanistan in support of the 11th MEU (Marine Expeditionary Unit) deployed there, he was ready to sail home, but welcome to the Marine Corps, where one day you're heading home and another you're sailing towards Somalia for no apparent reason. Brennan chuckled to himself when he thought about his conversation with Dietz the night before.

Corporal Vickers and Corporal Klyde, two NCOs (noncommissioned officers) in his platoon and the best friends a man could ask for, took seats just behind him.

"What's the word, Sergeant?" Vickers asks in a thick Texas accent, his trademark which grew even more pronounced after a few beers.

"You know about as much as I do. I shut my eyes last night and we were heading home; now we're sailing towards Africa. I hear it's Somalia, the armpit of the world."

"Hold on, there's more than two armpits, because last time I checked, we just got back from armpit one and Vickers is from armpit two," Klyde joked, nudging Vickers.

"I'll have you know Wilco, Texas, is a fucking paradise of flat dry brown fields, tumbleweeds and one-hundred-and-ten-degree days during the long summer months. Oh, and our shopping, the Flying J, has some of the best there is," Vickers said mocking his own hometown.

"Are we handing out MREs or something?" Klyde asked.

"Guys, I don't know shit," Brennan said, his tone snapping with irritation.

"Okay...looks like someone woke up on the wrong side of the rack," Klyde whispered to Vickers.

Klyde and Vickers were close friends but an unlikely duo. What brought them together was the Marine Corps, and what made them inseparable brothers was the bond of combat. They couldn't have grown up more different. Vickers was from a small Texas town, a typical corn-fed white kid, while Klyde was a black kid who grew up in what could only be described as the ghetto with a single mom. Yes, it was all stereotypical but their friendship wasn't. Theirs was a bond forged in brotherhood under fire. Brennan complimented their unique friendship but he sometimes felt like an outsider. He had been in the Marine Corps three years longer and had seen good friends come and go.

The hatch to the briefing room opened.

First Sergeant Riley barreled into the room, briskly walking to the front. Behind him, Captain Arnold, Alpha Company's commanding officer, walked in.

"Officer on deck!" someone hollered.

Everyone jumped to their feet and stood at attention.

"At ease," Arnold said, his south Boston accent barely present but still audible. "At twenty-three thirteen zulu yesterday, a dynamic, multipronged terrorist assault was carried out in Copenhagen, Denmark. The targets were civilians and the locations targeted were cafés, theaters, a music venue, a train terminal and a prominent art gala. In all, eleven locations were struck. Right now, we don't know the number of assailants but the estimate is over thirty, many of whom were able to flee. The weapon of choice in these attacks were small arms, nothing more. The attacks weren't sophisticated in nature but the coordination was impressive, specifically for a new group. The Bloody Hand, a splinter group of ISIS, conducted this attack. This was not inspired but funded with detailed instructions from their haven in Syria. We don't know much about TBH, but it seems each time the terrorists evolve, they become more ruthless.

"Let me pivot to what's really on everyone's minds. You're all hearing the rumors and it's true, we're a little over fifty miles east of southern Somalia. Why? We received critical intel from one of the dead terrorists in Copenhagen that leads to a facility on the island of Juula," Arnold said and turned around.

First Sergeant Riley hit a couple of buttons. A bright screen turned on behind Arnold.

Arnold pointed at a small dot off Somalia on a map and continued, "Gentlemen, we've been tasked with providing support to JSOC. A team of SEALS accompanied by a squad of Raiders will go ashore here and here via zodiacs. They'll move on this structure here," Arnold said pointing at a large white-roofed building. "If you'll notice, a klick and a half south is a small airfield. What makes this special? It didn't exist eighteen months ago. We discovered that when referring to older satellite images. We believe this airfield is providing support to this facility. We have eyes on it now in real time and see equipment that shouldn't be on a shitty little island like this. First platoon, your job will be to seize this airfield and hold it. We can't have anything going out."

Vickers leaned in close to Brennan and whispered, "Now we'll get to show those Rangers how you *really* take down an airfield."

"Ssh," Brennan scolded.

"Corporal Vickers, you have something to say?" Arnold snapped.

"No, sir," Vickers replied sheepishly.

"Let me go on, then. It's imperative that nothing leaves this airfield. The objective of this mission overall is to gather intelligence on the terrorist operation at this facility. The ROE is simple, you're weapons free. You see a hostile, take them out. We are considering this area to be very hostile. We must assume there are no friendlies here. This island has few inhabitants, approximately five hundred locals call this home, and we must assume they work for TBH now or are somehow associated with it. Once the SEALS and Raiders secure what intel they can, they'll head back to the beach and extract. First platoon, you'll be inserted by fast rope at the south end of the airfield. Extraction will be done in the same area unless circumstances on the ground dictate differently. Once we're clear of the target after extraction, we're going to level it with a few Tomahawks."

Arnold turned to Riley and said, "You got anything, First Sergeant?"

"No, sir."

"Sergeant Brennan, your squad will be first on the ground," Arnold said.

"Yes, sir," Brennan replied.

"First platoon squad leaders, I need you to make sure your squads are ready to go in two hours, the birds are taking off at zero one thirty. Get them to the armory ASAP. I need you to also get HE grenades. You're being tasked with destroying two small aircraft there and anything you find in that hangar. Have your men lined up on the flight deck at zero one. I'll have all your comm frequencies there as well. Something else, Lieutenant Frank will have contact with the SEAL team leader so you can be apprised of their status and if they need any support."

"Yes, sir," Frank said, chirping up.

"Any questions?" Arnold asked.

Brennan asked, "What exactly do we know about the intel that led us here?"

"The terrorist had a diary on him. In it he mentions spending time here on a weapons research project. Can you believe it, the dumb shit had a diary that's leading us right to one of their secret bases?"

"What if it's a trap?" Vickers asked loudly.

"We've considered that, but the chance to gather highly sensitive intel on a weapons research facility is worth the risk," Arnold replied.

"Sounds good to me. I especially love the part about being weapons free." Vickers laughed.

"Did the diary mention what types of weapons they were researching here?" a voice asked from the group.

"No, but because we're not sure what to expect, we are going at MOPP level one," Arnold said.

Groans from the group.

"At ease," Riley barked.

The room grew silent.

"I know wearing protective gear is a pain in the ass, but it's for your own protection," Arnold said.

Always one with the quick-witted remark, Vickers cracked, "So the frogmen should shave their nasty beards. It's tough getting a proper seal on your mask with one."

"Corporal Vickers, keep your mouth shut," Riley snapped.

"Sorry, First Sergeant," Vickers replied.

"Gentlemen, I know you're counting the days until we get home to our loved ones. I'd be lying if I said I wasn't. But when we're needed, we go, plain and simple. If there's no other questions, let's get going," Arnold said.

The room was silent.

"Attention on deck," First Sergeant Riley sounded.

The Marines all stood.

Arnold exited with the same brisk and deliberate stride he'd entered with.

Riley followed him out.

When the hatch closed, cheers rose from the Marines at the prospect of getting some action.

San Diego, California

BRETT SAT SPEECHLESS STARING at the television. He and the guests that had gathered for their party huddled around him, many silent, others mumbling above a whisper.

Seeing his brother discuss his harrowing ordeal only added to the uneasy feelings he had. Knowing that his brother was almost killed struck home, making it deeply personal. If someone as close to him could almost become a victim, why couldn't his sons or Madison? he asked himself.

Madison knew Brett well enough to know he would be affected by seeing his brother. She walked over and sat next to him. "You good?"

"Yeah, I'm good, crazy, huh?"

"Sure is."

Chris Simmons, a new acquaintance of Brett's, shouted, "Okay, let's get this party ramped back up. God, that was a buzz kill!"

Brett scowled at Chris, who was oblivious to the death stare Brett was giving him.

"I'm going to turn some music on, okay?" Madison said to Brett as she reached past him and grabbed the remote.

"Sure, let's have a good time," Brett replied. He shifted his gaze from Chris and put it on Madison.

Madison hit a few buttons on the remote. Suddenly the room filled with poppy-sounding music.

The volume of conversation rose immediately.

"Now we're talking. Let's have fun!" Chris hollered.

"Did we have to invite him?" Brett asked, referring to Chris.

"It's a package deal," Madison said.

Chris was married to Kristin, and Kristin was one of Madison's best friends.

Madison rubbed his shoulders and said, "I know you're upset, but try to have a good time."

"I will. Now go, entertain," he said, nudging her away.

She gave him a peck on the cheek before heading off to do her duties as a host.

Brett looked around the room. Everyone was laughing, chatting, and completely disengaged from what they'd just seen. *Are they feeling like me? Do they care? Or is it easy to put aside because it's all so far away?*

Chris came over and patted him on the shoulder. "Your brother looks like you, a few pounds lighter, but I can see the resemblance."

"Yeah, he's kept in better shape than me. I guess when you're bouncing around the world you don't eat as well as we do here."

"What are you drinking?" Chris asked.

"Beer."

"What flavor?" Chris asked, walking away.

"No, hold on, this is my party, I should be waiting on you."

"Nonsense, I have two good legs," Chris said, hovering over the cooler. "IPA or Corona?"

Brett stood up and went to the cooler. He looked at the beers but none looked good. "Neither, I've changed my mind. I think I'll have a whiskey."

Chris' eyes widened with excitement. "Now we're talking, whatcha got?"

"A decent selection, Bulleit, Templeton Rye, Buffalo Trace and a new favorite, Four Roses."

With a robust laugh, Chris replied, "All of them. But to be more specific, I'll try the Four Roses."

"Good to finally meet a whiskey drinker," Brett said as he placed the bottle down and grabbed two glasses.

"My mouth is watering," Chris said.

"Neat or rocks."

"Rocks," Chris replied.

"I'm liking you more and more." He put ice in the glasses and poured a healthy amount of whiskey.

Chris took his glass and said, "Nice pour, cheers."

Brett raised his glass and went to tap Chris' but stopped when Chris blurted out, "Death to all those Islamic savages."

Brett took pause because he never was a man who held such views that targeted a specific group or religion but his feelings were in flux and anger was one of them. He tapped Chris' glass and said, "Death to the Islamic savages.

Rancho Bernardo, California

THE CONFRONTATION with his father only amplified Mo's hatred of all things American. While in lockdown in his bedroom, he spent the hours cruising pro-jihadi websites, blogs and videos. He didn't care what his dad said, he was not going to turn his back on his *people*. As he bounced from one site to another, a feeling of pride began to well up inside him. Hearing the many different voices express their support for the Islamic State and The Bloody Hand was motivational. Many cited and described how they were fighting the good fight. One site had dozens of testimonials from men and women who had left their homes to go and fight. What struck him most of all was how similar he was to them. Most came from middle-class homes in Europe, Australia, Canada and the United States. As they put it, *'had tossed aside the chains of those cultures and embraced the ways of the caliphate'.*

Mo couldn't get enough. As soon as he'd finish one video, he'd click on the next. It was intoxicating. These were people his age, but they had one thing he didn't, *a purpose.* He longed for something greater than him, a cause to put his energy towards and one that promised adventure.

He clicked and there at the top of the screen was a video titled *'Manifesto of THE BLOODY HAND'.* He clicked on the video.

An ad popped up, making him wonder how YouTube allowed such stuff to be viewed, but there it was regardless. The ad concluded and the screen went dark. A synthesized voice began to speak.

The end of days is coming. Which side will you be on after Israfil blows his horn? Will you be on the side of the infidel or will you be on the side of Allah and his prophet, the most holy twelfth imam. He is here. He is working diligently to prepare only those true to Allah and his teachings. The others, including Islamic State, have failed. We, The Bloody Hand, are Allah's true warriors. We fight alongside our imam to destroy the infidel and the Great Satan. Be prepared, for the day that will end all days is fast approaching. Praise be The Bloody Hand, praise be Israfil, praise be our prophet the twelfth imam, and glory on high to Allah for he shall give us the victory we have so long sought.

An image of a bloody hand appeared on the screen just before the video ended.

The dark and foreboding video hooked Mo. There wasn't anything to see, it lacked the grisly images so often found in ISIS videos, but for some reason the mysterious element attracted him.

A notification popped up at the top of his screen. It was a text from Malik.

"What you doing?"

"My dad put me on restriction. Can you believe?" Mo texted.

"Sorry, bro."

"What are you doing?"

"Heading out to the party."

Mo had forgotten about the party Malik's friend Ali was having. He grunted and stared at the popcorn-textured ceiling. Disgust and anger began to rise in him.

"Gotta go. See you Monday?" Malik text.

"What's the address?" Mo asked.

No response came.

Mo texted again, "What's Ali's address?"

"You coming?"

"Yeah. Fuck my dad."

Malik sent the address and finished the text by saying, *"Glad you're coming. I want you to meet someone."*

Lake Arrowhead, California

RAMSEY WATCHED the flames of the campfire dance. There was just something about an open fire that he found alluring. Was it the smell, the crackling sound or the unique heat a fire gave off? Did it matter? Not really, he thought.

Across from him, Cassidy sat slumped in his chair. A can of beer dangled from his fingertips.

"You're awful quiet," Ramsey said.

"Just tired," Cassidy replied.

"Sucks that Scott had to completely cancel," Ramsey said

referring to a message he had received on his phone from Scott earlier, informing him he wasn't coming at all.

"Yeah, it does," Cassidy replied as he took a sip of beer.

"You mentioned the school called. What's up?" Ramsey asked. He was desperate to draw any amount of conversation from Cassidy that he could.

Cassidy took a big swallow, crushed the can in his hands and tossed it in the fire. "They want to meet with me on Monday."

"Oh."

"I'm guessing it has to do with something I posted on Facebook. I took it down but not before a teacher from the school railed against me in a post. It appears I'm in trouble for expressing my opinion."

"No shit?"

"Yep. At least that's what I think it's about. They just wanted to discuss something that concerned the administration and staff."

"What did you write that was so bad?"

"After the terror attack in Copenhagen I posted a meme. I guess the snowflakes began melting at the school when they saw it," Cassidy said, cracking another beer open.

"And...what did it say?"

"Something like *'Ten out of ten terrorists shot in the face don't commit terrorism'*. Something stupid like that."

"Hmm, well, it's true." Ramsey laughed.

"Yeah, it's true...ly got me in hot water now." Cassidy sighed. "I just don't know when to shut up. I'm such a dumbass."

"Why can't you have an opinion?" Ramsey asked.

"I can, mine is just the wrong one compared to the administration's is all. Trust me, if I was slamming a white guy or a

Christian for murdering people, I'd probably get a damn raise," Cassidy said just before chugging half the beer.

"Fuck them, man, it's all bullshit. You'll be fine," Ramsey said trying to make Cassidy feel better.

"If I lose this job, Sophie will be pissed. I just need to be quiet, learn my place."

Ramsey couldn't believe what he was hearing. His old friend looked and acted like a man defeated. It was hard to imagine this was one of the toughest, smartest and most confident men he'd ever known in the Marine Corps.

Cassidy gulped down the beer, crushed the can and tossed this one into the fire next to the other one.

Ramsey searched for what he could say to ease Cassidy's mind, but nothing came to him, so he thought it best to reminisce. "Remember that time in Thailand when Corporal Brown had his clothes stolen from that prostitute's room?"

"God yeah, he stepped out, happy and proud in his birthday suit, not a care in the world." Cassidy laughed.

"No shit. When you're hung like a horse, you can walk around like that," Ramsey quipped.

Cassidy laughed hard but quickly fell back into a mood. He looked across the flames and asked, "I'm a loser?"

"Huh?"

"Look at me. I lost my selection for that State Department gig, I got a DUI, which prohibits me from jobs I want to apply for and I might lose my job as a janitor. A fucking janitor at a damn elementary school. I'm scared, man, I'm scared if I lose this job, I'll lose Sophie," Cassidy confessed.

"You'll be okay. Toss me a beer," Ramsey said. All he wanted was to change the topic but Cassidy was making it impossible.

A ping sounded on Ramsey's iPhone. He picked it up and looked. "I can't believe I have a signal up here."

"There's a tower across the lake, that's why. The town of Lake Arrowhead is just over there maybe three miles way of the crow," Cassidy said, pointing south.

"Speaking of losers, those fucking protestors are causing chaos all over. They've shut down freeways and are smashing people's cars and businesses in Phoenix, LA, Seattle, New York, Houston and Chicago."

"What now?" Cassidy asked.

"I guess they're protesting the president's new executive order and his reaction to the terror attack in Copenhagen. You know, I have to wonder which side those people are on."

"Executive order? He hasn't even signed it yet," Cassidy mocked.

"I guess that doesn't stop these goons from rioting."

"Let's not mince words, they're on the side of the terrorists, period. They hate America almost as much as those Islamists do. The media loves to wrap these people in the Constitution and say they're peaceful. Clearly, they're not," said Cassidy.

"I can't imagine they're all bad. Some are just misinformed," Ramsey said.

"Useful idiots is what Hitler used to call his Brown Shirts."

Ramsey kept reading the news flash article and said, "Get this. A bunch of mask-wearing protestors in Philadelphia torched part of Independence Hall."

"See, they hate our country. Nothing like burning down the very building our Declaration of Independence was signed in."

Ramsey clicked his phone off, shook his head and said, "You know, I'm beginning to think those protestors are more a danger to our way of life than the terrorists."

Rancho Bernardo, California

Mo HAD BECOME a master of sneaking out; it was always getting back in that he feared. He tiptoed to the side window of the dining room and pushed, but it was locked. "Shit," he mumbled under his breath. This could only mean his father had found it unlocked and secured it. He tried again, fully knowing he wasn't getting inside. After failing, he pondered just how he'd get in.

Back and forth he paced. The high he had earlier was gone. He most assuredly would receive his father's wrath and the courage he'd displayed before leaving and at the party had vanished. No matter how many times he tried to convince himself that he was tough and fearless, his father struck terror in him.

A back-door patio light turned on.

He jumped behind a bush and hid.

"Mo, come now," his mother called.

He hesitated.

"It's okay, son, come," she called out just above a whisper.

He lifted his head and, like a beaten dog with its tail between its legs, stepped from behind the bush and walked towards her.

The bright light cast behind her, allowing him to only see her silhouette.

He walked up and stopped at the bottom of the stairs. "I'm sorry, but I—"

She grabbed him and pulled him close. "Don't apologize. Men don't apologize for being men. Come inside."

He was shocked and didn't know how to act.

She pulled him up and nudged him to go inside.

He resisted for fear his father would be just on the other side of the door.

"It's okay. Your father is asleep," she said pushing him more forcefully inside.

He stepped across the threshold and into the living room.

She came in behind him and closed the door.

Both were in the shadows of the darkened house.

She stepped in front of him, took his hands and said, "I believe in you. You're a good young man who will bring honor to our family."

"I don't understand," he said.

"I know, I know what you're doing and I approve. You must bring honor to our family and glory to Allah."

"You know?"

"This is our secret," she said, squeezing his hands.

"How do you know?" Mo asked, confused.

"How long have I been friends with Malik's mother, hmm?" she replied.

"Malik's mother knows?" Mo asked.

"Yes, and she told me after I called over looking for you."

"That doesn't make any sense. Why would she just tell you something as sensitive as that?"

"It's not for you to worry."

"We're lying to father."

"Allah allows us to be untruthful to the infidel and those who have lost faith. It is fine."

He was more confused than ever. The power he felt from being rebellious was zapped somewhat but it was replaced with pride that his mother, whom he adored, supported what he was doing.

She placed a hand on his face and said, "I'm so proud of you. Now, go upstairs and get some sleep."

He walked away and swiftly scaled the stairs to his room. Inside, he lay on the bed and tried to put his arms around everything that had occurred tonight. From meeting Kareem, Malik's secretive friend, and now the actions of his mother, he had much to process.

As he closed his eyes to sleep, he concluded that Allah was truly guiding him. If it was his will, then his plan would be shown to him and he'd have to let it play out.

When he finally drifted off, a slight smile crept onto his face, for he could see he was being given something that few teenagers had, a divine purpose.

CHAPTER THREE

Sunday, April 23
Island of Juula, Off the Coast of Somalia

BRENNAN'S BOOTS hit the tarmac. He let go of the thick rope and raced to his position. The insertion of first squad couldn't be more precisely choreographed. One by one as they fast roped down, the Marines peeled away to cover their responsible areas of fire.

First squad's main job now was to provide cover for the rest of first platoon as it followed.

It took only minutes for the remaining squads to get on the ground.

Brennan peered through the green-tinted terrain, made so by the night vision attached to his helmet.

"Sierra One and Two, move your squads north and secure those buildings. Sierra Three and Four, make a secure perimeter from west to east. Radio when you're in position," Lieutenant Frank radioed.

Brennan got up and tapped Vickers. "Let's go."

The Marines of first squad moved at the ready along the

western edge of the makeshift airfield with Brennan leading the way.

They reached the hangar and stacked up alongside the wall.

Brennan watched second squad with Frank leading them move along the eastern edge, stopping to secure the two aircraft before they too reached the hangar.

A wide opening spanning fifty feet separated the two squads.

"Sierra One, you'll go in and left. Two, follow me. On the count of three, let's move," Frank radioed.

"Roger that," Brennan replied.

"One, two, three," Frank radioed.

Feeling he needed to be point, Brennan led his squad into the darkened hangar. He walked straight ahead, his rifle raised at the ready. The second Marine peeled off to the far left and one by one, each Marine of first squad entered, calling out the direction they were heading.

Inside, they found an empty hangar save for a few crates and tables.

"All clear," Frank called out.

The Marines looked around, many hoping they'd encounter at least one bad guy to take down.

"Sierra Two, move north off hangar and set up a perimeter," Frank radioed.

Second squad exited the hangar and spread out along the north edge.

Frank walked over to Brennan. "That was easy."

Brennan had six years on Frank, who was a second lieutenant. While he was younger and had less experience, their time in Afghanistan had christened Frank and proved to his men he could be a leader.

"Easy for now, sir. I recommend we keep our heads on a swivel. There's no telling when a skinny will pop up. Those

Ospreys aren't the most silent things. I'm sure we got someone's attention," Brennan said, using the derogatory term of *skinny* to describe the Somalis.

"You got that right, Sergeant," Frank said.

"Any contact with the Raiders or SEALS?" Brennan asked.

"They're almost there. Other than that, a lot of shit talking between the two groups."

"Of course," Brennan replied.

"When we move to extract, you're responsible for blowing the two aircraft out there," Frank ordered.

"Roger that, sir," Brennan said.

Frank put his hand to his ear and said, "Hold on, I'm hearing they've made it and they have contact with some hostiles."

"Lucky bastards," Brennan joked.

Minutes passed. Taking the airfield had proven to be quite easy and with zero contact with any locals or hostiles.

Lieutenant Frank hovered in a far corner of the hangar, listening to the communications from the SEAL team and Raiders.

All seemed like it was going smoothly until...

"Sergeant Brennan, ready your squad!" Frank hollered.

"Yes, sir," Brennan replied. He turned and called out, "First squad, rally to me."

In seconds, Brennan was surrounded by his squad.

Vickers leaned in and whispered, "Either we're leaving this boring-as-fuck place or please get us some action."

Brennan ignored his friend.

Frank hurried over. "Sergeant Brennan, we're needed at the

research facility. They came under heavy resistance and they're trapped."

"Okay, what's the plan, sir?" Brennan asked.

Frank pulled a map out of his sleeve pocket, unfolded it and turned on a flashlight with a red lens. "We're here and this is the site. The fastest route there is directly north, but we have to go through this village just south of the facility."

"How far?" Brennan asked.

"About a klick and a half," Frank replied.

"Do you have a layout of the village?" Brennan asked.

"No."

"Can one of the SEALS or Raiders illuminate with IR?" Brennan asked.

"I'll find out, but you need to get moving now," Frank said, urgency in his tone.

"Roger that, sir," Brennan said. He turned to face his squad when Frank grabbed him by the arm.

"It sounds bad, real fucking bad. One of the Raiders is topside. He said the rest are down below, floors below."

"Okay, sir."

"You're going to think this is crazy and keep this to yourself but he said something about monsters."

Brennan chuckled then realized Frank wasn't joking. "What the fuck does that mean, sir?"

"I don't know, but they need support. Once we get them out of there, we'll put a bird right down on top of you and pull you guys out."

"Have you thought about sending two squads, sir?" Brennan asked.

Frank chewed on his lip as he pondered the idea- "We need to hold this just in case those villagers go crazy."

"But, sir, they are receiving heavy contact and are now

trapped. We should focus all of our attention on getting them out," Brennan stressed.

"There's no more time to waste. Take your squad and go," Frank snapped.

"Copy that, sir," Brennan said.

"Now get going," Frank ordered.

Brennan turned and said to his squad. "You heard the LT, the SEALs and Raiders need us. It sounds like we're stepping into a serious gunfight."

Vickers leaned into Brennan and said, "We're running a mile in MOPP gear, through a village of savages and into a fire-fight of unknown numbers? Have you ever seen *Black Hawk Down?*"

"Do you ever stop cracking jokes?" Brennan asked.

"It wasn't a joke."

"Let's go. I'll lead the way," Brennan said, stepping off.

WITH HIS SQUAD BEHIND HIM, Brennan ran across the relatively flat terrain that separated the airfield and the small village. As they came up on the south end of the village, he slowed.

"All stop, take a knee," he ordered.

He knelt down and looked for any movement.

Vickers came up alongside and said, "I don't see shit. Looks clear."

"Let's keep moving," Brennan said, stood and ran.

His squad followed.

They entered the village from the south. Brennan immediately beelined for the right side and hugged the structures close as they proceeded north.

Something seemed off. There wasn't any light coming from a single house, hut or building. It was as if it was a ghost town.

In no time, they cleared the village.

Brennan slowed and radioed Frank. "Sierra Actual, where's the IR? Over."

"One sec. Over," Frank replied.

A stream of light appeared to the northeast of their position.

"Got it, looks like we're two hundred meters southwest. I'm switching over freqs to contact them. Over," Brennan said.

"Copy that. Stay frosty," Frank said and went silent.

"Romeo team, this is Sierra One. We're two hundred meters southwest of your position. What's the situation?" Brennan radioed.

"This is Romeo Eight. You're clear, hurry," the Raider Marine replied.

"Let's go," Brennan said, stood and ran towards the streaming light only he and his squad could see through their night vision.

BRENNAN and first squad reached the chain-link-fenced perimeter of the facility.

"How do we get in? Over," Brennan radioed.

"West side," the Raider Marine replied.

Brennan instantly thought how quiet it was for supposedly entering a hot site. He led his squad around and into the small compound that surrounded the large cinder-block single-story building. Near a row of thousand-gallon propane tanks sat the Raider Marine. Brenna jogged over and took a knee. The remaining members of his squad fanned out in a circle, all facing out.

"Thank God you're here," the Raider Marine said.

"I'm Sergeant Brennan. Tell me what's going on."

"Corporal Marzelli, um, that first floor is just empty. The

only thing in there is a fucking single door that leads to a stairwell. It goes down three maybe four or more levels. I can't remember."

Brennan noticed Marzelli's labored breathing. "Are you injured?"

"My shoulder, I got bit."

Brennan turned and called out, "Corpsman up."

In seconds, Petty Officer Third Class Perino appeared. "Who's hurt?"

Marzelli raised his good arm. "Here, my shoulder."

Perino flipped on a headlamp and looked. "What happened to you?"

"I was bitten," Marzelli said.

"Yeah, you were. How odd," Perino said as he opened his kit.

"Tell me more, hurry, I don't want to walk in there blind," Brennan said.

"Um, three levels down we enter some office spaces. We begin to start bagging everything. Drives, binders, folders, you name it. Others in the team proceed further down. There wasn't any contact until we reached level five." Marzelli paused.

"And that's when you came under heavy contact?"

"There were cages, must have been dozens, hell, maybe a hundred. There were people in them. We thought...we thought they were prisoners. One of the SEAL members found the switch that opened them up, you know, like they have in prisons." Marzelli paused and cringed as Perino applied a gauze to his wound.

"So are the rest trapped? I need an answer," Brennan snapped. He wanted Marzelli to hurry up and get the story over with.

"As soon as the doors to the cells opened, all hell broke loose. They just...attacked us. They went through us so quickly.

They were so fucking strong and fast. It was crazy, man, fucking crazy."

"Are you the sole survivor?" Brennan asked.

"I don't know. We fell back but they kept coming. They were so vicious. There were a dozen men left, me with them, as we raced up the stairwell to the surface. One by one they got picked off. I reached the door at the top, got through, but one jumped on my back and bit my fucking shoulder. I shot it in the face. It fell off. I killed it, so I know they die. I slammed the door and radioed for support."

"You're telling me everyone else is dead?" Brennan asked.

Marzelli looked up with crazed eyes and said, "I don't know how anyone could have survived that."

"You said some were trapped," Brennan barked. He grew frustrated with Marzelli and his rambling.

"I don't know who radioed that but..." he said staring at Brennan with wide eyes. "I don't know how anyone could have survived that."

Vickers had walked up and heard the tail end of Marzelli's remarks. "Sergeant Brennan, what's the word?"

"We hold tight until I hear back from the LT," he replied.

"What the hell is he talking about?" Vickers whispered.

"I don't know, but it sounds like everyone is dead," Brennan answered. He turned back to Marzelli and asked, "The intel, did you get anything?"

"No," Marzelli answered.

"Nothing?"

"It took everything for me just to get out of there. You weren't there. It was crazy; they weren't people, they were like... like fucking mutated humans or something fucked up like that, fucking monsters. They were monsters, man, monsters."

Brennan shook his head. He was confused by Marzelli's account and chalked it up to shock.

"Any station on the net, this is Tango Actual. Come in. Over," a voice crackled over the radio.

Surprised by the transmission, Brennan replied, "Tango Actual, this is Sierra One. Go."

"We need assistance. We're barricaded in a room but we're out of ammo and we can't hold off these things much longer."

"Where are you?" Brennan asked.

"Third level down, west hallway. I think we're the second room on the right. You can't miss us. We're in the room those things are trying to get into."

"Copy that," Brennan said. He turned to Vickers and ordered, "Ready the squad. Get them over here." Brennan couldn't help but notice Tango Actual kept referring to *things*. What exactly were these *things*?

"You're fucking crazy, man. Don't go in there," Marzelli urged.

"Just shut up and tell me the layout," Brennan snapped.

Marzelli told him to the best of his recollection the facility's floor plan.

Brennan turned to his squad, who encircled him. He opened a map, turned it upside down and began to draw with a black Sharpie. "We'll enter the stairwell here. On each level there are three hallways. A north, south and west. On level two down the north hall, Corporal Marzelli says there are bags full of intel. Dietz and Harmon, your job is to gather that intel and immediately take it to the surface. Everyone else, we're going down to get those guys on level three. We're facing, from Corporal Marzelli's account, a lethal enemy. We're weapons free; kill anything that gets in your way. We'll snatch these guys, get topside and get the fuck out of here."

Copenhagen, Denmark

DAVID DIDN'T KNOW what was worse, his head pounding from the intense hangover or the fact he had fallen off the wagon and broken the promises of so many people he pledged sobriety too. He couldn't stop thinking about his betrayal with each drink but the more he consumed the less he cared. Like usual with anyone who has awoken with hung over, the regret now took center stage.

The light of the day was streaming through the edges of the drapes with the hum of cars from the street below telling him he had missed an interview he was supposed to shoot with the *Today* show. He picked up his phone on the nightstand but found it dead. He scrambled and found the cord and plugged it in.

Unexpectedly the bathroom door opened and a woman draped in a towel came out.

He was shocked to see her and sat up in the bed, not knowing what to say. He recognized her but not from anything that would have led to them being in his room.

"So sorry I have to run. There's been some arrests north of Paris. I need to meet my team," the young woman said, dropping the towel and putting on her clothes.

David looked at her slender body and now wished he remembered the night before. He placed his hand on his head and squeezed to rid himself of the crushing headache. "Ah, no problem, um, I know this is bad but we, um..."

"Great, way to make a lady feel special." She laughed.

"I, um, sorry, I drank way too much last night."

She pulled on her boots and faced him. "We both did, but luckily for me I remember because it was good, in fact, real good. I wish I had more time this morning."

A grin cracked his stoic face. Having a woman declare your bedroom abilities always could brighten a man's day. "Glad I could be of service."

She grabbed her jacket, bag, and headed for the door in a hurry. Stopping just before leaving, she purred, "Let's do this again tonight." She blew him a kiss and exited.

"Hmm, this time I won't drink too much so I will remember," David said out loud.

His phone pinged, reminding him of the missed interview he had that morning. He unlocked it and scrolled to Max's number. He needed to call him and apologize.

Notifications suddenly popped up: twenty-three voicemails, fifty-eight texts and the inbox of his e-mail was filling fast. "Shit, I'm such a fuckup."

Before he called Max, he decided to see what the texts had in store for him. Of course, most were Max screaming at him with all caps but one caught his attention, it wasn't a number he recognized. He opened it up and began to read. The more words he read, the more his pulse rose. Not waiting, he replied.

Excited, he stood up and began to pace the room. "Holy shit, this is it, this is it."

The phone rang. He sprang over and grabbed it. "Please be him." His hopes were dashed when he saw it was Max. Knowing he had to pay the piper, he answered, "Sorry, I overslept, but I've got good news."

"What the hell, Dave, that was a huge interview but luckily for you they're forgiving considering the circumstances you've been through. I've got you slotted for tomorrow same time."

The phone buzzed notifying him another call was coming in.

"Max, hold on." He pressed to answer it. "This is David."

Silence.

"Hello, this is David."

"David, my friend, glad to hear your voice," a man said with a thick Middle Eastern accent.

"Who is this?"

"I saw you on the television. I see you're becoming famous."

"Who is this?" David again asked.

"You forget so easily. Remember two years ago, we shared tea at the Saffron Ankara Hotel."

David raised his eyebrows and dropped his jaw when he realized who he was talking with. "Oh, my God, why are you contacting me? The last time—" David said but was interrupted.

"I defected."

"What? How?"

"That's exactly why I'm calling you. I have a story and you're the only person I'd tell it to."

"Where are you?"

"Come to Ankara immediately. I don't have much time. Hurry, my friend."

"Yeah, sure, I'm on my way. Um, hold on, how will I find you?" David asked.

"I'll find you. Hurry, my friend, hurry."

The phone clicked and went dead.

David was shocked. Joram was the last person he expected to hear from. He stared blankly for a second before realizing he had left Max on hold. He clicked over. "Cancel all the interviews and book me a ticket to Ankara, leaving as soon as possible."

"What?"

"Fucking do it."

"Hold on, wait a minute."

"Do it, no time to explain."

"Give me something."

"I just got off the phone with Joram. You remember him, don't you? The guy from Syria. His dad is a low-level bureaucrat in Assad's regime."

"The guy you interviewed a few years ago just before he went to join ISIS?"

"Yes, he's defected and needs to meet, no time, he sounded concerned. I have to go now."

"But these interviews are more important," Max insisted.

"I'll get even more interviews after meeting with Joram!"

"Is your visa still valid?"

"Yes, now hang up and book me a ticket and get me a room. I must pack," David said and hung up.

His face was flush and the headache was gone. He walked to the drapes and pulled them open, allowing the warm rays of the sun to come in. He instinctively knew this was what he was looking for. The information he could get from Joram could jump start his documentary film and give him the media spotlight to secure the funding he sorely needed.

Island of Juula, Off the Coast of Somalia

BRENNAN STOOD at the top entry door. He pressed his eyes closed, said his usual prebattle prayer, opened his eyes and gave Dietz a nod.

Dietz flung the door open.

Always insisting on leading the way, Brennan raced into the stairwell, rifle at the ready.

Right behind him, his squad followed closely.

The lights in the stairwell flickered on and off, making it impossible to use their night vision.

The top flight of stairs was riddled with bodies, friendly and foe.

At the bottom of the first flight, Brennan radioed, "Dietz, Harmon, get as much intel as you can. Just keep bagging."

"Roger that," Dietz replied.

Guttural growls, teeth gnashing and banging echoed from below.

Brennan's stomach tightened. He was never afraid to admit

being fearful going into a combat situation, but this just felt different, and his body was sending him plenty of warning signs.

They proceeded with diligence down the stairs, being careful not to trip over bodies nor slip on blood.

With each step he took, the grotesque noises grew louder.

The lights flickered out.

Brennan paused. His heart was thumping. The noises seemed louder when the lights were out. *How odd?* he thought.

Standing in the darkness seemed like an eternity.

Brennan contemplated going to night vision.

The lights flickered on.

He swiftly but stealthily moved down to within a few steps of the third-floor landing.

The sounds of the *monsters* were now so loud he found it hard to think. He looked down at his hand; it was shaking. *Get it together,* he said to himself.

He looked behind him and saw fear in his men's eyes. Together they had seen battle against the Taliban in Afghanistan, but something here was out of sorts and they all could feel it.

He motioned with his left hand that he would take a position at the north hall and west hall intersection and provide cover as the others came down.

He gulped and took the last steps but stopped just before the bottom. He slowly peered around the corner and caught sight of a large pack of those *things*. They were grunting, pounding and grinding their teeth outside what must have been the door that led to Tango Actual. He took a quick head count. *Shit, there's thirty plus.*

He looked back to his squad and gave a hand signal showing the number down the hall. With nothing holding him back but his own fear, he took two large steps and cleared the span of the hallway. He lifted his rifle and took aim. To his great fortune, they hadn't seen him. He looked to the second man to come, but as they were stepping off, the lights flickered out.

Damn, he thought.

Fear rose in him. Like a scene from a horror movie, he fully expected to see several of them in front of him when the lights came on.

He sat. His heartbeat was pounding so hard he wondered if those things could hear it.

The lights came on suddenly. To his delight, the things hadn't moved.

He signaled for his men to move.

Everything was going smoothly until Lance Corporal Shaw tripped and fell, his rifle smacking the tile floor. The sound echoed down the hall.

Brennan mouthed, *Fuck.* He looked up and saw several of those *things* running towards them. He raised his rifle, flicked off the selector switch and began engaging. "Here they come. Open fire!"

The Marines from first squad poured down the stairs, took various positions on the landing and immediately joined the fight.

Through the ear-smashing hail of gunfire, he could hear Marines crying out, "Reloading."

A smoky gunpowder haze soon enveloped them, making it hard to see.

Brennan cried out, "Cease fire!"

The Marines stopped firing. The clangs of empty magazines dropping followed by the audible clacks of new magazines going into the mag wells and the bolts going forward were the only sounds Brennan could hear. He stood and took a couple of cautious steps forward past the haze.

In the west hallway, a pile of bodies lay.

"Vickers, you and two others watch our six. Everyone else with me," Brennan called out.

"In here!" a voice cried from behind the second door.

"We're clear out here. Come on out," Brennan yelled back.

The sounds of heavy furniture moving came from the other side.

Unsure of what he expected to see coming out, Brennan stood back a few feet.

The door flew open. Two men stepped out. Just from their appearance, gear and weapons, Brennan knew they were SEALs. He looked at the name tag in the center of his chest. *CPO L. Owens, USN.*

"Boy, am I glad to see you," Owens said.

"No time to waste, we have a bird coming on station any minute," Brennan said. He pulled two spare thirty-round magazines from his vest and handed one to each of them.

"Thanks, brother," Owens said, inserted the magazine into his M4 and slapped the mag-release button on the slide.

"Anyone else alive down here?" Brennan asked.

"Just us, man," Owens replied.

Groaning sounded behind them.

Owens looked back and saw one of the *things* crawling. "One sec," he said and walked back to it. He stepped on its back and pushed it to the floor.

It growled in pain.

He knelt, grabbed its arms and put them behind its back, and with a pair of zip ties, he restrained its arms and legs together in a hog-tie. Owens then removed a roll of duct tape and wrapped it around its head multiple times to tape its mouth shut.

"Are you taking him with us?" Brennan asked.

"Yeah, we came to get intel on what they were doing and I

think we have it right here. And, by the way, I think this one is a she."

Vickers craned his head back and gave a disgusted look. "It's drooling everywhere."

"I think it likes you too," Owens said. "Help me carry it."

Lance Corporal Wallace slung his SAW over his back and came over.

The thing squirmed violently.

"Christ, she's strong," Wallace said. He lost his grip, causing the thing to fall to the floor hard.

It let out a wail and thrashed violently.

Vickers looked at the thing intently as they walked by with it. "Either that thing is fat or its pregnant."

Brennan walked to the front of the group and keyed his radio. "Dietz, we got the survivors. We're heading up. Is the bird here?"

Silence.

Brennan was concerned. He radioed again as he quickly scaled the stairs to the surface. "Dietz, this is Sierra One. Come in. Over."

Silence.

His concern grew. He turned around to his squad and barked, "I'm not reaching topside. Something might be wrong. Heads on a swivel, we may not be out of this yet."

First squad, with Brennan leading, raced to the surface, stopping at the exit door. He paused and tried to radio one more time. "Dietz, this is Sierra One. Come in. Over."

"Dietz here. Sorry, we're having some issues with Corporal Marzelli."

Breathing a sigh of relief, Brennan with his squad following exited the facility only to be greeted by screams. He sprinted out of the building to find Dietz, Perino and Harmon holding a convulsing Marzelli down.

"Fucking do something, Doc!" Dietz barked.

"I gave him a sedative already," Perino roared.

"Give him another one!" Dietz yelled.

Brennan ran over. "What happened?"

"Not sure, he just started to convulse. I've given him a sedative but it's not working," Perino explained.

"Hit him with a morphine injector. Dose him up," Brennan ordered.

"But..." Perino said wanting to object but was interrupted when Marzelli stopped moving.

"Is he dead?" Brennan asked.

"I don't know. Everyone back the fuck away," Perino snapped. He placed two fingers on Marzelli's neck. "He's got a pulse, fast too."

Marzelli opened his eyes, cocked his head towards Perino and lunged. He clamped onto his hand and bit down on the fleshy part of his palm.

Perino cried out in pain while retracting his arm, but Marzelli wouldn't let go.

"What the fuck!" Dietz hollered out.

Harmon tried to pull Marzelli off, but was pushed back hard when Marzelli lashed out with his right arm.

Owens stepped up, pushing past everyone, and swung down hard with his rifle, the butt slamming against the side of Marzelli's head.

Marzelli took the hit, but instead of letting go, latched down harder.

"He's fucking going to bite my hand off. Get him off!" Perino screamed.

Owens hit Marzelli again, but still he wouldn't let go.

Brennan didn't need to think about what to do any longer. He raised his rifle and squeezed off a single shot.

The round struck Marzelli in the side of the head. His body went limp.

Perino pulled his bloodied hand from Marzelli's jaws and crawled away in pain.

The unexpected shot startled everyone.

Owens looked at Brennan and said, "It's official, you don't fuck around."

San Diego, California

SURPRISINGLY BRETT WOKE FEELING GOOD. He fully expected to wake with a raging headache but he hadn't.

Up before the kids, he took the time alone to investigate the opportunities Chris had suggested the night before.

Chris and he were not really friends but more associates. Madison and Chris' wife, Lyndsey, knew each other from the kids' school and volunteered in one class as well as served on the school's PTA together. They had bonded almost instantly, and with their friendship blossoming, it was only appropriate to get the husbands together too so they could do couple dates. Brett's first encounter with Chris had been good, but nothing was there for Brett to want to pursue it further. This was mainly due to Brett's own prejudice. He claimed he had enough friends and didn't have time for more. However, after last night, he was ready to waive that rule for Chris.

Chris had recently retired from the San Diego County Sheriff's Department and was now working with a private security firm providing executive protection services for Japanese executives in Mexico. This work pulled him away but he loved it. After twenty-two years in the sheriff's department, Chris still had the itch.

After a few whiskeys, their conversation had quickly

focused on the terror attacks in Copenhagen and Chris' worldview.

Chris wasn't shy about his opinion and told Brett that these sorts of attacks were coming to American soil and probably soon.

This was exactly the opposite of what he needed to hear and only further galvanized his anxiety.

Chris was a big believer in being self-reliant and touted himself as a prepper of sorts.

This confused Brett because his image of preppers was different than Chris. He kept imagining images of camo-clad, beer-bellied rednecks living off the grid in the middle of nowhere.

Chris had assured him that wasn't the case and gave a compelling and reasonable case on why everyone should be prepared.

Brett listened intently and by the end of the evening was sold on the idea of becoming more prepared.

Happy to know this, Chris invited Brett to go to the gun range.

Brett happily accepted, but he hadn't told Madison yet of his intentions.

Clicking through various prepper websites, Brett found himself a bit overwhelmed. Like anything in life, the more you discovered about any topic, the more you realized you didn't know.

Doubt began to enter his mind as he questioned whether he was overreacting.

The television was on in the background with the news still reporting on the terror attack. It was an endless loop of photos, video and analysis from every talking head the newscasters could find.

A news alert sounded and pulled his attention to the screen.

'This is a FOX NEWS alert; French authorities are in a pitched gun battle with what is believed to be terrorists in a neighborhood north of Paris.'

What doubt he had vanished. He grabbed his phone and texted Chris. *'We still on for the range today?'*

"THE GUN RANGE?" Madison bellowed as she followed Brett to the garage.

"I've never shot a pistol before and Chris is going to teach me."

"What is wrong with you? Is this because of those stupid attacks in Copenhagen?"

"Did you see what's happening in Paris right now?" Brett said.

"So what?" Madison groaned.

"So what? That sorta stuff is coming here. I mean, it's been here with those smaller attacks last year and the year before, but big ones like Copenhagen are coming. Chris believes it and so do I," Brett said.

"You're crazy. Nothing is going to happen. You're being paranoid and Chris has put things in your head. I have the nerve to contact him and tell him to stop freaking you out with fear-mongering."

Brett put on a pair of boots and laced them up. "I've been wanting to learn to shoot and now seems like a good time and with someone who seems capable."

"Chris is kooky," Madison labeled.

"No, he's not. He's a good guy."

"He's a redneck, if you ask me." Madison groaned.

"Now you're calling him names? I bet if you had an issue

and called 911 and he showed up, you'd love kooky then," Brett challenged her.

She folded her arms and replied, "I like him but not enough to have him indoctrinate my husband. You know how I feel about guns."

"I'm quite aware, but I don't hold the same views you do, you know this. I don't have a problem with them and it's about time I learn what they are and how to use them," Brett said standing up and widening his shoulders boldly.

"Honey, I love you just the way you are. I know you feel tense about this whole thing, and with your brother almost getting killed, it's made you a bit emotional. I like that side of you but this is bordering on irrational," she said softening her tone and stepping closer to him.

Eddie poked his head into the garage and asked, "Where are you going, Dad?"

"I'm going—"

"Out with a friend, guy time," Madison interjected, interrupting him.

"Where?" Eddie asked, still curious because Brett never usually left the house on Sundays.

"I'm going shooting with Adam's father," Brett answered honestly, seeing no need to lie.

"Brett!" Madison scolded.

"Cool! Can I come?" Eddie exclaimed.

"Your dad has only shot .22-caliber rifles before. Today I'm going to shoot a 9mm and a .45-caliber pistol."

"Can I come, please?" Eddie squealed with excitement.

"Maybe soon," Brett said, kneeling and looking Eddie in the eyes.

"Never, ever, ever going to happen. Brett, how dare you!" Madison barked, grabbing Eddie's hand and dragging him inside.

"But, Mom," Eddie complained.

"Don't listen to your father. He's being an idiot!" Madison declared.

"Mom said a bad word, Dad," Eddie yelled from further in the house.

"I heard," Brett hollered back, shaking his head. He was shocked she would use those words in front of Eddie but not really surprised she was upset. Ever since childhood she was told guns were bad. She didn't have any negative experiences with them nor had she ever shot a gun, she just held a very passionate belief they were bad and anyone who owned, shot or liked them were ignorant hicks. Her belief wasn't borne or built on experience of using them but merely what she was told. If anyone was acting like they had been indoctrinated, it was her, he thought.

For Brett, he never held a belief either way. In many ways he was indifferent, but with everything happening, he felt it time to discover them and with someone like Chris, who could be a valuable teacher.

A car horn blared.

Brett stuck his head back in the house and hollered, "Bye, guys, love you. I'll be back in a few hours!"

"Bye, Dad," Eddie and Will both screamed from the playroom on the opposite side of the house.

Brett closed the door and exited the house. Outside, he found Chris behind the wheel of his Chevy Silverado pickup truck. He chuckled because Chris and the truck only added to Madison's stereotype of him being a redneck.

Brett jumped in the truck and nervously began tapping his fingers on his legs. "Thanks for doing this."

Chris looked at him and grinned broadly. "You good?"

"Yeah, why?" Brett asked, his hands clasped tightly.

"You look a bit out of sorts."

Adjusting his posture, Brett cracked a half smile and replied, "I do?"

"Is the old lady getting on you? I heard she's not a big gun person."

"She's not completely happy about it, but I'm my own man."

"That you are." Chris peered through the windshield and said, "Let's do this."

CHAPTER FOUR

Monday, April 24
USS *Anchorage*, Off the Coast of Somalia

SERGEANT BRENNAN MARCHED into the briefing room alone. He proceeded to a small table at which sat Arnold; Captain Devarow, the USS *Anchorage*'s commanding officer; Colonel Nellis, his battalion commander; and two other officers, both naval. He stopped in front and stood at attention. He had no doubt that when he left, he'd be a corporal or, even worse, a lance corporal. The verbal lashing he'd received upon his return yesterday was anything but welcoming. However, if he had to do it all over again, he would.

Seated in chairs against the far wall were Owens and Lieutenant Frank.

"Sergeant Brennan, we've read your account as well as the others' accounts from the raid. You're here because of your singular action to shoot and kill Corporal Marzelli," said an unidentified naval officer.

Brennan said nothing; he just stared ahead.

"Can you tell me why you did what you did?" the officer asked.

"Sir, I shot him because after repeated attempts to get him off Petty Officer Perino failed, and after what we saw in the facility, I made a quick decision to terminate him."

"Interesting word choice, and terminate you did."

"Sir, if I may continue," Brennan said.

"Go ahead."

"Petty Officer Perino is a great corpsman and a needed asset in our unit. If he were to lose his hand, we'd lose him. I'd also like to add that Corporal Marzelli's state resembled those of the droolers we encountered in the facility. For whatever reason, I deducted that Marzelli had..." Brennan said then paused.

"Had what?"

"Sir, that he had turned into one of them and therefore was a threat to us, all of us," Brennan answered candidly.

"Your brief contact with what you're calling droolers gave you the expertise to make that determination?"

"Sir, I'm not trying to be disrespectful, but those things went through an entire Marine Raider squad and almost took out an entire SEAL fire team. Those are some of the best and well-trained warriors we have, but they were cut down easily."

The room grew quiet.

Colonel Nellis cleared his throat and asked, "Did you think you should have requested permission to take such an action?"

"No, sir, not at all."

"And why not?" Nellis asked.

"There wasn't time to, sir. I did what I felt best at that very moment and I have to say that I'd do it all over again."

Again the room grew silent.

The unidentified naval officer said, "That's good to know."

Brennan wondered what that meant.

"Sergeant Brennan, your actions yesterday, while questionable at first, were the right ones. Your gut instincts told you that Corporal Marzelli had turned into one of those things and you were correct. At 2215 last night, Petty Officer Perino mutated and was killed within seconds."

Captain Arnold looked down the table and asked, "Can I interject here?"

"Sure," the naval officer said.

"Sergeant Brennan, when this inquiry was first called, we had something else in mind, but as more information became available and when the intelligence the raid acquired bore fruit, we shifted the rationale for having you here. You're a good NCO and a great squad leader, but I think you have a greater purpose now. Alpha Company is going to miss you."

Brennan was completely confused as to where this was leading, but it clearly was going in a direction of him leaving First Battalion Fifth Marines.

The unknown naval commander jumped back in. "The intelligence gathered yesterday has led us to a huge facility in Mexico. We're putting together a special team to tackle this and we'd like you to be a part of that team."

Brennan nodded, unsure of what to say.

"We'd like you to pick members from your squad that you think will be assets to this team. You'll work under Senior Chief Petty Officer Owens. Once the final elements of the team are assembled, you'll depart the MEU and head to Mombasa, Kenya. There you'll be taking a transport to Diego Garcia to deliver the specimen to a team from the CDC. After that your team will head to Coronado."

"Sir, I have a few questions," Brennan asked. A look of confusion was written all over his face.

"I'm sure you do. Proceed."

"Why me?"

"Because you've proven you're the kind of man we need. You're deliberate and thoughtful in your actions."

"There's a lot of men out there more qualified for these types of missions than me, sir."

"Don't undercut yourself too much. Yes, we have highly trained teams for this sort of action but..." The naval officer paused and looked at the other officers.

Several nodded for him to continue.

"What I'm about to tell you comes all the way down from the president. We need to keep this under wraps. The fewer that know about these droolers, the better. That's until we know for sure what we're dealing with."

Brennan shook his head.

"Is there something wrong, Sergeant?"

"That can't be all of it."

"All of what, Sergeant?"

"The truth."

The officer recoiled from Brennan's sharp response.

"I asked for you and your squad," Owens said from the side of the room.

Brennan turned and looked at Owens. "Why?"

"It's true they want as few people to know as possible. But to be quite honest, you showed me right away you know how to fight whatever these things are. I need someone like you. Someone who will act and not be sorry for it. And let me be clear, we're not going to make you go. If you don't want this, just say so."

Thoughts of Jenna came to Brennan. He had no doubt this new assignment could delay his return, but his nation was calling on him personally. If he turned down the assignment, he'd be home and holding his new baby soon, but what was this new threat? Would there be a home to return to if it got out? This was a chance for him to keep his family safe. He would be on the frontlines of stopping this and that was where he needed to be.

He gave Owens a nod, turned to the officers seated and said confidently, "I'm in."

London, United Kingdom

JORGE PACED the room with the phone to his ear. It rang until it disconnected. "Son of a bitch!"

"Sir, do you want me to try another number?" his assistant asked.

He tossed the phone onto a leather couch and said, "They tell me the time to call and then they never pick up. I hate waiting. I hate, hate, hate it!"

Just as he finished complaining, the phone rang.

Jorge marched to the couch and picked up the phone. He looked at the screen and saw it read BLOCKED NUMBER. "Must be them," he said and answered. "Yes."

"Sorry, I'm late calling. I've been tied up." It was the same voice from the other day.

"I wanted to make sure you received the cash," Jorge said.

"We did."

"And to let you know I have a judge that's ready to place an injunction on President Shade's executive order the day it comes out."

"Good."

Jorge walked to a massive window that looked out over the River Thames. "Are we on schedule still?"

"Yes."

"When?"

"Soon."

"You're a man of few words today. I would like to speak with Israfil, not now but can you make it happen?" Jorge asked.

"Soon, you'll see Israfil, I promise."

"I've cancelled all my travel to the States. I can assume that's wise?"

"You assumed correctly."

"Can you give me something, a date, time?"

"You'll know when it happens, trust me."

Jorge paused. He hated being the anxious one, but he couldn't help it. He had invested so much into this endeavor and soon it would pay off. Soon, his dream of crushing the capitalist regimes in the United States and Europe would be complete. It had been a lifelong vision and now he was close.

"The reports we're seeing of the protests are good, but we need more. We need your people to be violent, extremely violent."

"I've deployed my people. They've hired as many as possible to hit the streets."

"We need more. We need every major freeway in every major city in the United States shut down. We need to bring the United States to a crawl. This needs to happen over the next few days, culminating in a historic show of violence and civil disobedience May 1."

"I'll redouble our efforts, but you must promise me that I'll get to meet Israfil."

"You will, that I can guarantee. If that is all, I need to go."

"You will set up a meeting, a face-to-face with Israfil?" Jorge again pressed, anxious to meet this mystery man.

"Yes. There is something else I need of you."

"Something else?"

"Yes. We know you have contacts in DC, contact them. There's a military unit that's gathered information from one of our sites. We need to know what they know, and if you can, shut them down. Do whatever you can to stifle their efforts."

"Does this have to do with Somalia?"

"If you wish to see our endeavor succeed, you'll do what I ask."

Jorge fumed. He hated being told what to do. "I'll see what I can do."

"Good."

"May 1, is that the day?" Jorge asked.

"We'll let you know soon enough, I swear. Now if that is all, goodbye, Mr. Sorossi."

"That is all," Jorge replied.

The phone clicked dead.

Jorge tossed the phone, stuffed his hands in his pockets and stared out at the boats cruising along the river. The pedestrians strolling its banks and the cars zooming past on the streets above would soon come to a halt and it would all be because of him. A smile slowly stretched across his face as that fact hit home. He had become so rich and powerful that he alone would stop the world from moving. He would end the world as he knew it and usher in a new one.

Ankara, Turkey

DAVID LOOKED at his watch and grunted in frustration. Joram was running hours late. He began to wonder if he had been caught by his former compatriots and at this very moment was being tortured or was possibly dead.

Even if Joram didn't show, the trip wasn't a waste of time. Max had rescheduled his interviews with various networks via Skype and phone. And he also had the opportunity to chat with Dylan Grim, an old friend and intelligence source who worked at the United States Consulate. He informed Grim that he was meeting with someone who could potentially provide critical information and that he'd be back in contact soon.

In the far corner above the bar, a television news flash appeared.

Breaking news. President Shade has officially signed his controversial executive order banning all travel from any nation on the United States terror list, any passport holder from those nations, and has increased the vetting on all non- US passport holders coming from anywhere. He said and I quote, 'Today, I fulfilled a campaign promise. America will be safer for this increased vetting and ban. We will reevaluate the situation in six months.'

David watched the remaining segment and smirked and said, "Good luck with that."

The waiter approached him but before he could speak, David interrupted.

"No more, thank you."

"Sir, is your name David?" the middle-aged man asked, his arms folded behind his back, his Turkish accent delicately hidden.

David looked around nervously to see if anyone was watching him but the small café in the Saffron Ankara Hotel was nearly empty save for two old men huddled in the corner. He studied them but from all appearances they looked like two fellow Americans.

"Sir, is your name David?" the waiter repeated.

Wary, David lifted his head and replied, "Yes."

The waiter unfolded his arms and in his right hand held a small white envelope. "This is for you."

Nervously, David took the envelope and examined it. "Who gave this to you?"

"The gentleman at the bar," he replied.

David looked past him towards the ornate wooden bar, but no one was there and he hadn't noticed anyone there earlier.

"Can I get you anything else or just the check?" the waiter asked.

His curiosity piqued, David ripped the envelope open and pulled out a folded sheet of paper, the hotel letterhead crowned it.

Seeing that David was distracted, the waiter walked off without an answer to his question.

David quickly read the note. As his eyes passed over each word, his eyes widened more with excitement. He folded the note, pulled some coins from his pocket, put them on the table and raced out of the café.

San Diego, California

THE WEEKEND HUNTING trip had been just what Cassidy needed. He hated to see it end but all good things must.

He had prepped all his responses for the hypothetical questions he was certain he'd receive concerning the Facebook post. His bravado on Saturday was now gone. He wanted to keep his job and was ready to give a mea culpa.

Over and over he ran different scenarios until he pulled into the parking lot of the school. Even as he made the two-hundred-yard walk from his car to the front office, he played out what he imagined would happen. He practiced the various ways he'd apologize and kept reminding himself to make sure his facial expressions matched.

He strolled into the front office.

There he was greeted by Amy, the principal's assistant. "Hi, Trevor."

The other two women in the office looked up briefly then tore their gazes away.

Oh, shit, it must be bad, Cassidy thought.

"Kathy's waiting for you. Go ahead," Amy said, pointing at the principal's closed door.

Cassidy went up and knocked.

"Come in," Kathy said.

He opened the door. The first thing he saw was a uniformed police officer from the San Diego Police Department. Maybe they were having another meeting. Then he saw the man, the Muslim-looking man he had referred to the police, sitting next to the police officer.

"Trevor, please, come take a seat," Kathy said with a smug grin.

She and the other two were sitting at a small circular table in her office.

Now his being summoned made sense.

Cassidy took a seat opposite the man.

"Trevor, you're probably wondering why I called you in early," Kathy said, her hands clasped in front of her on the table and on top of a manila folder.

He looked at her then the other two. "I think I have a good idea."

"Then I'll just get down to it. Did you send this letter to Sergeant Haggen?" Kathy said opening the folder and handing him a copy of the very letter he did send.

"Yes."

"After you came to me with your unfounded suspicions and after I told you to drop it, as we don't practice racial profiling, you took it upon yourself, as a representative of the school, to go and do just what I forbade you to do."

"Yes," Cassidy answered, his stomach knotting up.

"Why? Why would you do that?"

"Because I saw this man here observing the school for two weeks," he answered.

"Have you taken it upon yourself to report everyone you see drive past the school and park near it?" Kathy asked rhetorically.

"He is a single man who is constantly around the campus. I've seen him six times parked in clear view of the front of the school. I've watched him watch us," Cassidy said, defending himself.

"I ask you again, have you reported others? Or just him because of his ethnicity?" she asked.

Cassidy clenched his jaw.

Kathy sighed and looked at the man. "Mr. Basher was confronted at his place of work and humiliated on Friday by San Diego police officers because of your letter implicating him as a potential terrorist. After the fine officers talked with him, they concluded that Mr. Basher is no such thing. He works nearby and happens to park so he can enjoy a cigarette before arriving at work."

Cassidy just wanted to yell *what kind of bullshit answer is that?*

"The police did run a background, and Mr. Basher is clean, no records, not even a traffic ticket."

"You see, I told my coworkers I quit, but I just can't seem to be able to. I'm embarrassed."

"Please, Mr. Basher, no need to justify your actions. It's Mr. Cassidy here that does," Kathy said warmly.

"I'm sure he's just doing what he feels best," Basher said.

"Please accept my apologies," Kathy said. She looked at Cassidy and said, "Trevor, you also owe Mr. Basher an apology."

"Where are you from?" Cassidy asked.

Kathy's eyes widened and her mouth opened in shock.

"Yemen."

Cassidy grinned.

"That's enough, just apologize to Mr. Basher," Kathy snapped.

"I'm not sure if I can apologize for protecting this school and all the kids here. I see something that looks suspicious and I say something. Aren't we supposed to be doing that, see something, say something?"

"Yes," the police officer replied.

"That's not what this is. You racial profiled Mr. Basher for no other reason than because he looked Muslim," Kathy snarled.

"Correct and I'll do it again," Cassidy said defiantly.

Kathy clasped her hands again and squeezed them tight. "Mr. Basher, again, please accept the apologies of Hacienda Elementary."

"Thank you," Basher said, a slight grin on his face.

"Thank you for coming down, Lieutenant Holden. I'm sure you could be doing more productive things," Kathy said.

Basher and Holden stood.

"Good day to you," Kathy said, shaking their hands.

The two men left.

Cassidy got up to leave but was stopped.

"Trevor, close the door," Kathy ordered.

He did as she said and turned around.

"Trevor, I'm afraid I have to let you go, effective immediately. Your actions are inexcusable, downright outrageous and offensive to the diversity we're trying to instill in the children here. We don't tolerate bigotry and refuse to manifest a culture of fearmongering. Go empty out your office and leave campus."

Anger welled up inside him. He wanted to scream but he knew that would only lead to him being arrested and that was the last thing he needed. He nodded and said, "Okay." He turned around and exited her office.

Outside, he caught sight of Basher getting into his car.

Basher looked up and saw Cassidy staring. He began to nod slowly as a grin began to stretch across his face. He lifted his hand and waved.

Cassidy scowled. He knew Basher was mocking him.

As Basher drove off, Cassidy swore he'd find a way to prove he was right.

Rancho Bernardo, California

MALIK RAN UP TO Mo. "Big news, big fucking news!"

Mo looked at the passing students all rushing towards homeroom so they could make it before the bell. "I haven't seen you this happy since you got laid."

"This is better." Malik smiled.

"Better than getting laid? This must be good," Mo joked.

"Kareem likes you. He wants to bring you in!" Malik said enthusiastically.

Mo looked around, nervous that others might hear. "Ssh, don't tell the whole school."

"We're having another meeting tonight. I hear things are moving up and that they've identified a target," Malik said.

Nervous, Mo pulled Malik aside and said, "You need to be quiet."

Malik laughed. "Fuck them, they won't do anything. Cowards all of them." Malik raised his hand and gave people walking by the middle finger.

Lowering Malik's arm, Mo warned, "Don't draw attention to yourself."

"Can you believe it, brother? Soon we'll strike at the heart of the fucking infidels. If we're lucky, we'll die a glorious death and be taken to heaven."

"I can't go," Mo said.

"But you must go. Either you're in or not," Malik said.

"My dad is home," Mo said.

"Fuck him. Plus, I heard your mom supports this, right?"

"I'm still freaked out about that. I just never imagined my

mom would say, '*Hey, son, go join a terror cell and become a martyr.*' So fucking weird."

"Who knew our mothers would be the ones with balls." Malik laughed.

Mo chewed on his lip nervously. His eyes darted over his shoulder to ensure no one was eavesdropping. "I'll be there, but if I'm late, you'll know my dad busted me."

"You'll be fine. Gotta run. Be there, okay?" Malik said pushing Mo out of the way. He raced down the hall and turned around. "Just think about fucking all those virgins in heaven!" he hollered as he moved his hips back and forth.

Mo shook his head. He liked Malik for many reasons, his lack of decorum wasn't one of them.

San Diego, California

BRETT DIDN'T SEE the balled-up paper coming his way until it hit him in the face. Surprised, he stepped back and bellowed, "Hey, what's going on?"

"That's the printout from our bank statement!" Madison snapped.

Brett put his briefcase down, bent down and picked up the crumpled piece of paper. He knew what was on there but still went through the motions.

"So you thought I wouldn't find out? How dare you make a purchase like that without consulting me!" Madison barked, her face flush and nostrils flared.

"I was thinking about how I'd word it," Brett replied, looking down, embarrassed by being caught purchasing a gun without discussing it with her.

"You go to the range with Chris once and buy a gun the same day? Who does that?"

Brett walked further into the house, steering clear of her and heading straight for the refrigerator. He opened it and took out a beer. "Where are the boys?"

"Upstairs."

"I just don't want them to hear this."

"Maybe they need to hear so they can know their father lies," Madison barked and came into the kitchen.

"Whoa, that's unfair," Brett replied, holding up his arms, disarmed by her last comment.

"You know how I feel about guns but you go and buy one! You think that you run this household exclusively? We have two small children here and you want to bring in a dangerous weapon?"

"It's just a tool, nothing more," Brett countered.

"A tool? A tool? You sound like Chris. It's a damn tool of war, nothing more. I just don't get you lately. Ever since those damn attacks in Amsterdam you've been withdrawn and disconnected from your family."

"I have a lot on my mind."

"So much that it's clouded your judgment. You go out once with Chris, so what do you buy on your second trip?"

"Nothing, I didn't buy anything my second time," he said confiding he'd seen Chris again.

"What?"

"I went to the range at lunch. I want to make sure I'm proficient when I pick it up."

"You went again?"

"Yep."

"It's like you're having an affair."

"Don't be so damn dramatic."

Flustered, Madison sat down on a stool and sighed heavily. "Brett, Brett, Brett."

Brett walked over and sat next to her. He put his hand on her shoulder and gave it a slight squeeze. "I'm sorry but I knew you'd flip out. My plan was to train extensively and get a safe to secure it at home so that when I took possession of the gun you could have a great peace of mind."

She glared at him and said, "There is nothing you can do. That gun is not coming into this house, period."

"Madison, please, stop being so excited."

"No."

"Madison, the pistol will be in a safe. No one will get—"

"NO!"

Brett opened his mouth but she again silenced him.

"Don't, no! You don't need a gun, you need a shrink. You need to talk to someone about why you're paranoid."

"Madison, come on, you're being too hard on me."

"No, I'm not."

"Yes, you are. You're not being fair."

"Brett, wake up, no terrorist is going to come in this house and kill us. We're not that important. The police and authorities are working overtime to protect us. I know you think you're helping your family but you're not. Let the professionals do their jobs; let them keep us safe. You need to be focused on your job and being a father and husband."

Brett listened but his feelings were mixed. He regretted that he hadn't been honest about purchasing the gun but he also felt a sense of pride that he had done it. It wasn't just about the recent attacks, it was also about the facts he didn't have the proper tools to protect his family, and soon he would once the firearm was released to him following the ten-day waiting period.

Madison slumped over the kitchen counter bar, her head hanging low.

Brett put his hand on her but she shrugged it off.

"I promise it will be in a safe place," Brett softly said.

Madison jerked her head up towards him and with her teeth

clenched seethed. "That thing will never come into this house, you understand me? Never."

Brett recoiled. He had seen Madison upset before but never like this. "You're being stubborn."

"I'm taking care of my family."

"So am I," he shot back.

Madison pushed away from the counter and stood up. "I suggest you go find another place to sleep because you're not coming into my bed." She stormed off and out of the kitchen.

"By the way, the attack was in Copenhagen, not Amsterdam!" he hollered after her.

"No one cares!" she barked back.

Brett sat, shocked at her extreme reaction. A multitude of emotions flooded through him. The one he focused on was his irritation with her.

He grabbed his phone and sent a text to Chris. "You available to grab a drink?"

Promptly Chris replied, *"Sure, where?"*

"Karl, in 20," Brett replied, referencing the Karl Strauss brew pub a few miles away.

"Let me check w/ the ball n chain."

Chris' response made him chuckle. Not feeling welcome in his own home, he immediately left and headed towards the bar to clear his mind.

Ramona, California

Sophie entered the darkened house. She flipped on the lights and jumped when she saw Cassidy sitting on the couch.

"Oh, my God, you startled me. Why are you sitting in the dark?" she asked, concerned.

"I've been sitting here thinking how I'd tell you and none of it sounds good," he confessed.

She rushed over and sat down. "What's wrong, baby?"

"I lost my job."

"What? How?"

"I was fired today for reporting that Muslim man to the police."

"Are you kidding me?"

"I wish I were," Cassidy replied somberly, his head hung low.

Sophie took a deep breath. She searched for the right words, but couldn't find them. Unwilling to just offer the standard predictable responses, she put her arms around him and squeezed. "I love you, Trevor."

"I'm so sorry, I'm such a fuckup, I'd understand if you left me. I get it. I'm a loser. I can't even hold down a job as a janitor. What in the hell is wrong with me?" Cassidy groaned. His pledge earlier to discover the truth about Basher was now gone when the reality of what had happened to him hit home.

With sincerity, she answered, "Nothing is wrong with you. The thing is, you haven't yet found your place out of the Marines, but you will, please believe that."

"I don't know if I can. I'm worthless."

"You're nothing like that at all. You're a strong man, an honest man, a good man," she said as she lifted his head and stared into his eyes. "I need you to pull it together. You're a fighter. You will come back from this and I'll be there right alongside of you."

Never in his life had he felt so lost and so vulnerable. The Marines had given him an environment to exploit his God-given talents of leadership and grit, but Sophie gave him something the Marine Corps never could, a place to call home. She was a safe harbor for him to reside while not out on the open sea of life. He hugged her tightly and whispered into her soft ear, "Thank you for being you. I will rise above, for you."

She pulled him away and poignantly stated, "Let me be your muse, but do it for you."

"I will. I'll go looking for a job first thing," he said.

"Don't just look...create. I know these words always sound so cliché, but you can truly be what you want. You just have to know who you are, know your true self, then go be."

He smiled and joked, "Are you my girlfriend or a motivational speaker?"

"To you, I'm both and more."

San Diego, California

BRETT PUT his drink down and sighed heavily.

Chris knew Brett had the weight of the world on his shoulders and that was before the dustup with Madison. "She'll get over it."

"Ha, I wish. You don't know Madison."

"You're right, I don't, but I just can't believe she'll hold this that long."

Brett picked up the pint glass and swished the contents. He marveled as the caramel colored ale fizzed with each twirl creating a foamy white head. Thirsty for the IPA, he tossed back what was left in his glass.

"Want another?" Chris asked.

"I better not. She's already pissed. Me going home half-cut won't help my cause."

"You think you can get in more trouble than you already are? This seems like a good time to leverage tying one on."

"I can't. Plus I have to work tomorrow."

"I understand. I know it's a bad time to ask, but are we on for the range at lunch tomorrow?" Chris asked.

The two stopped talking and turned to the television.

This is a Fox News alert. Sources in the intelligence and

defense communities are telling us tonight that over twenty United States Special Forces troops and Marines were killed in a surprise raid on a compound in Somalia the other night. When the White House was asked for comment, none was given. As of right now, we don't know if this raid was in response to the terror attack in Copenhagen. Until we get a confirmation from the White House or Department of Defense, we don't know for sure what's transpired. So the story is still developing. Shifting to the terror attack in Copenhagen, we have more information concerning this new terror group that has taken credit for that attack. They call themselves The Bloody Hand. What we're hearing is they're even more radical than ISIS. We're hearing they're an offshoot of ISIS that splintered off earlier in the year and have been able to go operational rather quickly. When we get more information, we'll update. We'll now return to your regularly scheduled programming.

Brett looked at Chris, his bald head reflecting the yellow glow from the pendant lights above their heads. "What do you make of all this stuff?"

"I keep saying it, and I know I sound like a skipping record, but something big is coming," Chris replied.

"Like what?"

"Nuclear, biological, something big. Those cocksuckers won't stop until they hit us so hard we finally buckle over. Pay no attention to those who say we have nothing to fear, we have everything to fear. Our borders are wide open. Talk to any border agent, they're capturing more than Hondurans or Mexicans coming in to pick strawberries. They're getting many Muslims. For years, they've been coming in and setting up shop. Hell, the FBI is tracking threats in fifty states and that's just what they'll tell you. Believe me, after over twenty years in law enforcement, it's always worse than what they're telling you."

"That bad, huh?"

"Yes, and it's only a matter of when."

"If it's going to be so bad, what can I really do to prepare, then?" Brett asked.

Chris gave him an odd look and answered, "Am I hearing doubt?"

"No...well, yes, a bit, if it's nuclear or, god help us, a biological-type thing, what can I really do to protect me and my family?"

"More than doing nothing, that's what. Pay no mind to the social media appeasers who say our only weapon to fight terror is through hugs and colorful memes. Those people are fucking idiots, pure and simple. Morons of the grandest form. As if changing your Facebook picture to the flag of Denmark is doing anything. It's bullshit, total. It's lazy and shows a blindness or even an ignorance."

"Wow, you're on a tear," Brett joked.

"Just the truth, buddy. If there's one piece of advice I can give you, it would be that no one, and I mean not a soul, gives a flying fuck. They act like it on Facebook, but when push comes to shove and if a nuke goes off in LA or a terrorist goes crazy in a mall, people don't care about you or me, they care about themselves. Yes, I'm overgeneralizing, as some people will stand up and help, but for the most part, we're a selfish species. If you are putting your family's fate in the hands of others, you're an idiot. Do you put your family's financial security in other people's hands? No. You work, save, and invest, all to make sure they're fine. You get my point?"

"I do and it makes sense."

"Good."

"What do you make of all the bomb threats and heightened alerts that started this morning?"

"It's one of two things. Either some assholes are pranking,

which is fucking stupid because you get caught doing that shit now, or it's being done to overwhelm the system."

"Isn't that a good thing? If everyone is looking, won't it be harder to pull off an attack?"

"The fact of the matter is we only have so many people working to prevent an attack. If you get them distracted and jumping from one place to another, it provides cover for something spectacular to occur."

"Then this could be all part of an orchestrated plan?"

"Yep. Get us all lathered up, get the American people freaked out, get law enforcement working overtime chasing down dead leads just so you can pull off the mother of all attacks."

The bartender walked up and said, "Last call."

"Last call?" Brett asked looking at the time on his phone.

"I'll take one more," Chris said.

"Screw it. I'll have another too," Brett replied to the bartender who took their empty glasses and headed towards the tap. Putting his head in his hands, Brett massaged his forehead. "This all sucks so much. Maybe Madison's right. I'm getting a bit obsessed about this. I have to admit it, I'm scared."

Chris could see the fear emanating from Brett. He put his hand on his shoulder and said, "Don't be afraid, be prepared."

"Is it that easy?" Brett asked, his head still hanging low.

"You can't control anything in this world but how you react to situations that confront you. You have no power over what a homicidal maniac does or the politicians back East. All you can do is ensure your family is safe if something does happen, whether that be from a terrorist or some douchebag coming into your house trying to rob you. Getting the tools and training for protection and being self-reliant are just more insurance policies. You have life insurance, I'm sure; you have car and health insurance too. Why do you get *those* insurance policies?

Preparing for a calamity is no different. There is nothing worse than having something occur and not being ready. Even Madison will look at you and ask, 'Why don't' you do something?' I guarantee it. I'd bet she's never been in a situation before that requires having a gun. That's the problem with our society. We're so far removed from having to protect ourselves and the days of living under tyranny are in the distant past that they think it's just history and can't repeat itself. People have what I call normalcy bias."

The bartender came back and placed full pint glasses in front of them.

The television broke into another breaking news story. *Circuit Court Judge Allen in Washington State has placed a temporary restraining order on President Shade's controversial travel ban and extreme vetting executive order. The restraining order stops the enforcement of the president's order, allowing those from designation terror nations to come to the United States under the normal visa restrictions. Many on Capitol Hill and across the country, specifically immigrant and Muslim groups, are hailing the judge's action. The protests still continue across twenty-seven different cities. We will now go back to your regularly scheduled program.*

Chris took his beer and took a large gulp. "Unfucking believable."

"I saw that coming. Things are so polarized, it's not about what's right, but what's politically expedient to appease a loud and vocal minority," Brett said.

"It's the shit right there, that's what's going to get us all in trouble," Chris growled.

Brett took a long drink and thought back to something Chris had mentioned earlier. "What's normalcy bias?"

"It's when people have a false belief that everything around them is the way it's always been and always will be. You meet those people every day. I see it in the eye rolls of people when I tell them I'm stocked up for anything."

Brett took a long drink. He could think of several times he was the eye roller in his past.

"Do you have a large supply of water? Food? I ask people all the time and again they think I've lost my mind. I then ask them if they think a big earthquake could happen in their lifetime. Their answer. Yes. But think stocking up is crazy. I'm over trying to convince the inconvincible."

"That's something else I need to do."

"My advice is to just do it, don't ask permission from your wife, just buy the stuff and put it in the garage."

"I'm not too worried about her response with that stuff."

"Good, you should get on it, then," Chris said putting down his beer and picking up his phone. "I'm texting you a couple of places to order some stuff. Don't go too crazy and try to be *tacticool* by buying a bunch of garbage that looks neat but you'll never use."

Brett's phone buzzed. He looked down at the phone sitting next to his beer and saw it was Madison texting.

You coming home?

"It's Madison," Brett said, picking up the phone, and replied, "I can come home?"

Brett watched in anticipation as he could see she was replying by the bubble on his screen.

"What's up?" Chris asked.

"Ah, nothing," Brett said, still looking at the screen, waiting for her response.

Sorry flashed on the screen followed by a frowny face.

He quickly replied, "Coming home." A smile stretched across his face, knowing she felt just as bad as he did about their fight.

"A smile! Nice, glad to see you're happy again," Chris

blared.

"Me too, I just hate it when we fight. I love her so much but sometimes she can just be so damn stubborn," Brett confessed.

"Aren't all women?" Chris joked.

Brett took a large gulp and put his beer down. "Listen, I'm going home."

"You do that. Makeup sex is always great."

"Exactly," Brett said with a broad smile.

"Remember to start ordering your other stuff and get some ammo," Chris advised.

"I will," Brett replied stepping away from the bar but not before tossing a couple of twenty-dollar bills on the bar. "My treat."

"Not necessary."

"Nope, my pleasure," Brett said, happily striding away.

"Lunch tomorrow at the range?" Chris hollered.

"I'll be there," Brett said as he happily walked off.

Rancho Bernardo, California

Mo DIDN'T KNOW what to expect from his first formal meeting as a member of an official terror cell. All day he kept thinking it was too easy to join a terror cell. *Didn't they do more vetting?*

Malik couldn't relax, he kept bouncing around and jabbering nonsense like earlier.

"Is he normally late?" Mo asked, looking at the time on his phone.

"Ahh, yeah, I think so," Malik said.

Mo cocked his head and asked, "Hold on, you've been to one of these so-called official meetings before, haven't you?"

Malik shrugged his shoulders and replied, "Not really."

"I thought you knew this guy," Mo said.

"I do, I mean, I met him a week before you did. I was introduced to him at our mosque."

Mo leaned in and grumbled, "How do you know he's not a cop or FBI? Huh? What if this is some sort of sting operation."

"It's not, chill out," Malik happily replied.

Mo glanced around the small back room of Amir's Smoke Shop, a local business run by a Pakistani immigrant. Sitting in pairs of two were three other groups, each conversing with themselves. Mo wondered if they too were having doubts like he was.

The door opened suddenly and in walked four very intimidating men.

A tall and lean man walked to the front of the room and said, "Welcome, everyone. Now can everyone stand."

No one hesitated. They all stood up.

"I need you to take off your jackets, sweaters. I then need you to empty your pockets, that includes your phones," he said as he snapped his fingers.

The other men walked by with large bins, collecting the phones.

"Are we getting them back?" Mo asked.

"Of course, you just don't need them where we're going," the man answered.

"Going?" Mo mumbled to Malik.

Malik responded by shrugging his shoulders.

After the men collected the phones, the man ordered, "Now strip down."

The group began to mumble to each other.

"Do it!" the man barked.

Like recruits in the military, they all began to undress.

"Hurry up," the man snapped. He walked to one of the young men in the group who stood with his underwear still on. "All of it, naked."

"But—" the young man sheepishly said.

"No one cares how little or how big your cock is. Strip or you don't go."

The young man dropped his underwear but covered his crotch with his hand.

The man laughed and continued. "When you're done, please line up at the door."

The group did as they were told.

Mo felt uncomfortable and his stomach began to tighten with nervous fear.

Before they could walk out the door, they needed to raise their arms and were subject to a quick examination.

"We're not perverts. We're just making sure you don't have a wire stuck up your ass. We can never be too careful," the man explained.

One by one they were examined, given shorts and a tee shirt and told to proceed to a van waiting out back.

"This is cool, isn't it?" Malik whispered over Mo's shoulder.

Cool was the last thing Mo would call this.

"Open your mouth, raise your arms and spread your legs," one of the men asked.

Mo did as he asked.

The man flashed a light in Mo's mouth and ran a gloved finger along his inner cheeks. After that he examined under his armpits, his crotch and the crack of his butt.

"You're good. Take these, get dressed and go to the white van," the man said.

Violated is the only word Mo could think to describe the ordeal. He quickly put on his new clothes and marched to the van.

EVERYONE SAT IN THE VAN, quiet.

Mo could feel the fear. It hung over everyone like a thick fog.

The man who led the inspection came out to the van and looked inside. "Put these on for the trip."

The other men handed out large thick brown canvas bags.

The group took them and looked at each other, bewildered what they were for.

"Cover your heads. Once that's done, we'll be able to depart," the man ordered.

Each new step was only making Mo regretful of his decision. He cautiously slipped the bag over his head. The earthy smell of the canvas filled his nostrils and the thickness made seeing impossible.

The side door of the van slammed shut.

Mo could hear others in his group breathing heavily, a clear sign they were panicked.

The driver's door opened then closed.

The van roared to life.

Mo closed his eyes and whispered to himself, "Allah, if this is your will, I am your humble servant. I put my life in your hands. Do with me what you desire."

The driver mumbled something unintelligible.

Mo's ears picked up the gear shift engaging. Seconds later the van lurched forward and sped off.

CHAPTER FIVE

Tuesday, April 25
Ankara, Turkey

DAVID SLOWLY WALKED down the long hallway. The hotel was nice for Turkish standards. The carpet in the hall was old, worn and faded with the center showing the deepest signs of wear. Small tears and peeling of the wallpapered walls was noticeable in the corners near the floor and the ceiling. This he could overlook, it was the musty smell that got to him most. The low textured ceiling and dim lights made him feel claustrophobic.

As he passed one door after another, he drew closer to room 506. There he hoped to finally meet with Joram and get an interview he needed for his film.

David stopped just outside the door and took a deep breath. A chill ran down his spine. He didn't know what to expect once the door opened. Fearful questions suddenly came to him. *Is this all a ruse to capture me? Am I to be used as a pawn in the war?* He immediately squashed them. *Why would Joram take me prisoner? Why me?* Unsure if he'd grabbed everything he needed, he hastily looked through his backpack. Seeing he had the tools of his trade, he deliberately slowed his breathing. Once he was confident he was ready, he knocked.

The door opened swiftly and there stood Joram.

Being a person who picked up on the smallest details, David instantly noticed several small razor cuts on Joram's neck. He imagined they came from having shaved for the first time in a long time.

"David, my friend, come in, hurry," Joram said stepping aside and motioning with his hand towards the back of his room.

David stepped across the threshold and stopped just inside.

Joram stuck his head out the door and looked in both directions. Seeing no one was in the hallway, he closed the door and locked it. He turned to David, who had his hand extended to shake. Joram pushed his hand aside and gave David an embrace.

This was entirely unexpected for David. His body tensed when Joram's arms wrapped around him and hugged.

"My friend, welcome to Turkey, so good to see you and thank you for coming," he said.

"Sure."

Joram let him go and raced into the room. "Can I get you something to drink? I have some tea."

"I'm good, thank you."

"Please come and sit," Joram said, pointing to a set of chairs in the back of the room.

David looked around the room, it was exactly like the standard room he had. The bathroom was the first room on the right and past that was one space with one queen-sized bed, across from it a dresser with an old analog television sat near the window, two chairs and a small table stood. The room was untidy, with trash, newspapers and dirty plates from room service beside the bed. Empty bottles of Coke covered the tops of the dresser and nightstands with ashtrays overflowing with cigarette butts on each table.

"David, sit, please," Joram insisted.

David walked towards the chair on the left and took a seat. He felt uncomfortable and hoped his body wasn't showing his apprehension. "Why am I here?"

"I told you, I defected."

"But why call me, why not go to Damascus, to your family, your father?" David asked curious as to why he hadn't gone back to the presumed protection of his father.

Joram grinned, his yellow-stained teeth showing a lack of hygiene. He grabbed a pack of cigarettes and pulled one out. He stuck the unfiltered Camel cigarette in his lips, but just before he lit it, he offered one to David.

David was tempted but refused. He opened his backpack and pulled out his camera and digital recorder.

"You're all business, I like that." Joram laughed.

"Let's get this straight, I'm not here to chitchat and swap stories. I'm here because you have a story to tell and I'm the perfect person to hear it and share it."

"All true, all true, that's why I called you," Joram said, exhaling a thick plume of smoke into the air above David's head. With his fingers, he picked a small piece of loose tobacco that lingered on his tongue and wiped it on his jeans.

David clicked the recorder and asked, "So you defected from ISIS?"

"Ha, you are all business."

"Timing is everything," David replied.

"That it is. Something is different with you, I sense fear."

"I'm fine."

"What happened in Copenhagen shook you?"

David thought about turning the recorder off but changed his mind. "Yeah, you could say that."

"That's to be expected. I was shaken too when I saw those ISIS butchers murder innocents," Joram declared.

"Looks like we share something," David said.

Joram paused and thought about what to say next. When he had made up his mind, he said, "I apologize for having you wait for so long. I needed to make sure you were by yourself. I wasn't sure if you told anyone. You see I can't risk being caught by your CIA. I don't wish to spend time in one of your American black sites."

"No one knows except me, you and my agent," David lied, having told Dylan Grim he was in Turkey to meet his ISIS contact.

"Max, right?"

"Yeah, Max, good memory."

With the cigarette between his fingers, Joram tapped his right temple and said, "Like a trap."

"The last time we talked you had fled Damascus and came to Ankara to meet with someone, a recruiter of sorts, for lack of a better word, who was going to ferry you back into ISIS-controlled Syria."

"Yes."

"Based upon the fact you've defected, it's safe to say you made it there and assimilated into ISIS?"

"Yes."

"When did you defect and why?" David asked.

"I defected a week ago. The why is a much longer answer."

"I've got time," David replied.

"Good, because you're going to need a lot of it."

Riverside, California

THE VAN STOPPED ABRUPTLY.

Mo woke. He couldn't believe he fell asleep. He opened his eyes but was only greeted by darkness. Unsure of how long he'd been out, he whispered, "Malik, Malik."

"Yes," Malik replied.

"Where are we?" Mo asked.

"How would I know? I can't see a damn thing," Malik answered.

The side door opened. An unfamiliar voice boomed, "Take off your hoods."

Mo ripped off the hood as fast as he could. He inhaled deeply, enjoying the fresh air.

"Out of the van, hurry," a man in the shadows ordered.

Mo climbed out and looked around the darkened space save for a single overhead light in the far corner.

We're in a large building, he said to himself.

The shadowy man stepped into view. "Follow me."

Everyone obediently did as they were told and shuffled behind the large man.

"Sit down," the man barked.

Mo looked at the rows of chairs and took a seat in the back. His eyes darted around and settled on a dry-erase board emblazoned with the emblem of The Bloody Hand.

"They're The Bloody Hand, can you believe it?" Malik whispered to Mo.

"This all seems so surreal," Mo replied.

The others talked amongst themselves in whispers.

The clang of a metal door sounded behind the dry-erase board out of sight of everyone. The clack of hard sole shoes echoed off the concrete floor.

All fell silent.

A well-dressed, tall and slender man appeared from behind the dry-erase board. He walked the edge of the chairs, looking carefully at each recruit, until he came full circle, stopping in front of the chairs.

He stepped aside and pointed at the image of the bloody hand. "This here isn't just an emblem. It isn't just a symbol. It is who we are. The great prophet Mohammed was Allah's heart and soul here on Earth. We are Allah's right hand, a hand covered in the blood of our enemies, Allah's enemies. We have and will strike down all those who oppose Allah's will. We will fight and destroy those who do not submit to God's laws. Our cause is holy."

All sat mesmerized by the man's words.

"You have been chosen to be an instrument, a warrior in this fight. Allah is proud and so am I. Together we will strike a blow to the infidels, a blow so deadly that the streets will flow with their blood. Soon, all of you will take to the battlefield in a battle that will finally end the Great Satan and usher in a new age of believers."

A roar of applause and cheers rang out.

"Sit down!" the man barked.

Everyone fell silent.

"This is not a game. This is not a pathetic spectator sport. Show discipline. You are warriors!" the man snapped.

At first, Mo felt a sting of pride, but it wasn't enough to overcome the nauseous feeling in his body. Something felt off, something felt...wrong.

Malik nudged him.

Mo looked and Malik was smiling, his eyes wide with joy.

"Are you truly dedicated to fight for Allah?"

Fearful, the room was silent.

The man smiled and said, "You may now respond."

"Yes!" everyone said in unison, including Mo.

The man walked up to the front row and looked down at the faces there. "Are you committed?" he asked to the first young face he saw.

"Yes," was the answer given.

The man stepped in front of the next and asked again, "Are you committed?"

"Yes."

Through the ranks, the man went, asking the same question over and over. When he was finished, he stepped back in front of them and said, "Today will be your first test."

Doors located far off screeched open.

Everyone turned to see, but couldn't.

Mo's stomach tightened.

Out of the shadows, a single file line of bound and hooded people appeared. They were paraded to the front.

The man hollered, "Right now, you will get to show your loyalty and commitment to Allah."

Mo looked down at his quivering hand and the urge to vomit was growing.

"Pick one and stand in front," the man ordered.

Many didn't hesitate, including Malik. He rushed and stood happily in front of a hooded person.

Mo followed and stood next to him. He gave Malik an uneasy look then fixed his gaze on the person in front of him. He could hear their labored breathing.

"Look, this one pissed their pants." Malik laughed, slapping Mo on the arm.

One by one, the hoods were removed. Their mouths were taped and gagged, but each one mumbled pleas of mercy. There wasn't a pattern to the soon-to-be victims. They were black, white, Hispanic and Asian. Men and women both. Young and old.

Mo looked at his victim, a young woman. Her begging eyes pleaded for him not to hurt her.

"Take a knife, hold it to the infidel's throat and repeat after me," the man said.

Several men handed out long-bladed knives.

When Mo took his, he had a hard time admiring it like Malik was. Doubt continued to fill him every second. The man was right, this was a test of commitment and he wasn't sure if he could do it. However, the question then turned to *what if he didn't?*

Mo jumped when the man appeared behind him and whispered in his ear, "Put the knife to the infidel's throat."

Fearful of what could happen to him, he did as he was told.

The woman's eyes bulged when the cold steel of the blade touched her tender throat. Tears began to well and flow from her eyes.

"Repeat after me, I am a warrior of The Bloody Hand. I take your life in service of Allah and the caliphate. Praise be to Allah!"

In a loud chorus, everyone repeated the words, including Mo.

More tears flowed from the woman.

Unable to look at her, he set his gaze upon the dry-erase board.

"Press your blade hard against their throat and slide it firmly across," the man instructed.

Malik laughed as he followed the order.

Mo didn't; he froze.

"What are you doing?" Malik asked ensuring he kept his voice low.

"I can't," Mo replied.

"Do it," Malik urged.

"I can't."

Yelling from the end of the row turned everyone's attention there.

One of the victims, unhurt, sprinted away after a recruit failed to execute the command.

"Stop him!" the man yelled.

The lone victim was chased down easily and executed.

Mo looked back to his victim, his blade still at her throat.

Seeing the opportunity, Malik pushed Mo aside and slid his blade across her throat.

At first the cut bled slowly, then gushed.

Mo watched as her life literally drained out of her eyes. She gave him one final look then dropped to the floor.

The man looked at the bodies in front of the recruits minus the one who allowed his to escape. He walked up to him and asked, "Brother, what's your name?"

"Mohammed."

Mo shuddered when he heard the name because it was also his.

"Mohammed, what happened?"

"I, um, I couldn't, I'm sorry. I don't want any part of this. Just let me leave," he said, his voice quivering.

"Let me see your knife," the man said.

Mohammed handed the knife to him.

"You're a disgrace. How dare your parents honor you with the name of the great prophet," the man said and, in the blink of an eye, took the man by the hair, pulled his head back and sliced Mohammed's throat.

Mohammed struggled at first but soon the loss of blood tempered his resistance.

The man kept cutting and with a single twist and pull, removed Mohammed's head. He held it up and yelled, "This is what we do to those who oppose us, because opposing us is opposing the will of Allah. We are The Bloody Hand, we are Allah's one true army."

Ankara, Turkey

DAVID RUBBED HIS SORE EYES. He and Joram had been up for what seemed liked countless hours. While he was exhausted, Joram was as fresh as when they started. His stories were not only informational and would give anyone who read them insight in the inner workings and day-to-day life of an ISIS member, but the way Joram told them, they were exciting. He sometimes caught himself leaning in with excitement and when he did he had to remind himself that these weren't just stories but the confession from a former member of one of the most lethal terrorist organizations in the world.

It had taken David a while to settle down. He had met Joram before and there were many ways to describe their relationship but trust wasn't a word he'd ever use.

The first hours of the interview covered his departure for ISIS and how he'd been received and processed. He described an organization that had a surprisingly sophisticated internal governmental structure. When he first arrived in Raqqa, he was shocked to see he wasn't alone in being a fresh recruit. He didn't expect he'd be the solitary newbie, but when he first stepped foot out of the back of the Toyota truck, he saw a group of well over a hundred new men and some women who had traveled far, some as far as Australia and the United States. What he found interesting was that a good number weren't Muslim by birth but converts. The ISIS Internet-recruiting campaign was working, it had been a success. He hadn't spent much time online but after conversing with many new recruits he found they had made their minds up after viewing videos and posts showing ISIS victories as well as the life they'd be living under the Islamic State. All the new recruits he spoke to gave similar responses, as if they were speaking from talking points. What was visible to him in all the fresh faces was a mixture of fear and excitement. None knew for sure if they'd ever return to their homes, but like him, they didn't seem to care because the promise of adventure and conquest was too alluring.

Joram described that his first few days in Raqqa were spent at the Homs embassy; this was where Syrian natives had to

apply for legal status in the Islamic State. He then was trans-
ferred to the Border Administration Department so he could be
naturalized. He found this humorous, as he was Syrian and
Raqqa was technically in Syria, but the Islamic State thought
differently. To them, he and all who traveled there were immigrants and had to be processed and documented. There he had
to pass a citizenship test, which was administered ironically by
an Iraqi. Through his first few days, a pattern emerged. Nearly
everyone he met, specifically those in the ranks of ISIS, represented dozens of nations around the world. The Islamic State
was truly an international destination.

His citizenship test consisted of a series of questions mainly
about why he wanted to be there and why he was seeking the
life of a holy warrior. He described how he was nervous about
his answers but decided to just be honest. For all his concerns,
his answers passed muster, allowing him to move to the next
phase, indoctrination.

Indoctrination was handled by the Sharia court. There he
gave David a vivid illustration of an intensive educational
program taught by several high-ranking clerics. Calling it education wasn't accurate, it was nothing short of brainwashing to all
new recruits that they should hate and seek to destroy all nonbe-
lievers, including fellow Muslims. They used Muhammad's
teachings found in both the Quran and the hadiths to help vali-
date their viewpoints. Joram described being fascinated by parts
of the hadith, specifically from the *Sahih Bukhari*, where it
described warfare and jihad. He had heard of the book before
but hadn't really studied it growing up.

Joram was born a Muslim and to say he practiced the faith
honestly was not true. Like many Christians and Jews worldwide they might associate themselves with a religion for cultural
reasons but many didn't truly practice their faith. He was like
many twentysomethings around the world, but he also had

many advantages that a lot didn't have. He grew up to a well-to-do family in Damascus, went to good schools, was well educated, liked music, movies, and just about anything that came from America. He often sported the latest fashions, was active on social media and was never caught without the latest tech gadgets. In fact, he was fortunate enough to have spent several summers in Europe. There he found friends and did as any young man would do away from his parents; he drank, played and flirted with women. When the clerics at the Sharia court showed him the direct quotes from the Bukhari he was shocked. Now immersed and surrounded by many who had become devote, he found it intoxicating to be a part of something much bigger than him. With each day, he examined his past life and concluded that it had been corrupted by the West.

Joram paused and sat looking down at his folded hands. The seconds turned to minutes, making it an uncomfortable situation for David, who sat patiently.

"Everything okay?" David asked, unable to control his desire to break the silence.

"Yes," Joram replied, taking another cigarette out and lighting it with the one he was already smoking. He inhaled deeply and closed his eyes.

David stared at him. He could see the creases and wrinkles on his face were more pronounced than he remembered. It was as if Joram had aged a decade or more. But what was to be expected after living a life he had for three years. The life, usually short, of a mujahedeen wasn't easy.

Joram opened his eyes and said, "I witnessed my first execution shortly after going to court."

"A beheading?" David asked.

"No, nothing as noble as that type of death for this man," he replied, taking another long drag off the cigarette.

David searched his thoughts for all the murders he'd heard

or seen on the Internet connected to ISIS. Many gruesome images came and he couldn't guess nor did he want to. "What happened?"

"The man, a Jordanian, was accused of providing coded messages to the Syrian government."

"So, he did it?"

"Yes, he was guilty, but his punishment was more severe than the crime."

"Was he a spy? Like a legitimate spy sent from Assad?"

"I don't know."

"But you're sure he was guilty?"

Joram paused. "Are you asking me if I saw the evidence against this man?"

"How do you know if he actually did it?"

"I don't. I never saw anything that connected the man to the crime, I just assumed that he had."

David nodded.

"I'm not saying this in any way to show support for his sentence, but how do you know anyone does commit a crime? You hear about a murderer and you see his face on the news but have *you* seen the evidence? Were you there?"

"I see your point."

"I mention that because you seemed to be making a pointed accusation that I should have somehow been privy to the evidence against this man."

David didn't respond, he just stared.

"Do you research every person's case to ensure they're innocent before your country executes someone?"

"Of course not, but—"

"You trust that the system works."

"Well—"

"Don't mince words. You trust the system, just say it," Joram pressed.

David didn't reply; instead he asked, "Can we move on? None of this is pertinent."

"I'm like you, I trusted the system I walked into," Joram said, defending his past actions and motives.

"Our systems aren't the same. You can't find moral equivalency in them."

"Oh, really?"

David put his pen and pad down and shuffled in his seat. "My country might not be perfect, but we don't go around murdering people."

"You don't?" Joram mocked.

"No, we don't."

"Tell that to the millions of innocents over the years who have died from your bombs or soldiers."

"That's war. There is always collateral damage."

"Islamic State is also at war."

Frustrated by the spin from Joram, David stood up and began to pack his bag.

"What are you doing?" Joram asked.

"I'm tired, hungry and I think it's best we continue this later."

"No, no, please stay. I have so much more to say."

David stopped and said, "No. I won't be subjected to condescending bullshit. If you have a story to tell me, then tell me and please leave out the parts where you find justification for what ISIS does or that the US and ISIS are no different."

"But there are similarities."

David slung his pack and glared. "We are not the same. I go searching for the truth regardless of affiliations; I don't join death cults who murder innocents in cold blood because they drew Muhammad on a piece of paper."

Joram stood and held out his hand. "Please, I'm sorry, don't leave."

"I'll come back later, but right now I need a break."

"No, please stay. Let's talk more. I'll just share my experiences, no politics."

David walked to the door but was stopped when Joram grabbed his arm. "Please stay."

David looked at his grasp and said, "I'm tired and hungry, I'll come back in a bit."

"Please return quickly. I have much to tell and not enough time to tell it," Joram said.

David hesitated.

"Are you staying?"

"No, I'll be back soon, but you worry me. Are you safe?"

"No one is ever really safe, are they?"

David scrunched his face, unsure what that comment meant. "I need a break. I'll be back soon."

Joram grabbed David's arm again and said, "Make sure no one follows you back. I can't stress the importance of our privacy."

"I value privacy. I won't say a word and I'll be careful. Now, please let me go."

"Fine, I'll see you soon."

"Yes, soon, bye," David said, rushing out. After the door closed he sighed heavily. Their hours-long interview had drained him. He needed some food, rest, and a shower; then he'd be back. He looked both directions down the hall. A bit of paranoia gripped him then. Was he truly safe? And what would happen if ISIS found them together? He shrugged off the concerns. He needed Joram's story and nothing was going to stop him.

Over the Indian Ocean

BRENNAN FOUND the hum of the C-17's engines soothing. With his head rested against his pack, he began to drift off.

"What the fuck!" Vickers yelled.

Brennan sprang up and looked.

Near the aft of the plane a group of Marines and SEALs were standing, all huddled around Princess, the name they'd given the female drooler.

"What's going on?" Klyde said, rushing past Brennan to see what the commotion was about. Even though he hadn't encountered the droolers during the raid, Brennan insisted he join the team. He needed men he could trust, and Klyde was just that.

Vickers hollered, "Sergeant Brennan, get over here."

Muffled screams and howls drowned out much of the cross talk and chattering.

Brennan hurried over. He pushed past several people so he could see.

Owens was shaking his head and chuckling. "I think we're about to have a baby."

"Seriously?" Brennan asked as he finally got his eyes on Princess.

Straining under the restraints, Princess gnashed her teeth and howled in pain. For their protection, she was strapped to a gurney, which was encapsulated in a thick clear plastic to ensure no contamination. It was all attached to a metal cargo pallet and secured to the floor.

"It's hard to tell," Brennan said, trying to get a good look, as the plastic distorted his view.

"Look at her belly," Owens said, unzipping a small section. He inserted a long rod and lifted her shirt.

"Don't unzip that. We don't know if we'll get contaminated," someone hollered.

Owens looked back and said, "They think it's blood borne. We're fine."

"Fuck that," the man said backing away.

Several Marines recoiled when they saw the violent thrashing and movements in her lower abdomen.

"Where's Sanchez?" Owens asked referencing Petty Officer Third Class Sanchez, the team corpsman.

"I'm here," Sanchez answered.

"Well, Doc, thoughts?" Owens asked.

"I'd have to say the child is in distress," Sanchez replied.

Owens chewed on his lower lip. He gave Brennan a look and asked, "I don't think we should do a thing. We can't have you getting in there with her."

"I agree, but what if she and the baby die," Brennan asked. Taking Princess to Diego Garcia was their mission, period.

Princess wailed in pain.

"I should do something, maybe a shot to ease the pain," Sanchez said.

Princess cried out in pain. She looked at her stretching and expanding belly and growled.

Sanchez took a step closer and grabbed the zipper. He was torn about what to do. He struggled as competing instincts played out in his thoughts. *Should I provide care, or should I get away?*

"Sanchez, step back," Owens ordered.

"But she needs help."

"She? I don't think so. I'm not letting you inside that enclosure," Owens said.

Sanchez hadn't deployed to the island and was one of the few on the team who hadn't had direct contact with the droolers.

Princess' body tensed as she tried to free herself from the tight bindings. Her stomach heaved and grew even more. She cried out and feverishly tried to get loose.

"We do nothing?" Sanchez asked.

"Nothing, just observe. I can't risk any of you getting infected."

Princess began to convulse and scream.

Brennan watched her belly in horror. He could clearly make out what looked like a hand pushing up.

The men groaned and showed their own disgust at what they were watching.

The distinct sound of bones crushing and grinding came from Princess. Her screams turned to whimpers then silence. Her body went limp.

"I think she's dead," Brennan said.

"I'll check," Sanchez said stepping towards the enclosure.

Owens grabbed him. "No. Leave her be. Look at her mouth, look!"

Sanchez cocked his head and watched in amazement as thick dark red blood began to pour out of her mouth.

"Are we sure this thing is zipped up tight, no holes?" Brennan asked.

"I guess, fuck, I don't know. But we can't let her contaminate the plane and all of us," Owens said.

"Holy shit, look at her belly!" Vickers cried out.

She was dead, but the child was still alive and struggling to free itself of the womb.

Sanchez reached to unzip the enclosure.

"NO!" Brennan snapped.

"But the baby," Sanchez said.

"For all we know that baby is not a baby, but one of those things," Brennan said.

"But what if we're wrong," Sanchez said, his gaze going back and forth from Brennan to Princess.

Princess' belly stretched and expanded with greater intensity.

Brennan could now make out the baby's head pushing

straight up. He forcibly pushed Sanchez back and asked, "Would a normal baby do that?"

"What the fuck?" Klyde blurted out, his hand over his mouth.

Other men howled and vocalized their disgust.

Brennan looked back at Princess. Her stomach was stretched to the max, like a balloon ready to burst.

A tear appeared just above her belly button.

Freaked out, Owens said, "What the hell?"

No one moved as they stared at the gruesome sight. It was like they were in a trance, their gaze fixed on the horrific scene.

The split tore wider and suddenly a head pushed through the ripped flesh. It looked at them and let out a hellish scream.

A couple of men began to vomit.

As if he was acting the part in a low-budget horror movie, Klyde screamed in fear.

In all his years and after witnessing some of the worst a battle zone could offer, Brennan was in shock. This wasn't like anything he'd ever seen.

The baby pulled itself out of the belly and, with remarkable agility for a newborn, lunged onto the floor.

That was enough for Owen. He ripped his pistol from his holster and pointed it.

"No, you can't shoot in here," Brennan barked.

Owens knew Brennan was right. He lowered the pistol and put it back in his holster.

Vickers pushed his way through the huddled men, a large wrench in his grasp.

"What are you doing?" Brennan asked.

"Killing that fucking thing," he replied.

The baby stood up and started to claw at the plastic.

Vickers swung and hit it in the head.

The baby fell back, shook its head and got back on its feet.

"Shit's gone sideways, man. I've never seen a baby walk in my life!" Klyde rambled.

"That's not a normal baby," Dietz said wiping vomit from his mouth.

The wails of the baby bounced off the walls. It stepped towards the plastic screen again but was stopped by its entangled umbilical cord. It pulled hard and ripped the placenta from the gaping belly. The bloody mass hit the floor with a splatter.

The sight caused more men to vomit.

"C'mon, you little bastard!" Vickers barked.

"We gotta toss this thing out the back," Owens said looking at a crew chief.

The crew chief radioed to the pilots.

"We don't have time for this. You, you, and you, help me push this entire thing to the back. When we get at a lower altitude, we'll toss this fucking thing out," Owens ordered.

Brennan could feel the plane descending.

Vickers was determined to kill the thing. He took a wide swing, again striking the baby in the head.

The swing jolted the baby. It fell and lay in a pool of thick blood, coughing and hacking.

The crew chief released the pallet, looked at Owens and said, "It's ready."

"Hurry! Push!" Owens commanded.

Using every ounce of strength fueled by adrenaline, the men pushed the gurney towards the back.

The crew chief ran past them to a panel. He flipped a switch and hit a large button.

Lights began to flash inside the fuselage. A whoosh of cold air swept in from the rear of the plane as the back opened like a pair of jaws.

"One sec," Brennan said.

"What?" Owens yelled.

Brennan ran back to his pack and came back promptly. He held up his hand to show a fragmentation grenade. "Let's send it off with a bang."

"Good idea," Owens said.

"Push it just near the edge. I'll toss it in," Brennan instructed.

The baby howled, grunted, and scratched at the plastic.

"Stop right there!" Brennan hollered.

Everyone did as he said.

Brennan popped the thumb clip and pulled the pin. "Someone unzip."

Owens carefully unzipped the enclosure near the top.

The baby jumped up and thrust its arm through.

Owens flinched.

Vickers stepped forward, wrench still in hand. He slammed it down on the mutant baby's arm.

The child screamed and fell back on top of Princess.

Seeing his opportunity, Brennan tossed the grenade in the opening and hollered, "Hurry, push it out."

Everyone shoved hard and pushed the gurney down the ramp. It slid and fell off the lip and disappeared.

Brennan watched as it tumbled towards the expansive ocean below.

Seconds later it exploded.

"We're closing it up!" the crew chief barked, referring to the ramp.

His head spinning from the ordeal, Brennan walked back to his pack and plopped down.

Vickers raced over and asked, "Did you see me hit that fucking thing?"

"Not now, Vick, not now," Brennan said, waving Vickers off.

Owens came up and sat next to him. "Good call on the grenade."

"Let's hope."

"You think that was the right call on getting rid of her?"

Brennan let out a little chuckle. "We're in uncharted territory. I'd say yes, it was."

"Good, 'cause I'll need you to back me up 'cause when we land and we don't have Princess, there will be a shit storm."

"I got your back, don't worry," Brennan answered.

"Thanks," Owens said. He stood up.

"Owens," Brennan said.

"Yeah."

"What the fuck just happened?"

"That, my friend, was a nightmare come to life," Owens answered.

Poway, California

BRETT DIDN'T WANT to admit it, but he liked the smell of gunpowder. He thought about telling Chris but didn't want it to sound odd. He finished packing up the gear and cleaned the bench. He took his last target, and just as he was about to toss it away, he looked at it proudly. His groupings were about nine inches wide but enough to stop someone if they meant him or his family harm. He decided against throwing it away; instead he folded it and stuffed it in his pack.

When Brett emerged from the range, he found Chris still on the phone. He pointed towards the front door, motioning that he'd meet him outside.

Chris gave him a thumbs-up.

The midday sun felt great on Brett's face as he leaned against his car, waiting for Chris to come out. He pulled his phone from his pocket and sent Madison a text. *Love you.*

No reply.

Chris exited the range and briskly walked over to Brett. "You won't believe what happened."

"Don't tell me there was another terror attack," Brett replied.

"I said you won't believe it," Chris said, getting into his car. "C'mon, hurry up. We only have a little time to get some food."

Brett got in.

Chris started the car and pulled out.

"What's the exciting news?" Brett asked.

"Our school's janitor was fired."

"And why?"

"I just got off the phone with an old friend of mine from the PD. He says the janitor, a former Marine mind you, contacted them about suspicious activity at the school. Some guy, a Muslim-looking guy, was casing the place for two weeks."

"Okay."

"The school's administration fired the poor guy."

"Why did they fire him?" Brett asked, his curiosity piqued.

"Some PC shit."

"And what about the guy?"

"Yeah, right, the guy casing the place. They checked him. Seems he came here nine months ago as part of a refugee resettlement from Yemen. They say he's legit, but they don't have much to check. There's hardly anything to cross-reference in Yemen."

"Since when do we take refugees from Yemen?"

"My friend says the guy sought political asylum."

"What's he doing casing the school?" Brett asked, concern in his voice.

"Not sure, but I want to talk to the janitor," Chris said. "I want to get his side of the story."

"If you get in touch with him, I'd like to join you, okay?" Brett asked.

"Sure thing. But can you believe it? Canned the poor guy for saying something. I thought we were supposed to say something if we saw something," Chris said mocking the phrase.

"Now I'm nervous as hell, man. Maybe we need to set up a security watch at school," Brett said.

"Maybe so."

Brett looked out the window at the passing cars, his mind spinning with various hypothetical scenarios of attackers at the school. The thoughts horrified him.

Chris switched topics and asked, "How did you shoot?"

"Oh, um, good, I did good," Brett replied.

Chris could see the information about the school had freaked Brett out. He didn't want to press him, so he turned up the radio.

"...San Diego police have been responding to numerous calls today concerning spray-painted markings on buildings around the city and county. What gives the police concern is the symbol painted is that of a red hand..."

Chris tapped Brett's arm and said, "You look out of sorts."

"Hold on, I'm listening to the radio," Brett said.

"...so far police do not have a suspect or suspects and cannot confirm if these red handprints are in anyway connected to the terror group The Bloody Hand or just vandals using the symbol..."

"The Bloody Hand, that group, the ones who almost killed my brother. Did you hear that?" Brett said.

"I did."

"Do you think those spray-painted hands are from the terror group?"

"They could be, but it could also be a bunch of teenagers tagging shit because they think it's cool."

Brett jumped on his phone and searched the news story.

"What are you doing?"

"Seeing if there's more info on where those handprints were located," Brett answered.

Chris could see the fear on Brett's face. He wasn't sure what he should say or do. Maybe Brett needed to work through the issue on his own.

Brett frantically scrolled through the search results.

Unsure what to do, Chris changed the radio channel and put on some music. He looked at Brett, smiled and said, "Just remember, don't get scared, get prepared."

Ramona, California

CASSIDY SCROLLED through the employment ads online. The jobs listed that he knew paid well required background checks. He was tempted to apply, but like before, if there was competition, his past DUI would help the anonymous human resources person weed him out of selection.

He cursed his prospects as he slammed the laptop closed.

The television blared an endless stream of updates and personal stories from the terror attack in Copenhagen.

He sat back and began to watch.

Images of the terrorists appeared on the screen. Their faces, many old happy photos from social media, showed different people than the killers who had taken to the streets to murder indiscriminately.

Basher's devilish grin popped into his mind.

He had zero doubt that Basher was up to something, but the police were overwhelmed and political correctness had permeated down from the higher offices, preventing the average cop from doing his job.

Thoughts of Kathy and her smug attitude ate at him. He wanted nothing more than to walk up to her with proof he was right and shove it in her face.

Tired of hearing about the incident in Copenhagen, he picked up the remote and began to flip through the channels. A movie caught his interest; he stopped and began to watch.

The image of Basher was stuck in his mind, though. His intuition screamed out that he was right and Basher was casing the school for nefarious reasons.

A sense of determination gripped him. He turned the television off, grabbed his coat and headed out. If he was going to fail, at least fail miserably, he thought as he got behind the wheel of his truck.

Ankara, Turkey

DAVID SHOT UP, sweat dripping off his brow. He swung his legs off the bed and rubbed his eyes. The nightmare he'd just woken from had been intense. He'd been having bad dreams since the incident in Copenhagen., but this one was by far the worst.

It was nighttime. His room was drenched in an amber hue from the two streetlights below his open window.

He stood, stretched and walked to see what was happening outside.

A cool breeze swept in and cooled his skin.

He pushed the drapes fully open and stood gazing out. The sounds of the city washed over him.

Joram came to mind. David looked at the clock on the nightstand. It was almost nine. He had taken more than a nap, he had been asleep for many hours, a clear indication his body needed the rest, but now he needed to go back to the reason he had traveled so far.

His thoughts were broken when his phone began to vibrate.

The glow of the screen partially lit the room. He glanced and saw the screen, it read, UNKNOWN CALLER. Curious as always, he picked it up and answered, "Hello."

"David, it's Dylan. You able to talk?" Grim asked.

"Sure, what's up?" David asked.

"Face to face. Meet me in the hotel bar in ten, okay?"

David glanced at the clock again. "Sure."

"See you then," Grim said and hung up.

"Well, this has gotten more interesting," David said out loud. He put the phone in his back pocket, grabbed his jacket and headed out the door.

DAVID LOOKED around the smoke-filled crowded bar. It was a different scene than the other day. The seats were filled with a menagerie of faces. A collection from around the world, many he suspected were government workers from dozens of nations all chatting and enjoying a drink. Around them were young attractive women, no doubt prostitutes looking for a john or intel officers conducting countersurveillance with hopes of securing a new asset.

David scanned the room but couldn't spot his old friend. Something jabbed into his back. He jumped.

"Stick it up," a voice boomed behind David.

"You got me." David laughed and turned around to see Grim, a large smile stretched across his aging face.

"Good to see you. How about we grab a table in the corner," Grim said pointing to the far end of the bar.

"Sure," David said.

The two walked to the table, Grim leading the way.

Grim took the seat with his back to the wall.

David sat across from him.

A young waiter promptly arrived. "Drinks?"

"Two beers," Grim replied without asking David what he wanted. He appeared to be in a hurry.

"We have Budweiser—"

Grim interrupted the waiter. "Bud is fine, thanks."

The waiter left as fast as he had shown up.

David folded his hands and placed them on the table. He leaned in and said, "You seem on edge. You good?"

Grim mirrored David, leaned close and replied, "I need your help."

"Let me guess, you want to know about my conversations with the defector?"

"You could say that."

"Fine, what?"

"First, tell me you're not recording this."

"Not at all."

"I can trust you, right? This is off the record. We need info and your guy might be able to shed light on something critically important."

David raised his hands and said, "Not recording and this is off the record. To be quite honest, I'm more than happy to help."

"That incident did change you," Grim said astonished at David's willingness. "I was fully expecting I'd have to arm twist a bit."

"When we talked the other day, I told you if I can help, let me know."

"Good, your country appreciates it."

The waiter suddenly appeared. He placed the beers down and said, "Can I interest—"

"No, now please leave us alone," Grim snapped.

The waiter nodded and shuffled off.

David picked up his beer and tipped it back.

Ignoring his drink, Grim said, "What I'm about to tell you is classified. You cannot, at all, repeat what I tell you."

Those words perked David's interest. He held the beer in his grip and leaned even closer.

"When we talked, you said you were in Ankara to interview and update a story concerning an ISIS recruit who turned defector. I didn't think much of it until this morning. We received a list of names from a source in Syria. On this list was the name Joram. I began to wonder where I'd heard that name. I then remembered your defector. I pulled up your old *Economist* story and there he was, Joram, the recruit turned ISIS soldier, who turned ISIS commander."

"ISIS commander? That's news to me."

"That's not it, though, his name appeared on an ISIS special missions roster. He was the lead for this team."

"Okay."

"Hold on. The thing is, this team went missing two years ago. ISIS listed them all as killed in action."

"Okay, that's weird. Maybe it's another Joram."

"Let me finish," Grim snapped. "It wasn't just his name that stuck in my head, but the picture you had of him. We received this in the packet today as well," Grim said and pulled out a photo showing a group of smiling faces, their hands raised, palms out. All were standing in front of a dilapidated building. "Right there, that's your guy, center, standing."

David took the photo and stared at the face. "Yep, that's him. But I can assure you he's not dead. I was just with him this morning. Apparently, ISIS can't keep good records, or you are looking for a different Joram."

"Has he mentioned anything about a group called The Bloody Hand?"

"No."

"Nothing?"

"You think he's a member of the group who carried out Copenhagen?"

"Yes."

"But this photo could be an old photo from Syria. There's

nothing on it to verify when it was taken, and like I said, there could be dozens with that name."

"We used facial recognition on the photo. The names came back and matched the roster for the special missions team that was purported killed two years ago."

"The photo could be older, when he was with ISIS."

"Look more closely."

David did but couldn't spot anything that would help identify the timing. "I see a photo of ISIS goons, all waving in front of a war-torn building, probably taken in Raqqa."

Grim snatched the photo, placed it on the table, pointed and said, "Nope. To the right, look in the distance over the building."

David leaned close and said, "Is that a billboard?"

"Yeah, how many billboards do you think there are in ISIS-controlled Raqqa?"

"But that photo could be from a lot of different places, maybe Syria before he left for ISIS. Where did you get this?"

"From a smartphone we found in an apartment in north Paris after an anti-terror raid days ago."

"But that doesn't say anything."

"The billboard in the background. We zoomed in. It's an advertisement for a large flea market that's held annually in Laredo. You can't see with the naked eye, but in the lower right, the dates for the show are listed."

"And they were?"

"This past fall."

"I know, as you do, that ISIS has sent cell members across the border from Mexico. You're not telling me anything that's beyond top secret."

Grim sighed. "The Bloody Hand is an offshoot of ISIS. It separated because they've become disenchanted with the internal politics and corruption. They believe it lost its way. I think the core members of it are in this photo. Joram being one of them. They defected years ago and formed The Bloody Hand. They're now operational but we know they've begun work on other projects...projects of the biological kind. That raid in Somalia, it was on an old research facility."

"Bioweapons, you're fucking joking?"

"That's what we think their special missions were, but we don't know for sure. What makes sense is Joram and the men in the photo were all part of this team that went missing, were presumed killed, then show up in Mexico over a year later, all flashing the hand gesture of The Bloody Hand, see look, they're not waving, their fingers are outstretched. It's the sign of The Bloody Hand."

"The Bloody Hand, really? The guy I'm talking to seems regretful, at odds over what he's done, but again he does seem scared. He said they were looking for him. Maybe he ultimately defected from The Bloody Hand and is now being hunted by both," David wondered out loud.

"We need to talk to him immediately," Grim confessed, his true intentions now confirmed.

"You?"

"Where is he?"

"You're going to rendition him?" David asked, his tone signaling his concern.

"You sound hesitant."

"It's just that I promised him that I wouldn't jeopardize him or have him sent off to a black site somewhere."

"It's critical that we interrogate him as soon as possible."

David ran his fingers through his hair and grunted.

"Is there a problem?" Grim asked.

"Yeah, I, um, I want to help but he's just a kid."

"A kid? He's in his late twenties and is a member of a notorious terror organization that just murdered hundreds of people and is plotting a major attack, according to all the chatter."

"What do you mean by a major attack?"

"The chatter across all electronic gathering is off the charts. Something big, fucking huge, is coming and they're behind it. We need to find their leader Israfil, cut the head off the snake and work our way backwards."

"What do you need to know? I'll find out for you."

"No, just tell us where he is?" Grim insisted.

David sat speechless.

"You said you wanted to help and now you're just sitting there. Where the fuck is Joram?"

"I promised him that I'd assure his safety," David insisted.

"He's a fucking terrorist, David."

"And he's a source. I need to protect my sources."

Grim leaned in very close. He was inches from David's face. "Tell me where he is or—"

"Or what?"

"Goddamn it, David, this is national security."

"This is also about protecting my sources from unwarranted interrogation, even torture," David said in a righteous tone.

"You've got to be joking, right? You're fucking joking right now," Grim exploded.

Several people seated close turned and looked.

Grim barked, "Turn back around. Nothing to see here."

A man approached the table. "Excuse me, is there an issue?"

"Yeah, your being here is a fucking issue. I'm trying to have a conversation with my friend and you're interrupting."

"I'm the manager, sir, and your voice is getting loud, too loud. Please calm down."

With the manager hovering, David saw his opportunity. He stood up quickly.

"Where are you going?"

"I need to think about this. You're asking me to jeopardize my journalistic integrity." David moaned.

"Integrity? We're talking about a life-and-death thing here."

"Sir, please keep your tone down," the manager scolded, still present.

Grim gave the manager a stern look and replied, "Go away or I'll ruin you, do you understand?"

The manager stepped back. He mumbled something unintelligible and marched off.

David followed closely behind him.

Grim shot up from the table and pursued him. "David, tell me where he is?"

The urge to turn and offer up Joram was there, but David's need for a hot scoop to help his career was stronger. He kept walking away.

Grim caught up and took David by the arm. He swung him around and snapped, "You leave me no other recourse but to take you in."

"Get off me," David protested trying to pull away from Grim's firm grip.

"You've given me no choice."

"You're making a scene. You can end up blowing your cover," David warned, referencing Grim's official capacity in Ankara as a cultural enrichment liaison.

"It doesn't matter. This is too important," Grim replied pulling David with him towards the door.

Three large men appeared in front of Grim. They all were dressed in hotel attire.

Grim stopped. "Get out of my way."

The men circled Grim.

The manager rushed up. "That man right there. He's causing a disturbance."

Seeing the best opportunity to flee, David pulled away from Grim and said, "He's trying to hurt me."

The men converged on Grim, taking him forcibly by the arms.

As they marched Grim out of the bar, he turned around and yelled, "You're going to regret this, David! You hear me? This will come back to haunt you!"

David watched as his old friend was taken outside. He didn't like that it had to go that way, but David couldn't allow anything to jeopardize his story, his one possible chance to get his documentary back on the tracks. He had no doubt this would come back to bite him, but he was willing to take that risk in hopes the dividends returned on this explosive exposé would boost him to journalistic glory.

His phone vibrated in his jacket pocket. He removed it and saw a text from Grim.

"Since you won't help, at least ask him about the twelfth imam. Who is he? Who is Israfil?" Grim texted.

"I will."

"If he tells you, tell me, ASAP."

Seeing a compromise, David replied, "OK, I will."

No other reply came from Grim.

A sense of paranoia came over David. He exited the bar and quickly shuffled down the street. After a few turns he slipped into a small side street. He let his phone fall from his grip onto the pavement. He stomped on it multiple times, picked it up and tossed it into a flowing storm drain.

He hated having to destroy his phone, but he was given no choice. He just prayed this all worked out, because his life and career depended on it.

Rancho Bernardo, California

Mo DIDN'T EVEN CARE what his father would do to him. After what he had just experienced, nothing his father could dish out would match it.

He shut the front door and proceeded to his room slowly, a weary look on his face.

"Where have you been?" Mo's father barked from the kitchen.

"Not now, Dad," Mo said, his tone subdued.

Mo's father scurried towards Mo but stopped when he saw his son. "What happened to you?"

"Nothing. I'm tired. I need to go to bed," Mo answered. He was tempted to tell his father everything in hopes his honesty could cleanse him of his part in what happened but fear of reprisals prevented it. He disliked his father, however not so much he'd want him hurt or worse.

"Mohammed, where have you been? You didn't come home last night and when you do, you look as if you've been up all night," his father said.

"Let the boy sleep. He can talk to you tomorrow," Mo's mother said, walking up beside his father.

"But he disobeyed me. He missed school today," his father said.

She took Mo's father's hand and said, "I remember you being a bit of a rebel too at his age."

"Looking back now, I realize I was foolish. I don't want him repeating my mistakes."

Mo stood watching his parents. His fatigue weighed on him like heavy chains.

"Are you mixed up in anything?" his father asked.

Mo sighed again. He was tempted to just speak honestly but stopped when he saw his mother ever so slightly shake her head, signaling for him to remain quiet. "No, Dad, I just went to a party. I messed up. I'm sorry."

"How dare you disobey me!" his father barked.

"Dear, let him get some rest. You can deal with him later," his mother said softly.

"We'll talk later, Dad, I promise," Mo said and continued to his room.

Mo's HEAD hit the pillow and he began to swiftly fall asleep until he heard his bedroom door open.

He looked and saw his mother enter. She came to his bedside and sat down.

"Are you okay?" she asked.

"Fine."

She petted his arm and asked, "Are you doing as I asked?"

"Meaning what, Mom?"

"Have you found your holy purpose? Is that where you were?"

"I don't want to talk about it," Mo grumbled.

"Okay, I just needed to check on you. And don't worry about your father. Like I said before, I'll take care of him."

"Thanks, Mom, now please go. I'm exhausted."

She stood but hesitated from leaving. She leaned down, gave him a kiss on his forehead and whispered, "I'm so very proud of you. You will restore honor to our family. You're a man now. Just give me some time to convince your father of that."

"No, don't tell Dad. He won't understand," Mo said, fearing she wanted to confess his actions.

"I would never divulge that. It's just time for him to recognize you as a man. I'm proud of you son... my mujahedeen," she said and kissed him again.

"Love you, Mom."

"Love you too. Sleep well," she said, leaving.

Mo lay there. The image of the woman's face screamed at him in his thoughts. He could still see her pleading eyes so clearly, as if she were there. It was a moment, an event, he'd never forget. He was afraid, there was no denying it. However, he was committed. He had to continue because not doing so would most likely lead to his family's demise.

As he drifted off, one thought kept banging around in his head. *What am I doing?*

CHAPTER SIX

Wednesday, April 26
Diego Garcia, British Indian Ocean Territory

IT TOOK everything Brennan had not to laugh out loud. He sat with his arms folded, watching Owens get scolded by several people they had only met minutes before.

"She was your responsibility. You had one job, one, and that was to get her here," Tracy Dalton barked, her temples throbbing with each word she uttered. Tracy was a research biologist from the Centers for Disease Control in Atlanta. She and two others had flown from Atlanta to pick up Princess.

"Ms. Dalton, we had no choice," Owens said defensively.

"It's my understanding she was contained in ten-millimeter sheeting," Tracy said.

Brennan couldn't hold back. After listening to Owens inadequately defend the team's actions, he had to speak up. "She was dead anyway."

Tracy cut Brennan a hard look. "So what. We could have still conducted research on her body."

"And the baby's too," Mark Warren said. He was another biologist from the CDC.

"Thanks, Mark, and yes, the baby too. We are dealing with something unique, some form of parasite that mutates the host, but you throw it out over the ocean. What were you thinking?"

"All I can say is you weren't there. We don't know anything about those parasites, so we didn't want to take a chance and get infected," Owens countered.

"Now we have nothing to study, you military boys are so quick to blow things up," Mark said, referring mainly to the Tomahawk strike against the facility in Juula, which destroyed the underground facility.

Tracy mumbled something unintelligible and walked off.

Brennan looked at his watch and was shocked when he saw the time. He tapped Owens and said, "We're wheels up in thirty-five. Let's go."

Owens nodded at Brennan, acknowledging what he said, but he was more interested in finding a solution for Tracy, as he did understand their frustration. "Ms. Dalton, hold up," he said, walking up behind her.

"Yes, what is it?" she asked turning around, her hands on her hips.

"How much do you know?"

Shaking her head, she returned his question with one. "About the mutants? I'm not sure what you're asking me."

"Have you been briefed on everything?"

"I was told they, the mutants, came from a weapons research facility in Somalia, beyond that, nothing more and it looks like I'll never know," she lamented.

"Did they tell you about Petty Officer Third Class Perino and Corporal Marzelli?" Owens asked.

"No," she replied, her lips pursed with curiosity.

Owens looked around to see who might be listening. When

he was sure it was just them, he said, "Both of those men were turned into droolers."

"Please stop calling them that," she said.

"What do you want me to call them?"

"It doesn't matter. What happened to those two people?" she asked.

Owens told her what had occurred with both men and that their bodies, from what he knew, were still on board the USS *Anchorage*. Finishing he said, "I suggest you contact whoever you have to and get their remains."

"I will, thank you," she said.

Out of the corner of his eye, Owens caught Brennan waving him over. "I have to let you go. Let me know if I can help with anything," Owens said and walked away.

Tracy tucked loose strands of hair behind her ear and smiled as Owens walked away. She liked his swagger.

"What did you tell her?" Brennan asked sensing something was divulged.

"I told her about Marzelli and Perino. Apparently, she wasn't made aware of them," Owens answered.

"Oh, okay. Um, we've been summoned to the headquarters building," Brennan said.

"Then let's go see what's up," Owens said.

Ankara, Turkey

David had repeatedly gone back to Joram's room after the encounter with Grim, but Joram didn't answer.

Fear rose in him. *Is Joram gone? Did Grim find him?*

He banged for an extended period on the door. "Are you there? Open up, please."

Nothing. No reply.

"Fuck," David snapped. He looked both ways to see if

anyone was coming. With no one in the hallway, he made a rash but decisive decision. He was going to kick the door down. He stepped back, lifted his leg and thrust it forward.

His foot landed perfectly just to the right of the handle. The door exploded open.

David rushed into the brightly lit room. "Joram, are you here?" David asked as he began to frantically look around. He half expected to find Joram's body.

Joram was not there.

Frustrated, David walked to the table he had been sitting at hours earlier and sat down. He decided he would stay until Joram returned. Fatigue began to grow and his eyes soon started to close. Just as he nodded off, David caught a glimpse of a piece of paper taped to the screen of the television. He shot up, ran over and ripped it off the screen.

The note read *"Dear David, I called you because I thought I could trust you. You even sat here not long ago and told me that no one would know I was here. You lied. I know you met with your CIA friend. I can't express how disappointed I am with you. You failed me. You failed yourself. Goodbye old friend. – Joram"*

Disheartened, David stepped back and let gravity pull him to the edge of the bed. He slumped over and crumpled the note in his hand. "Damn it!" he groaned.

And just that fast, what he had hoped would be an interview that could reboot his career was gone. The opportunity had come and gone just as fast.

He tossed the note on the floor.

A tap on the door startled him. He looked up and saw Grim standing there.

"Howdy," Grim said with a grin.

"You followed me, how?" David asked.

"I can't tell you that. I'd never compromise my sources and methods," Grim replied stepping into the room.

"He's gone. He knew, somehow he knew I had met with you," David said.

"He's a clever guy," Grim said.

"What now?" David asked.

"I suggest you pack your stuff and put yourself on the next plane home, wherever that is for you," Grim answered.

"So that's it, I go home?"

"Yeah, I highly doubt he'll raise his head around you again. You betrayed him, but if he ever does, please let me know," Grim reminded him.

"Let you know? It's because of you that I've lost the best story of my career," David spat, standing up.

"Nice to see your patriotic colors shine. Now go pack your shit and leave before I have your visa pulled and you're stuck in this Godforsaken place," Grim said.

David walked past Grim, brushing his shoulder.

"Excuse you." Grim laughed.

"Fuck off," David said as he exited the room.

Rancho Bernardo, California

MO ROLLED OUT OF BED, exhausted. The first few hours of sleep were sound but the remaining hours were nothing short of horrible. He couldn't push the images from his initiation out of his mind. As he lay in bed during the wee hours of the early morning, his tormented thoughts turned to fear then panic.

He jolted up, his breathing rapid and his heart pounding hard. He clutched his chest; a dull but intense pain was growing. *Am I having a heart attack?* he wondered.

He swung his legs out of bed, his hand still on his chest. He focused on his breathing to control it, but the pain in his chest grew and was now emanating in his back and shoulders.

I'm having a heart attack. I'm dying, he screamed in his thoughts.

He stood up quickly and took a couple of steps but felt uneasy. His panic grew as his pain did.

"Mom! Mom, help!" he cried out.

The pain was now in his neck and jaw. *It is a heart attack. I'm going to die,* he thought.

Stomping feet sounded in the hallway.

He took more steps to the door, but the pain was too much. His knees buckled; he crumpled to the floor.

His door opened. The light from the hallway spilled over him.

"Mohammed, oh dear, what's wrong?" his mother cried rushing towards him.

His father came in right behind her. "What's happening? Son, are you okay?"

"My chest, it hurts, and my shoulders. I feel like I can't breathe..." he said, his voice sounding labored.

"Calm down," his mother said as she cradled him in her arms.

"I think I'm having a heart attack," Mo mumbled.

"Ssh, now be quiet and calm down. You're not, you're just having a panic attack, nothing more," his mother said in a reassuring voice.

"Are you sure?" his father asked.

"Yes, I've had them before, so did my father. He's just upset. Probably had a bad dream," she said softly as she caressed his arms.

"Bad dream?" his father asked mockingly.

She leered and said, "If you're going to be no help, please go back to bed."

His mother's embrace was easing his symptoms. The pain in

his chest was ebbing and his heart rate was slowing. "I'm feeling better."

She ran her fingers through his thick black hair and said, "Good. You just rest in your mother's arms until you fall back to sleep."

His father grumbled something under his breath and barged out of the bedroom.

Mo looked at his mother and said, "I don't think I can do it."

"Are you still having doubts? Please, son, just relax. You're stronger than you know."

"I'm scared."

"It's okay to be scared, but you're also very courageous. You always have been," she mused as she remembered a moment from his early years. "Did I ever tell you about the time an older child was bullying your cousin?"

He nodded.

"I did?"

"Only a hundred times," he said softly.

"It's because I love that story. I was so proud of you. I heard the commotion and came out of the house to see you standing up to the older boy. He must have been a good foot taller than you. You told him to leave your cousin alone. Of course, the boy pushed you and said that he wouldn't be told what to do. I thought about coming to help but I saw you clench your fist and hit that boy right in the mouth. Oh, that was one of the proudest moments. That boy fell back and you didn't stop. You jumped on top of him and kept hitting him. You yelled, 'Never touch my cousin again!' over and over. Oh, how I was so proud. I knew then that you were going to be the one who would bring honor back our family. You're my warrior, the fighter, you have the heart of a lion."

"I can't do it, Mom. I can't," Mo confessed.

"Ssh, you still need more time is all," she said, petting him.

"Why? Huh? Why are you pushing me?"

"Because our people need warriors. We've lost our way. Many of us are becoming Americanized. The way of Allah is lost on so many of our people now. They've given in to the indulgences and wretched behaviors and lifestyles of American culture. It's corrupt and decadent. It must be overthrown," she replied forcefully.

"Who are you, and what have you done with my mother?" Mo asked, half joking, half serious.

"I have always been here, hiding, waiting for the moment, and I knew that moment was when I heard about you and Malik."

Mo sat up and looked deeply into her eyes. "You really want me to do this?"

"More than anything."

"But I could die. I will murder innocent people."

"If you die, you die a warrior in the eyes of Allah, and those you kill, they're no greater than sheep and Allah gives you the right to cut them down."

He put his head in his hands. Confusion and doubt filled him. The pain and rapid heart rate were gone. He was having a difficult time processing his mother's wishes and beliefs; it wasn't anything he'd ever heard her say. "In all my life I've never heard you speak this way. Does it have anything to do with your uncle being killed in Afghanistan?"

"He was a good man. I wish you could have met him," she said, reminiscing about her beloved Uncle Raffi.

"That's it, you're angry that he was killed in a US-led bombing. What I don't understand is you hadn't seen him in twenty-five years."

"Time doesn't make one love one less. He helped raise me when I was a little girl, as my father was always gone."

"It's fine you're upset, angry even, but I just don't think I can go forward with this plan. I have doubts and I won't lie, I'm terrified."

She pursed her lips and growled, "Enough whining. I heard you already. Stop being a baby. It's time for you to grow up and be a man."

He raised his hand in objection to what she just said. He stood and walked to his bed. "I'm going to bed. We'll talk later."

She sighed and got up. She walked to him and with a more subdued tone said, "I'm sorry. You get some rest."

"Goodnight, Mom," Mo said.

She kissed him on the forehead and said, "Goodnight, son."

San Diego, California

MADISON RUSHED DOWN the stairs and found Brett with the boys. She looked at him strangely and asked, "What are you still doing here?"

"I decided I'm going to walk the boys to school."

"Hmm, that's a nice surprise, isn't it, boys?" she asked, tousling Will's hair.

"I want Daddy to walk us every day," Will said.

"Me too, but unfortunately that's not really possible, so let's just enjoy this morning," Madison said as she leaned in close to Brett and gave him a kiss.

The family all exited the house via a back gate. It was a short walk to school. Normally, Madison made the trip with the boys. She loved the lifestyle of strolling every day, talking and sharing in the unique experience of having the school close by.

They cleared the last corner near the school and were greeted by a massive boisterous crowd of parents, teachers and students all huddled at the entrance.

"What do you suppose is going on?" Madison asked.

"Dad, did something bad happen?" Eddie asked.

"I don't know, buddy," Brett answered.

They walked up to the crowd.

"Did you hear?" Lyndsey asked, appearing suddenly.

"What?" Madison asked.

"The school got tagged," Lyndsey said.

"Tagged?" Madison asked, unsure what the term meant.

Brett pushed his way through the crowd until he got a clear view. When his eyes settled on the large red spray-painted hand, a chill shot through him. He immediately turned around and rushed back to his family. "Let's go."

"Huh?" Madison said, alarmed by his urgency.

"We're going home, now," Brett said, taking Will and Eddie by the hand.

"Hold on, what?" Madison asked, following them.

"Home, we're going home. The kids can't go to school today," Brett frantically said.

"Brett, stop. What the hell are you talking about?" Madison asked. She ran up and jumped in front of him. "What's going on? What did you see?"

He pointed behind him to the crowd and replied, "That's not just some tag, that's their symbol, their logo, whatever you want to call it, of that terror group The Bloody Hand."

She shook her head and sighed. "Again. We're doing this again?"

"They're marking targets, I know it!" Brett snapped.

"Enough, stop. C'mon, boys, let's go before you're late," Madison said, taking the boys by the hands.

"No, not today. They can play hooky," Brett said, stopping her this time.

"No, they can't, you have to go to work and I have appointments I can't miss. They need to go to school."

"I'll stay home," Brett said.

"Stop the crazy talk, Brett. Nothing is going to happen.

176

Whatever you saw is nothing more than teenagers spray painting graffiti. It's not some grand conspiracy," Madison scolded.

"NO!" he barked.

Several people turned and looked at him.

"Brett, stop it. You're making a scene. Now, boys, let's go."

He ran up and jumped in front of their path. "Maddy, please, just give me this. Let me keep them home, I beg you. I'm not the only one who thinks that's legit. They're taunting us, and we won't do anything about it. Look around, there's no police. No one cares; the administration doesn't. As a society, we've talked ourselves into forced complacency. And they're trolling us. They're laughing at us," Brett rambled.

"Brett, you're embarrassing yourself. You sound unhinged," Madison snapped.

"Daddy, I'm scared," Eddie whimpered.

"See, you're freaking out the kids now. Brett, get out of the way!" Madison roared.

"No."

"Is there something wrong?" Kathy, the principal, asked. She had heard their quarrel and saw the need to interject herself.

"Hi, Kathy, nothing is wrong. We're just—"

Brett interrupted Madison and asked, "Why is the school open? Where are the police? That symbol is a terrorist marking. It's a threat."

"Oh my God," Madison groaned.

"I can assure you everything is fine. We did contact the police, but they're delayed due to a large protest on the interstate," Kathy said.

"Delayed? Boys, come with me," Brett said motioning Eddie and Will away from the school.

"Stop it!" Madison yelled.

"I can see there is a problem. Madison, Brett, please step over here. Let's discuss this," Kathy said, motioning her hand towards a barrier.

"It's not necessary. Brett is a bit nervous. His brother was almost killed in Copenhagen and he's having a hard time with that," Madison explained.

"I'm sorry to hear about your brother," Kathy said.

"Don't patronize me. The police are finding those hands painted all over and it's not just here in San Diego, it's everywhere. Go online, search it. It's in every city," Brett said, his voice elevated.

"Brett, please keep your voice down," Kathy warned.

"No, I won't. That is a problem for me, for my kids. The police can't come because—"

"Because they're dealing with a protest, something that's clearly more important. This is simply a prank, nothing more," Kathy said.

"Boys, come," Brett said, snatching Will's and Eddie's hands. He was done debating.

Madison grabbed his arm and pulled hard.

He yanked his arm out of her grip.

"Brett!" Madison hollered.

"Brett, stop or I'll call the police," Kathy threatened.

He marched off, kids in tow. "Good luck with that. They're busy taking care of more important things, as you said."

Ramona, California

Sophie came into the kitchen to find Cassidy stuffing a bagel in his mouth on his way out the door.

"Where are you off to so early?" she asked.

"I have some interviews," he answered.

"Dressed like that?" she asked, looking at his clothes, which consisted of running shoes, blue jeans, T-shirt and a black hoodie.

"Oh, um, warehouse jobs. They don't care what you look like. Hell, this is dressing up for them," he joked as he tried to make sure his fictitious story sounded believable.

She walked up and stopped inches from him. "You forgot something."

"I did?" he asked, looking around.

She pointed to her lips.

"Ha, sorry," he said and gave her a kiss on the lips.

"Good luck, babe, call me and tell me how it goes," she said.

He raced out the door. Guilt riddled him, as he hated lying to her. But if he could prove Basher was up to no good, he'd be hailed a hero and all would be forgiven.

Unfortunately, yesterday's surveillance discovered nothing. His plan today was to go to his place of business and trail him anywhere he went from there. He was determined to find something that he could present to the police as hard evidence.

Diego Garcia, British Indian Ocean Territory

OWENS, Brennan and the team stood on the flight line, waiting to board their transport.

More intelligence had come in and now the team was being sent to Coronado. There they would link up with some additional assets and go to a facility run by The Bloody Hand in Mexico.

Owens and Brennan were discussing some of the details of the pending mission when Owens looked up and caught sight of Tracy and her team heading their way. He tapped Brennan and said, "Look."

Brennan craned his head over his shoulder and asked, "What do they want?"

Tracy strolled up, dropped two large bags and said, "When are we leaving, gentlemen?"

"We?" Brennan asked.

"Yeah, we're going with you?" Tracy replied.

"Did you contact the *Anchorage*?" Owens asked.

"Yes, and they seemed a bit annoyed that you told me."

"Well, are you getting their remains?" Owens asked.

"No. Apparently, they destroyed the bodies. So stupid," Tracy complained.

"This reminds me of a joke," Brennan chirped.

"I love jokes," Owens said.

"Military intelligence," Brennan said with a straight face.

Both Owens and Tracy waited for the punch line.

"Guys, that's the joke, military intelligence, get it?" Brennan said.

Owens narrowed his bright green eyes and cracked a grin. "Really? That's the oldest joke, ever."

"I'm not sure we should consider that a laughing matter," Tracy said.

"Why?" Brennan asked.

"Because it's true," Tracy snarked.

Brennan tapped Owens arm and said, "I'm going to see what the holdup is."

"Sure," Owens said and put his attention back on Tracy. "Are you just making a quick turnaround in San Diego, or will you spend a day or so, maybe see the sights. It's a great city."

"Um, about that," she replied.

Owens raised his right eyebrow and asked, "What?"

"I made a pretty big stink about you losing the female and the destruction of the other bodies."

"How big?"

"I guess the president heard about it and he's not happy."

"Jesus, seriously?"

"Um," Tracy said and paused, her normal confidence gone.

"Spit it out."

She held out her hand and said, "We didn't really get properly introduced before, I'm Tracy Dalton, senior biologist, CDC liaison and a new member of your team."

Rancho Bernardo, California

MO HEADED TO HIS LOCKER, his head hung low.

Like many times before, Malik raced up and jumped on his back. "Bro, how fucking amazing was the other night?"

Mo shrugged him off.

Seeing Mo was in a bad mood, Malik chose to taunt him. "What's up with you, poopy pants?"

"Nothing."

Malik tickled Mo under his ribs and asked, "C'mon, what's wrong?"

Mo jerked away from Malik, slammed his locker and yelled, "Leave me the fuck alone!"

"Whoa, chill!" Malik barked back, his hands raised high in the air.

Mo aggressively stepped towards Malik and snapped, "Leave me the fuck alone. I don't want any part in this...this...I don't want anything to do with it. You tell Kareem and those other people I'm out. I don't want anything, nothing at all to do with your plan."

Malik recoiled initially then came back at Mo. "There's no out. You're in now. That's how it is. We're being activated soon, so unless you want to have your head and your family's heads cut off, I suggest you show up when they call us."

Mo stormed off.

Malik followed. "What's wrong, man?"

"What's wrong? Is that a serious question? I thought, hell, I don't know what I thought. I imagined it was something different. Something glorious. I don't know, maybe I didn't think this was actually real, but it is."

Malik took Mo by the arm and spun him around. He jabbed his finger in his face and said, "You need to keep quiet!"

"Quiet? Quiet? Coming from you? The person who is always yelling this and that everywhere!" Mo barked, his voice carrying down the bustling hall.

Malik shoved him against the wall and snapped, "Tread carefully, bro. If Kareem or the other brothers heard you now, they'd take your head."

Mo pushed Malik away from him. "I'm out. I can't do this. I won't!" he wailed and took off running down the hall. He saw the entrance and raced for it. He burst through the doors and out onto the parking lot, he kept running until he reached the street. Out of breath, he stopped and looked back.

No one followed.

The woman's face flashed in his mind. He shook his head vigorously and hollered, "Get out of my head!"

His phone began to ring. He looked and saw it was Malik. He couldn't talk; he needed a place to think. He shoved the phone into his pocket and took off down the street.

San Diego, California

CASSIDY QUICKLY PULLED over and got out his phone to take photos of Basher walking into a mosque, as if a Muslim going inside a mosque was incriminating evidence.

He snapped photos until Basher disappeared inside.

The sun was hovering near the horizon and he'd been out all day. Like the day before, he didn't have anything that was solid, but he was confident if he kept on Basher, he'd come up with something.

He thumbed through the dozens of photos he'd taken, looking for something that stood out. Was there a pattern? Who knew, he'd have to do this daily until one appeared.

He looked up and caught sight of Basher exiting the mosque.

"That was a quick stop," he mumbled. He started his car, put it into gear and waited.

Basher approached the street slowly. He looked both ways before turning right out of the mosque parking lot.

Cassidy promptly pulled out behind him and was three car lengths behind.

A flash of red and blue lights followed by a loud wail sounded behind Cassidy. He looked into his rearview mirror and saw a San Diego police cruiser.

"Shit!" he hollered. He slowed and pulled over.

The police car parked behind him.

Cassidy did as he had always done, kept his hands on the wheel at a ten and two position. He did this as a courtesy so the cops always knew where his hands were.

The police officer walked up to just behind the driver's side window and ordered, "Step out of the car."

"Officer, what's the trouble?" Cassidy asked.

"Step out of the car. Keep your hands where I can see them," the officer ordered.

"Was I speeding? What did I do?" Cassidy asked. He looked in his side mirror and saw the officer had his hand on the backstrap of his holstered pistol. Not wanting to escalate the situation, Cassidy opened the door and stepped out with his hands clearly visible.

The officer stepped back and said, "Face the vehicle and place your hands on it."

"What did I do?" Cassidy asked while he did as the officer commanded.

The officer stepped behind Cassidy, patted him down quickly then took his right arm and pulled it behind his back.

"Hey, what did I do?"

"You're under arrest for stalking and harassment," the officer said as he took Cassidy's left arm and placed it behind his back.

"Stalking?" Cassidy asked but knew he'd been compromised. He'd been seen for sure.

The officer placed handcuffs on Cassidy.

When Cassidy heard the unique clicking of the cuffs, he saw his life with Sophie flash before him. He let out a heavy sigh as the officer led him to the police car and placed him in the back.

Sitting in the back of the cruiser, he began to question his stupid and impulsive behavior. He stared out the window and caught sight of Basher, who was in his car parked across the street.

Basher gave Cassidy the same shitty grin and waved before driving off.

Cassidy had been outmaneuvered, there was no other way to put it. He was fucked.

CHAPTER SEVEN

Thursday, April 27
Coronado, California

BRENNAN, Vickers, Klyde and the rest of the team walked into the briefing room. There they saw Owens at the front of the room, talking to an unknown officer.

Tracy was present as well; however, she was sitting at a table in the far corner, crouched over a laptop.

Grouped in the center of the room, thirty men sat. Their uniforms told Brennan they were SEALs and other Marines.

Owens saw his team and called out, "Take seats, all of you, hurry up."

The team did as Owens said.

As he often did, Vickers sat next to Brennan. He leaned in close and asked, "Do you suppose that zero is our new commanding officer?"

"Who knows," Brennan replied.

"And who are these motherfuckers?" Vickers asked, pointing at the other men.

"Who knows?"

Owens took a seat at the table in the front.

The officer, a naval commander, looked to the back of the room and said, "Can someone close the door?"

Dietz jumped up and did it.

"My name is Commander Shenkman and I'm now the commanding officer for Unit 5."

As usual, Vickers leaned in and said, "What's Unit 5, is that us?"

"Ssh," Brennan said.

"Unit 5 is now an official QRF, with a singular mission, to address the mutant threat."

"They're calling them mutants," Vickers whispered.

Brennan glared.

"Due to the hasty nature of how this unit was formed, it started with inadequate resources and manpower. It began with you gentlemen, because you had firsthand encounters with the mutants. However, that is not enough. For you to be effective, you need more men."

Brennan looked at the others in the room.

Shenkman continued. "We're also reorganizing Unit 5 into four platoons, each platoon consisting of three five-man fire teams. Each team will have a team leader, machine gunner, demolitions and two riflemen. First platoon will be commanded by Owens here. The other three platoon leaders are Senior Chief Jones, Senior Chief Dillon and Senior Chief Alvery. We'll operate from Coronado here, which is to our advantage, it gives us access to air and sea assets we'll need."

Tracy raised her hand.

Shenkman gave her an odd look.

"Excuse me," Tracy said.

"Yes, Ms. Dalton."

"Where does my team fit in to the org structure?"

"You're not actually an operational element of Unit 5,

you're just being attached for a single mission, nothing more. And I'll get to that in a bit. Just please sit patiently, Ms. Dalton."

"Hmm, not what I understood, but no need to discuss it now," she said.

Shenkman waited for her to continue, but she remained quiet. "With that out of the way, let's get down to our next mission. Intel gathered in Juulu points to another facility south of Cuidad Juarez, Mexico. What we know about the facility is it appears to be another secret laboratory and research facility that we must assume houses these mutants. Your job will be to secure that facility. However, we need you to use caution so that you can preserve as much evidence as possible," Shenkman said. Picking up a remote, he clicked a button and zoomed in on an aerial photo that appeared on the screen behind him. He pointed and continued, "We don't know what to expect or what you'll encounter once you get there, but time is of the essence, so we haven't had a lot of time to conduct reconnaissance. All four platoons will deploy on this." He pointed at a large warehouse and said, "First platoon, you'll be the lead element going into the actual labs, which we believe is this building due to the volume of HVAC equipment outside the building." He clicked the remote. A second image appeared; a red line encircled three buildings and a large courtyard. "Second platoon will provide over watch and secure the perimeter. Third platoon, you will secure this building here."

Everyone sat taking in all the information.

Shenkman went through more details of the raid, pausing near the end. He took a drink of water and went on. "We will be taking Ms. Dalton and her team of biologists from the CDC on this. Treat them like you would any imbed journalists. Ms. Dalton and her team will go in with first platoon."

"Now we're babysitters, great," Vickers mumbled under his breath.

"We're wheels up in three hours, and remember once we touch down at Fort Bliss, we're going straight to the birds. Make sure you have your shit together, and first platoon, let's not kill the specimens this time," Shenkman said with a tinge of sarcasm.

Ramona, California

SOPHIE PUT the car in park in front of their garage. She put her head in her hands and started to cry.

Cassidy, just released on bail, looked at her sorrowfully. He thought of words to help ease her pain and disappointment but nothing came. It all sounded like bullshit in his head. He reached out with his hand and touched her.

She recoiled from his touch.

He tried again.

"Don't touch me!" she barked.

"I'm sorry, I'll keep saying it, I fucked up. I just thought I could salvage my reputation and prove—"

"Prove what? You're an idiot? Listen, I don't know if that Basher guy is a terrorist. He could be, but is it really your responsibility now to stop him? You tried; the police brushed it off. I would imagine the cops know more than you. Did you ever think of that?"

"What if they're under pressure, you know, political pressure not to really do their jobs as it pertains to Muslims?"

"What am I supposed to do? Huh?" Sophie complained wiping tears from her cheeks.

"I'll fix this, I promise."

"The job interviews, those were lies. You lied to me?"

"I had every intention of going to some. I just needed...I just felt—"

She held up her hand and shouted, "Stop! No more. I

can't sit here and listen to more of your bullshit." She opened the car door, got out and slammed it shut with all her strength.

He cringed.

She marched into the house, slamming the front door to the house as well.

Cassidy sat in his own self-inflicted misery. He wasn't sure what his next step should be. He now had to worry about what the outcome of his hearing would be and how bad it would impact his record, which in turn would complicate his job prospects.

His phone began to vibrate in his pocket.

He pulled it out. It was a number he didn't recognize. Normally he wouldn't answer but after dealing with the police, bailiffs and everything related to being arrested, he thought it could be something that pertained to that. With great reluctance, he answered, "Hello."

"Trevor Cassidy?" the voice asked.

"This is him."

"Hi, my name is Brett Silver. I'd like to speak to you about the incident at school."

"Who is this?"

"Brett Silver. My kids go to Rancho Nopal Elementary. I desperately need to speak with you," Brett said.

"How did you get this number?"

"I really need to talk with you. It's urgent. There was an incident yesterday."

"An incident, what happened?" Cassidy asked, his curiosity piqued.

"Someone spray painted the symbol of that terror group The Bloody Hand on the front of the school. I think it's a message, a warning. I desperately need your help. I need to know more about this man you thought was a threat."

189

Cassidy got excited, here was a man just as concerned as him.

"Mr. Cassidy, can you meet with me? Can you help me?"

The front door of the house opened. Clothes, shoes and a suitcase flew out and onto the deck and lawn.

Cassidy's heart melted. "I'm sorry, I can't. Don't call me again," he said and hung up.

The front door slammed again.

He sat looking at his life strewn across the front lawn. He had reached a new low in his life. What was left for him? He wanted to feel angry and blame Basher or Kathy or his damn friends for offering him those last few drinks years ago, but he couldn't, he was to blame. He was taught at a young age that he was the master of his own destiny and that only he could alter his path. But how?

He opened the door of the car and got out. He looked at his things and thought about gathering it all up, but why? They were just that, things. What he needed to do was gather his shattered life and that began by trying to make things right with Sophie.

San Diego, California

BRETT LOOKED AT THE PHONE. "He hung up on me," he grunted.

He began pacing through his house, his thoughts going from taking extreme measures like directly confronting Kathy to passive approaches like seeing Madison and begging for forgiveness.

The ring of his phone gave him respite from his conflicted thoughts. He raced over and picked it up. Seeing it was Chris, he answered.

"Hey, buddy."

"Hi. Any word from Trevor Cassidy?"

"Yeah, he said no."

"No shit, he won't help us?"

"Yeah, he was pretty adamant too."

"I've been reaching out to all my old buddies in the force and they're saying it's a total shit show inside the ranks. The brass is being told to all but stand down against these fucking protestors and they're being told to keep the investigations on the tagging quiet. The rank and file are pissed but there's not much they can do."

"It's like we're living in an alternate universe. What the hell?" Brett exclaimed.

"I've never seen anything like it. One of my old friends told me the tension between the street cops, detectives, and the brass is explosive. He said it's as if they're being given orders from someone higher up. It's so weird. So not like when I was a deputy."

"Then we need to protect our own," Brett said.

"Agreed."

"This damn ten-day waiting period is killing me. I hate to ask..."

"Don't say it, I got you. Let's meet for lunch. Okay, gotta go. See you at the usual place. Bye," Chris said and hung up.

Brett looked at the time. He still had a good several hours. In the meantime, he'd wait but outside the school. He wasn't going to sit around and idly do nothing. He grabbed his car keys and headed for the garage.

Rancho Bernardo, California

AFTER HAVING a good night's rest, Mo was ready to take on the day. He was still struggling with the images from the other night, but needed to put it behind him.

He expected he would have been on the receiving end of an endless streams of texts from Malik but suspiciously, none after the last he'd received midday yesterday. Maybe Malik was going to give him the space he needed.

His stomach grumbled as hunger pangs signaled it was time for breakfast.

He raced out of his bedroom and down the stairs. He turned to head to the kitchen but froze when he saw his mother, Kareem, Malik and the unknown man from the other night sitting in his living room.

"What?" Was the only word he could muster.

"Mohammed, please come and sit down," his mother said, patting the empty space next to her on the couch.

"Where's Dad?" Mo asked.

"He left for work. Now come, sit down," his mother urged.

"Mom, that's the man from the other night. He...he murdered someone," Mo said, his voice cracking.

"I did no such thing, for it is not murder to take the life of an infidel. You have much to learn, my young friend. Sit, go sit, like your mother said," the man said.

"Mohammed, come sit next to me. We have much to discuss," his mother pleaded.

"Mom, I can't," he said, still in shock at seeing everyone there.

"C'mon, bro, sit, you're safe. I talked to Kareem and Farouk. Nothing will happen to you," Malik said, waving Mo over.

Mo shook his head.

Farouk stood and approached Mo.

"No, get away from me," Mo barked.

"I won't hurt you. I promise," Farouk replied. He stopped feet from Mo and continued. "Your dear friend Malik contacted us concerning your doubts. We thought it best to have, oh, what should we call it?"

"An intervention," Kareem blurted out.

"Yes, an intervention, that's the word. You see, your mother, the beautiful sweet Nahid, has been a believer and follower of ours since 2004, right after the Americans killed her brother. She has been instrumental all these years in supplying us with much-needed resources," Farouk said.

"Mom?" Mo asked, stunned by the revelation.

"It's true. I didn't, I couldn't tell you. I needed you to want this on your own. When Malik gave you the opportunity, you didn't hesitate. I couldn't have been prouder. But now, in your hour of doubt, I thought I needed to let you in on my secret and to beg you to continue. You're on a holy path, you just need to see it through," she said.

"But I...do you know what happened the other night?" Mo asked.

"I am aware. It's ugly, but necessary," she acknowledged.

"I feel sick," he mumbled. He stepped back and sat on the stairs.

His mother raced to him. "Mohammed, are you okay?"

"I don't feel well," he answered.

She whispered so no one else could hear, "I need you to stand. You need to go along or we're all dead. Nod if you understand?"

He nodded.

"Come, get up," she said in a normal voice, helping him to his feet.

He wiped his clammy forehead and said, "I've not been feeling well."

Farouk approached closer. He placed his hand over his heart and said, "If your mother wasn't who she was, we wouldn't be here talking. You've been given one chance, something we rarely do. You are with us or you're not. We need an answer...now."

Mo blinked heavily, opened his mouth but nothing came out.

Malik pressed his eyes closed in prayer that Mo would give the proper response.

"Answer," Farouk ordered.

"I'm with you. I'll do what you need," Mo replied. His mind spun. It all made sense now. Why would a terror cell take him so quickly? Because he was already known, he had already been vetted, same for Malik.

"Good, we'll be in contact soon, very soon," Farouk said. He then stepped up to Mo, placed his hand on his shoulder, leaned in close and whispered, "That was your one chance. You get no more and, Mohammed, we're watching." He slapped him on the back and walked out of the house.

Paris, France

DAVID LUGGED his bags up the three flights of stairs, only dropping them when he reached his front door. He pulled the keys from his pocket and unlocked the door.

When he entered his apartment, he was greeted by a musty but familiar odor. He tossed his bags onto the bed and headed for the bathroom. He had been looking forward to a hot shower since before leaving Ankara. He turned on the water to warm it up, then stripped down. He caught sight of his reflection in the mirror. He leaned close and gazed at the dark bags under his eyes. He swore he looked older than he was. Such was the life of a foreign correspondent and photographer.

Steam began to fill the small space.

He climbed in the shower. The hot water felt great against his skin. He stood for what seemed like minutes under the steady stream of water as his mind wandered back and replayed everything that had occurred in Ankara. He had been so close to the story that would remake his career. But just like that, good fortune was replaced with bad luck.

Max, the ever-supportive and bottomless reservoir of optimism, was ready to help with more interviews and a possible contributor position on Fox News. All he needed to do was be available later and tomorrow morning.

With the grime from Turkey washed away, he exited the shower, toweled off and headed for his bed. A few hours of sleep would give him the boost he needed to tackle the interview later. He pushed his bags aside and lay down. Normally he'd start flipping through his phone, checking out social media or news sites, but he didn't care, all he wanted was sleep. But what he couldn't risk was oversleeping. He set the alarm on his phone, closed his eyes and drifted off.

———

THE STEADY BEEP from his phone alarm woke him. He rubbed his eyes, stretched and turned off the alarm.

The honks and whizzing of cars below on the busy street sounded like a beautiful chorus. He loved Paris and was happy to be back in his adopted city.

He sat up, but just before he could get out of bed, he caught a glimpse of a figure hiding in the shadows of his bedroom. "Who's there?"

The figure emerged; it was Joram. He raised his index finger to his lips.

"What are you doing here?" David mouthed silently.

Joram turned on the television on the dresser and raised the volume high. "Sorry to alarm you," he said, his voice now shielded by the sound of clapping and laughter coming from the television.

"What the hell are you doing here and in my apartment?"

David asked, he looked around, confused, and then asked, "And how did you get in?"

Joram stood up and walked out of the room. "Come, let's finish our conversation. I don't have much time."

David jumped out of bed.

A glow from the kitchen caught David's eye. He looked and saw Joram standing in front of the open refrigerator. "I'm thirsty. I need something cold."

"What are you doing here? And how on earth did you even get here? The border controls have to be tighter since Copenhagen," David said.

"Ha, border controls, this is France, there are no border controls. Same goes for much of Europe," Joram declared, laughing.

"I thought I'd never see you again after that note you left. I thought that was it," David confessed.

Joram grabbed a can of Diet Coke and opened it. "This will do." He took a long drink.

David tore open his backpack and removed his recorder and notepad.

"Oh, that hits the spot," Joram said, wiping his mouth off on a hand towel. He belched loudly and laughed.

"You have to tell me how you got here. How is it so easy? You're a—"

"A terrorist," Joram said finishing David's sentence.

"Well, ah, yeah, that's what the authorities would call you."

"I'm not here to waste time talking about that. I need to finish my story, the story you've been dying to get your hands on, the one you're hoping will resurrect your floundering career."

"I wouldn't describe—"

Joram raised his hand. "I wasn't trying to offend you. It doesn't matter."

"But my career—"

"Like I said, there's not much time. We need to finish this story, plus I know you have better questions to ask."

David sat searching for a good question but suddenly he found himself speechless.

"David, really? It's okay, you can ask. Go ahead and ask," Joram said giving David a 'stop bullshitting around' look.

Joram's tone and look jogged David's thoughts. He now remembered the questions he needed to ask. "I want to start this by asking about everything you told me before. How you came to be with ISIS, your family life, why you joined years ago, was that all true?"

"All true."

"Did you defect from ISIS, or is that a lie?"

"True, I did."

David thought for a second and asked, "When? When did you defect?"

"About a year and a half ago."

"Were you part of a secret or special missions group in ISIS, working on biological weapons?"

"Yes."

David gasped.

"Your CIA friend, he told you some stuff, didn't he?"

"Yes," David answered.

"What else did he tell you?" Joram asked.

"Who's asking who here?"

"You tell me what he told you and I'll corroborate it or not," Joram said.

"Are you a member of The Bloody Hand?"

"How about we do this. I don't want to get out in front of anything. That's why I was telling you my story chronologically. Everything has context. Let's go back to where we left off. I promise I'll answer everything you want to know just by telling you my story."

David thought and said, "Okay, that works."

"Good, now where did we leave off?"

"An execution, you were disturbed by it."

"Yes, I was, but I soon could understand why they did so, and in fact grew to appreciate the uses of capital punishment."

"Hmm," David mused, his head bobbing as his right brow rose.

Joram paused. "Why did you do that?"

"Do what?"

"This, with your head along with that grunting sound," Joran said using his head to replicate the motion David made.

"I didn't do anything."

"Yes, you did," Joram said, his tone shifting to one of annoyance.

"I didn't."

"I'm here to help you and in return you're helping me. I'm not going to be mocked, do you hear me?" Joram blasted.

Shocked by his sharp tongue, David worked to ease the situation. "Sorry, I didn't know I did something to offend you. I won't do it again."

Joram didn't reply right away, he only stared.

"I promise I'll make sure I keep my body language in check."

Grabbing a cigarette from his half-empty pack, Joram lit one and took a long drag. He exhaled, blowing a smoke ring, and continued, "Once I became educated, I saw the wisdom in the harsh punishment. What eventually caused me to lose respect for the imams and mullahs was the corruption. You see, they weren't principled. It was more about power than principle. I was disgusted by that, but where else was I to go. The other groups out there were really no better."

"So that's when you decided to start The Bloody Hand?"

"You're determined, aren't you?"

"It's just a question."

"Do you want to hear my story, or do you just want to interrogate me?"

"Go ahead, my journalist side gets in the way," David confessed.

Joram sat back and grinned.

Suddenly David felt uncomfortable. "What?"

"You, you're interesting. I picked you because you don't have allegiances per se, odd in this world. Many people take sides with large groups, but you, you don't. You're on David's side. Even though you've been warned that I could be a dangerous terrorist, getting the story is more important. More important than what I may know that could possibly stop attacks like Copenhagen. I find that interesting but valuable to me at this very moment."

David didn't know if he should be offended or thank him. He found some of his word choices interesting, so he pressed. "Are you planning further attacks?"

"And if I were to say yes, what would you do with that? Hmm?"

David felt conflicted. Joram's question struck a nerve, one that made him briefly question his own morality.

"No answer?" Joram asked.

"Let's get back to you telling your story," David said.

Joram smiled broadly. He sat up and said, "I like you, David, I really do."

Unable to look at Joram, David looked down at the pad of paper in his lap.

"I'm sorry, where were we?"

David scanned his notes and replied, "You didn't like the corruption."

"Yes, the corruption. I found that even the mullahs were susceptible to bribes and greed like any Westerner was. It was one thing that made us all human. I detested that. How can one say they follow the word of Allah but will turn a blind eye simply for the sake of money or favors? You can't. It's impossible. As I became more entrenched in the bureaucracy of the Islamic State, I uncovered many situations where graft and bribery were used to sway judgments and to force an outcome. I soon began to realize that the Islamic State is no different than any other government. That eventually power does corrupt. I wasn't alone in this disgust. As I ascended the ranks, easily by the way. Being fluent in French, English, Farsi and Arabic made me valuable. I guess those years in private school in Damascus paid off," Joram said. He took a long drag of his cigarette and continued. "On my year anniversary, I was brought before Imam Hassan, he was the defense minister for Islamic State. He liked me and wanted me to work for him directly. What could I say? It was an honor, so I took the position."

"What was the position?"

"I was more of an aide, but soon I was giving orders and making strategic decisions. One day, not long after working for him, I discovered a library hidden in his house and it was there I found journals that detailed a weapon so amazing I needed to ask why it wasn't being explored."

David fidgeted in his chair when he heard this revelation. "What was it?"

"Years before a gentleman by the name of Aashiq Abdullah Aziz had acquired some research documentation on a couple of bioweapon projects. He tried to get them off the ground but he got nowhere..."

"Why, what happened?"

"Not sure, all I know is the project was terminated weeks after he started it. The rumors are he disobeyed a wealthy Saudi prince by the name of Yasser Mohammed Faudi. This disobedience resulted in not only his project being terminated but Aashiq as well."

"How did Islamic State get the documentation?"

"Who knows, but what I do know everything has value on the black market."

"You used the word *amazing*; that makes it sound like you were excited about these potential weapons."

"I was. I was impressed. Page after page described a weapon that if created could utterly bring—"

Thinking he knew the next phrase, David interjected, "The United States to its knees?"

"No, the world."

"What was it?"

Joram sat back, his eyes looking around as he took himself back to that day in Mullah Hassan's library.

"Joram, what was this weapon?"

"I'll explain it a bit. After discovering these journals and the weapons they possessed, I brought them to Mullah Hassan's attention. He wasn't happy that I had violated his private library, but he also was curious as to my thoughts on the journals. I told him that the Islamic State should pursue it. At first, he didn't like the idea. He imagined a weapon like it could get beyond their control, but after weeks of pressing, I convinced him if done right and done with an antidote or cure, you could say, he gave me the go ahead. However, we were to do our research in private. No one on the council, no one at all must know what we were doing. He said that few could be trusted."

David scribbled frantically.

Joram grew quiet. The grin he had been wearing melted away. He looked down and sadly said, "Two months later, Mullah Hassan was brought up on charges of conspiring with the government of Turkey, a lie, and was beheaded. They got rid of him. Someone wished to have his position; someone wanted more power so they contrived a false charge against Mullah Hassan. It was then I was done with Islamic State, the corrupt and decadent knew no bounds. My team and I fled Syria, we disappeared. That was eighteen months ago."

"And you took this weapons program with you?"

"Yes."

"And you formed The Bloody Hand?"

Joram didn't reply right away. He looked out the window, his thoughts racing back to the time he was told of Mullah Hassan's execution. "I wasn't in Raqqa when they killed him. If I was, I would've been killed too. I knew my days were numbered. Mullah Hassan liked me and trusted me. He told me I had great promise. That Allah had a plan for me…"

"Does he have a plan for you?"

"David, Allah has a plan for everyone."

"And what's mine?"

"You're a messenger, that's what I believe your purpose is."

"That would be true."

"Of course it is. As far as Mullah Hassan, the part Allah gave him was that of a leader, a nurturer of sorts. I've come to reconcile what happened to him. He was supposed to die the day he did, I see that now. But I wasn't, so I fled."

"You fled to save your own life."

"Yes, but later I came to realize it was for more. Poor Hassan though, I miss him dearly. He was innocent of the charges but he was guilty of being naïve about politics. He wasn't a man born for that kind of world. He didn't know how to navigate it properly, so therefore it consumed him and eventually killed him."

"You seem upset. You two really were close?"

"He had become like a father figure, a spiritual father."

Joram rose quickly and walked to the refrigerator. He

opened it and took out a block of cheese he'd seen on the shelf earlier. Putting it to his nose, he smelled. "I love this stuff. We could never get good cheese in Syria."

"Help yourself," David said. A question suddenly popped in his head, one that Grim had brought up. "Joram?"

"Yeah."

David hesitated, as he wasn't quite sure how he should phrase the series of questions he had. But after listening to Joram and, more importantly, trusting his instincts, he needed to know. Deciding there wasn't a fancy way to put it, he just spit it out, "Is Israfil the twelfth imam and..."

"Go ahead, finish your question," Joram said.

"Are you Israfil?"

Coronado, California

BRENNAN WAS USED to hurry up and wait. It was the second motto of the Marine Corps, right after Semper Fidelis.

Owens burst through the door, walked to the television mounted on the wall and turned it on. He flipped to a cable news channel and waited.

Brennan was caught off guard by Owens' behavior. He strode over and asked, "What's the word?"

With a clenched jaw, he jabbed his finger at the television but said nothing.

Vickers and Klyde came over.

"Can we get some chow?" Vickers asked.

"One second," Brennan said, staring at the television screen.

The commercial break ended. A newscaster appeared. "*Unnamed anonymous intelligence and defense sources are telling the* New York Times *that the president has ordered a military strike into Mexico. Details of the strike are unknown but the sources told the* Times *that they're related to the raid in Somalia and deal with intelligence gathered in Copenhagen..."*

Owens turned the television off.

"What the fuck!" Brennan snapped.

"It's one thing we have to fight these savages, but now we've got our own snitching on us," Owens barked.

"But why? Why would they do that?" Brennan asked.

"Not sure, must be fucking politics, always is. They disagree with the president and suddenly they think they get to fuck with national security," Owens railed.

"Aren't we on the same team?" Vickers asked.

"Unfortunately, that doesn't appear to be the case," Owens replied.

"That sucks. They'll be waiting for us now," Klyde said.

"It's off. The raid is off right now and all because we've been compromised. Some asshole analyst who was appointed by an opposing political party thinks he knows best and has jeopardized our mission and the potential for gathering valuable intel against a terror organization," Owens barked.

"Now what?" Brennan asked.

"We sit and wait. Brass doesn't want us going in now that we've been compromised. It's too risky," Owens said.

"But we need a specimen, we need it," Brennan said.

"Fuck it, I say we go in," Vickers said.

"There's another issue. The Mexican government is pissed that we didn't brief them on the raid."

"Because we can't trust those bean eaters," Vickers said.

"I heard that!" Vasquez, a Marine from first squad, hollered.

"You know I love you, Vee," Vickers said, blowing a kiss to Vasquez.

"What you guys need to know is the mission has been scrubbed. It's off," Owens said.

"Any chance of it being revived?" Brennan asked.

"Nothing is a hundred percent, but they did tell me to pass on for everyone to turn in their weapons at the armory."

"It's off." Vickers laughed.

"Yep," Klyde said.

"I'm truly shocked," Brennan said.

"Get used to it. This has become business as usual now," Owens said.

"The leaks?" Brennan asked.

"Yeah, the leaks, but I never thought they'd blow up a mission like that," Owens said.

"I guess we can never truly trust those spooks," Brennan said.

"No shit, remember Sangin," Vickers said.

"What happened in Sangin?" Owens asked.

Brennan exhaled loudly. "I don't want to talk about it," he said and walked off.

Owens gave Vickers and Klyde a look and asked, "What's up with him?"

"He got triggered," Vickers joked.

"Huh?"

"What dumbass is saying is Sergeant Brennan doesn't take kindly to politics interfering in our missions. It always ends up fucking shit up," Klyde answered.

"So what happened in Sangin?" Owens asked.

Klyde replied, "Back in Afghanistan we got a report that the Taliban had surrounded a group of locals in Sangin. Our company was called up to go and rescue them. It was a simple, cut-and-dry deal; we'd go in, engage the Taliban and free the locals. Everything was going smoothly until we reached phase line echo, which was also a large field where poppy grows. It was there that shit went south. We were instructed to stop. Word then came that we couldn't cross even though it was the most direct route to the village. While we wasted time, the

Taliban had gone through with their threat and burned the locals alive inside the building. When we finally arrived, we discovered the locals were all school-aged girls, as young as four and old as twelve. They had been murdered solely for the fact they were girls, nothing more. I can still see the ash floating through the air. It sticks with me; it's seared into my mind. Those sick fucks murdered them for nothing more than their gender. That's barbaric, it's sickening. When we got back to Leatherneck, rumors circulated that the reason we couldn't cross where the poppy grows was because the land was owned by the interior minister and our transit could potentially destroy some of the crop. The CO pushed the issue but was told it was classified and to back down."

"Fucking bullshit politics killed those girls." Vickers groaned.

"You know who stopped us at phase line echo? American contractors, guys just like us but now making six times as much working private. I was never more pissed off in my life," Klyde confessed.

"Makes me see red every time I hear that story," Vickers said.

Klyde looked over to Brennan, who was now sitting along the far wall. "From that day, Sergeant Brennan...all of us swore nothing would stop us from helping innocents like those girls again."

"Hmm, makes sense why that pissed him off," Owens said referring to the news their mission had been compromised by political leaks. Owens walked over to Brennan and sat next to him.

"I assume those chatty kathys told you," Brennan said.

"Yeah."

"That shit pisses me off. It's unnecessary and costs lives. I hate it," Brennan growled.

"I've been meaning to ask. I heard the guys talking about you yesterday," Owens said and paused.

"And?"

"They said you have a ritual of sorts before you go into a gunfight. What is it?"

"They're talking about my prayer. I always take a good twenty seconds to recite a prayer if I think the lead is going to fly. It helps to calm me, and now, I've been doing it so long that it's just what I do."

"Sort of like ball players who wear the same underwear during play-offs," Owens said in a weak attempt at comparison.

"I wouldn't say it's like wearing the same boxers for weeks, but as far as a ritual, yeah it's the same," Brennan said.

"What is it? What's the prayer?" Owens asked.

Brennan gave him a leery look and asked, "You really want to know?"

"Yeah, I do, but if you want to tell me to go pound sand, I'll understand," Owens said.

"My old man taught it to me. He was in Vietnam in 1974; it's what he'd recite too. He told me his old man, my grandfather, used to say it too."

"You're from a family of warriors?" Owens asked.

"Yeah, my dad was a Marine, my grandad and even my great-granddad, all Marines," Brennan said.

"Same for me, all sailors though, going back generations. My dad was a frogman too, an old UDT guy."

"It's good, it really is," Brennan said.

"What is?"

"The family thing, carrying on traditions, I like it, but I do question whether I want my son to join. It's so fucked up now," Brennan confided.

"Don't get yourself too worked up. It's always been fucked up; this is just our generation's version of it."

"Hey, I'm going to get my guys to the armory. We'll chat later," Brennan said standing up.

"Hold on, the prayer?"

"I'll write it down for you. See ya," Brennan said and walked off.

A Marine in first squad turned on the television.

"*...from all over the country, more and more reports of bloody hands being spray painted on buildings. Some say it's just pranksters while others say it's a sign, a harbinger, and others that these places are being targeted by the terror group The Bloody Hand. When we return from our break, we'll sit down with a terrorism expert to discuss this and the latest on the leak concerning a possible military strike in Mexico and if the president has possibly violated international law.*"

Disgusted, Owens hollered, "Turn that shit off!"

San Diego, California

"Before I give this to you, please promise me you won't do anything stupid with it?" Chris asked, holding the gun box in his hand.

"I'm not going on any rampage. I just need something now. That waiting period is leaving me defenseless," Brett said.

"This is the same model handgun you purchased and have been using. I thought it best to give you the exact one you're going to get and have been training with."

"I can't thank you enough," Brett said.

"No worries."

"I don't know how I can repay you," Brett said.

"How about a six-pack of PBR, the twenty-four-ounce cans," Chris said.

Brett furrowed his brow and asked, "You serious?"

"Yep."

"Pabst?"

"It's an old tradition going back twenty-some years. Something my friends and I do to say thank you."

"But Pabst, that's shit beer," Brett replied.

"It's not bad, and on a super-hot day, an ice-cold PBR tastes mighty fine." Chris smiled.

Brett stuck his hand out.

Chris took it.

The two men shook.

"Oh, I've got something else for you," Chris said, pulling out a piece of paper and handing it to Brett.

"What's this?"

"Trevor Cassidy's address, just in case you want to pay him a visit. Don't go stalking him with my gun now," Chris warned.

"I'm not crazy."

"If you go over there, let me know what happens. Also, I'll take the morning shift at the school," Chris said, referring to the security patrols they were doing during the beginning and end of school.

"You'll be the first to know. That used to be Madison," Brett moped.

"So how is she, any word?"

"Nope, she won't even take my calls and no replies to my texts. She's really pissed off."

"Oh, she just needs more time. My wife will stay pissed at me for a week just for not putting down the toilet seat," Chris joked.

Brett tapped the gun case, smiled and said, "Thanks again. I'll be in touch."

"No lunch?" Chris asked.

"Can't, sorry, maybe tomorrow," Brett answered and walked off.

Chris watched Brett leave. He wanted to help but having

been married for seventeen years, he knew these domestic issues could take a while to mend.

Brett got in his car. Normally they would have done lunch, but he had somewhere to be. He unfolded the note and started to plug the address into his phone's mapping system when a text popped up.

"*I need your help.*"

It was Madison.

He immediately replied, "Okay."

"*I won't be able to pick up boys from school. Traffic is a mess, highway is shut down.*"

"I'll do it, no problem."

"*And we need to talk. I'll pick up dinner.*"

"Sounds good," he answered.

"See you later," she texted.

He stared at her texts. A feeling of joy began to rise in him. He hated fighting with her and he missed his boys dearly. He glanced at the note with Cassidy's address. He folded it and placed it in his pocket. He'd wait to go by, the last thing he wanted now was to mess up his chance with Madison.

Paris, France

JORAM JUST WOULDN'T GIVE David what he wanted, the answers to the questions Grim had sought. David was selfish though, he wasn't asking for Grim, but because he thought it would be good for the documentary.

Joram had spent the past several hours going over the lives of the men whom he'd defected with. He gave David insightful details that would provide good filler content for the documentary but nothing that was earth-shattering. Every time David would bring the conversation back to the bioweapon, Israfil or the twelfth imam, Joram would deflect.

David's patience was wearing thin.

Joram exited the bathroom and once more proceeded to the refrigerator. He opened it and took out a package of presliced salami. He read the ingredients and remarked, "You're health conscious."

"Why do you say that?" David asked.

"No nitrates," Joram said, holding up the package of salami.

"You might want to check the date on that," David warned.

Joram stopped chewing on a piece and read the packaging carefully. "Hmm, says it's past due by several weeks but it tastes fine. Or maybe my taste buds were ruined after eating all that horrible food in Raqqa." He walked back to his chair and sat down. He gave David a glance and could see weariness written all over his face. "You look tired. Shall we call it a night?"

"No."

"Then let's continue. I was telling you about the time we were in Mexico."

"Stop, please."

"What?"

David rubbed his face and lamented, "What am I really doing here?"

"I chose you to tell my story. I want the world to know how it all happened."

"What happened? Your defection from ISIS and your creation of The Bloody Hand?"

Joram winked at David and said, "You don't give up. You just want to jump ahead, spoil the story."

"I need to know who I'm speaking with."

"Why? Will that change anything...anything at all?" Joram asked curiously.

"Ah."

"If I told you that I'm the twelfth imam and that I'm the holy leader of The Bloody Hand, would it make you pause?

Would you want to continue, or would you run out of here screaming bloody murder and call your friend the CIA officer?"

"I just need to know."

"Why?"

"I just do."

Joram pulled a slice of salami from the package and stuffed it in his mouth.

An awkward silence filled the room.

"You're not going to tell me," David said.

"I will, but patience, my friend. Answer me this, you're one of those people who picks up a book, you read the first chapter then skip to the last chapter."

David put the pad down on the coffee table and stood up. He began to pace the room.

"Sit down. Let's continue," Joram urged.

"I can't place it, but every time we talk, you're different. It's like I'm speaking to a different person every time. You're clearly not the man I met three years ago. I would expect you to be different after your experiences, but the man in Turkey that first day was different than who is sitting in front of me now."

"How so?"

"You're...more confident. I don't know, you're different. You seem like..."

"Like what?"

"Like...this is all orchestrated...like...how did you know I spoke with Grim? Huh? How did you know that? Did you follow me? How did you get here so fast? How did you know where I lived? How did you find me and get my phone number? You just seem to know everything. You're too..."

"Too what?" Joram asked. He was enjoying this analysis very much.

"In control," David blurted out.

"Because I am."

David's eyes widened. "You are, aren't you? You're in control of it all?"

"Control of what, David? You seem to have a grand theory at play in your head."

"How did someone like you—a man on every terror watch list, a man known to the CIA, MI6, Interpol—get to Paris so quickly. How could you fly? It's impossible with all the facial recognition out there. They would have spotted you."

"Do you want me to tell you?"

David rushed to his chair, sat down and picked up his notepad. "Yes, please."

"I flew private."

David's pen was pressed against the page with earnest, but when he heard Joram's reply, he lifted it and asked, "Private?"

"Yes, David, I flew private from Ankara to Slovenia, a car was waiting for me there. I then simply drove to Paris. Very easy, David, now does that answer your question?"

"Is that a common route?"

"Common? No. We vary our arrival cities when we fly but we always make sure we land in countries with limited customs. The Balkan states are very weak on immigration and customs, and if you do run into an issue, they all can be bought off. Greed is a wonderful thing when you need it."

"Europe truly is porous? Easy to get in and out of?" David asked.

"Yes, and so is Latin America and Mexico. It's ridiculous how easy it is. It's gotten tougher under the new president but fortunately the previous American administration's policies were so lax we were able to exploit them."

David paused from writing. He looked up and asked, "The way you're talking right now. You've been inserting jihadis through the U.S. southern border?"

"Did I say that?" asked coyly.

"You said we were able to exploit them."

"Well, we were also able to exploit the refugee flows and the visa programs. Did you know last year over seven hundred thousand visa holders overstayed and are still in the United States? Do you want to know how many were ours?"

"Right there, you're admitting you are The Bloody Hand and you've infiltrated the United States," David declared.

"I see that you're never going to let this go and, well, I did kind of give it away," Joram said before pausing.

Waiting on pins and needles, David sat, his leg bouncing up and down with nervous energy.

"To answer one of your questions, yes, I am part of The Bloody Hand."

San Diego, California

"CITY AND LAW *enforcement officials are telling us that May 1 is likely to be one of the worst and quite possibly the worst day for protests we've seen in San Diego. The reason? Around the world, May 1 is recognized as International Worker's Day. It's already a prominent day for protest and civil disobedience by workers' groups, unions and other special interest advocates. We're hearing now that immigration groups plan to join these protests to voice their opposition to the recent controversial actions by the president and what many see as his overreach in regard to recent military actions taken by his administration. Law enforcement officials are saying if you don't need to travel, don't. They're predicting that the freeways will be shut down again as protestors target them..."*

The front door opened.

Brett quickly grabbed the remote and turned the television off. The last thing he wanted was for Madison to hear the television news and assume he was obsessing again. He rushed out of the kitchen and hollered, "Hey, boys, your mom is here. Get cleaned up for dinner."

Madison strolled past him into the kitchen, holding a couple of bags in her hands. She held one up and asked, "How does Thai food sound?"

"Excellent," Brett said, coming in behind her.

"And I picked up some ice cream, mint chocolate chip," she said, holding up the second bag.

"Wow, you do still love me," he joked as he went for a kiss.

She didn't recoil. She let his lips touch hers and followed with one of her own.

"I missed you," Brett said softly.

"I missed you, too," she replied, putting the bags on the counter.

"After dinner, let's talk," she said.

"But don't the boys have to be in bed?" Brett asked.

"Of course, I thought we'd sleep at home tonight. The boys are missing their home. They love staying at Mom's but nothing is like home."

"So true," he said.

"Upstairs, wash up, brush teeth, then bed," Madison said to the boys as they sprinted up the stairs, happy in the knowledge they'd be sleeping in their own beds.

"Glass of wine?" Brett asked.

"Yeah, why not," she answered.

Brett opened a bottle, grabbed two glasses and headed for the couch.

Madison joined him. She sat opposite him and put her feet up on the coffee table.

"Maddy, I'll just come out and say it, I'm sorry I upset you, but please know my intentions are pure," Brett said.

"I know they are. I was just embarrassed, and to be quite honest, you were acting a bit manic. I was scared."

"Sorry, it's just that I worry."

"I love that you care so much, but we can't let all of this stuff, the terrorists or protestors, affect our lives. There's only so much we can do."

"But aren't you the least bit concerned about that handprint being spray painted?" Brett asked, concerned she was too laissez-faire.

"I'm not. I think it's just one of those idiot protestor type people. You give them one excuse and they act like children. Do I think it's some grand plot or conspiracy? No."

"But they're popping up everywhere, all across the country."

"Remember a couple of years back, people dressing up like clowns. It started with one or two, then morons were copying them. Soon, dozens and dozens of sightings of creepy clowns," Madison said.

"I remember."

"It's just like that, nothing more. Social media spreads these things like wildfire and losers don't have better things to do than go and do stupid stuff. These viral things come and go. What about the time people were planking everywhere. You couldn't look on Facebook without seeing some idiot kid doing it."

Brett thought hard about what she was saying. There was truth in her words. People were sheep like in their behavior and if it got them attention or could rack up likes on Facebook, they'd do it. "Maybe you're right."

"I'm not saying there aren't bad people out there. I'm not saying we shouldn't be concerned for our boys' safety, but at what point does concern turn to paranoia?"

Brett could easily see her point. *Have I become paranoid? Is there a balance?* He thought.

"I want my husband back," Madison said softly and scooted closer to him.

"I need to ask," he said.

She stopped moving and asked, "What?"

"The gun I purchased, I want to keep it," he said.

She squinted and pursed her lips. "I suppose so, but you need to get a safe first and you need to train...a lot."

"Deal."

"And one more thing," she said.

"You need to take me shooting."

"What?" he asked in shock. He never imagined those words coming out of her mouth.

"I've done a lot of thinking. You're a good man, I love you, I loved you from our fourth date. If you want to own a gun and go shooting, I need to support you in that as long as you ensure it will be handled safely in our house."

"Of course."

"Good, now come here," she purred pulling him close. "All this talk of shooting has made me miss you even more."

He wrapped his arms around her and said, "One of the greatest things ever invented was makeup sex."

"Who said we were having sex?" She laughed.

He pulled away and asked, "We're not?"

"How about we cuddle first, see where it goes."

He squeezed her tight and said, "Deal."

Rancho Bernardo, California

MO HAD GONE TO SCHOOL. He wasn't sure why, as he didn't learn a thing. His mind was clogged with what had happened this morning and what could end up being his ultimate fate.

Upon returning home, he decided he was done with school. Why bother going if he'd never see graduation anyway.

In the hours he'd been home, he secluded himself in his bedroom. He had no appetite and all he could do to keep his mind off all the recent events was to play video games.

A tapping on his door pulled him away from his game.

"Yeah."

"It's your mother. Can I come in?"

"Yes."

She opened the door, stepped in and closed it promptly behind her. She walked over to him and sat on the edge of the bed.

He couldn't look at her, it was too hard; instead he kept his focus on the game.

"Mohammed, I need to talk to you," she said.

"Okay."

"I need your attention," she urged.

"I'm playing. Go ahead and tell me what you need to tell me."

"Mohammed, look at me."

He ignored her and kept playing.

Frustrated she stood up and walked in front of him to block his view of the television.

He tried to look around her but she kept moving. "Get out of the way. I've never played this level," he barked.

"Look at me," she snapped.

"Just get out of my way and just say what you came to say," he snapped back.

She turned around and turned off the game console.

"What the hell!" he yelled.

She swung around and slapped his face. "Don't you dare yell at me."

He put his hand to his cheek; her hit stung his face. "Get out of my room."

"Not until I talk to you."

He glared at her and said, "There's nothing to say. Nothing!"

"There is. Let me talk."

"I said talk, go ahead. I'm doing what you wish, not because I want to, but because they'll kill all of us!"

"Keep your voice down. Your father will hear," she barked.

"So what!"

"Mohammed, I swear," she said, raising her hand.

He stepped towards her and stuck out his face. "Go ahead, hit me. That's nothing. Soon I'll be dead and it won't matter."

His remarks struck her hard. She tried to take his hand but he pulled away. "Son, please know that I love you. I know you're upset, but I need you to fully understand everything."

"There's nothing to understand. I made a huge mistake. I was an idiot. I thought it sounded cool, rebellious, but it was all a big mistake. What really hurts is you knew and let me walk into that. You're okay with letting me die."

She again stepped towards him, but for each step she took, he backed away.

"I'm just a stupid kid. I didn't realize just how...how real this was. I never imagined it would actually happen. I thought that Malik and I would just get together and talk shit, maybe meet with others, but I never in my wildest dreams believed it was real or would ever happen."

"Mohammed, please let me explain."

"Mother, I was a fool. When I look at this country, it's not perfect but it's not evil. I'm not sure why it took what I've seen to realize that, but what you're asking me to do, what those men are asking me to do is not better than what they say Americans have done to them; in fact it might be worse. I don't know what's in store for me, but what I do know is soon, I'll be asked to murder innocent people in cold blood and for a God, a religion, I don't really care about."

"Take that back," she snapped, her tone becoming harsh.

"I won't take it back. I'm going to die soon and I might as well tell you exactly what I think."

"Take it back now."

"No."

"Allah will forgive you, I know. I will pray for you," she said, marching past him and out of the room. She closed the door and stood in the darkened hallway. She was sure her God would forgive her son, he had to, especially after he sacrificed himself for him.

Mo stared at the closed door. His temper was only as great as his disappointment in his mother. She was not the woman he grew up knowing. The thought she would support and advocate his supposed martyrdom was shocking but his destiny had been written.

He sat back down and turned his game console back on.

His phone beeped.

He picked it up to find a text from Malik.

"U good?"

"Fine."

"U sure?"

"Yes. Tired."

"Ok, just checking on you. Allahu akbar, brother. Soon we will fight."

Mo stared at the text. At first, he thought about texting back something derogatory. That thought shifted to not replying at all, but then he grew concerned that could signal something negative. To play it safe, he went along and texted, "Allahu Akbar." He tossed the phone on the bed, picked up the game controller and began playing.

CHAPTER EIGHT

Friday, April 28
Coronado, California

"Sᴇʀɢᴇᴀɴᴛ Bʀᴇɴɴᴀɴ, ᴘssᴛ, Sᴇʀɢᴇᴀɴᴛ Bʀᴇɴɴᴀɴ, ᴡᴀᴋᴇ ᴜᴘ."

Brennan opened his eyes to find Dietz hovering over him. He rubbed his eyes and asked, "What is it?"

"You're being summoned, Commander Shenkman has requested all squad leaders to report ASAP."

Brennan swung his legs out of the bed and stood. He grabbed his trousers and put them on. "What the word?"

"I heard we're being called up. The mission is back on," Dietz answered.

"You sure?" Brennan asked as he laced up his boots.

"That's the scuttlebutt."

"What time is it?"

"Zero three twenty-three, Sergeant."

"So you're on duty the rest of the morning?" Brennan asked.

"Yes, Sergeant."

"Okay, go back. I'll call if we are getting called up. Don't wake the guys yet," Brennan ordered as he headed out the door.

———

BRENNAN WALKED out into the cool brisk early morning air. The base was dead; the only thing moving was the ocean breeze across the island.

He threw open the door to the headquarters building and walked into a buzz of activity, a contrast to the sleepy base outside.

Owens walked around the corner and spotted Brennan, "Good, there you are. You're the last squad leader. Hurry, we have some developments."

Brennan followed Owens into the command briefing room. He took a seat next to another Marine and fixed his attention to the front.

"Sir, everyone is here," Owens shouted out to Shenkman.

Shenkman was chatting with another officer. He finished and looked up. "Thank you all for rushing over as quickly as possible. Gentlemen, since the op in Mexico was shut down, we have been keeping an eye on that facility. We've seen trucks enter, over a dozen, but none leave. At first we were unsure why, but now we believe they have a tunnel, probably built by the cartels, that is connected to the United States somewhere. We contacted our good friends at the DIA, who contacted our very dear friends at the NSA to see what they could do to help us figure out where these trucks might be popping up. Well, magic happened, that's all I can say about their conclusions." he said and nodded to a young officer.

A screen behind Shenkman turned on.

"I'm not even going to begin to try to explain to you how they figured it out. They were telling me and I was lost, so I'll skip to the sweet stuff," he said. He clicked on his laser pointer. The red dot instantly popped onto an aerial photograph. With his arm extended, he leveled the pointer's dot onto the top of a large building just across the border. "This is where they say the bunker exits, under this building. We pulled the records on this building. It's owned by a company called...ISRAFILS HORN. They acquired it over two years ago. We know the name is not coincidental." Shenkman lowered his arm and faced the men. "Fourth platoon, you will go down there and take this building."

Several men began to mumble and cross talk.

"Everyone, be quiet. I'm not done. The other three platoons, you're being tasked with another mission. This one took us by surprise after we confirmed it." He nodded to the young officer running the multimedia. The screen changed from the large tans and browns of south Texas to lush green. "Gentlemen, this is a map of northern Minnesota." He put the dot of his laser pointer on a large fenced compound. "In several decrypted messages we found in an e-mail account, the location of this compound was mentioned as well as its purpose, a staging and training facility."

Brennan was stunned, as were others.

The Marine next to Brennan gasped.

Shenkman paused and continued, "Believe me, I was just as shocked as you are. This facility is active too. We have eyes on and there's a ton happening there. Gentlemen, we are green for taking this facility down."

Several of the men in the room mumbled their approval by saying, "Yeah," or, "Good."

Shenkman paced for a few seconds and continued. "There's one sticky point. This compound is listed as a children's camp." He picked up a piece of paper and read, "It's officially listed as the Upper Midwest Children's Islamic Enrichment Center and Camp, and when we pulled title on the property we found

something curious, the titled owner is a corporation, called...
ISRAFILS HORN. Clearly this property and the warehouse in
Texas are connected. We're currently researching other proper-
ties or land owned by that corporation by conducting searches
via the secretary of state's nationwide database for corporate
entities." He tossed the paper on the table and said, "We've verified that the site is actually used as a children's camp. What we
have here is a terror training, staging and research center
disguised as a children's camp. If you look, the compound covers
over four square miles of land, with the main children's camp
located here and what we believe is the research buildings here
and here. Gentlemen, there are kids here. We have confirmed
that." Shenkman paced more and said, "This puts us in a tight
spot. The president has personally ordered we take this site
down, but with children located on-site, this could become a
fucking PR nightmare if this goes south. So, keeping that in
mind, third platoon will secure what we believe are the buildings used for the camp. Once secure, they'll ensure no children
exit those buildings, hence keeping them away from the main
thrust of our raid, which will be conducted on these buildings."

Several men grumbled audibly.

"First platoon, we suspect this building here houses any
research that might be happening on-site. We believe this
because of all the HVAC and power along the side of the building. Also, we have found building permits from the county and
submitted architectural plans. This is a subterranean structure,
actually, it's a fucking super-structure when you examine the
plans."

The squad leader for third squad leaned over and said to
Brennan under his breath. "All this under our noses and right in
the good ole US of A."

"Yep," Brennan replied simply.

Shenkman continued, "We've contacted local and state law

enforcement that we will need their support but we didn't give them any specifics yet. They told us they'll be ready to move to assist once we give them the call. We'll use them to process any children. It's sad that we can't have a more active role for them, but we can't trust anyone with these fucking leaks happening. In fact, only the Secretary of Defense, Secretary of Homeland Security, president and we here know about the raid. Once the intel went up, nothing came back down alerting anyone we were going green on this mission. We can't afford to let those cocksucker reporters at the *Post* or *Times* blow this for us."

"Lock 'em up," a sailor blurted out, referencing the leaks.

Several others mumbled their agreement.

"Men, our objective is twofold. Intel and eradication. First platoon is there to locate, find any mutants we can secure as specimens, scrounge up intel and to capture any scientists that can provide us critical information. Everyone else, our secondary objective is to terminate without prejudice any threat there. You will be weapons free."

Brennan was happy to hear his squad would take point against the mutants. His only concern was the children being used as human shields.

"First platoon, you will not be babysitting the team from the CDC, as we can't have you focused on taking care of their safety. Also, Sergeant Brennan, you will oversee first platoon, as Senior Chief Owens will be the OIC for the mission. I'll be accompanying fourth platoon in Texas. So, fourth, when I finish this briefing, stay seated. I'll cover some other details and discuss the coordination we'll be getting from customs agents for our raid in Texas."

"Owens, you're wheels up in two hours. You'll fly to Grand Forks Air Force Base, there you'll link up with air assets that will take you to the site. When the sun sets later today, you'll go in," Shenkman said as he turned off the screen behind him. He faced the men and finished, "I can't stress enough that these missions are critical. We are facing a new threat with these mutants, like nothing we've ever seen before. We believe a massive coordinated attack is coming. We don't know where or when, but the Pentagon believes these mutants will be part of this attack. We need as much on them as possible."

Brennan couldn't resist, he needed to ask a question that had been dogging him. He raised his hand.

"Yes, Sergeant Brennan," Shenkman said pointing at him.

"Why were the other mutants' remains destroyed, sir?"

"The captain of the *Anchorage* cited a dated protocol on shipborne contaminants It's a shame, we could have been that much further ahead. It also didn't help that you and Senior Chief Owens tossed the female mutant and her offspring out over the Indian Ocean."

"To be fair, sir, as you know, in battle things happen. Decisions are made based upon the situation as it's unfolding," Brennan blurted out.

Owens tapped his leg and whispered, "Not the time."

"Sergeant Brennan, you and your Marines were put on this team because you were highly recommended from your brief encounter with these mutants. What happened on that plane gives me pause that you and your men aren't up to the task. These mutants pose a potentially grave threat. We desperately need a sample."

"I agree, sir, on the last point; but may I add, sir, that we'd have another sample if some desk jockey wasn't leaking critical and sensitive classified information to their buddies in the media."

"You're right, Sergeant. Now if you're done, we can move on. We have a couple of missions to prepare for," Shenkman said, then dismissed the men.

Owens immediately turned to Brennan. "What the fuck was that?"

"I'm curious."

"That wasn't curious, that was borderline insubordination."

"Take it easy. It wasn't. I just want to know why things aren't lining up. First the captain of the *Anchorage* destroys all the remains, then a leak."

"I don't want to hear crazy conspiracy theories. No one forced us to toss Princess from the plane."

Brennan thought and replied, "True. I guess we're just having bad luck."

"Go get your boys ready. We're leaving in less than two," Owens said, getting up, a tinge of irritation in his voice.

"Hey, Owens, here," Brennan said, handing Owens a folded piece of paper.

"What's this?" Owens asked.

"The prayer you asked about," Brennan answered.

Owens unfolded the paper, read it and said, "Good stuff, thanks. And, Brennan, don't do that shit again. I vouched for you and your guys."

"I won't, I swear."

"I know shit isn't going as planned, but sometimes that's life. We just have to roll with it," Owens said.

"Agreed," Brennan said.

The two men walked side by side out of the briefing room and exited the building. As the darkness enveloped them, Brennan couldn't help but ask something that plagued him from the mission brief.

"How the fuck does a terror organization operate a sophisticated training camp and research facility right under our noses?"

Owens thought on it for a minute and replied, "That is the big question. I don't know. It does make you wonder if they've had help, you know, on the inside."

"Look who's wearing a tinfoil hat now," Brennan quipped.

"Not this guy. I just can't believe that. Large conspiracies like that are too big not to collapse under their own weight. Someone is bound to squeal, but then again, how does that happen?"

"See, me asking those questions and being skeptical isn't so crazy."

"Maybe so, but there's a bigger question. Are there more?"

Paris, France

DAVID OPENED his eyes and flinched when he saw Joram towering over him.

"You dozed off," Joram said, a big smile stretched across his face.

"Oh, ah, sorry, I, um, where did we..."

"Sleep, my friend, I need to go do a few things," Joram said putting on a hooded jacket.

"No, no, let's keep going," David insisted as he rubbed his weary eyes.

"Get a few hours of sleep. I'll return."

"You sure?" David asked, the idea of getting a few hours of sleep was sounding good now.

"Positive," Joram replied as he headed towards the door. He opened it, turned around and said, "Don't make any calls, okay?"

David raised his hands and shrugged. "I'm just going straight to bed."

Joram nodded. "Good, because when I get back, I'll finish my story."

"I like the sound of that."

"Me too," Joram said and left.

David stood and stretched. He sauntered to the bedroom and fell into bed. For a brief moment, he looked at his phone on the nightstand. *Should I make a call to the embassy?* he thought.

Joram had divulged a lot of good information that would bolster and add entertainment value to his documentary. His declaration of membership in The Bloody Hand was a big moment for the night, so was the fact he verified having worked on a secret bioweapons program. Otherwise, the rest was filler. He talked about the others on his team and explained how they initially fled Syria and their travels around the world.

As David played back Joram's story, something began to appear. He hadn't given away any real actionable intelligence. He'd never told him exactly what they had been working on or where they had gone, specifically. He'd used generalities like Mexico, East Africa and so forth. There wasn't any doubt in David's mind that Joram had been until recently an active terror member.

He began to ponder whether he did have a responsibility to turn Joram over to the authorities. But if he did, he didn't have the final pieces of his story. It was too soon. He needed a bit more information; then he could think about doing it.

Thoughts of his journalistic integrity gripped him then. By turning Joram over to Grim and the others at the CIA, he was violating Joram's trust. Could it be that Joram was seeking redemption for anything he'd done by sharing his story and exposing The Bloody Hand? By turning him over, could he be sending Joram to a fate he didn't deserve. He'd heard a lot about the CIA black sites and rendition. Many in the civilized world considered those things a clear violation of human rights. If he turned Joram in, then he'd be party to such things.

His eyes grew heavy. He needed to sleep, but his thoughts were now torturing him. *What should I do?* he thought. He ran through various scenarios until he found the one that was a win-win. He would contact Grim about Joram, but not until he had gotten everything he needed, that seemed fair. He only needed a few major items explored and once he got them, he'd make the call.

Grand Forks Air Force Base, North Dakota

FIRST SQUAD HUSTLED from the transport towards their chopper.

Brennan reached the chopper and counted as each of his men got on board. After the last boarded, he went on. He took a seat near the aft and put on a headset.

"This is Sergeant Brennan, platoon leader, first squad," he said.

"Good afternoon, Sergeant Brennan. I'm Captain Tillis, your taxi driver to Minnesota."

"We're all loaded up back here," Brennan said.

"Copy that. We'll be airborne in ten mikes. I'll stay in touch," Tillis said.

"Roger that," Brennan said.

Vickers rushed over and sat next to Brennan. "I'm pumped."

"Good."

"So I've been thinking. I hate the name. We need to come up with something tougher, more badass."

Brennan looked at him and asked, "What are you talking about?"

"The name, Unit 5, I hate it. It's fucking boring."

"I think it's cool. Look at SEAL Team Six, just a number."

"Yeah, yeah, yeah, so I'm thinking Team Killer or Task Force Valiant."

"Seriously? Those sound stupid."

"Maybe not those, but you get the point?" Vickers asked.

Klyde hollered over from across the chopper, "Is Vickers boring you with dumbass names for the team?"

"How did you guess?" Brennan shouted back.

"The only stupid name was yours, Klyde," Vickers blurted out.

"Well, your mother liked screaming my name when I was fucking her," Klyde shot back.

"Fuck you, man," Vickers groaned, showing something unusual for him, annoyance.

"Hey, Vick, how about focusing on the task at hand," Brennan recommended.

"I haven't lost focus, just passing time. We've got an hour-plus flight, what else am I supposed to do?"

"Sleep, maybe," Brennan said, pointing across to Dietz, who was already sound asleep.

"Liftoff in two mikes," Tillis said.

Brennan hollered, "Two mikes!"

"You think we'll encounter more of those things?" Vickers asked.

"Who knows, I think you need to be prepared for it."

Vickers smiled and replied, "You know me, Sergeant Brennan. I'm always prepared."

San Diego, California

BRETT WATCHED with fascination as the two media pundits debated the president's recent executive order and the subsequent restraining order against it by a federal judge.

"The president has the clear executive authority as the

commander-in-chief of this country to allow in or block anyone who he thinks threatens our national security. There isn't a debate here, this has been established law for many years," the woman said.

"The only one threatening our national security is the president. His executive order is nothing more than an insult to all Muslims. He has proven once again to be a demagogue. He's disgraceful and thankfully that federal judge has stopped it. Once more, justice has been served," the man countered.

"If there is an attack here and it's carried out by someone from one of these targeted nations, that judge will have blood on his hands," the woman snapped.

"There you go again, always blaming the refugees or immigrants. Studies show that most attacks are committed by US nationals not immigrants," the man replied.

"I know we have trouble with our own people, so why on earth would you import more trouble," the woman countered.

Brett heard Madison's footfalls. Not wanting her to see him engrossed in the show, he turned it off, picked up his phone and pretended to be thumbing through. He was still concerned about the potential of terrorism but having Madison and the boys back made him happy and the last thing he wanted to do was turn the apple cart over.

Madison entered. "When do you go back to work?"

"Oh, next week, I decided to knock out a few honey do's that I've been neglecting."

"So you don't mind if I take your car to work on the first. I need the space to carry some items the foundation is donating," Madison said.

He enjoyed having her and the boys home, so he just agreed without thinking it through. "Sure, that's fine."

"Good, thank you."

"You know, I'm gonna go for a run. When is dinner?"

"In about an hour."

"Good, I'm going to go change and hit the pavement," he said.

She took him by the arm, pulled him close and presented him with a big kiss.

"What's that for?" he asked.

"Do I need a reason to kiss my husband?"

"No."

"I'm just happy and consider it a deposit for later," she said with a wink.

"Oh yeah." He grinned like a schoolboy.

"Now go get your run on."

He gave mock salute and said, "Yes, ma'am."

As he left the kitchen she hollered, "And thanks for getting those honey do's done, whatever they are."

Brett sprinted upstairs, his mood expressing itself in his springy step. He turned towards his bedroom but stopped when he heard the boys chatting. "What are you guys talking about?"

"Daddy, are we going to die?" Will said plainly.

"What?" Brett asked, stunned.

"Eddie says we are."

"I did not, brat. I said we might die," Eddie replied angrily.

"Whoa, whoa, whoa, what is going on?" Brett asked, taking a knee. He looked into Will's tender eyes and said, "Listen, you're not going to die. No one is."

"But, Dad," Eddie barked.

"Not right now," Brett said, giving him a stern look.

"But, Dad, I heard you, and other kids at school are saying it could happen," Eddie continued, ignoring Brett's wishes.

"I don't want to die, Daddy. My birthday is coming up and I want to go to Disneyland," Will cried.

Brett brought him close and whispered, "You're not going to die."

Eddie opened his mouth, but stopped short of saying a word when Brett raised an angry finger and pointed it at him. "This is so stupid. I'm only telling him what I've heard and some of that from you." Eddie stormed off.

Brett put his attention back on Will. He wiped his warm tears and softly said, "Son, you're safe."

"Nothing is going to happen to me, to you or Mommy?"

"No, we're all going to be fine."

"Then why is Eddie lying to me?"

Brett sighed, frustrated that he had to again have this type of conversation. "Eddie isn't lying, he's just...let's just say he's not communicating effectively. He's right that there are bad people and they do hurt people, but we're safe here. We live in a nice area; good people live here."

"But can't the bad people come here?"

"They..." Brett paused. His mind quickly processed the answers that would least upset Will. "The police keep them out."

"Then who painted that thing on the school?"

"Just some silly kid, nothing more," Brett lied.

"Nothing bad is going to happen?"

"No."

"Okay."

"Go to your room and play. I'm going to talk to your brother now," Brett said giving Will a kiss on the forehead.

Will raced off.

Brett went to Eddie's room. The door was closed. He knocked and opened the door. "Hey, buddy, can we talk?"

"No."

Brett entered the room, closing the door behind him. He sat on the bed and watched as Eddie fiddled with Legos. "I want to talk to you about what you told Will."

"I'm not lying, Dad," Eddie growled.

"I know you didn't mean any harm."

Eddie didn't look up or respond.

Brett leaned over and lifted Eddie's head so they could look eye to eye. "You need to be careful what you say to your little brother."

"But it's true."

"To be precise, and I'll do that with you, we really don't know for sure what's going to happen. Some bad people have done some horrible things, but that doesn't mean we're all going to die."

"But I heard you say—"

"I'm not sure what you heard me say exactly, but I don't believe I've said we're going to die. Am I concerned a little bit? Of course, just like I'm concerned about bad people, strangers who like to take little kids. It's the same."

"Why did you and Mommy get into that fight in front of the school?"

"Because I got really nervous, but I don't know for sure anything will happen."

Eddie sat up and stared into Brett's eyes, looking for honesty. "Are we safe?"

Maintaining a poker face, Brett answered, "Yes."

BRETT BOLTED DOWN the hall towards the back door.

"What took you so long?" Madison asked.

"The boys, they were bickering. I had a talk with them," Brett replied. He didn't want to tell her what it was about.

She dipped a spoon into the sauce and sipped, "Mmm, that's good."

"Smells good."

"Hurry back. Dinner will be ready in thirty."

235

"I'll do a quick three miler."

"Before I forget, I was meaning to tell you. The principal sent an e-mail out about that spray-painted hand. The police came back and reported that it's nothing more than a teenager's prank. See I told you, nothing to worry about."

Brett nodded and said, "Thanks for letting me know." In his thoughts, he was highly skeptical but he wouldn't tell that to Madison. He promptly left without saying another word.

London, United Kingdom

"Sir, there's a call on the private line," Harris said, interrupting Jorge.

Jorge hit the mute button on the phone and asked, "Who is it?"

"It's them, sir," Harris said.

"Tell them I'll be right there," Jorge said. He unmuted his other call and said, "Sorry, gentlemen, I have to step off the call. I'll follow up again shortly," Jorge said to the others on the phone before disconnecting.

Harris leaned over the desk and handed him a small mobile phone. "Do you need anything else, sir?"

"Yes, make sure you open a bottle of the Chateau Lafite Rothschild for dinner tonight," Jorge said.

"The 2009?"

"That will be perfect, thank you," Jorge said.

Harris nodded and promptly left Jorge's office.

"Hello," Jorge said.

"You called us," the voice said.

"It's almost May 1 and no word, nothing from you. If May 1 is the day, I need to know now."

"We will let you know, but not by phone."

"You promised I'd meet Israfil."

"And you will, please, Mr. Sorossi, show patience."

Jorge's nostrils flared. "I've held up my end of the bargain, I've given you a ton of cash, I've leveraged my assets in the United States judicial system, gotten politicians to look the other way and obstruct, and right now I have tens of thousands of protestors on the streets, many paid. I've done everything you've asked but I get nothing from you!"

"Mr. Sorossi, you will hear from us soon."

"When?"

"Soon. Now I don't have time for this. Goodbye."

The phone went dead.

In anger, Jorge threw the phone across the room.

Harris entered the room, cleared his throat and asked, "Everything fine, sir?"

"No, it's not."

"Anything I can do to help?"

"If you can conjure up this man Israfil or tell me the exact day my project will start, then yes; otherwise, I'm afraid you can't, old friend."

"Sorry, I can't help, sir."

Jorge sighed.

"Sir, dinner will be served in the green room in thirty minutes," Harris said, turned and walked out.

"One second," Jorge hollered.

"Yes, sir?" Harris asked, turning back around.

"You've been good to me, Harris. I want you to join me."

"Where, sir?"

"Soon the world will become a better place, a more peaceful place, I'd like you there with me...for that world."

"If you wish, sir."

"That will be all, thank you."

Northern Minnesota

"OKAY, FIRST PLATOON, SHOWTIME!" Brennan hollered just before racing down the ramp of the Osprey and onto the gravel lot adjacent to their target building.

Around him the thumping of rotors from multiple Ospreys filled the early evening air.

Soon yelling and screaming sounded all around them.

He crouched, his rifle in his shoulder. "Straight ahead, go!"

First platoon sprinted towards a set of side doors. When they reached them, they stacked up.

Brennan stepped forward, his rifle pointed at the door. "Let's get it open!"

With his SAW slung on his back, Dietz stepped up with a breaching sledge. He swung hard and struck the door near the handle. The door burst inward.

As he always did, Brennan took the lead. He walked into the brightly lit space. Ahead was a long hallway with doorways lining the entire expanse. He stepped to the first door, touched the handle but flinched when a massive explosion from outside shook the entire compound.

"What the hell was that?" Vickers asked.

Klyde, who had the tail end of the stick, called out, "Our bird, it's down, struck by an RPG."

"These motherfuckers have RPGs?" Vickers hollered.

"Shit just got real! Clearing first room," Brennan said kicking in the door.

Sporadic gunfire around the compound rang out.

Brennan entered the first room, followed by two others. "Clear," Brennan called out.

First platoon went from room to room, the cries of 'clear' ringing out.

Brennan ran ahead to the door at the end of the hall. He peeked through a small window to find a stairwell was on the other side. "Stairs, right here!"

His platoon lined up behind him.

Vickers grabbed the handle and threw the door open.

Brennan raced in, his rifle pointed down the concrete steps.

A volley of gunfire cracked from below.

Chunks of cinder block exploded around Brennan. He crouched and maneuvered to a spot where he could get a better vantage point.

Several more volleys rang out. The sound was amplified by the narrow stairwell.

Brennan saw a single man, armed with an AK-style weapon, step out and fire shots toward him. "One guy, two floors down!"

Vickers came into the stairwell. Unafraid, he leaned over the railing and waited, his rifle in his shoulder.

The man stepped out.

Vickers squeezed the trigger of his M4, striking the man squarely in the chest.

The man recoiled and fell backwards.

"He's down!" Vickers called out.

"Moving down," Brennan said, racing down the stairs to the first level down. "I've got a single door."

Gunfire came from the hall. Bullets ripped through the door, striking Lance Corporal Higgins, who was behind Brennan, in the legs.

Higgins collapsed. "Fuck, I'm hit!"

"Corpsman, up!" Brennan called out.

All the men of first platoon repeated the call for the corpsman.

Another volley of bullets ripped through the steel door, this time striking Higgins in the neck and jaw.

"Fuck!" Brennan hollered. He grabbed Higgins by the back of his tactical vest and dragged him clear of the door.

Vickers came down to the landing and pulled a fragmentation grenade from his vest. "Fuck this guy. Frag out!" he yelled as he opened the door and tossed the grenade in.

A loud explosion followed seconds later.

Vickers threw the door open and stepped into the cloud of smoke. He spotted the shooter crawling on the floor. Without a second's hesitation, he squeezed the trigger, putting several well-aimed shots into the man, killing him. He looked around and hollered, "I've got more rooms down here!"

The corpsman sprinted down the stairs to Higgins.

Higgins coughed up blood and wheezed heavily.

"You're going to be okay," Petty Officer Third Class Wendall said, examining Higgins.

Higgins grabbed Wendall by the arm, coughed up a large amount of blood and died.

Brennan and the others in first platoon were already in the hallway, clearing rooms.

"Higgins is KIA," Wendall radioed.

Hearing Wendall's transmission boiled Brennan's blood, but there wasn't time for remorse, they had a mission to complete.

Like the floor above, the offices on this floor were empty except for random furniture.

"Kilo Actual, Kilo Two, I'm hearing a lot of voices down on the third level," Vickers radioed.

"Take your team down. Teams one and three will stay on level two," Brennan replied.

"Roger that," Vickers said.

Brennan watched Vickers and his team disappear back into the stairwell.

Klyde ran up to Brennan, his eyes wide. "You gotta see this." He turned around and headed towards the last doorway on that hall.

Brennan followed on his heels. When he entered the room, he found it was a large laboratory. "Bingo. Okay, guys, pull out your trash bags, start tossing anything that even remotely looks like intel. Bag and tag, boys!"

"Sergeant Brennan, over here!" Klyde called out.

Brennan looked and saw Klyde standing in front of a large walk-in freezer. He rushed over. "What do you have?"

The ground shook.

Both men flinched with Klyde looking towards the drop ceiling. "You suppose they tagged another bird?"

"God knows," Brennan replied. "What do you have in here?"

"Vials, a shit ton of them," Klyde said, pointing inside the twelve-by-twelve-foot walk-in.

Brennan pushed past the thick vertical plastic sheeting and into the bone-chilling space.

Seven-foot-tall metal racks lined the walls. Stacked two deep on the five-shelf racks were boxes marked *Printer / Copier Replacement Toner*. Brennan saw a box open and peered inside to find exactly what Klyde described. He pulled out a single vial and examined it. Inside was a thick brown liquid. There was nothing marking or identifying what it was on the outside. He placed it back and tore open another box. There he found more. He did the same to three other boxes, the contents all the same.

"Kilo Actual, we've got contact, say again, we've got contact with our friends," Vickers radioed.

"Copy that. What's your location?" Brennan replied.

"Level four. They came out of nowhere. We were engaging people. Things went quiet for a moment; then they came at us. It was weird, as if those people were turning into those things, and fast."

"I'll send team three."

"Negative, I'm making the call. We're sealing this floor off, too many."

"Kilo Actual, this is Mike Actual. What's your sit rep?" Owens cut in on the radio.

"Gathering intel on level two. Team two is engaging droolers on level four," Brennan replied to Owens.

"Copy that. We're securing their barracks on the west side of the compound. They're fighting back hard."

"You need us?"

"Negative, get as much intel as you can."

"Owens, be advised. Vickers gave an odd report. He said that at first he was fighting people, things went silent, then those things showed up. He thinks the people mutated."

"Roger that, I'll pass that down. Keep your head on swivel. Out," Owens said.

A scream came from the far end of the hallway and gunfire erupted shortly afterwards.

Brennan turned to Klyde and ordered, "Bag a box. Destroy the rest."

"Copy that," Klyde said.

Brennan ran out of the walk into the hallway.

The gunfire was heavy, as were the screams.

He peered out the door and saw several droolers sprinting from the stairwell.

Several Marines began to engage.

The drooler in the lead was struck. It fell and splayed out in the hall. The one behind it leapt over it, kicked off the wall and hurled itself towards one of the Marines.

Four more droolers burst from the stairwell.

"Where the fuck are they coming from?" Brennan hollered leveling his rifle and shooting.

The second drooler's gymnastic-like maneuvers allowed it to reach Lance Corporal Whitney. With its left hand, it grabbed Whitney by the throat, picked him up, and with its right, thrust it up underneath his vest and body armor into Whitney's lower abdomen.

Whitney cried out in pain.

The drooler twisted and turned its right arm and pulled out a glob of Whitney's intestines.

Brennan aimed and shot, striking the drooler in the head.

It wailed and dropped dead, its right hand still clinging to Whitney's guts.

"Frag out!" a Marine called out, tossing a grenade.

Brennan ducked behind the door jamb.

The grenade detonated with an ear-smashing concussion.

Screams came from within the smoke and haze.

"No, no!" a man cried out then fell silent after the sound of bones crushing.

A screeching wail filled the darkened hall.

Brennan knew it was one of them. The grenade hadn't killed it.

A volley of gunfire rang out followed by the sounds of tussling.

He tried to see but the smoke was still too thick. "First platoon, call out!" Brennan yelled.

Silence.

"Fuck," Brennan said under his breath.

The screeching continued.

Brennan pulled a grenade from his vest, thumbed the clip, pulled the pin and tossed it. "Eat some shrapnel, motherfucker."

Almost instantly the grenade came back, bouncing off the edge of the door jamb.

Seeing the grenade he had just tossed spinning feet from him, Brennan scurried away. He curled up into a ball behind a cabinet.

The grenade went off.

Gunfire came from the far end, near the stairwell.

Brennan heard a thump on the floor. He looked and saw a drooler laid out in the doorway.

"Kilo Actual, this is Kilo Two. What's your location?" Vickers radioed.

"Hunkered down, far room on left," Brennan replied.

"Copy that. You good?"

"Yes."

"All clear in the hall."

"Klyde, you still in the back?" Brennan called out.

"Yep."

"Grab what you have. Let's go," Brennan ordered as he tugged at his MOPP suit collar. "God, I hate this thing. Feels like I'm suffocating."

Klyde stepped out of the back with a large sack slung across his back. He slammed the thick heavy door and hustled away.

A loud thump came from inside the walk-in freezer.

"Good job," Brennan said.

Klyde pointed to the sack. "I feel like Santa Claus."

Brennan led them out of the laboratory, stepping over the dead drooler in the doorway. In the hall they discovered a gruesome scene.

Vickers and several others were gathered at the end of the hallway, guarding the stairwell.

From floor to ceiling, blood, guts and various body parts ranging from small to large covered the entire hallway.

"Where's everyone?" Brennan asked.

Vickers looked back and hollered, "C'mon, Sergeant, hurry up."

Brennan's ears were ringing from the two grenade blasts. He felt something warm and wet sliding down behind his jaw. He reached back, touched it and brought his hand forward. It was blood.

His eyes bounced around the hall. There were so many bodies it was hard to count. "Members of team three, sound off."

Silence.

"Team one?"

"Here," Dietz said, stepping out of a side room, his MOPP suit covered in soot and blood.

"I'm good," Wendall called out. He was two steps behind Dietz.

"And Klyde, you're here, team one is mostly good. Is there anyone at all here from team three?" Brennan said loudly.

No one sounded off.

Vickers looked over his shoulder and said, "We lost one."

"Copy that," Brennan said. "Wendall, see if any of our guys are alive."

Wendall had a shell-shocked look on his face. "Roger that."

Brennan walked up to Vickers and patted him on the shoulder. "I thought there was like six maybe seven of those fucking things, looks more like twenty plus."

"They must have come from up above," Vickers said. "We did our best to clear the other levels below and lock them down. You should've seen it. We were shooting at these raghead bastards, they disappeared into a room, and seconds later those things came running out. They're different too. They're stronger, faster; it was crazy how fast they were."

"I noticed that too. One seemed to walk on the wall before pouncing on Whitney and ripping out his guts with its bare hands. And get this, I tossed a grenade but had it come back at me. I swear the thing caught it and tossed it back at me."

"These droolers aren't like the ones we fought in Somalia," Vickers said.

"I agree, we're dealing with a better...for lack of a better word, version."

"Yep."

"They've got contact above too, same situation. In fact, let me update Owens," Brennan said. He keyed his radio, "Mike Actual, this is Kilo Actual. Come in. Over."

"Go for Mike Actual."

"We've secured this building, have intel, ready to come topside."

"Proceed to the children's housing. We've fallen back there. Hurry," Owens said.

"What's the situation topside?"

"Shit show, it's like we stirred up a hornet's nest. Dozens of droolers. Exit through the east doors, come directly across the parking lot, enter the north entrance," Owens said. *"Gotta go."*

Vickers chuckled and said, "Never a dull moment."

"Never is," Brennan replied.

"But I wouldn't want to be anywhere else, buddy. Now, let's go fuck some shit up."

Rancho Bernardo, California

Mo HAD GIVEN up on school. *Why bother?* he thought. Today he had sequestered himself in his room, playing video games and just relaxing.

He heard his father leave for poker night and wondered if he'd even noticed he hadn't gone to school. Probably not, he mused.

A text popped up.

"Where have you been?" Malik texted.

"Been home, why go to school?" he replied.

"Not like you," Malik said.

"I thought I'd enjoy what time I have."

"Always a Debbie Downer. School is fun. Especially all the easy white girls."

Mo wondered why someone like Malik, who seemed to love

American culture, wanted to destroy it so much. Or was something else driving him? He came from a good family. They had money. He was educated. They didn't want for anything. So what was it?

Mo heard footsteps in the hall. He lowered the phone and readied for his mother to knock and enter, but the footfalls came and went by.

He listened, but nothing. He went back to scrolling through his phone.

A loud knock sounded from the front door.

He sat up and rushed to the window to see who it might be. He peered down and saw it was the UPS delivery driver. He sighed and went back to lounging on his bed. He began to wonder if his mother even knew he was home. That had to be the reason she didn't stop by his room.

Their argument the other night was eating at him. He had to make it right. He tossed his phone on the bed and exited the room. He walked to her bedroom and tapped on the door.

"Who's there?" she asked, her voice showing alarm at someone being there.

"It's me, Mom."

She threw open the door and asked, "Come to apologize to your mother?"

"Yes."

She frowned, a tear in her right eye.

"I, um, wanted to say I love you and I'm sorry for yelling at you," he said, his head lowered.

Her frown became more pronounced as more tears welled up in her eyes. She grabbed and pulled him close. "It's okay, my big and beautiful boy, it's okay."

Knocking again at the front door.

She pulled away and said, "Probably a delivery. I was expecting something."

He stepped out into the hallway and said, "Can't be. I saw them stop by already."

More banging at the door, heavier this time.

He raced down the stairs.

She was fast behind him, curious as to who it could be.

Mo took the doorknob in his grip. He knew who it was.

"Open the door," she said.

"It's them," Mo said.

She placed her hand tenderly on his arm and said, "Open the door, son, and embrace your destiny."

He turned the knob and opened the door. There in front of him stood Kareem and two other men he'd never seen.

Kareem smiled and said, "It's time."

Ramona, California

CASSIDY SAT PARKED in his truck on the street in front of his house. He had spent last night in a hotel and wanted desperately to come home.

He glanced at his phone, the twenty-third time he'd done so in mere minutes, hoping to see a text from Sophie, but like the other twenty-two times, nothing.

He had never seen her so mad, but he prayed that if he could talk with her, he could smooth things over, hence why he sat waiting for her to return home from work.

Growing impatient, he turned on the local talk radio channel.

"Welcome back to our program, tonight in our In-depth segment we'll explore and try to answer the question plaguing the intelligence and law enforcement communities. Who is Israfil? The new terror group The Bloody Hand came on the scene with the grisly Copenhagen terror attacks last week. As the intelligence community strives to find out more about this new

group, one name has surfaced, Israfil. Many believe he is their leader, yet no one has seen him or knows where this mysterious figure came from. Tonight, my guest is Bradley Figueroa, a retired CIA analyst, who will help us go in-depth to unmask who this Israfil just might be..."

A pair of headlights streamed into the cab of his truck. He looked and waited to see if it was Sophie.

The car slowed, but instead of turning, it pulled up alongside him. He caught a glimpse and noticed it was her.

He rolled down his window.

She pulled up beside him and lowered her window. "What are you doing here?"

"Soph, I'm sorry. Please, can we talk?"

"I told you I'd let you know when I was ready. I'm still pissed at you."

"Please, just let me talk to you, try to explain."

"I don't want excuses. I'm hurt that you betrayed my trust. I know you're angry at your old work and I agree that what they did to you was chicken shit, but you turned around and made the problem worse. You just can't let it go."

"I, um, I just wanted a chance to prove I wasn't wrong about that guy."

"You should have thought more about what you were doing. It was already difficult for you to get a job that required a background, now it will be impossible."

"I'll do whatever you say, please."

"You've known me how long?"

Cassidy thought.

"Never mind, it's not important. Don't grovel; don't come over here and do what you're doing now. I can't stand that. What you can do is show me, prove to me you can go get a job. I don't want talk, I want action."

"Can we at least talk?"

249

She put her car into gear and replied, "I need you to be strong. But right now you're being weak."

Those words struck him very hard.

"I want the man in my life to be determined, strong, discipline, focused. I'm not one of these women who want a whiney, groveling and pathetic version of a man. I'm sorry if I'm being harsh. You need to stand up. If you can't do it for me, at least do it for yourself."

"You're saying I'm not a man?"

"Not right now, no."

"That's so messed up."

"I do love you, but I'm at a stage in my life that I want the man I'm with to be just that, a man. Don't come groveling. Don't come begging to come home. Show me you can, prove to me you can get back on the saddle. Maybe my dad spoiled me but he was an inspirational and influential person in my life. He was present and always striving to be better. You know they say little girls end up wanting to marry a guy like their father...and right now, you're nothing like my dad."

Cassidy shook his head in disbelief at the forward and direct way she was confronting him. He loved her and if she wanted him to prove he could stand up on his own, then he would do it. "I hear what you're saying. I'll go be that man. I promise."

She broke a faint smile. "Good. Call me when you've secured a job; then we can talk."

"Okay," he replied.

"And if you want to stay at the house, you can tomorrow night."

"Really?"

"I'm leaving tomorrow for Boise. I'll be gone a few days. The interview is on Monday. I thought I'd see my cousin who lives in Kuna."

"Boise? You're thinking about taking that job?"

"Yeah, I think I need a change. I at least owe it to myself to go see the city, visit the branch office and see if it's something that makes sense."

"How soon would you have to leave if you took the job?" he asked, shocked to hear the news.

"Soon."

"You don't mess around. I screw up and you're now leaving?"

"I just think I need to look, that's all. I need to get away for a few days. Stay at the house while I'm gone. And, Trevor, I do love you, I'm just...what happened with you and the police, it really disappointed me. You know trust is a big thing with me."

"You go from wanting to stay to now possibly moving, in the matter of days."

"Circumstances changed."

"Don't leave. Give me a chance."

"I'm not leaving yet, and I am giving you a chance. Go prove yourself to me," she said, looking at the clock on her dash. "It's late. I'm tired and hungry. Goodnight, Trevor," she said before raising her window and pulling off.

She had risen the stakes for him. If he truly wanted her back, he needed to do not talk. Now was a time for action and he was going to show her he could be that man.

Northern Minnesota

"WHERE'S OWENS?" Brennan asked when he first entered the children's housing, a two-story wood-sided building meant to look like a huge log cabin.

"Roof," the SEAL replied.

Brenna turned to Vickers. "Put the platoon into action; fill in any holes defensively. I'll be right back."

"Copy that," Vickers said.

Brennan raced up the stairs. On the second floor, the sounds of whimpers and cries from children could be heard. He ignored them and proceeded up until he reached the roof. Outside, he heard Owens before seeing him. "Senior Chief, first platoon is here. Where do you need us?"

"Your timing is perfect, there's a lull. For some reason those things stopped attacking us. It's like—"

"They're devising a plan," Brennan interrupted.

"Exactly."

"These things are smarter, stronger, faster. They're not the same things we fought in Somalia," Brennan said.

"Tell me about it. We failed to secure the barracks. Eventually we were pushed back to defending the children's housing. I've called for air support but they're refusing. I've called for evac, but they're working out details to get us out of here," Owens informed him.

"Working out details? What the hell does that mean?" Brennan asked, shocked to hear the update.

"In all the years I've been doing this, I've never heard that. I'm sure it has something to do with the fact we're operating on US soil."

"Ha, they're calculating the political risks now that this has gone sideways," Brennan said.

"Sideways? We aren't finished yet," Owens said.

Brennan peeked over the pony wall and said, "Two downed Ospreys, dozens dead and more injured, I'd say this op has gone sideways."

"I disagree, this is just combat, brother. Thing is, we're finally fighting a formidable enemy," Owens said.

"What's the plan?"

"While we have this lull, we need to get these kids out of here."

"Where?"

"Anyplace but here. There's a school bus parked over there," Owens said, pointing northwest to a building just past the research building Brennan had cleared. "We need that bus to haul these kids out of here."

"Keys?" Brennan asked, looking in the direction Owens pointed; however, he couldn't see the bus from his vantage point.

"A woman, a guidance counselor of sorts, she's been helpful, says the keys are in the main office on the first floor here."

"I'll send Vickers and Dietz," Brennan said.

"Once you get back, we'll load up the kids, and we'll all get the hell out of here."

"Sounds like a plan," Brennan said.

"How's your platoon holding up?"

"Not good, team three is gone, lost one in team two, and I'm down two," Brennan replied.

"Second platoon suffered about the same trying to take those barracks. Third platoon is solid, no fatalities," Owens said.

"I'll get those guys ready to go—"

"Here they COME!" someone hollered out from their rooftop position.

Brennan looked over the wall and saw a wave of droolers racing towards them. He was in awe of their speed.

Gunfire erupted from all positions.

Brennan leveled his rifle and began firing.

The halogen streetlights that lined the compound and the corners of the buildings gave them plenty of illumination to see the droolers.

"Reloading," Brennan cried out as he dropped the empty magazine from his rifle and loaded a fresh one.

"Cease fire, cease fire!" Owens hollered.

The gunfire stopped.

Owens looked out. Drooler bodies lay strewn across the parking lot. "That was fast. I think they're testing our defenses."

"Call command. We need support; we need evac. What happened to them providing local and state law enforcement?"

"I'll try again, but in the meantime, we need to think about getting out of here ourselves. We have the intel, we have the kids, now let's catch a ride."

"You're right. I'll send my guys out ASAP," Brennan said, running off.

THE PLAN WAS SIMPLE. Make a run for the bus and bring it back to the children's housing.

Brennan recruited Dietz, Vickers, Klyde and himself to get the bus. The idea was for Klyde to provide over watch from a building rooftop that overlooked the bus while the three would get to the bus and bring it back. Dietz's primary role was to provide cover on the ground with his SAW if any droolers came their way.

"Klyde, make for that building and get on the roof. Signal us when you're in place. We'll cover you," Brennan said.

"Roger that," Klyde said before sprinting off.

"These keys better work," Vickers said, holding the single key attached to a rabbit's foot. "I never guessed they believed in such things."

"He's made it," Dietz said of Klyde, pointing to the single flash from the rooftop.

"Okay, I'll lead the way. Dietz you'll be last. On the count of three. One, two, three," Brennan said and sprinted from the north door towards the far building.

Vickers and Dietz were right behind him.

Brennan's heart pounded harder with each step he took on

the gravel. The lights of the compound were a blessing and a curse. They had good visual, but that also meant they could be seen.

"Kilo Actual, I'm not sure that bus is going to be adequate," Klyde radioed.

Brennan rounded the corner to find Klyde was right. The bus was there, but it was a short bus and wouldn't hold everyone. He ran for the door and pried it open.

Dietz ran past and took up a defensive position to the west.

Vickers ran onto the bus and got behind the wheel. He inserted the key. "It fits, that's a good sign. Now let's see if she starts."

"Stop talking and get it started," Brennan snapped.

Vickers turned the key and pressed the accelerator.

The bus roared to life.

He looked at Brennan and said, "Everyone on board the short bus!"

"Dietz, come on," Brennan hollered.

Not hesitating, Dietz ran back and jumped on the bus.

"We have movement, west, coming your way," Klyde radioed.

Brennan looked in that direction but couldn't see anything past the shadows. "I've got nothing."

"They're coming. I'm engaging now," Klyde said.

Several shots rang out.

"Get on!" Vickers barked.

Brennan ignored him. He raised his rifle and pointed it west.

Klyde fired again. *"I've got ten, maybe more, coming your way."*

Out of the shadows the droolers emerged.

Brennan aimed and began to fire.

"Sergeant Brennan, get on the bus!" Vickers hollered.

More droolers came.

"Shit!" Brennan yelled. He stepped back and got on the bus. "Drive!"

Vickers slammed on the accelerator; the bus lurched backwards.

Klyde kept firing, but he kept missing the fast-moving targets.

Dietz lowered a window, stuck his SAW out and began to fire.

Vickers was more focused on the advancing droolers, and he didn't see the stacked empty wooden pallets behind him.

The bus crashed into the pallets and came to a full and sudden stop.

Brennan, who had been standing in the open doorway, slammed into the door and fell out of the bus.

Dietz smacked his face against the window, cutting open his forehead.

Unfazed, Vickers put the bus in drive and hit the accelerator.

Brennan jumped up and got his bearings, but not before a drooler was on top of him. "Ah, fuck!" he cried out.

The drooler snapped its jaws as it tried to bite him in the face. The only thing preventing it was Brennan had its neck in his hands and the drooler extended out from his body. "Somebody help!" Brennan called out, feeling his muscles start to give.

A single shot rang out.

The drooler's head exploded. Its body went limp.

Brennan tossed it off him, looked up and saw another only feet away.

Klyde fired again; this shot struck the drooler in the chest. It lunged forward using its momentum and landed on top of Brennan.

Vickers turned the bus around and was headed towards

Brennan. However, he had company now, as several droolers were clinging to the sides.

Brennan found his rifle and began to shoot at the droolers dangling from the bus.

Vickers slammed on the brakes near Brennan.

One drooler lost its grip and fell off.

Brennan quickly shot it several times.

"Get on!" Vickers hollered.

"No, get the bus back, go. I'll cause a diversion!" Brennan yelled before sprinting towards a large metal-sided building.

Vickers hated to leave him, but he sped off.

With Klyde's support, the two droolers hanging on the sides of the bus were shot.

Brennan ran to the building, screaming and hollering with hopes he'd draw the droolers towards him.

It worked. They broke off from pursuing the bus and went after him.

He reached a side door of the building, prayed it was unlocked and tried to open it.

It opened.

He tossed the door open and ran into the darkness. Thinking quickly, he locked the door using a dead bolt. "Klyde, I need you to stay on post. You're my eyes," he radioed.

"I've got you," Klyde called back.

"What's happening?" Brennan asked.

"You know me, Sergeant, I never sugarcoat, so I'll give it to you straight. You're in a bit of trouble."

Chula Vista, California

LIKE THE LAST time he'd been taken, Mo was forced to wear a hood. He hated it. The smell of old sweat, saliva and canvas made for a putrid smell.

The van came to a stop. By Mo's count, this would be the fourth time.

The driver and passenger doors opened and closed.

"I don't think they wash these things," Malik joked.

"Why have us wear them?" an unfamiliar voice asked.

"Precautions, prevents anything bad happening. They're safe, nothing more, don't take it personal," another unfamiliar voice replied.

The side door opened.

"Take off your hoods," Kareem ordered.

Mo did but was greeted by the bright beam of a flashlight. He recoiled and shielded his eyes. "Where are we?"

"No questions, just get out," Kareem said.

Mo, Malik and two others got out and stood in the cool evening air.

"Follow that man inside," Kareem ordered pointing to a long figure walking towards an abandoned warehouse.

Mo glanced around to get his bearings but nothing looked familiar.

Kareem stepped up beside Mo. "I've got my eye on you."

"You do?"

"I don't trust you, but Farouk does, so you're here. I think we should have killed you."

"Oh."

"Where are we?" Mo asked.

Kareem grabbed Mo firmly by the shoulder and spun him around. "Always with the questions. I suggest you just do as we ask, no questions."

"Can't I ask? It's not like I'm going anywhere until we go do what we're going to do," Mo quipped.

Kareem licked his dry lips and said, "This place will be your home, your final home. Here you'll be taught what you need to know about being a martyr for Allah." Kareem spun him towards the building. "It's not much to look at but this will be where you spend your last days. Enjoy them."

Northern Minnesota

BRENNAN STOOD SILENTLY, listening for any sound or movement in the building. In all the confusion and chaos, he didn't think about what might wait for him inside, but he did know what was outside. Never in all his years as a Marine had he felt so alone, so vulnerable.

Growing up, hunting was a part of life. He enjoyed it, but now he felt like the animals he hunted. He was no longer the predator, he was the prey. It was a role reversal he didn't care for one bit.

Tiny fragments of light broke the darkness but wasn't enough to allow him to see anything.

His heart pounded and sweat poured down his face. He'd managed to elude the droolers, but his experience told him his time would run out.

Something stirred outside the door.

He began to walk backwards, unsure of where he was going, putting any distance he could between him and the door.

The door handle jiggled, followed by the sound of nails scraping on the metal door.

Should I just shoot through the door? he thought.

He wasn't completely alone. He had his radio and contact with anyone from Unit 5.

The door handle jiggled more then stopped.

"Kilo Three, status? Over."

No response.

Where are you, Klyde?

He took several more steps backwards and ran into a table. A glass bottle wobbled but didn't fall over.

259

His heart about jumped out of his chest.

"Kilo Three, come in. Over," he said.

No response, the radio was silent.

Is he dead? Did they kill Klyde?

"Mike Actual, this is Kilo Actual. Come in. Over," Brennan radioed Owens.

"Go for Mike Actual," Owens replied.

"I'm in a bit of a situation," Brennan said.

"Talk to me," Owens said.

"I'm stuck in a building. Tangos on the outside. I'm by myself. By last count I think I saw seven, maybe eight."

"Just hold tight. We're loading the bus now. We've had to secure a couple of trucks too, can't fit everyone."

Heavy banging at the door.

"I don't think you understand," Brennan stressed.

Gunfire began to roar in the distance.

"Gotta go. We're under attack again," Owens said and went silent.

"Shit," Brennan said out loud.

He reached back and felt the table behind him. Like a blind person, he navigated his way around it by touch.

"Kilo Actual, Kilo Actual!" the radio boomed. It was Klyde.

Hearing Klyde's voice gave him hope. "I'm blind in here. What's it look like out there?" He anticipated a prompt response but none came. "Damn it, Klyde, you're my eyes. What's going on?"

At first his ears heard a distant patter coming from outside near the door. It grew in volume with each second and kept building and building, like a crescendo.

Brennan knew something was coming.

The sound grew louder.

"Klyde, I hear something. What's happening? Talk to me."

"Run! Run!" Klyde yelled over the radio.

The far wall was hit by what sounded like a wave of bodies all striking it simultaneously.

Brennan did as Klyde said; he turned around and sprinted to the opposite wall. He reached it and began to feel for a door.

The sound of stressed metal tortured his ears.

"Sergeant Brennan, run, fucking run! Get out of there!" Klyde barked.

Gunfire cracked from outside. It was closer than the heavy gunfire in the distance coming from the assault on the children's housing.

Brennan found the door handle, pushed hard and raced out. He ran full force into a drooler.

They both fell.

It stood and shrieked, raising its arms above its head.

He raised his rifle and shot it in the face.

The back of its head exploded and it fell to the ground like a heavy sack.

He got to his feet, looked and saw the west door to the laboratory building.

The door to the building he was just in gave way. A flood of droolers sprinted through it, shrieking and screaming.

He grabbed the handle of the laboratory west door and pulled.

It didn't budge.

Using both hands, he pulled harder.

Still the door wouldn't move.

"Shit!" he hollered.

The shrieks and screams grew louder. They were closing in.

"To your left, small shed!" Klyde hollered over the radio.

Brennan looked. The shed was mere feet from him. He got to it. The single door was open. He stepped in and closed it, but it wouldn't lock.

Heavy footfalls, panting and growls came from outside the shed.

Several shots sounded.

A heavy thump hit the ground just outside the door of the shed. Klyde was back in action and providing much-needed cover.

More gunfire.

The footfalls moved away from the shed door.

Brennan closed his eyes, slowed his breathing and prayed. The funny thing was, he had nothing else but prayer, because if they found him, he'd be dead.

BRENNAN WASN'T sure how much time had gone by, but when he felt confident the droolers had moved on, he radioed out. "Mike Actual, this is Kilo Actual. Come in. Over."

"Go for Mike Actual," Owens replied.

"What's the situation out there?"

"Where are you?"

"Still locked in a small shed."

"Get your ass out of there and get back here. The bus has left; all the kids are gone. I'm here with a few stragglers, some women staff members. We're loading up in trucks. We managed to repel the last assault, but if they come at us again like last time, we might not be able to stop them."

Brennan pushed the door open slightly. He peeked through the crack. "Kilo Two, do you see anything?"

"Negative, you're clear," Klyde answered.

Brennan opened the door enough for him to slip out. He looked in both directions. Seeing it was clear, he started for the children's housing.

"Kilo Actual, contact left, I say again, contact left. You've got three tangos," Klyde said.

Knowing he couldn't outrun them, Brennan took up a defensive position behind several fifty-five-gallon drums and leveled his rifle in their direction. "I see them. Damn they're so fast!"

Klyde fired first. The seven-point-six-two-round from his rifle struck the lead drooler. It fell and splayed out on the gravel.

Brennan put his reticle on the next one and squeezed. The round struck the drooler squarely in the chest.

"Good shot, Sergeant," Klyde said.

"I've got this one too," Brennan said and released another well-placed shot.

The drooler flinched and fell dead.

"Damn good shooting!" Klyde said.

"Can you all stop patting each other on the back and get back here," Owens chimed in.

"Heading in your direction now," Brennan said. He stood and began the trek back.

"Sergeant Brennan, stop! I'm counting multiple tangos heading your way," Klyde radioed.

"How many?" Brennan asked.

"Too many to count, I believe they're heading towards the housing for an assault. Mike Actual, do you copy? Over," Klyde said.

"I copy, multiple tangos. Are they coming towards the north entrance? Over," Owens asked.

"Affirmative. Kilo Actual, you need to find a place to hide. You'll never make it, they're coming in fast," Klyde said.

"I'm tired of hiding, I prefer a good fight. And when are we going to get some damn support here?" Brennan barked.

"I'm contacting command now," Owens replied.

"Sergeant Brennan, you're not going to make it. You need to take cover, now!" Klyde said.

Brennan looked around, the north entrance to the research laboratory was the only thing close by. He ran for it. The door was open.

"Kilo Actual, they spotted you going in. A few have broken off to pursue," Klyde said. *"I'll work my magic from out here."* Klyde aimed and let a round fly.

Brennan didn't remember this wing of the research laboratory. Had they not secured this? Uneasy, he had his rifle at the ready. The bright fluorescent lights bounced off the white eggshell-white walls and garish white tiled floor.

Single gunshots sounded from outside.

"They're at your door," Klyde said.

Brennan hadn't yet cleared the hall. He turned to see two droolers coming through the door. He fired at them.

It took more than a few hits to take them down.

The door opened again, and several more came through.

"Kilo Actual and Mike Actual, I'm counting nearly forty tangos with about fifteen coming after you, Kilo," Klyde radioed.

Unable to reply, Brennan stood his ground and fired at anything that entered the building. By his count he had downed seven when his bolt locked to the rear. He reached for a fresh magazine but found none. He dropped his rifle, letting the two-point sling hold it in front of his body as he transitioned to his Beretta 92F, nine millimeter. He aimed and began to fire.

The pistol proved not to be as effective. He went through a single magazine and only stopped one. He reloaded and began to fire again.

Seeing he was now at a great disadvantage, he turned and ran into the stairwell. Again, he didn't remember seeing this stairwell. Somehow, his platoon hadn't been in this wing of the laboratory. For him, there was no time to fret, he was out of rifle ammunition, had no grenades and only three fifteen-round pistol magazines left. To put it plainly, he knew he was in trouble.

He sprinted down the stairs to the second level, stopping only to peek through the small window in the door to ensure he wasn't walking into more droolers or terrorists, as if they were any different.

The hall was clear. He threw the door open and ran inside. The last thing he wanted to do was get trapped inside a room with no secondary exit.

"*Kilo Actual, what's your location? Over,*" Owens asked.

"Second level of the lab building, but in a wing we didn't clear. Over," Brennan replied.

"*I've got some good news and some bad news,*" Owens said.

"I always like my bad news first, makes the good that much better when I hear it," Brennan said scouting each room.

"*Command is sending support...*" Owens said.

"I said the bad news first," Brennan said.

"*I'll rephrase it, command is going to level this entire compound,*" Owens informed him.

"Still, that's not bad news."

"*The air is heading here now. They'll be on station in five mikes. Can you make it to us in time? I need to get these noncombatants out of here,*" Owens said.

"Um, one sec. Kilo Three, what's going on?"

"*All forty of those things went into your building. Apparently, they like you. Mike, you're clear, no tangos coming your way,*" Klyde said.

"*Brennan, I don't want to leave you, but can you get out of there and topside? You've got four mikes to get here,*" Owens said.

Brennan stopped and leaned against the wall, deflated by the news. "You said I had five mikes."

"We need a minute to be clear of the ordnance," Owens said.

"Sergeant Brennan, I'm coming to get you out of there," Klyde said.

"No, go link up with Mike Actual. Get out of here," Brennan said.

"Negative, you're my brother. I'm coming for you," Klyde said.

The stairwell door burst open; droolers began to pour through.

Brennan turned and started to fire. He turned and ran into a room and closed the door. He shoved a desk and other furniture behind the door. When he looked, he noticed the room was a laboratory like the one where they had found the cases of vials. He ran to the back and found a walk-in freezer.

The droolers pounded and clawed at the door.

"I'm on the first floor, heading to the stairwell," Klyde said.

"Negative, Klyde, go. I'm screwed. I'm not getting out of here. The best thing I can do is find a place to hunker down. Maybe I'll survive the bombardment."

"No, I'm not leaving you. You wouldn't leave me," Klyde replied. *"I'm in the stairwell."*

Brennan could hear Klyde's gunfire.

"I'm drawing them to me. They're coming up. Christ, they're so fast," Klyde said.

"Air will be on station in two mikes. What's your situation? Over," Owens asked.

"Go, get out of here. I'll never make it to you. I'm going to barricade myself in this freezer and pray it protects me," Brennan said, entering the walk-in.

"Mike Actual, I'm heading your way. They're coming after me now," Klyde said, out of breath.

Brennan closed the freezer door and got comfortable. There

wasn't much else he could do now. "Kilo Three, what's your situation? Over," Brennan asked.

No response.

"Kilo Three, Klyde, come in. Over," Brennan radioed.

Nothing.

"Kilo Actual, Kilo Three is down," Owens said. *"We're oscar mike, those things are coming after us. You might be clear. Kilo Three drew them out of that building,"* Owens said.

Brennan lowered his head in despair. He couldn't believe Klyde was gone.

"Air on station in sixty seconds," Owens said. *"Sorry."*

"No need to apologize, it's all in the job description. Get those civilians clear. Take care, my friend," Brennan said.

"You'll be fine, you've got a hard head. It'll take a big bomb to crack that skull," Owens joked.

Brennan knew his odds were slim. Command knew this building was a massive subterranean structure and would drop a bunker buster. His thoughts went to Jenna. He prayed she was fine and, if he didn't survive, she'd find love again. He wondered what his baby would look like, a thought all parents have. Would the child look like him or her? How would they sound when they first started to talk?

The first bomb hit. The ground shook.

Brennan looked up instinctually.

The second bomb struck and all the lights went dark.

He now sat in the pitch black and began to wager with himself which one would be the bunker buster that would hit his building. Bomb number three, four, maybe five or six.

The building shook violently. The ceiling caved in on top of him, a large chunk of something struck him in the back of the head and out he went.

OWENS WATCHED the bright flashes of the explosions in the rearview mirror. Leaving Brennan was one of the toughest things he'd ever done.. Brennan was right though, it was all part of the job. Getting the civilian noncombatants to safety wasn't their first priority, but it did rank high.

"Kilo Actual, come in. Over," Owens radioed.

No response.

"Brennan, are you there? Over."

Silence.

The truck shook.

Owens looked out and saw a drooler clinging to the side. "You bastards are relentless."

A loud thump struck the passenger side.

He looked and saw one staring at him through the side window. He raised his rifle and fired at it.

The rear window exploded as one leapt into the truck. It scaled the seats and jumped in the passenger seat.

Owens drew his pistol and shot, striking it in the head.

The drooler shrieked and began to flail.

He lifted his foot off the accelerator, raised his leg and kicked it hard. The door flew open and the thing fell out.

The one on the driver's side punched through his side window and grabbed the wheel. It pushed it hard to the right.

Owens put his pistol to its head and pulled the trigger.

Its head exploded and it fell off the car.

He looked in the side mirror and saw it tumbling on the road. He put his eyes on the front and saw the guardrail coming towards him fast. He hit the brakes, but it was too late.

The truck slammed into the guardrail, coming to a full stop.

His head bounced off the steering wheel, knocking him out.

CHAPTER NINE

Saturday, April 29
London, United Kingdom

JORGE LOOKED at the handwritten note. His hands were shaking. He picked up the phone and dialed. "Answer the phone, damn it."

The phone connected.

"Bradley Shipman, Infinity Wealth Management, how can I help you?"

"I need you to sell everything. Put all my accounts to cash."

"I'm sorry, who am I speaking with?" Shipman asked.

"This is Jorge Sorossi."

"Oh, Mr. Sorossi, hello. I'm sorry, I don't understand," Shipman said.

Jorge stood from his desk and walked to the expansive window in his office. He looked out. His hands were sweating. "Liquidate everything. Put it all to cash."

"Mr. Sorossi, are you sure you want to do that?"

"Just do as I ask. I then want you to transfer those monies to my Cayman account."

"Yes, sir. I'll forward the documentation immediately."

"Send it to my confidential email. The encrypted one," Jorge ordered.

"Of course, sir."

"Thank you, Bradley," Jorge said.

"Will there be anything else, sir?"

Jorge lowered his voice and asked, "Do you have any family, you know, kids?"

"I do."

"I know it's weird I'm asking. I just never knew. You've handled my personal portfolio for years and I've never thought to ask."

"Two little girls, six and eight."

"How sweet."

"Thank you. Now is there anything else I can help you with today?"

"Ah, no."

"Have a good day, sir."

"Hold on, Bradley. Take a holiday with your family. Get out of the city."

"Excuse me?"

"Take a holiday with your family. Take them to the coast or north to Scotland for a couple of weeks. In fact, I want to cover the costs. You've been so good to me over the years."

"I'm sorry, Mr. Sorossi, but I can't. My firm has a lot going on. I'm afraid any holidays for me and my family won't be until later this year."

"You don't understand, you need to get your family and leave the city."

"Excuse me? I'm sorry, sir, I don't understand what you're trying to tell me," Shipman said, confused.

A strong sense of sentiment hit Jorge; he again pleaded for Shipman to leave. "I'm paying for it, take advantage, go, leave the city. I'll have a car service take you and your family to the coast in Wessex. I have a nice cottage over there you can use."

"*I'd love to take you up on that, but the timing just isn't right, Mr. Sorossi. You're very generous but I can't.*"

Jorge gripped the phone tight. He wanted to tell him but stopped just short of doing so.

The phone suddenly went dead.

Jorge turned around to find his assistant hovering over the phone's receiver, his finger pressed down on the switch hook. "What are you doing?"

"Saving you from making a mistake this close to the finish line, sir."

Jorge looked down at the handset in his hands and let out a heavy sigh. "God, you're right. I just was overcome with a wave of odd emotions for the man. He has been so nice to me over the years. I just thought..."

"Forgive me, sir, but you weren't thinking."

"You're right, thank you, Harris. You're another person who's been indispensable. I don't know what I would have done without you."

"It's been my pleasure."

Jorge walked back to his desk and put the phone back on the receiver. He picked up the note next to it and reread it.

Notre Dame, Paris, tomorrow, 1015, fifth pew on left from the back. Israfil will be waiting. Look for a man wearing a red shirt.

"Sir, shall I pour you a glass of scotch?"

"Are my bags packed like I asked?"

"Yes, sir."

"Contact the crew of my G-4. I want to leave for Paris first thing in the morning. Arrange a car for our arrival."

"Yes, sir, and will I be going too?" Harris asked, wondering if this was the *trip* Jorge had mentioned before.

"Yes, from there we'll head to George Town, Grand Cayman."

Harris nodded. He turned to leave but stopped. "Is this it, sir?"

"Meaning?"

"Your project, sir?"

Jorge took a lighter from his top desk drawer and flicked it on. He ran the orange flame beneath the note until it caught fire. He held it in his hands until he could no longer, tossing the charred and blackened remains into the metal waste bin. He looked at Harris and replied, "Yes, the hour is almost here."

Chula Vista, California

Mo OPENED his eyes but he couldn't see a thing. The room was pitch black, not even a sliver of light was coming in from anywhere.

Frightened by his situation, he called out, "Is anyone there?"

"Yes, I'm here," Malik said from a far corner.

"Where are we?" Mo asked.

Another voice called out from the darkness, "We're in a holding room. You're not alone. I was just brought here maybe an hour ago. There's five others in here with us."

"What's your name?" Mo asked.

"Saleem and yours?"

"Mo...Mohammed," Mo replied.

"I'm Malik," Malik said from his corner.

"I'm Amir," a voice said near Malik.

"Anyone else?" Mo asked.

"Ssh, I'm trying to sleep," a voice grumbled.

"That's my brother Rahim. He's always an asshole. I'm Razi."

"That's six. Who is number seven?"

"I agree with Rahim. Can everyone shut up," a voice mumbled near Mo.

"What's your name, friend?" Mo asked.

"Lateef, now shut up. We have a long night ahead of us," Lateef said.

"Were you all with us that one night?" Mo asked.

"The night that Mohammed got his head cut off?" Saleem asked.

"Yes, that night," Mo replied.

Around the darkened room, everyone said, "Yes."

"Just seven of us, is that all?" Mo asked.

"Mo, Mohammed, whatever you call yourself, shut up, I'm tired and I don't want to hear you wetting your pants over there," Lateef snarked.

"I'm not wetting my pants," Mo challenged.

"I can hear it in your voice, you're practically in tears. You don't like dark rooms. I bet your mommy leaves a night light on for you," Lateef mocked.

"Shut up," Mo shot back.

"I will if you will," Lateef said.

"You're an asshole," Mo snapped.

"And you're a pussy. Probably a homo, we should toss you off the top of this building instead of taking you with us." Lateef laughed.

"Fuck you," Mo said.

"I bet you want to," Lateef chided.

Mo didn't reply. He sat immersed in total darkness, stewing.

Loud creaking, like the sound of metal scraping against itself, came from the far side of the room. A thump followed; then daylight spilled into the room.

Everyone shielded their eyes.

"Oh, c'mon, I need more sleep," Lateef complained.

Kareem stepped into the room. "Time to get up. We have much to do."

Paris, France

DAVID COULDN'T WAIT ANY LONGER. He had spent the entire day waiting for Joram to return, but he didn't. He shrugged it off and exited his apartment. Joram had shown he could gain access, so he didn't need to be there if he did come by.

He walked onto the bustling street. It was evening, but Paris was like New York, it never slept. He turned right and headed for his favorite local café, there he'd be able to get a glass of wine and indulge in a delicacy, foie gras.

He reached the intersection but as he stepped to cross, a black sedan pulled up. The doors opened and several men stepped out. They grabbed him and shoved him into the car. The car sped off.

"What the hell?" he barked, lashing out at his abductors.

"Take it easy, David," Grim said from the front seat. He turned around and gave David a smile. "I hope we didn't disturb your dinner."

"What do you want? I told you I wasn't going to cooperate."

"We tracked your friend here. Have you met with him?" Grim asked.

"I don't know what you're talking about?"

The car made a hard right and accelerated.

"I tried to be nice, but Joram is a dangerous man."

"I haven't seen him since Ankara."

"Right now, this very second, Homeland is combing through a compound in northern Minnesota. This wasn't some random day camp, it was a terror base and distribution center. In Texas yesterday, our forces took down a transport center. Do you know what they were transporting? Hmm?"

David straightened his clothes and said, "I'm sure you're about to tell me."

"A bioweapon, we're sending it to our labs to learn more about it. In Minnesota we lost a lot of men. I won't go into further detail but if you're talking to Joram, you need to tell us. We need him, we need him to tell us who Israfil is and where we can find him. A major attack is coming and we're just pecking along at the edges of it. All of this is happening while our resources in the States are tapped dealing with these leftist protestors. We're desperate, David. We need you more than ever."

"I imagine you were watching my apartment, so you'd know if he came to visit me or not."

"We have been watching but we haven't seen him, unless you're hiding him, hence why when you return to your place, you'll find we visited."

"Oh c'mon, are you trashing my place?"

"Sorry, but you left us with no other recourse."

"Tell me, what is this bioweapon?" David asked.

"It's classified, but I will tell you it's lethal. We need to find Joram. He and he alone can lead us to Israfil. At least find out, if you talk to him, when they might be planning their attack."

"I said I haven't been in contact since Ankara. Now drop me off at the corner, I'm done with this interrogation unless you plan on using enhanced techniques. I know how much you agency guys love to use them."

Grim looked at the driver. "Pull over."

The car swerved to the right and stopped suddenly.

David was sandwiched in between two men. The man on the right got out of the car, allowing David to exit.

Grim grabbed David's arm. "I hate begging, but we're coming up with nothing. We hear the chatter but we don't know anything; these Bloody Hand people are tight as a virgin."

"Nice metaphor," David mocked.

Grim wouldn't let go. "Help us and we'll help you with your project. I can get access to info that will be beneficial for your documentary, I'll make sure of that."

"I'll think about it, but the problem is I haven't seen him. Good night," David snarked and got out of the car.

Grim rolled down the window and said, "I know you're lying, and if this attack happens and you could have helped stop it, there will be blood on your hands. Just know that."

David raised his hands and quipped, "Look clean to me."

"He's playing you, David. You're playing the part he wants you to play. You just don't see it, you can't. You're blinded by your own selfishness. Just remember, if something happens and we find out for sure you were in contact, I'll make sure you disappear into the blackest of sites in some shit-hole country you've never heard of."

"Nice to see you too." David waved.

Grim shook his head. "At least take this. We know you destroyed your phone," he said, handing him a small flip phone.

"How did you know?"

"Do you have to ask?"

David took the phone.

"You still have time to do the right thing, David, just remember that," Grim said.

The car took off.

David watched it turn and disappear. His bravado slipped away into heavy breathing and panic. *Is Grim telling me the truth? Am I being played?* Now that his apartment building was being watched, how would he get in contact with Joram? His hunger was gone. All he could think about was Joram and finishing his interview. He turned around and raced back home.

Northern Minnesota

276

OWENS WOKE WITH A GASP.

Where am I? What happened? He hastily looked around but his vision was blurred. He then remembered the fierce battle at the compound, leaving, then *boom*, the crash.

He repeatedly blinked until his eyes focused. He looked through the shattered windshield and saw gray smoke coming from the crushed engine compartment.

He then remembered losing control after several droolers attacked him on the road. He peered beyond the crumpled hood. *Where am I?*

He quickly examined himself, but didn't find any broken bones or puncture wounds. He tried to open the door but it was stuck, no doubt the result of the collision with the guardrail. The metal screamed as he pushed hard against the door. Inch by inch the door creaked open until it was wide enough for him to slip out.

He stood on the deserted road. The sun was high, signaling it was midday. Off in the distance he heard the roar of water. *A river or stream?*

An eerie sensation suddenly gripped him, sending shivers down his spine. He paused to listen, but he heard nothing, absolutely nothing.

The forest and surrounding area were deathly quiet; nothing moved. *Where are the birds?* They and all manner of creature sat silent.

His eyes widened when the answer came.

The animals were hiding from them.

With his sixth sense on high alert, he scanned the area. He knew he wasn't alone.

Are they watching and waiting? These questions plagued him, but his gut and crawling skin screamed loudly, *They are there.*

He pressed his eyes shut tight and listened more closely.

Nothing.

He took a few steps, stopped and listened while his eyes scanned the opposing tree line and slope.

A loud pop and crack echoed from further down the road.

He looked carefully towards the direction of the sounds, but saw nothing.

Up and down and back and forth, his eyes scanned each branch, rock, and tree trunk, but still he saw nothing unusual or out of place.

A strong uneasy feeling struck him. He turned back and grabbed his rifle. With a gentle tug, he pulled the bolt back to find a round was seated in the breech. He pushed it back and tapped the forward assist.

A subtle movement across the road caught his attention. He stared intently, examining each inch. Then he saw it, a pair of eyes fixed on him from behind a thick bush.

He recoiled from the sight, raised his rifle and flicked the selector switch to semi-auto.

A lone figure emerged from behind the bushes and stepped onto the road. It was one of them, but its actions were different than the others he'd encountered. It didn't rush him or signal it was about to attack.

Owens' instincts were telling him to run, but he stood fast. He gripped the rifle tighter, keeping the reticle of his optics squarely on its chest.

The drooler tensed its body before releasing a guttural scream. It cocked its head to the left, then to the right and let out a series of wails.

It was a unique cry, nothing he'd ever heard before.

Why is it just standing there? Owens thought. His palms began to sweat. The thing freaked him out, more because it was just standing there, both of them locked in a deathly staring contest. Owens index finger touched the trigger. He began to apply pressure. "Time to get smoked, motherfucker."

Loud crashing sounded around him.

There are more? he thought, and just like that, his thoughts were answered. The opposing tree line came alive. One by one, droolers stepped out and onto the road. They fell in behind the first one and stood, their chests heaving, mouths open, drool dripping out onto their tattered clothes.

Owens had first experienced this level of discipline the night before when they'd tested their defenses and later attacked the obvious weak positions later.

The first drooler grunted several times.

Owens watched with a tinge of curiosity as the others began to shuffle and line up alongside the first one. *They're taking cues.* This told him everything he needed to know. The first was their leader, a weird thing to think, but that would be his initial target.

When the last one stepped out, Owens peered over his rifle at what he knew was his fate. He quickly counted, twenty-three, not a lot but more than he'd be able to handle.

Owens sighed loudly as the reality sank in that this was it, this was his last stand. He'd never see his friends or family again. How weird it was to know your own death was coming and that it would be brutal and violent. Resolved to his situation, he decided he wasn't going down without a fight.

"Come on, you motherfuckers!" Owens screamed as he took a step towards them. His gut tightened and a cold sweat began to bead on his forehead. He gripped the rifle firmly and put the reticle of the optics back on the chest of the leader.

The leader examined Owens intently. Besides its eyes moving, it remained as still as a statue while the others behind it weaved, bobbed and fidgeted with pent-up anger and blood rage.

"Come on!" Owens barked.

The leader raised its head and howled loudly.

"Come on, you fucker!" Owens screamed.

Making his first move, the leader broke his stoic stature and raised his arms.

"This is it. Who would have thought I'd be eaten by monsters." Owens laughed out loud. He firmly squeezed the forearm of the rifle, readied himself and recited the prayer Brennan had taught him, "Lord, make me fast and accurate. Let my aim be true and my hand faster than those who wish to harm me and mine. Lord, if today is truly the day you are to call me home, let me die in a pile of brass."

The leader shrieked and lowered his arms. The others raced towards Owens.

Just before Owens squeezed off the first round, he swore the leader smiled, but he wasn't sure. His first shot struck it in the chest squarely. He took aim on another and fired, then another and another.

Pop.

Pop.

Pop.

Pop...

La Jolla, California

SUSPECTED TERROR-RELATED INCIDENT IN MINNESOTA flashed as a news notification on Brett's phone, making him anxious. He picked it up and unlocked his phone to read more about the story.

Madison saw Brett out of the corner of her eye. She leaned over and whispered, "Don't be rude. We're out to dinner with friends."

Brett skimmed through the story and got the information he

was looking for before turning his phone off. He looked up to the couple they were having dinner with, Michelle and Tom Finton. "Sorry, guys, my curiosity got the better of me. Won't happen again."

Tom leaned in and asked, "Now I'm curious. What was it?"

"Nothing. Just silly stuff," Madison chimed.

Brett cut her a look.

"Oops, I saw that. What is it?" Michelle asked.

"It really is nothing," Brett said. "I saw a news flash about another terror incident, this one in Minnesota."

"Brett," Madison groaned.

"I swear, every time I turn on the news, there's another terror attack," Tom said.

"Right," Brett replied.

The waiter approached the table. "Good evening, folks. Can I get you started with a drink or cocktail?"

Madison breathed a sigh of relief. She'd take this interruption to turn the topic to cocktails and the restaurant in general. "Tell us about your specialty drinks."

The waiter rattled off a small list.

"I think I'll try that jalapeno margarita," Madison gushed.

"Good choice," the waiter said.

"I'll just take the IPA," Brett said.

"Me too," Tom said.

"And you?" the waiter asked Michelle.

"I'll just have a vodka gimlet, please," Michelle answered.

"Sounds good. I'll be right back with those," the waiter said and walked off.

"Thanks for making the reservation. I've been looking forward to coming to this place," Tom said.

"Me too. Um, Tom, how's business?" Madison said.

"Good, can't complain. But I'm still curious about what we were talking about before."

Tom's answer deflated Madison. The last thing she wanted tonight was to talk about terrorism.

"What I read happened in Minnesota is interesting. They're not saying too much, but it appears the military conducted a raid on a property. They said something about it being a possible training camp," Brett said.

"A training camp in the States, crazy," Tom said.

"Scary is what it is," Brett said.

"Agree, but our military will take care of us. I'm not too concerned," Tom said.

The waiter approached and set the drinks down. "Are you ready to order a starter?"

"Yes, we'll take the calamari," Madison answered.

"Good choice," the waiter said and walked off.

"So you don't think we should do anything to protect ourselves?" Brett asked.

"I'm not saying that. I believe we should do what we can, but what are you asking me? Should I go out and hunt terrorists?" Tom asked.

"Not that. I'm saying—"

"What Brett is saying is you should get a gun, tons of survival gear and be prepared to fight a terrorist on every corner," Madison said mockingly.

"I don't believe that," Brett challenged her.

"Yes, you do!" Madison said, her voiced raised.

"No, I don't. I just think—" Brett said but was cut off.

"Did you know he bought a gun after that terror attack in Copenhagen. He thinks he needs a gun to protect us from terrorist, like ISIS wants to come to our home and kill us."

"They do want to kill us," Brett said.

"They want to kill us? Like we're so special," Madison snarked.

"I'm not saying they want to kill us because they know who

we are, but they, the terrorists, want to kill us because we're Americans. I'm not saying we're special."

Tom and Michelle sat back and uncomfortably watched Brett and Madison argue.

"Can you believe he bought a gun without telling me and ordered thousands of dollars' worth of freeze dried food, sleeping bags, tents, a bunch of survival stuff, like we're going to have to live in the woods after the scary terrorists try to kill us," Madison mocked.

"Enough," Brett shot back.

"We're trying to enjoy a night out and you just can't stop talking terror this, terror that. You're right, enough already," Madison said loudly.

Brett fumed.

The waiter walked up. "Okay, folks, have you had a chance to look at the menu?"

"No, come back in a few," Brett barked.

The waiter raised his brow and said, "Okay, I'll come back."

Tom leaned in and joked, "How about those Padres?"

Madison folded her arms and huffed.

"Sorry, guys, we've been debating this issue since my brother was almost killed in Copenhagen," Brett said.

"Your brother almost died in Copenhagen?" Tom asked, curious.

"I've had enough. Michelle, you want to go to the bar? How about you boys get me when you're done talking about this stupid shit?" Madison snapped and stood up. She tossed her napkin on the table and stormed off.

"Madison, come back," Brett said.

"I'll go check on her," Michelle said. Getting up, she hurried off behind Madison.

Brett scowled and said, "Sorry you had to experience that."

"Oh, shit, that's nothing. You should see Michelle and I go

at it. The thing is it's over a topic not as exciting or important. She'll ride my ass over the trash cans getting left out too long." Tom laughed.

Brett chuckled, but he couldn't help but regret getting into a fight with Madison. He had wanted a nice evening, but of course his obsession with all the recent events had proven to be too much for his relationship once more. She was right; he should have just ignored his phone. Timing was everything and he knew that. He also messed up by entertaining the conversation with Tom. He should have just dropped it, but he didn't imagine she would lose it. He had calculated wrong and it backfired.

Michelle walked back. "She'll be fine. She just needs a minute."

The waiter returned with the calamari. He placed it on the table and said, "Enjoy."

Tonight was supposed to be one of those moments for he and Madison to *enjoy* but again it was spoiled. He needed to find a way to balance his concerns about the current affairs of the world with his private life or he'd lose the latter.

Chula Vista, California

"WE'RE A TEAM," Malik said, smiling.

Mo gave Malik a lukewarm smile as he gave Malik a once-over. "You literally look like a terrorist."

"Terrorist, no, I'm a holy warrior. You really need to stop talking like them," Malik warned.

"But you look like a—"

Malik put his hand over Mo's mouth. "You don't sound like one of us. If you're not going to say something fitting, don't say anything at all."

Mo nodded.

"It fits good," Malik said, admiring his suicide vest and belt, minus the explosives.

"How do you feel knowing you'll be blown to a million pieces soon?" Mo asked.

Malik sighed and asked, "You're not going to stop, are you?"

"What? It's a legitimate question."

"No, you should be asking how does it feel to know you'll be blessed by Allah with seventy-two virgins?"

Mo turned away from Malik and put his attention on the AK-47-style rifle on the table. He had spent the better part of two hours learning how it worked. He had been given a vest to wear as well, but his would be loaded with loaded magazines.

Malik walked up to the table and picked up his rifle. "This is so cool. I finally get to shoot a machine gun. I'm so excited." He put the rifle in his shoulder and pretended to shoot. "Pew, pew, pew. Die, infidels, die."

Mo looked around the room. It was stark, the white walls barren except for a white dry-erase board, and the only things in the room were a dozen chairs and four folding tables. The seven had been divided into three teams with the one odd man, Lateef, being chosen as the driver. No one yet knew the target or when they'd launch their attack.

The door opened and in came Kareem and Farouk.

Kareem took a seat in the corner while Farouk walked to the front of the room, stopping in front of the dry-erase board. "How is everyone doing?"

In unison, everyone replied, "Good."

"Take a seat," Farouk said.

Everyone did as they were told.

"First, let me thank you for what you're about to do. You are holy warriors, mujahedeen of The Bloody Hand. Allah thanks you and will bless you and your families for your sacrifice, your martyrdom. The hour is now very near. We have received the call from our holy imam, the last of his line, to assemble. Soon we will strike out at the infidel. It will be a glorious attack, one that will finally destroy our adversary and usher in the great caliphate," Farouk said, his chest puffed.

He turned to the dry-erase board, took a marker and began to draw. He finished and turned back to the seven. "This is our target; it's a school. An elementary school. It is one of the softest targets there is. It's so sad that in America they put more security on a jewelry store than their own children. It tells you a lot about our enemy, doesn't it? We will exploit their incompetence and strike at their heart.

"This is how the attack will proceed. Lateef will drive onto the property here. This is a one-way drop-off lane; it exits here. He will drive a cargo van with you in the back. He will proceed through until he gets to the exit. You will exit and head to the front. You'll find at the hour of our attack, hundreds of children and their parents will be present. Once you're clear of the van, Lateef, you will blow the van. This will prevent anyone from exiting, trapping them there. Lateef, you will begin shooting all those trapped in vehicles behind the van. Two of our teams will head inside the school. Team one, that's the brothers, you will kill everyone at the entrance, then blow yourselves up, again, preventing anyone from fleeing. Inside, the other two teams will split up. One will head to the administration office. There you'll detonate another vest. The last team, Mohammed and Malik, you'll go to their multipurpose room, this is where the children gather in the morning before going to their classrooms. Mohammed, you will escort Malik there, gunning down anyone that gets in your way. Once in the room, Malik, you will blow yourself up. When the bombers are gone, you four remaining with rifles will go classroom to classroom, picking off anyone who is left. You will not have to worry about the police. They will be tied up dealing with protestors. We have assurances that large protests and riots will occur that morning. This will give you plenty of time. It's a very simple plan. Any questions?"

No one raised a hand or said a word.

"I'll repeat it; then one by one, I'll have you come forward and repeat what I've said. You will know this plan inside and out. Do you understand?"

"Yes," they said.

"Good, let me start over again. Lateef, you will drive onto the campus..."

Ramona, California

CASSIDY FOUND it difficult to watch television. Nothing could hold his attention. Even the news reports coming from Minnesota concerning a possible terrorist raid couldn't keep him from thinking about Sophie. He wanted her to be happy above all else, and if that meant her moving to Boise, he'd support her, but he desperately wanted to share in that happiness and be by her side through it.

His phone rang.

He looked and saw it was Sophie. He quickly muted the television and picked it up. "Hello."

"Hi."

"Hi, how are you? Everything good?"

"Yeah, I made it fine. Flight was super easy."

"Good."

Silence.

"Sophie, what's up?"

"I just spoke to my brother. He's got me freaked out."

"What do you mean?"

"He told me to stay in Boise; don't come back. He wouldn't say why."

"He did?"

"I've never heard him sound so...scared. He knows something but won't tell me."

"He didn't give a hint at what it might be?" Cassidy asked although he suspected what it could be.

"Nothing, he just told me that some bad things might happen and that Boise, being a smaller city, would be safer."

"It's terrorism. He must know of a credible threat, one that's imminent. I heard something happened in Minnesota," Cassidy said.

"What else could it be?"

"Listen to him. Stay longer, stay past the interview. Take your time."

"You sure?"

"Yes, your brother is in the know on these things; heed his advice. Make it a little vaca; go see some sights."

"Now I'm really freaked out because you think my brother is right."

"Honey, I don't know anything, but if your brother, who works for Homeland, says not to come back to San Diego for a bit, I'd listen to him."

"Okay, I'll stay longer, through to, say, the second or third. I'll look at changing my return flight," Sophie said.

"Good. Take lots of pictures."

A long pause.

"I wish you were here," she said.

"I can come up," he offered.

"No, I don't want to trouble you."

"It's no trouble at all, plus...if you're moving there, I want to scout possible jobs up there."

"But what about your court hearing?"

"I spoke to my attorney today. Nothing prohibits me from leaving or moving. I just need to come back for the hearing. It's not scheduled for a few more weeks."

"What a total mess." She sighed.

"Sorry."

"Stop apologizing, please. I hate that."

The urge to apologize for apologizing came, but he didn't utter the word. "Let me come up, see Boise, look for something there. I think the change of locales can do us both good."

She paused. *"Sure, come up Monday. My interview is in the morning, downtown. I'm staying at the Marriott. Just take an Uber from the airport."*

"Good, I'll book my tickets as soon as I get off the phone," Cassidy said, his mood lifted.

"And, Trevor, don't think you're off the hook just yet. I need you to take everything I said the other night seriously. I need you to step up," she warned.

"I will, I mean, I am. I'll get a solid job. I'll stop messing up."

"Hey, I've got to go. I'm meeting my cousin for lunch. I'll see you tomorrow afternoon."

"Love you," he said.

Once more she paused before she said, *"Love you, too."*

CHAPTER TEN

Sunday, April 30
Paris, France

THE CAR STOPPED.

Jorge looked out the window at the gothic bell towers of Notre Dame. They stood out against the deep blue sky dotted with puffy white clouds.

"We're here," Harris said, sitting next to Jorge.

"I know, I'm just appreciating the view. Isn't it beautiful?"

"Yes, sir, yes, it is," Harris said.

Jorge looked at his watch, a rare Frank Mueller, and saw it was ten on the nose. "Let's go."

"Shall I join you?" Harris asked.

"Ahh, no, stay here with the car," Jorge said, stepping out. He closed the door and adjusted his slacks before stepping off.

Like any other day, the plaza in front of Notre Dame was bustling with people, many tourists enjoying the vibrancy of Paris.

He weaved his way through the crowds until he reached the

front. A line of people stood waiting to enter. He casually got in line and waited.

The line proceeded slowly, but soon enough he was inside.

He gazed up at the high peaks of the ceiling and the towering stained-glass windows. It was more impressive inside than out. He was amazed at the architectural achievement, especially given that people eight hundred years ago didn't have the tools they had today.

He tore himself away from sightseeing to look for his target, the man in the red shirt. He scanned the back pews, and just as promised, in the fifth pew from the back, a man wearing a red shirt sat.

Jorge made his way toward him.

Seemingly out of nowhere, a man bumped into him.

"Excuse me," Jorge said.

The man kept moving.

Irritated by the lack of manners, he shook his head and continued. He stopped at the end of the fifth row and asked the man in red, "Israfil?"

The man looked up, a perplexed look on his face. "No," the man said, standing. His accent told Jorge he was French not Muslim. He handed Jorge a small package. "This is for you."

"What is it?" Jorge asked, looking down at the taped cardboard box. It was heavy, oddly heavy, in fact, for something as small as it was. An envelope was taped to the top of the box.

The man pushed past Jorge and hurried away.

"Hey, where are you going? Where's Israfil?"

Not stopping, the man disappeared into a crowd of people.

Jorge shook the box. Nothing moved or shifted. He sat down, placed the box next to him and removed the envelope off the top. He tore it open and pulled out a single folded page. He unfolded it.

The note read, *"Thank you, Mr. Sorossi, for everything.*

Without your help we could not have achieved our mutual goals. Allah blesses you with goodness."

Jorge flipped the page over. Nothing was there. Frustration rose inside him. Where was Israfil? He was promised he'd get to meet him. He crumpled the note and tossed it on the floor. He pulled his phone from his sports coat pocket. He was going to call and voice his opposition when the box caught his eye. He lowered his phone.

Curiosity grew as he wondered what could be in there. A clue maybe? He set his phone down and picked up the box.

Thick clear tape sealed every edge. How was he going to open this? Using his fingernails, he scratched hard at the edge of the tape on the top until he pulled up a corner. He grabbed it and tugged; the tape peeled back. The box top was ready to open; however, when he tried, it seemed stuck. He shoved his fingers inside the flap and yanked hard.

The box exploded.

Jorge never felt a thing, never had a chance to flinch.

The explosion was so powerful that it practically vaporized his body and took everything within a forty-foot diameter with it, leaving a small crater filled with smoldering debris.

Jorge's journey was over. He'd never get to witness his dream come to fruition. Like many others, he was but a pawn and now a victim of The Bloody Hand.

Chula Vista, California

BLOOD DRIPPED from Mo's fingertips. He had always had a bad habit of chewing his nails when nervous and now, he'd chewed them raw. Clueless that he had ripped the flesh from his fingers, he sat staring in an almost trancelike state at a lone palm tree through a small cracked window in their break room.

"You're bleeding," Malik said.

Mo wiped the blood on his jeans.

"You don't look good," Malik whined.

"You don't say," Mo snarked.

Malik raised his hand and snapped, "Nope, don't, I don't want to hear it. You're here now. Just suck it up."

Mo leaned to within inches of Malik's face. "Children, fucking children, Malik."

"Fucking small infidels, nothing more. They'll grow up and one day bomb our children. It's only right we kill them before they kill ours."

"I don't know if I can," Mo said.

"You're going to die regardless. Do you want your family to die too?" Malik asked, reminding Mo of the alternative.

"Of course not."

"Then shut up, already."

"You love it here. You love everything about America. The clothing, the television, movies, food, fuck, man, pizza and Coke, it's like your favorite meal. Why are you suddenly ready to go murder people for a religion you don't even practice?"

"I can ask the same of you. I didn't see you asking these questions when I first had you meet Kareem. You stood there acting tough, talking tough, then shit got real that night. Now you're second-guessing everything."

"I am, and yes, shit got real that night. I realized it's not a game. This is life and death. I thought the idea of being a warrior was noble, was honorable, but we're nothing but—"

Malik put his hand over Mo's mouth. "Stop right there. I love you like a brother, but if you say another word, I'll tell Kareem. I'm done with your bullshit. You're either with us or not. I'm in, fully. If you're not, so be it. Die and have your parents die too. I don't care anymore. This will be the last time I stop you from saying something that will kill you and your family. This is your final warning," Malik barked. "Do you understand?"

Mo nodded.

Malik removed his hand. "Are you done? You're not going to convince me. So if you're going to preach, then know I'm going to Kareem first word out of your mouth."

Looking down at the half-eaten sandwich, Mo felt a surge of emotions hit him. He looked up at Malik and cried, "I'm sorry. I'm just so scared. I...I don't want to die. I...thought..."

Malik embraced him. "It will be fine, brother. I'll be there with you."

San Diego, California

EDDIE AND WILL jumped on Brett, waking him from the few hours he did sleep. He rolled over and said, "Morning, you two wild men." The sun's early rays were beaming through the plantation shutters in the living room. He squinted and looked around; a tinge of a headache reminded him of the one too many beers he'd had at dinner.

"Why are you sleeping on the couch, Daddy?" Will asked.

"Yeah, why are you sleeping here?" Eddie followed up.

Not wanting to concern the kids, he lied, "Oh, I was watching TV and fell asleep."

"What were you watching?" Will asked.

"Something on the History Channel, I can't quite remember."

"Can we watch it?" Eddie asked.

"Ahh, maybe. Um, is the TV on in the kitchen?" Brett asked.

"Yeah, we woke you because we can't find the remote and it's on your channel," Eddie said.

"Look in the drawer next to the utensils," Brett said.

"We did," Eddie replied.

"...the bomb went off at approximately ten fifteen local time in Paris. At the moment, the authorities aren't confirming it's terrorism or linked to ISIS or The Bloody Hand, but some of my sources say they highly suspect it is," the newscaster said.

Brett sat up, craned his head around and glanced into the kitchen. The boys were right, it was on his channel, and once more there was another terror attack, this time Paris. "What time is it?"

"I don't know, early," Eddie said.

Will jumped off Brett and sprinted away.

"Go turn the TV off. I don't want to wake up Mommy," Brett said.

Eddie raced into the kitchen and did as he was told. "I'm going to go play."

"Okay," Brett said. He found his phone on the coffee table and picked it up. The screen was loaded with news flashes about the bombing in Paris. He swiped to go read the story, but paused. No, he wasn't going to get excited about it. His first action this morning was to go upstairs and apologize to Madison. He tossed his phone back on the coffee table and headed upstairs.

He entered his bedroom to find Madison sitting up in bed on her iPad. He waved and said, "Good morning."

She gave him a playful scowl and went back to watching her iPad.

He jumped on the bed and crawled over to her.

She rebuffed him.

Determined to make amends, he got up and ran downstairs. He went out front of his house, picked a white rose, the only blooming flower he could find, and came back to the bedroom. He re-entered the room, this time with the stem of the rose clenched between his teeth.

She tried not to look at him, but his valiant attempt at humor mixed with romance won. She paused her show, pulled her earbuds out and asked, "What?" Her tone was a mix of irritation and playfulness.

He dropped the rose in her lap and with puppy-dog eyes said, "I'm sorry."

"I'm still mad at you," she growled.

"I know, but do you forgive me?"

"I have to think about it."

Taking a serious tone, he said, "I really am sorry. I just saw the news flash and once more got worried."

"There's going to be news flashes of bad things all the time. This is just the world we live in. There's no grand conspiracy to kill us all."

He wanted to say there probably was, but he'd never convince her, so he skipped past her comment. "I say we get the boys and go to the beach today. Let's just make it a family day."

She thought for a moment and replied, "Good idea. Let's do that."

He picked up the rose and placed it again between his teeth. He leaned in and rubbed her nose with it.

She giggled, looked over his shoulder, then back into his eyes and asked, "Are you trying to get some?"

"Let me think...ahh, hell yes."

"Go lock the door. We don't want the boys to walk in on us," she said.

He jumped up, shut the door and locked it and climbed back into bed. "So where were we?"

"You were telling me how sorry you are, now show me," she said, tossing off the sheets.

Paris, France

DAVID RUBBED his eyes and stretched. He couldn't believe he had slept this late.

Sirens blasted in the distance. A lot of them.

Curious, he turned on the television. There he saw the news concerning the bombing in Notre Dame. *Was this Joram's doing? Is it a coincidence? Joram is in Paris and now a bombing here too?*

He fell into his cushioned chair and watched the scenes of police and EMS surrounding the iconic cathedral. Memories of Copenhagen came to him. He shook them off. There was a story to document and he was still in his underwear. He bolted for his bedroom and changed.

With his pack loaded with cameras and all the tech he'd need, he made for the front door. He stopped when he saw the envelope on the floor. He picked it up. There was nothing written on the front. He tore it open, pulled out the single folded paper and read it.

Meet me at the Carrousel du Louvre, in front of the Golden Arches, tomorrow at 1745. Leave your apartment via the basement laundry room. There's an emergency exit. Follow it all the way to the end. It exits into the adjacent building. Go through the restaurant and take a cab. Don't be late. I don't have much time. I'm being pursued. – Joram

PS: Backup my interview. Everything you have on me. Put it on a thumb drive and bring it with you. That will be your payment for the final exclusive access. All will be revealed then. If you don't bring it, don't bother coming.

David frantically fumbled trying to unlock his door. He dropped his bag but finally succeeded in getting it open. He stuck his head out and looked in both directions.

When did he drop this off? Was he seen by Grim?

He stepped back inside his apartment and closed the door. He reread the note. *Emergency exit in laundry room?* He'd never heard of it or seen it. He was going to see where this room was. He grabbed his bag and headed out.

THE ELEVATOR DOORS SLOWLY OPENED. The bright white lights of the basement were almost blinding. He followed the hall until he reached the laundry room. On the wall, a sign was posted with an arrow, *EMERGENCY EXIT*.

He followed the signs until it led to a single door. He opened it. A passageway led him to another elevator and a narrow stairwell. Wary of riding the unknown elevator, he climbed.

At the first level, he found himself in the kitchen of the Café Jardin, a swanky eatery next door to his apartment building.

"Who are you?" a sous chef asked.

"Sorry, made a wrong turn. Where's the exit?" David asked sheepishly.

The man pointed.

David went in that direction and soon found himself on the street in front of the café. He looked around. He was a half block from his apartment building and out of sight of anyone possibly watching it.

A smile creased his face. "You tricky bastard. Always one step ahead." He saw a cab and hailed it.

The cab pulled over.

David jumped in the back.

"Where to?"

"Notre Dame."

The driver gave him an odd look and mumbled under his breath, "Crazy Americans."

Del Mar, California

THE COOL OCEAN air felt good. Brett closed his eyes and faced the crashing waves. "I love the smell of the ocean. Good call on coming to the beach."

"Me too, and how awesome that it's not too packed," Madison said, taking his hand in hers.

"Hey, I promise I'll find balance with my concerns—"

"Paranoia," she interrupted.

"Whatever, and make sure I don't do what I did the other night," he finished.

"I told you the other night, I can understand your paranoia, *cough*, concerns. Just don't be so consumed by them," Madison said softly.

"Are you afraid to die?" Brett asked.

"What kind of question is that?"

"I am, I wasn't before, I mean, not until they came along," he said, pointing at the boys playing in the sand.

"I guess, if I really think about it, I'd be afraid of what would happen to them without a mother," she said.

"You said it perfectly. That's what scares me most of all. Not my own death, but their lives without me in it."

"Daddy, let's go swimming!" Will called out, running towards the surf.

"Be careful," Madison hollered.

Eddie walked up. "Do you have gum in your car?"

"Yeah, it's on the top of the console," Brett answered.

Before she could say a word, Eddie ran off. "Make sure you get a piece for your brother."

"I will," Eddie cried out.

"That kid has good ears." Brett laughed.

Will jumped around in the crashing waves, laughing and squealing with joy.

Eddie walked up and said, "Dad, why do you have this in your console?"

Madison looked and gasped. "Dear God, put that down, now!"

"What?" Brett looked around and saw Eddie holding a pistol.

Afraid, Eddie dropped the gun in the sand.

"Where did you get that?" Madison scolded.

"It was inside the console," Eddie whimpered.

"Brett, Jesus Christ, what's wrong with you? You had that in the car? You said you were going to lock it up," Madison barked.

"I did. I had it in a case, locked in the console," Brett said defensively.

"Then how did he get it?" Madison asked. "Eddie, how did you get this?"

"I saw the box and opened it."

Brett grew angry. "That's impossible, the case was locked."

"How dare you have a gun in the car, unlocked."

"It was locked."

"No, it wasn't. I was looking for gum and couldn't find any, so I opened up the console. I saw the box; the lock was just hanging on it, unlocked. I opened it up and found it."

"Is it loaded?" Madison hollered.

"Keep your voice down, Maddy," Brett snapped, carefully picking up the pistol and hiding it in a beach towel. "I'll be right back."

"Why do you have it, Dad?" Eddie asked.

"No questions. Go play in the water with your brother," Madison ordered.

Eddie stormed off.

Madison gave Brett a deathly stare as he walked away.

Back at the car, Brett found the case sitting on the car seat. He put the pistol back in and locked the case. This time he put the case in the trunk. "Stupid, stupid, stupid," he mumbled to himself. He knew he left that case locked, he just knew it. He glanced over the trunk and could see Madison still leering at him.

If it wasn't one thing, it was another. Ever since that damn attack in Copenhagen, the wheels had come off his relationship and his nerves. In just a little over a week's time he had managed to make Madison angry multiple times and had even gotten himself barred from the school campus. He was not doing well these days and he was sure to hear about this the rest of the day. He slammed the trunk and said, "Looks like it's the couch again tonight."

CHAPTER ELEVEN

Monday, May 1
San Diego, California

To AVOID the highway shutdowns and gridlock. Mo and the others had left well before dawn.

Lateef found a quiet place to park the van, nowhere anyone would find it suspicious.

Mo hated not being able to see out, something in him wanted to know where he was, which school it was. Not that it mattered because knowing the name wouldn't prevent the attack. In fact, it would only make it more personal to him, but he didn't care, he wanted to know.

How can the others sleep? he asked himself. He glared at each snoring and slobbering face and just wanted to shoot them. Yes, those thoughts entered his mind. What if he just killed them all? He could prevent the attack, but his survival would only highlight to The Bloody Hand who had done it and would most assuredly get his family killed. Not one scenario where he played the hero did he and his family survive. Maybe they should die? Maybe his family, including himself, should sacrifice themselves to save hundreds of innocent children. His thoughts spun and twisted, but each time he settled back to his fate and his life ending at the school.

Lateef's alarm on his phone began to beep. He reached out and stopped it. Yawning, he turned around and barked, "Wake up. It's show time."

The others stirred.

Malik opened his eyes, smiled and said, "Good morning, Mohammed."

"Good morning," Mo replied, his head low.

"Go over your gear," Lateef ordered. He had been given the title of cell team leader and took it seriously.

Everyone, including Mo, did as he said. They counted their magazines, checked the wiring on their explosives, ensuring not to arm them until they exited the van. Each bomber was equipped with a dead man's trigger. Once armed, the bomber would depress the trigger and hold it; if he released the pressure, the bomb would detonate. This ensured the bomb would go off regardless if the bomber was shot dead.

"All good?" Lateef asked.

Everyone acknowledged they were ready.

"It's eight forty-five. Let's get in line for school," Lateef joked and drove off.

Paris, France

DAVID PUSHED past several slow-walking tourists. "Sorry, in a hurry."

He glanced at his watch. It was seventeen forty-five and he was late but not by much. He could see the McDonald's, or as Joram had referred to it, the Golden Arches. Out of breath and out of time, he made it to the entrance, but looking around, he didn't see Joram. He walked inside the restaurant, but Joram wasn't there either. Frantic, he exited and almost ran into him.

"You're late," Joram said.

"I'm sorry, um, not by much, seconds," David pleaded.

"Come, let's sit," Joram said and walked to a bench.

The two sat down.

Joram cocked his head and asked, "Did you bring what I asked?"

David reached into his pocket and pulled out the blue thumb drive. He handed it over. "Here. Everything is on there. All the recordings, my notes, everything."

Joram held the thumb drive and marveled, "Isn't it funny how something so small can contain so much information?"

"Technology."

"I love technology. It can be used for good and bad, don't you think?"

"Yes, it can."

"Look at the splitting of the atom. It can be used to blow up entire cities, killing hundreds of thousands, or it can be used to provide much-needed energy to hundreds of thousands."

"It all depends on whose hands it's in, technology, that is," David said.

"Same goes for money. In some hands, it can be used to feed the hungry; in other hands it can be used to murder those same people."

David opened his pack and pulled out his digital recorder. He looked around and asked, "Are you sure this is a good place to conduct this interview?"

Joram smiled. "This is perfect."

"Aren't you afraid you'll be seen?"

"No, not really. Soon, they'll have their hands full." Joram laughed.

David clicked the record button and asked, "What do you mean by having their hands full?"

"Soon a dream that started many years ago will be realized."

"And what's that?"

"The end of the United States."

David recoiled slightly and said, "That's a big statement."

"Oh, it is and it wasn't easy, but using technology and money, we have devised a weapon so beautiful in its design that once unleashed will spread around the world like one of your teenybopper videos."

"You mean go viral?"

"Exactly."

"You sound different. You're not the same man I met years ago, and you're not the same man I first encountered in Ankara."

"You've said that before."

"Because it's true. When I first met you three years ago, you were an idealistic young man, not evil, just misguided. When I again met you in Ankara, you seemed like a hunted man seeking redemption. I felt sympathy for you. Now, I see..." David said but paused.

"You see what?"

"You are part of a diabolic scheme to kill many people and you seem happy about it, euphoric."

"All of us have schemes; I'm no different."

"Yes, you are. Yours is to kill people."

"And what are you doing but aiding and abetting me, purely for selfish reasons. You're willing to risk lives so you can get a scoop, a story that you hope to sell to make millions and receive praise from your friends in the media. And let's discuss the media, they're not journalists, they're propagandists who peddle agenda-driven stories. Do they care about people dying? They say they do, but when U.S. bombs kill our children by the thousands, it's never reported, but you know what is? Overhyped and outright fake stories so they can drive false narratives to perpetuate whatever the agenda is of their political and corporate overlords. You see, David, none are without sin. They just package it better and smile."

"Bravo, that was awesome."

"You're mocking me?"

David thought for second and defiantly replied, "Yes, I am."

"You said I was different, I am different. I was reborn when I went and joined the Islamic State. I was shown the true Islam. And soon, Islam will conquer the Earth."

"What the Islamic State preaches is not Islam."

Joram laughed. "So blind by your need to be politically correct. I have to say it has helped us, your willingness to look the other way and find excuses. While we killed in the name of Allah, many like you would say we weren't Islamic and that we were extremists. Do you know how much we have enjoyed watching many of you contort yourselves, doing back bends to make sure what we were doing wasn't associated with Islam. David, you helped us. You gave us cover. You allowed us to spread."

"Stop right there. I did nothing to help you spread, nothing. This is ridiculous."

"Is it? Every time we'd attack and kill, many like you would defend Islam, and to prove you weren't bigoted, you worked against your very own national security interests to allow us to come in, to live among you. David, we didn't need to sneak into your country, you rolled out the red carpet for us."

"What you preach is not Islam."

"David, you're a fool. We follow Mohammed's teachings and lessons to the letter. You're so blinded that you don't even know history. Let me ask you, how did Mohammed spread the word of Allah? Do you know?"

"Let's move on."

"Answer the question if you know."

"This is silly now. Let's move on to what you have planned."

"He spread Islam through conquest. He converted people by the sword and so shall we, although the sword has changed."

"Who is Israfil?" David asked.

"You will meet him very soon," Joram said, looking at his watch. "David, we don't have much time. Ask me anything, I will answer."

"Are you Israfil?"

"No."

"Are you the twelfth imam?"

"Yes."

"Are you planning, is The Bloody Hand planning a major terror attack?"

"Yes."

"Where?"

"Everywhere."

"How is that possible?"

"Let me go back to the beginning..."

"Again?"

"You said I was a different man than you met three years ago and even different than last week. It's true. Three years ago, you did meet an idealistic man. I was looking for a meaning to my life. I found it in Raqqa. I was reborn there. Allah showed me my path and I chose to take it. Since then I have been working hard to fulfill the dream of a one world caliphate, a world under Allah. Soon, in minutes, in fact, the first strike in a series of strikes will begin. By the end of the day tomorrow, the United States will be on its heels, bleeding out. Within a week's time, the United States will collapse," Joram said calmly with a slight grin plastered on his face. "Last week you met a fake me. I needed you to believe I was in need, a hunted man; I needed you to believe I was a victim. It was the only way I thought you'd help me. I was right but I was also bolstered by your own greed and selfishness. I played your sensibilities. Multiple times you have been approached, warned and given specific details that I was up to no good and part of a conspiracy to attack the West. It was all true. If I had shown you the man I have become, would you have been so warm, so inviting? I doubt it. Deep down the political correctness you espouse daily fought with your better judgment, as did your greed. It was a perfect cocktail for you to sit and listen to the ramblings of a terror leader who in mere minutes will launch an attack against the West never seen before."

In shock, David stood. "I won't sit and listen any longer."

"Yes, you will. Now sit down. I'm just about to get to the best part."

"I won't."

"Oh, but you will, don't you want to know how I did it? How I beat your system; how I concocted the most lethal bioweapon ever known?"

David internally struggled. He was disgusted by Joram, but the tease of the big reveal would make for a great story. He relented and sat back down.

"I told you you'd stay."

David looked at his watch, five minutes to six.

"With Dr. Schumarr's books, the ones I mentioned before, me and my partners went in search of the best and brightest virologists, biologists, anyone who was the best in their field that could help us. That took us a while, and when we found them, we ran into our next obstacle, money. I looked around the world. Who had the means and the mutual hatred for America? I said to myself. I found it in a man, a man with huge financial resources, a billionaire who desperately wanted to see the United States transformed, and to do so, it needed to be destroyed. I presented our plans, not all of them, but enough to get him enticed. He bought in and financed the further research we needed. Our financial backer—"

"Who was it?"

"You'll know him, Mr. Jorge Sorossi."

"I do, the billionaire hedge fund guy. He's very active in politics."

"That's him. With his backing, we could perfect our weapon. Mr. Sorossi came with a bonus that proved to be highly beneficial, his network and influence was deep and wide. We could get him to influence court decisions, policy, legislation, you name it. Over the past two years, he helped shape things that made it easier for us to create the infrastructure so our plan would be successful."

"This is a vast conspiracy?"

"It is, but the parts—or better yet, let me explain it this way. Let's say the hub of a wheel is the conspiracy and the spokes are all the people and organizations or groups that are assisting. The thing is, the spokes don't know what the hub really is and in fact don't know they're part of a bigger plan."

"Lies and deception?"

"Exactly," Joram said and pointed to the television. "You see those images of riots across the United States and in the UK? All a deception. They've been recruited, told the hub is about civil disobedience towards an administration they hate. The media is so willing to help they feed that narrative and fuel the outrage. Working in tandem, they help distract and overwhelm law enforcement and other emergency services. While this is all happening in the open, we move, slithering like a snake, putting our pieces into position."

"And the politicians?"

"Not all but some are bought and paid for. They will go against anything we tell them to. That judge in Hawaii who put

that injunction against the president's executive order, one of
our judges, or I should say, one of Mr. Sorossi's judges. He was
all too willing to help because he thought he was resisting the
president, but he also liked the money he got. Ever wonder how
many politicians enter rich and leave stinking wealthy? The
system is corrupt. We leveraged that. With that one judge's
injunction, we could keep flooding the United States with fighters. We used your freedoms and your Constitution against you;
we used it to destroy it."

"I just can't believe that judge is a paid agent of Mr.
Sorossi."

"Don't believe it, doesn't matter what you believe, it's true.
You don't want to believe because it runs counter to your own
political leanings. If it doesn't fit, you discount it. Another
failing of your media and politics. There is no truth in your
country, only political perspective."

"Our media isn't perfect, but we are not propaganda."

"If you say so," Joram said, catching the time was now five
fifty-eight.

"What is the attack? What are you planning?"

"Sticking with deception, and because it's just so perfect we
couldn't resist, we will strike conventionally. Our targets,
elementary schools and airports. The schools are an easy target,
not guarded, one can just walk up and begin shooting. The
airports? Because we want to shut them down, cut off all
commerce."

"You're going to attack and murder children?" David asked,
shocked.

"Depends on how you define murder."

"I think there's only one definition and what you're about to
do fits it."

"Yet you still sit here, listening. If you're so appalled, why
haven't you gotten up to find the closest security officer?"

David lowered his head because Joram was right.

"Once the first wave of attacks is over, Israfil will present himself. He will come forth and deliver the final blow."

"Who is Israfil?"

"Do you want to meet him?"

David gulped and hesitated. "Is he here?" He looked around.

"He is," Joram said. He looked up to see the time was six. "Before you meet him, I want you to watch. Look at the television monitors at the McDonald's."

San Diego, California

LIKE HE HAD SINCE COPENHAGEN, Brett was glued to the television. The news from Paris concerning the bombing inside Notre Dame Cathedral sickened him. A lover of history and architecture, seeing the historic building suffer, too, added to his anger. Yes, it seemed odd to be angry about that, but he was. In the lower right-hand side of the screen, a shot of the protests nationwide was being shown. The newscaster was flipping between the riots and the bombing in Paris.

There just seemed like so much was happening. A quickening of sorts. He could feel it, hell, he was watching it, but for Madison, she couldn't. In a weird way, she was blind to it. This was the normalcy bias Chris talked about.

Disgusted by it all and his current situation, Brett turned the television off. Today would be his first day back to work, but he planned on working from home, as there was no way he'd be making it in on time.

He strolled to his office and plopped into his leather roller chair. He turned the television on but put it on mute. He started his computer and waited for it to boot.

Yesterday had been an unmitigated disaster for him. How

stupid could he have been to leave the gun in the center console. He just never imagined Will would go digging in there for gum only to find a *gun*. Seeing his youngest holding up the Glock terrified him.

Madison had every right to lose it over that. He had messed up and that incident could have been very bad. Thankfully, Will hadn't tried to squeeze the trigger.

He bent over and stretched. After another night on the couch, his back was feeling it.

His e-mail folder began to populate with dozens of unread e-mails. After taking a week off, he'd be burning the midnight oil to catch up.

He stared at his computer screen. The motivation to work just wasn't there. "Fake it till you make it," he said out loud, taking a hold of his mouse and clicking on the first e-mail.

An image popped up on the television, catching his eye. He glanced over. It was a man dressed in a hooded cape, his face masked by shadowing.

Brett grabbed the remote and raised the volume.

"...a man calling himself the twelfth imam has just sent us this transmission. He claims to represent The Bloody Hand. We've reviewed this message and have forwarded it to law enforcement. After careful review and deliberation from our editorial staff, we have decided to show it to you. Please, this is sensitive in nature, only for mature audiences. If children are in the room, please turn off the television or make sure they leave," the newscaster said.

Brett leaned in. The disclaimer grabbed his full attention.

The screen went back to the man in the hooded cape.

"My name is Joram. I am the twelfth imam and I represent The Bloody Hand. We are Allah's right hand. The hammer that has been sent forth to destroy the infidel and usher the worldwide caliphate. For many years, we have warned the United States and *its Western European puppets to leave the Middle East, but you did not adhere. Today we strike back. Today we get our vengeance. Once this day is over, you will regret everything you have ever done against the Muslim people."* The voice stopped talking. A loud horn sounded and persisted for thirty seconds. *"And so it begins,"* the voice concluded. The screen turned black and a red hand appeared.

"What the hell was that?" Brett said loudly, astonished at what he had seen.

"As you can see, the video is dark, foreboding..."

A loud boom sounded not far off.

Brett sat motionless. "What was that?"

The rattle of automatic gunfire echoed across the sky to the south.

Brett leapt from his chair and sprinted towards the back door, his phone in his hand. As he ran, he thumbed to Madison's phone number and pressed *call*.

The phone rang.

Madison answered, "Yes."

"The school, it's under attack. Hurry home; it's under attack!"

"Not again. Are we doing this again? I've had it, Brett. Seriously, grow up," she said and hung up.

Brett shoved the phone in his pocket and opened his stride.

The roar of gunfire filled the air.

He cleared the last corner. The school was in view.

A smoldering vehicle sat at the single-lane drive in front. People were running and screaming in all directions away from the school.

A flash and loud boom shook the ground. The concussion of the blast struck Brett making him wobbly.

Cries and wails were everywhere.

The gunfire kept thumping.

Brett ran passed weeping and bleeding children, all hurrying to get away from the carnage. He jumped over a small fence and into the parking lot. He felt defenseless not having a weapon.

A plume of black smoke rose from the school entrance.

Madison had dropped the boys off early; that meant they were either lined up in the multipurpose room or already walking towards their classrooms.

Brett hurdled bodies and debris.

"Hey Brett, over here!" Chris cried out.

Slowing to see where Chris was, Brett didn't see Lateef run up to him.

"Allah Akbar!" Lateef hollered, he pulled the trigger of his AK47 but nothing happened. "Argh!" he bellowed.

Not waiting for him to reload, Brett sprinted off.

"Hey Brett, over here!" Chris again cried out from behind a parked car in the parking lot.

Lateef reloaded. He had seen Chris hiding and snuck up on him.

By the time Chris noticed Lateef was there, it was too late.

"Allah Akbar!" Lateef cried out and pulled the trigger. This time the AK47 roared to life.

Half a dozen rounds struck Chris in the back, killing him.

Brett didn't see Chris' demise. He pressed forward in hopes of finding the boys unharmed.

He hurdled a pile of bodies near the entrance and ran inside the campus. His first stop, the multipurpose room.

The rattle of gunfire came from behind Brett. It was Lateef executing more innocents.

Brett didn't look back; he kept moving. He turned a corner and there in front of him were two men holding AK-style rifles. It was Malik and Mo.

Malik was taking random shots at children as they fled.

Brett jumped behind a large column.

The scene was horrific. Little bodies lay everywhere.

Brett peeked around and scanned the bodies. *Are any of them Will or Eddie? Are they one of the bodies? Are they dead already?* He couldn't remember what they were wearing today.

His phone began to ring.

He ignored it.

Malik laughed as he took shots at fleeing children.

Mo, though, only stood and pointed his rifle; he never pulled the trigger. It was his way of defiance.

Brett saw one of the doors of the multipurpose room was wide open. Seeing an opportunity, he ran for it. Feet away, he slipped in a pool of blood and fell to the ground hard.

The shooter turned around after hearing Brett fall but was distracted by the sight of three children running. He aimed and gunned them down. When the children fell, he laughed loudly.

Brett struggled to get up. Each time he got his footing, he'd slip again in the slick blood.

Cries and whimpers came from inside.

Why didn't they lock down the school? Brett thought. *Don't they do training for this sort of thing?*

A third explosion rocked the campus. This time coming from inside the school near the administration offices.

Brett got to his feet and cleared the remaining distance. He was inside the room. "Will, Eddie!" he called out.

No reply, only cries and whimpering.

"Will, Eddie Silver, has anyone seen them?"

"Daddy!" Will whimpered from the far corner.

"Will, Will, is that you?" Brett hollered as he ran over to Will. He picked him and hugged him tight.

Will shook uncontrollably.

"Where's your brother?"

Will pointed to a gaggle of kids huddled under a table.

Brett ran over. "Eddie, are you here?"

"I'm here, Dad," Eddie replied.

"Get out of there. We're getting out of here."

Eddie stepped out but stopped short of going. "What about my friends, the other kids?"

Brett looked at the terrified faces. Eddie was right. He couldn't just save his own. He needed to do something to help the other kids. "Kids, everyone, listen up. I'm Mr. Silver. I'm going to get you out of here."

Several of the kids came up and hugged him.

"That back door, we're going through there. It leads to the lunch area and past that is the play yard and the fence. We're going over it and going home. You understand?"

The thirty-plus kids, all surrounding him, nodded or said, "Yes."

"Eddie, lead the way," Brett ordered. "All of you follow Eddie, now. No time to waste."

"Okay, let's go get your brother," Brett said and ran to the door with Will cradled in his arms.

"Where are you going?" Malik yelled.

Brett turned to see a rifle pointed at him. He turned back to Eddie and said, "GO! NOW!"

Eddie and the other kids in tow ran for the back door.

Malik pressed the trigger but nothing happened.

For the second time, Brett's luck was keeping him alive. But how long would that last. He needed a weapon, anything at this point.

Malik dropped the magazine and looked for a fresh one in his vest.

Mo walked in but stopped just inside the room.

Brett gave Mo a look.

Mo waved his hand, signaling for Brett to go.

"I'm out of ammo, Mo. Give me some," Malik barked.

"No," Mo said.

"What? Give me some ammo!"

"No, I won't," he said. He turned, pointed the rifle at Malik and pulled the trigger but nothing happened. He looked oddly at his rifle and tried again. Nothing. He dropped the magazine, saw it was fully loaded, reinserted it and pulled the bolt back. A round flew out of the receiver, he let the bolt go, which put another round in the chamber. He again pointed the rifle at Malik and pulled the trigger. Still nothing happened.

With Mo and Malik involved with each other, Brett saw his chance. He turned and ran for the back door.

"You idiot, they disabled your rifle. Only now you notice," Malik mocked. He saw the room was now empty, meaning his objective had disappeared. "Better go find someone else to blow up."

"I don't think so," Mo said, dropping his rifle. He ran and jumped on Malik.

"What are you doing?" Malik yelled.

"Stopping you from murdering anyone else," Mo said as he struggled to release Malik's hand from the dead man's trigger.

"No, stop, what are you doing?" Malik wailed.

Mo was bigger and stronger. He pried one finger after another off until only Malik's thumb remained. Mo bit down on it and began to chew.

"Stop, no, stop!"

Mo didn't feel the blast nor did Malik.

The intense blast blew them into millions of pieces.

Brett heard the explosion from the play yard. Ahead of him, Eddie had shown great courage and leadership.

Eddie and the other older kids were helping the younger ones over the fence.

Brett was so proud. He would forever remember this moment.

Searing pain suddenly jolted Brett. He collapsed and rolled onto his side. He wrapped his right arm around and felt something warm and wet. He brought his hand back and stared. It was covered in blood; he'd been shot.

Gunshots cracked over his head.

He looked back and saw Lateef coming towards him, firing.

The problem was he wasn't firing at him, he was shooting at the kids.

Brett rolled over and saw Eddie was down. "No! Eddie, no!"

Will ran to Eddie's side and shook his lifeless body. He turned to Brett and cried, "Daddy!" Will ran to Brett.

"No, Will, run away, run away. Don't come to me, no!" Brett yelled as he crawled.

"Daddy!" Will screamed, still running towards Brett.

"No, Will, run away, run!"

Brett watched in horror as four bullets ripped through Will's chest. He dropped to the ground, but was still alive.

"Will, my baby boy, no!" Brett cried as he tried desperately to reach Will.

"Dad...dy," Will gasped and exhaled his last breath.

"No, oh my God, no!" Brett screamed.

Lateef emptied his magazine on the remaining children, killing them all. He stepped over top of Brett, who was still crawling towards Will. He kicked Brett onto his back.

"You got away before, not this time." Lateef laughed, loading another magazine.

Brett's phone rang.

He imagined it was Madison calling. She probably had

gotten the word about the school attack and was now trying to find out anything she could. Problem was, she was too late.

Brett coughed up blood and stared blankly at Lateef.

Lateef pointed the rifle at Brett's head and said, "Die, infidel." He laughed loudly before pulling the trigger.

Ramona, California

CASSIDY STARED AT THE TELEVISION. He couldn't pull himself away from the sights of chaos and rioting taking place across San Diego County. The freeways were shut down as were many of the side roads. Those wishing to avert the frozen freeways by taking surface streets only clogged those, they couldn't escape the gridlock.

The city had come to a standstill.

He glanced at his watch. It was getting close to nine in the morning. He was packed and ready to go, but his flight wasn't scheduled to depart until twelve fifteen. He hoped the roads would be clear by then, but the scenes playing out weren't giving him much hope.

He clicked off the television, turned on his laptop and went back to scrolling through employment notices online in Boise.

Lost in the endless stream of job postings, he didn't notice the time until stomach pangs reminded him it was time to eat breakfast. "Hmm, almost ten. Maybe I should think about heading out soon."

He stood, stretched and sauntered to the kitchen. He grabbed leftovers from the night before, tossed them in the microwave, and while he waited for them to warm up, he picked up his phone. His eyes widened when he saw the numerous notices from Sophie. Fifteen missed calls, twelve texts and seven news flashes. "What the hell?" He didn't read the texts, he immediately called her.

He listened as the phone rang.

"Trevor! Where are you?" Sophie said, her voice cracking.

Instantly hearing she was stressed, he asked, "Soph, what's wrong?"

"They're killing kids, murdering them. It's horrible!" she cried.

"What are you talking about?"

"You don't know? Turn on the TV," she said.

He exited the kitchen, grabbed the remote and turned the television on.

"...more reports are coming in from all over the country. There seems to be a pattern. These attacks are targeting schools, primarily elementary schools..."

Cassidy wasn't surprised. In many ways, he felt vindicated. He thought of the school he worked for and wondered if they too were under assault.

"Trevor, I'm scared," Sophie whimpered.

"Where are you?" he asked.

"In my hotel room."

"Stay there. I'm heading to the airport now. I'll get an earlier flight," he said.

"What? You can't."

He raced to the bedroom, grabbed his bag and ran towards the front door. "I'll get out sooner or later, whether it's an earlier flight or my flight at twelve fifteen."

"Trevor, you can't leave. You're stuck," she said.

He slammed the door and headed for his truck. "It'll be fine. Just stay in your room and I'll get there as fast as I can."

"Listen to me, you're not flying anywhere!"

"Why not?" he asked, getting into his truck.

"They've also struck airports; San Diego was one. Some terrorists blew themselves up at the ticketing areas, and it's just

*been on TV that the president has shut down all air traffic. You're
not going anywhere."*

Shocked by the news, he turned on the local news station.

*"...that's right, Sharon. We're being told by SDPD for
everyone to stay indoors, stay home. Do not venture out. If you
have kids at one of the twenty-seven schools listed, please do not
go to the school, you'll only interfere. Designated safe zones are
being created now. They'll bus those children who are unhurt to
those safe zones. Once we have the names and locations of them
and the corresponding schools they'll service, we will report it. If
you're traveling today, San Diego airport is closed. The highways
are still jammed from the earlier riots and CHP isn't expecting
them to clear up for many hours. So, please, if you don't have to
travel, stay home."*

Cassidy ground his teeth.

"Get out of there, just drive. Come to Idaho," Sophie urged.

He thought for a second. "Good idea."

"I'm going to call my cousin. I don't feel safe here in downtown. There's been a couple of attacks here too. I can't believe it,
I just can't."

"Go to your cousin's house. She lives in the middle of
nowhere; you'll be safe there. Hurry, go. Call me from your taxi
the second you get in," Cassidy ordered.

"Okay."

"Go."

"Trevor, I love you."

"I love you too, babe."

"Hurry," she said before disconnecting the line.

He opened the garage with his opener and beelined for the
cabinets inside. Cassidy threw open all the cabinet doors and began
removing every item he imagined he might need. Sleeping bags,
camping gear, cases of water, a case of MREs he had left over from

the Marine Corps, lanterns, blankets and ammunition cans full of nine millimeter, five point five six rounds and twelve gauge shells. He hauled it all to his truck and tossed it in the bed. Back and forth he went until he had everything minus the most important items, his guns. Tucked in the corner was a large gun safe, he opened it and took out his Glock 17 and shoved it in his waistband. He grabbed the AR-15 and his trusty Mossberg 930 shotgun and slung them both over his shoulder. On the floor of the safe was his range bag. He tossed in every empty magazine, spare sling and his extra knives.

His phone started to ring from the truck.

He zipped the bag and raced to the truck. Once there, he dumped all the firearms in the passenger seat, grabbed the phone and answered, "Yeah."

"I'm in an Uber, headed to my cousin's," Sophie said.

"How are you?"

"Nervous. There's a lot of activity downtown. People out in front of a mosque, protesting it."

"Just ignore everything and get to your cousin's. I'm packing the truck. I'll be on the road shortly. I'll haul ass. I estimate I'll be there in, say, sixteen hours, give or take, all depends on fuel stops."

"Be safe."

"I will."

Sophie screamed.

"Sophie, you okay?"

"There's some man, he's deranged. He's attacking the car in front of us at the light," she said to Cassidy. *"Go around. Hurry, go around,"* she said to her driver.

Over the speaker, Cassidy could hear the driver debating what to do.

"Just go around...he's coming this way. Drive, drive!" Sophie screamed.

"Sophie, what's going on? Talk to me," Cassidy said.

"*He's attacking our car now,*" she said to Cassidy. "*Go around him, damn it. Drive! I don't care, hit him. Look at him, he's covered in blood. Just fucking drive!*"

The sound of glass shattering hit Cassidy's ears. "What was that? Sophie?"

"*He's smashing, oh my God, no, oh my God! Drive, dri—*"

The phone disconnected.

"Sophie, Sophie!" Cassidy yelled. He redialed. Nothing. Redialed again. Nothing. Five more times he tried, and like before, no answer. "Fuck, fuck, fuck!" He jumped behind the wheel, pulled out of the driveway and sped off.

Paris, France

DAVID'S JAW hung open as he watched the news reports coming from back in the States. It was exactly like Joram had said. It was like Grim had foretold. Joram was evil, he was a horrible person, and here he was sitting with the murderer of innocents.

A strong feeling of nausea came over him. He put his hand to his mouth and gagged.

"Are you okay?" Joram asked, putting his hand on David's shoulder.

David shrugged and barked, "Don't touch me."

"Shall we finish the interview?" Joram asked.

"No, I'm done. Why, huh? Why would you even want me to interview you if this was your plan all along. If you succeed, who will be around to watch it?" David asked, standing up.

"I wanted it for posterity, a record of how it all came to be. I could have just recorded myself but where's the fun in that. And I suppose I wanted to tell someone, someone I liked, someone like you who would listen."

"You used me."

"And you me," Joram said.

"You won't get away with this," David scoffed.

"I already have, but if I fail in the end, the world will know how it came to be. There is now a documented record."

"I'm leaving," David snapped.

"I thought you wanted to meet Israfil?" Joram asked.

"I don't want any of it. Leave me alone," David said, stuffing his things into his pack. His hands were shaking and he fumbled the pack. It hit the floor and its contents spilled out.

Joram bent over and picked up the flip phone David had received from Grim. "You brought this? Who were you planning on calling?"

"That's mine. Leave me alone," David snapped.

Joram gave him the phone with his right hand and with his left jabbed David in the neck with a needle.

"Argh! What the fuck did you just do? Huh? What did you just give me?" David hollered.

His yelling drew the attention of many in the mall around them.

Joram held up the syringe and said calmly, "Meet Israfil."

"Huh?" David mumbled as he tripped backwards over a small table. The seething from the pain throbbing in his neck was making it difficult for him to think.

"When Robert Oppenheimer, the scientist who created the atomic bomb, called himself 'death, the destroyer of worlds', he was wrong. I am." Joram smiled.

David's vision began to blur and sweat rose on his brow. He clenched the phone in his right hand and stumbled away from Joram.

"Goodbye, David," Joram said. He picked up David's things, put them in the pack, slung it over his shoulder and walked off in the opposite direction.

David reached out to bystanders in the mall.

They recoiled and steered clear of him.

"Help, please." He coughed. A deep pain in his chest began to emanate out to his limbs and a sharp pain in his head came on suddenly. It started from the base of his skull and moved up into the cradle of his skull. "Argh!" he screamed.

He leaned against a wall, opened the phone and hit the call button.

The phone dialed.

The pain in his head grew in intensity.

"Answer," he said.

He heard people talking about him as they passed by. He glanced at them. A strong urge to attack them raced through his mind. A hunger followed. A desire to bite them.

The phone connected. "David?"

"It's not a person," David mumbled.

"What? Who is this?" Grim asked.

"David, this is Daaaviiid," he repeated. His words began to jumble as they fell out of his mouth.

"David, what's wrong? Have you found Joram?" Grim asked.

"Isra...Israfil, it's...argh, the pain, it hurts so bad." David grimaced and crumpled to his knees.

A young woman came up to David. "Are you okay?"

The anger returned. "Get away from me!" he yelled.

The woman recoiled in fear when she saw David's eyes.

"David, what's going on? Where are you?"

"It's not...Israfil..is...ahh, the pain, I can't think," he groaned.

"What about Israfil?" Grim asked, picking up the fact David was referring to the elusive figure.

"Think, slow your thoughts," David said to himself.

"Where are you? I'll send someone," Grim said.

"Is...ra...fil is not a person. It's a virus, a bioweapon. It..." David said and buckled over in pain. "My head, it hurts so bad."

"What? Did you just say that Israfil isn't a person, it's a

virus?" Grim asked, finding it hard to know what David was trying to say.

"Yes," David answered clearly.

"Where are you?"

David's body tensed and began to shake violently. Seconds later it stopped. He looked up at the shoppers passing by, all staring. A deep-seated hunger backed with pure rage was boiling inside him. He stood up, tossed the phone and attacked the person closest to him.

North of Victorville, California

AFTER HOURS of repeatedly trying to reach Sophie, Cassidy tossed his phone on the seat and clenched his teeth with frustration.

When he called all he'd get now was, *'ALL CIRCUITS ARE BUSY, PLEASE TRY YOUR CALL AGAIN LATER.'*

The radio was an endless stream of frantic reporting about the terror attacks spanning from one coast to the other. Schools and airports were the main targets, but now reports of deranged people viciously attacking people randomly at malls, on streets, in their neighborhoods, and at their place of business were now becoming more frequent.

For Cassidy, he didn't know what to make of those reports, but they did sound a lot like what might have happened to Sophie.

His heart hurt at the thought of her being a victim of these terror attacks, but unable to reach her, he'd have to hold out hope she was fine.

The back-country roads to the east of San Diego County were proving to be wide open. Making his escape from the urban sprawl of Southern California easy.

Unsure of what he'd discover upon arriving in Idaho, he did the only thing that he could, pray.

He gripped the steering wheel tightly, looked towards long stretch of highway that laid out before him to the north, and said, "Lord, I don't call on you often. It's only because I don't feel worthy, but please, please look after my Sophie. Please keep her safe. If you do, I will never doubt you. I will be your humble servant."

He glanced at his mapping system, it read, nine hundred and fourteen miles.

The miles and the time to drive them, would be the longest of his life.

CHAPTER TWELVE

Monday, May 8
Coronado, California

BRENNAN OPENED his eyes and stared at the thick olive drab canvas above his head. After repeated blinks to clear his blurred vision, he rose and looked around at his unfamiliar surroundings. The only thing that was familiar was the musty smell, the signature odor of a tent. When he turned his head, a sharp pain shot from his neck down his back and across his shoulders, causing him to flinch.

"Ouch," he said loudly.

The flap of the tent burst open, letting in the midday sun. A woman he'd never seen before stepped in.

"You're awake!" she said, her eyes wide with excitement at finding Brennan sitting up and conscious.

Brennan touched his neck and only then noticed a bandage on the back of his head. He ran his fingertips over the course fabric, unaware of how he'd gotten hurt.

The woman took a few steps further inside the tent and asked, "How are you feeling?"

"Groggy, thirsty," he replied.

She rushed to his side with a bottle of water. "Here, drink."

Brennan hesitated. He looked at the woman intently while his mind tried to recall her youthful face.

"Drink. I won't bite, I promise," she insisted. She knelt next to him and put the bottle to his lips.

He took a small drink at first. The cool water tasted so good. His thirst took over, and he snatched the bottle and began to guzzle.

"Easy," she said.

He ignored her and finished the bottle. Feeling refreshed, he looked at her and asked, "Where am I?"

"You don't remember?"

"No."

"Nothing?" she asked with a surprised look on her face. "You were semi-conscious when they brought you back."

"I remember being chased. I took shelter. I...I then remember..." Brennan said and paused. His mind searched for what happened next. "There was an explosion..."

"How do you feel?" she asked, putting the back of her hand to his cheek.

"Confused," he answered.

"I can imagine; you were touch and go there for a while, but how do you feel? Queasy, headache, fatigue?" she said, taking a seat next to him on the cot.

He felt uneasy at her proximity. She was an attractive woman, but having just awoken in a strange place with unfamiliar people he was suspicious.

She reached for the bandage on his head.

He recoiled.

"Sorry, I just wanted to check it," she said.

"Who are you?" he asked.

"My name is Sherry."

"Where am I?" he asked, following up.

She tenderly looked at him and said, "You're safe, that's where you are. Now can I check the bandage?"

"Sure," he said.

She began to examine the wound.

"Where am I? How did you find me?"

"You were medevac'd back here less than a week ago. We got word you were in a local hospital in upstate Minnesota. The hospital staff called about you because you were wearing your uniform."

"Where am I?"

"You're back in Coronado."

"In a tent?" he asked, confused.

"We put those recovering out here while those with more serious injuries have priority inside," she said.

"I don't understand."

"Looks fine. You've healed nicely," she said referencing the wound to the back of his head. "You had me worried though."

"What's happening?"

She ignored his question.

"Tell me," he urged.

Brennan grabbed her arm, "What in the hell is going on?"

"Please, let go of my arm."

"Not until you tell me what is going on?"

"You almost died. The gash on the back of your head got infected and then you became unconscious, that's the best way to describe it. You've been out for a little over a week, like eight days." She lowered her head and continued, "Once we were sure you weren't going to turn, we took you out of quarantine and out here."

He looked over his body. His arms were heavily scratched with small scabs. "Are you talking about me turning into a drooler?"

"I hate that name. I just call them mutants."

"You know about them?" he asked.

She gave him an odd look and said, "Of course."

He stood up and immediately felt a surge of vertigo.

Seeing his unsteadiness, she grabbed his arm. "You really should take it easy."

"You're confusing me. What's going on?" he asked again.

"Maybe you should rest. You've been out for a while, so you shouldn't be up and running around," she warned.

Loud concussions came from outside. The ground shook and rumbled.

"What's that?" he asked.

"Sounds like they're bombing the city, finally," she replied, her tone showing no shock in what she said.

He shifted his eyes towards the entrance of the tent and started for it.

"You're not in any condition to go looking around," Sherry said.

"I need to find out what's going on," he snapped.

"As your doctor, I now insist you rest," she barked.

The ground rumbled again.

"I don't understand. I need to see," he said, racing outside.

He recoiled from the bright midday sun. With his hand shading his eyes, he looked out.

Spread out along the tarmac of the base was a sea of GP tents. His view of the downtown San Diego skyline was unencumbered to the north. There he saw large thick black plumes of smoke billowing out from the city.

A loud whoosh tore his gaze upwards.

A pair of F-18s were heading towards the city.

He watched as they barreled down, dropped their ordnance and each veered off in opposite directions. Seconds later, massive explosions appeared followed by the concussion from the blasts.

He turned to Sherry, who was standing just behind him. "What's going on? What's happened?"

She stepped up next to him, her gaze upon the city. "There's a lot of names for what's happened. The Bloody Hand says it's the end of days. Others simply call it the mutant apocalypse. Me, I think it was our reckoning. It was a matter of time, the writing was on the wall, literally in some cases," she said. Her eyes cast upon the towers of downtown and the ominous smoke that swirled out. "Seeing this for the first time but must shocking."

"Those things, the ones we were fighting, you're telling me they're everywhere?" he asked.

"I don't know what you were doing before you came to us, but it all started the day you were brought in to us. It was May 1; everything seemed normal that day until the first reports came in about an attack at a school in North Carolina. There was some confusion as another report came in from New Hampshire, then Pennsylvania, Oregon, Arizona. The reporting of the attacks on schools spread. By midday, there were over a hundred reported attacks with many going unreported."

"Those things attacked schools?"

"No, the attacks on the schools were your run-of-the-mill jihadis using regular weapons like guns; some had bombs. But regular terror attacks, the shocking thing was they were primarily targeting schools. It was horrific, the images coming across the television, so sad. We all thought the attacks...the slaughter of the kids at the schools was the worst of it, but it wasn't. It all appears to have been a ruse, a way to get us to look somewhere else. Later in the day, reports of odd, strange attacks began to be reported. Those reports spread and widened until we had them everywhere. It will be difficult if not impossible to know exactly how it all happened. The government is huddled down in a secret location, the military is fighting feverishly against these things, but they multiply...fast."

"You're telling me that this entire time I've been unconscious, the world ended?"

"In so many words, yes, I guess I am saying that."

Several jets flew overhead.

Brennan looked up and watched as they dropped their ordnance on some unseen target in downtown. He couldn't believe it. All of it was so much to take in. "My team, do you know anything?"

"I don't, sorry."

"Why are they bombing downtown, is it that bad?" he asked.

"It is, in fact it's dire. There's talk we're to be evacuated soon to San Clemente Island. They've set up a base there."

"I need to find my team. I need to talk to someone. I need..." he said almost hysterically.

She gently touched his arm and said, "What you need is rest." She pointed to the city and continued, "This isn't going to change, but if you plan on getting back in the fight, you need to heal."

"This is all so crazy," he mumbled.

"That's one word for it."

More jets flew by, headed towards downtown.

He looked up and watched as they delivered their payloads. She was right, it was shocking. "You, seem calm."

Laughing, she replied, "Don't mistake my demeanor as calm. I'm terrified, really, but if I give in to it, I'd be useless."

"What happens now?"

She stood in front of him, looked him squarely in the eyes and answered, "We fight."

"It's that simple?"

The ground rumbled from another wave of bombs.

"It's about survival now, we're not fighting for a country, a flag, apple pie or freedom. We're fighting for our very existence."

"Christ, it's really that bad?"

"Yes, it is."

He turned around and headed back into the tent. He began searching the tent. "Where's my clothes?"

She came into the tent. "What are you doing?"

"My clothes, I need my clothes," he said.

"Your uniform was thrown away, it was covered in blood," she answered.

"I need clothes, a uniform," he said.

"You need to rest."

"No, I don't. I've rested enough. You said that the world we knew had ended. You just told me a reckoning had befallen us and that we were fighting for our survival. I'm not going to just lay around while..."

"There's nothing you can do," she said interrupting him.

Nodding he said, "Yes there is, I'm a fighter and you said our only hope was to fight. That's exactly what I'm going to do and you are not going to stop me."

"The trunk," she said.

"Huh?"

"There's a fresh uniform in the trunk," she said.

He went to the trunk and opened it. As she said, a uniform lay folded inside.

"You really should rest, another day at least."

"Not going to happen, doc."

The ground shook.

Unconcerned about privacy, he dropped the hospital gown and quickly put on his trousers.

"Is there anything I can say to make you reconsider?"

"Nope. You said our only hope was to fight and that's what I'm going to do," he replied. He put on his shirt and exited the tent.

She followed him out. "Be safe, Sergeant Brennan."

He stopped and turned, "Doc, thanks for fixing me up. Much appreciated."

"It's what I do," she said.

"And fighting is what I do. It's time to get back in the game," he said and walked off.

He didn't know where he should go exactly, but he'd start by going to the command building.

The ground shook again and jets swooshed overhead.

He looked towards the smoldering city. She was right. The world he knew had ended. But as long as he was still standing, he'd fight and do whatever was necessary to win this new war.

Thoughts of Jenna and his yet unborn child came flooding in. *Where was she? Was she okay? Was she even still alive?*

The best way for him to answer those questions was to find his unit first. Only then would he have the support needed to save her.

He entered the command building. People were criss-crossing the halls; the volume of chatter was high.

"Can I help you?" a young sailor asked.

"I'm looking for Commander Shenkman," Brennan said.

"Second floor, room H."

Brennan got to the second floor and found room H. He didn't bother to knock, he just walked in.

"This is where we'll begin..." Shenkman said and looked up at Brennan with a surprised look on his face. "Sergeant Brennan, you're awake."

"Yes, sir."

"We're conducting..."

Brennan interrupted him and asked, "I'm ready, sir."

"Ready for what?"

"Fight sir, that's what you're planning, correct?" Brennan asked as he pointed at the map of downtown San Diego.

"Excuse me, gentlemen," Shenkman said walking around his desk. He walked up to Brennan and said, "Let's speak outside."

The two went into the hallway.

"Are you doing okay?" Shenkman asked.

"I'm good, sir, ready to come back to Unit Five."

"Glad to hear you're feeling better."

"How can I help with the offensive?" Brennan asked referring to the briefing he interrupted.

Shenkman gave an uncomfortable laugh. "My dear, boy, we're not planning an offensive. We're planning a mass evac."

"But the bombing, the city?"

"Report to hangar four, we'll get you on a transport to SCI," he said, SCI being a reference to San Clemente Island.

"But I'm here, I'm ready to fight."

Shenkman put his hand on Brennan's shoulder and said, "You've been unconscious for a while but I'll give you the abridged version. We're losing...badly. San Diego is lost. We're leaving, all personnel are to begin evac in four hours."

"Losing?"

"You fought those things, you've seen them firsthand."

"But.."

"Go to hangar four, we have a transport heading out in an hour, I want you on that."

"But.."

"Unit Five is there now, what's left of it. We're regrouping now."

"San Diego is lost?"

"I don't have time to explain it all, but San Diego is the last major city to fall. The others, all of them, gone. There's no other way to say it, we've lost control of our country."

"How?"

"Go to hangar four, get on the transport. I'll have someone waiting for you on SCI."

Bewildered, Brennan said, "Yes, sir."

Shenkman patted Brennan on the shoulder and said, "Good to have you back, sergeant. I'll see you on SCI." He disappeared back into his office.

Dazed, Brennan walked off. He exited the command building and sat on the steps.

He watched as multiple waves of jets came towards the city, all dropping bombs and flying away.

A massive explosion sounded to the east, he craned his head to see the Coronado Bridge collapsing, disintegrating and falling into the harbor below. The sight was surreal.

"Did you see that?" a man asked another walking by.

"That's not a good sign," the other man said.

"Hey, hold up," Brennan said.

"Yeah," one of the men said.

"Not a good sign, what do you mean by that?"

"Oh, we were told if they blow the bridge it means those mutants are getting close."

"Thanks," Brennan said.

The two men walked off.

Distraught, Brennan darted his gaze from the city to the remnants of the once expansive bridge. *Was this all a dream?* He wondered.

A flurry of activity in the tent city caught his attention. He looked and saw five ton trucks pulling up. Just past that he caught sight of the words, *HANGAR 4*.

A sense of urgency filled him. He needed to do as

Shenkman ordered. Get to hangar four and get out of here. He stood up and marched towards it.

His thoughts were jumbled with all the new revelations from both Sherry and Shenkman. Their words echoing in his head. *Losing. Reckoning. Over. Lost control of the country.*

He pushed those thoughts aside and pressed forward. His future wasn't in San Diego anymore. As Shenkman said, it was lost. His future was now on San Clemente Island and from there...well, he'd find out. He stepped into the hangar and hollered out to the first person he saw. "Where's the transport to SCI?"

A man pointed outside to a CH-53 Super Stallion parked alongside the east side of the hangar.

Brennan found the crew chief of the chopper sitting on the ramp smoking a cigarette.

"Is this the bird going to SCI?" Brennan asked.

"Yep, who are you?"

"Sergeant Brennan, with Unit Five."

"Take a seat, we're heading out in twenty."

"Copy that," Brennan said walking onto the chopper.

The crew chief took a long drag of his cigarette and said, "Let's hope that chick you caught will help bring an end to this shit."

Unsure of who he was talking about, Brennan said, "I've been out of it for a bit, took a hit to the head. Who are you talking about?"

The crew chief swung around and said, "You guys caught some bitch, I hear she worked with the motherfucker who created this."

"My team got her?"

"That's the word. She's being held over in SCI now."

"Oh."

"You all are good. Took you a matter of days to get her."

"That's good news."

The crew chief got up and walked onto the chopper. He stopped in front of Brennan and said, "You fivers, your good, that's the word. A band of badass mothers." He stuck out his hand and said, "Gunny Smithers, nice to meet you."

"Hi, Gunny."

"Well, let's get you over to the island. Looks like you're flying solo today," Smithers said walking back to a panel. He flipped a switch. The ramp began to rise.

"Wait! Hold on!" a woman's voice hollered.

"Oops, look like you'll have company," Smithers laughed lowering the ramp.

A hooded woman ran onto the chopper and took a seat across from Brennan.

"Anyone with you?" Smithers asked.

"No, just me," she said pulling the hoodie off her head. It was Tracy from the CDC.

"Tracy?" Brennan asked.

"Well, if it isn't Sergeant Brennan, the man who doesn't die," she replied with a big smile. She hopped up and came over to Brennan's side of the chopper. "How you doing? I heard you injured badly."

"Not too badly, I guess."

The rotors of the chopper began to turn.

"I'm glad you're back on your feet," she said patting him on the leg. "And next time, call, me ma'am," she joked.

Brennan raised a brow.

"That's right, you don't know. You all work for me now."

"What?"

"Yep, you and the others are now under my command, I know, it sucks but it is what it is," she said informing him of the new chain of command.

"And our mission?"

"You're my seekers, anytime we get intelligence on something or someone that can help us, we send you boys out. So far, it's paid off."

"I heard."

"Don't worry, you guys are getting plenty of action."

The chopper lifted off the ground.

"You should get some rest, you have a big night ahead of you," she said.

"We do?"

"Yeah, the woman we brought in, she's spilled the beans. We know who and where the mastermind of this whole thing is."

"Oh yeah."

"Yep. So, get some rest. It'll be a long night," she walked back to the other side of the chopper and sat down.

The chopper banked hard and headed northwest.

Brennan looked over his shoulder and down at the city. The number of smoke plumes had grown. As they flew further away, the entire coast came into view and all along it, similar black plumes of smoke rose. Southern California looked like a war zone, like something he'd only seen in Afghanistan or other faraway lands.

War had come to the shores of the United States.

The enemy didn't use tanks or fighter jets, but science and deception. They had leveraged our own political differences to get inside. They had manipulated the media and brainwashed many of its citizens through political correctness, forcing them to look away as plots were being formulated and executed.

Sherry was right. What had occurred was a reckoning. All the signs were there, but few took notice of them.

Survival was the focus now. How and why would have to addressed later.

The day of reckoning had come and with it brought; blood, despair, death and destruction.

Brennan wasn't thinking in those stark terms. For him, tomorrow was a new day, a day of retribution.

EPILOGUE

Tuesday, May 9
Thompsons Lake, New York

MAX PACED his small den countless times. He'd stop every time he was near his computer to see if any new e-mails had come through.

A man that lived by constant communication, he was finding life after the attacks sufferable due to his lack of contact with the outside world. Odd for a man who lived in the back-woods of Upstate New York.

The television media reports stopped almost a week ago but he found an old radio in his basement. Those broadcasts ceased two days ago. The emergency broadcast loop didn't suffice as contact, so he turned the radio off and stowed it.

His last bastion of communication was on his computer, but there he hadn't received an e-mail from anyone in days.

Growing impatient and frustrated, he was about to give up and go searching for people, anyone.

A car horn blared in the distance. He ran to the front door and looked out. *Was someone in need of help? Was one of those things there?* Frightened by the latter, he shut the door and locked it.

A ping came from his computer. He knew that sound, it was an e-mail.

He sprinted down the hall and into his den.

There on his computer, in bold font, was a new e-mail. He didn't recognize the sender and didn't care. He sat down and with excitement, opened it.

The e-mail read; *"Dear Max, David would have sent this but unfortunately, he couldn't. You'll know what to do with this. – Joram."*

Attached to the e-mail was a series of large attachments. He opened the first one to discover it was an audio recording of Joram and David talking.

After listening for a bit, he came to realize these were the unedited recordings of David's interview with Joram. This was pure journalistic gold, but what good was it now. There wasn't any media to broadcast it on.

With nothing else to do, Max decided to listen to the hours of recordings.

He thought. *Who knows, maybe there's something important here.*

ABOUT THE AUTHOR

G. Michael Hopf is a USA Today Bestselling author of almost forty novels including the international bestselling post-apocalyptic series, THE NEW WORLD. He has made a prominent name for himself in both the post-apocalyptic and western genres. To date he has sold over one million copies of his books worldwide and many of his works have been translated into German, French and Spanish.

He is the co-founder of BEYOND THE FRAY PUBLISHING and DOOMSDAY PRESS and a veteran of the United States Marine Corps. He lives with his family in San Diego, CA.

ADDITIONAL APOCALYPTIC BOOKS

HOPE (Co-Authored With A. American)

DAY OF RECKONING

DETOUR: AN APOCALYPTIC HORROR STORY

DRIVER 8: A POST-APOCALYPTIC NOVEL

THE DEATH TRILOGY (WITH JOHN W. VANCE)

THE DEFIANT SERIES (WITH JOHN W. VANCE)

LOCKDOWN: TALES FROM THE NEW WORLD (CO-AUTHORED WITH L. DOUGLAS HOGAN)

MOTHER: MISSIONS FROM THE EXTINCTION CYCLE

BINARY: ORIGINS OF HONOR (out of print)

ADDITIONAL WESTERN BOOKS

THE LAW MAN

THE RETRIBUTION OF LEVI BASS

JUDGMENT DAY

RIGHTEOUS KILL

HORROR/PARANORMAL

THE DOLL (CO-AUTHORED WITH SAVANNAH HOPF)

BEYOND THE FRAY: BIGFOOT (CO-AUTHORED WITH SHANNON LEGRO)

BEYOND THE FRAY: PARAMALGAMATION (CO-AUTHORED WITH SHANNON LEGRO)

Made in the USA
Monee, IL
17 January 2021

57878377R00204